Praise for the M

...SF on a broader scale...its metaphors apply to a very human tangle of loyalty and betrayal, politics and idealism—Wells and Orwell updated....
—*Locus*, June 2005

The third volume of the Marq'ssan cycle, *Tsunami*, confirms what the second volume, *Renegade*, made clear: the narrative drive and sheer invention of the work is more than up to the size, scope, and ambition of this extraordinary project. What a grand job! What a great read! It's been a long time since I've read science fiction with such a dramatic grip on the political complexities of our slow progress toward the better world we all wish for.
—Samuel R. Delany, author of *Dhalgren* and *Trouble on Triton*

"[Duchamp] overwhelmingly rises to the challenges she sets herself through the nuanced development of strong characters over the course of these first three volumes of the Marq'ssan Cycle..."
—Amy J. Ransom, *NYRSF*, April 2007

"...easily one of the best science fiction series I've read in years. It strips bare the arbitrary structures of our world (sexuality, gender, government) and rebuilds them in complex, new structures that are strikingly at odds with our experience...."
—Sean Melican, *Ideomancer*, March 2007

"...the closest comparison one might give is to some of Le Guin's later work—no small recommendation. Worth looking for."
—*Asimov's*, June 2006

"[T]hose with a serious interest in dystopias and particularly the feminist version thereof should find L. Timmel Duchamp's Marq'ssan Cycle a rewarding experience."
—*NYRSF*, December 2005

"Politically savvy and philosophically relevant, this title puts a human face on today's problems."
—*Library Journal*, June 15, 2005

Stretto

Books by L. Timmel Duchamp

Love's Body, Dancing in Time

The Grand Conversation

Red Rose Rages (Bleeding)

The Marq'ssan Cycle

Alanya to Alanya

Renegade

Tsunami

Blood in the Fruit

Edited by L. Timmel Duchamp

Talking Back

WisCon Chronicles, Vol 1

*WisCon Chronicles, Vol 2
(with Eileen Gunn)*

Stretto

Book Five of the Marq'ssan Cycle

by L. Timmel Duchamp

Aqueduct Press, PO Box 95787
Seattle, WA 98145-2787
www.aqueductpress.com

Library of Congress Control Number: 2008902365

ISBN: 978-1-933500-18-8
ISBN-10: 1-933500-18-2
First Edition, First Printing, July 2008

16 15 14 13 12 11 10 09 08   1 2 3 4 5

COVER ACKNOWLEDGMENTS
Cover Design by Lynne Jensen Lampe
Cover photos Ocotillo, Sunset, Prisoner: © Royalty-Free/CORBIS
Cover photo of Emma Goldman speaking in Union Square, © Bettmann/
CORBIS collection
Cover photo of Red Square, Courtesy University of Washington Libraries
Special Collections, UWC0121
Book Design by Kathryn Wilham
Fingers Touching by Lori Hillard

This book was set in a digital version of Monotype Walbaum, available through AGFA Monotype. The original typeface was designed by Justus Erich Walbaum.

Printed in the USA by Thomson-Shore, Inc, Dexter, MI

for Kathryn Wilham
and
Ann Hibner Koblitz

ACKNOWLEDGMENTS

In Chapter 10, Alexandra Sedgewick ponders the words of Friedrich Nietzsche. These are to be found in Twilight of the Idols, which Nietzsche wrote in 1888 not long before his forty-fourth birthday, just shortly before his physical collapse and complete mental breakdown.

It gives me great pleasure to thank the numerous individuals who, over the course of the two decades since I first drafted Stretto, read the novel in ms and offered me usefully frank comments on it. Among these I especially appreciate the efforts and support of Tom Duchamp, Professor Ann Hibner Koblitz, and Elizabeth Walter. The critiques they offered were a labor of love; I will always be grateful to them for their engagement with my work. Kathryn Wilham, who edited and typeset Stretto, was absolutely key from the beginning; her confidence in my vision for the Marq'ssan Cycle was vital to my completing and then deciding to publish it. I'd also like to thank Lynne Lampe for designing the covers for the Marq'ssan Cycle.

"Political claims rely on the ability to exercise imagination, to think from the standpoint of others, and in this way to posit universality and thus community. The universality of such claims depends on their being not epistemologically justified, as most feminists have tended to assume, but taken up by others, in ways that we can neither predict nor control, in a public space. This space called the world is an ever-changing one in which, positing the agreement that may or may not materialize, feminists discover—daily—the nature and limits of community."

   —Linda M.G. Zerilli, *Feminism and the Abyss of Freedom*

"All questions of politics, the ordering of society, educa-tion have been falsified down to their foundations because the most injurious men have been taken for great men— because contempt has been taught for the "little" things, which is to say for the fundamental affairs of life..."

   —Nietzsche, *Ecce Homo*

Chapter One

Sedgewick's Island, Maine
Thursday, January 12, 2096

Dear Elizabeth,

I'm charmed by your magnificent (not to say munificent) gift. I confess your largesse took me entirely by surprise, not least because of what happened with the last girl you sent me. I'll warn you right now, there's little hope I'll behave more properly this time; I hope you don't think I'll be shamed into it? We both know I'm beyond shame. But as for the girl herself, she's irresistible. How did you guess I prefer them cool and reserved? Her air of *noli me tangere* ravishes me. And for a service-tech she's amazingly elegant.

And so here I am once again facing the anniversary of Kay Zeldin's death. (Assuming—and one would be a fool to take my father's "facts" as unquestionable—that he gave me the correct date.) I always faithfully observe the old rituals of going out to stare at the statue and trudging up the stairs to the top of the house to that ghastly room. (If he never showed it to you, you must let me take you up there sometime, since you know as much about that room as I do.) I don't, however, get paralyzingly drunk. That's one, at least, of my father's vices that I eschew.

I should gracefully end this letter now and fall silent for another several months. That's the formula, isn't it. But this time I'll risk boring you, my dear, dear jailer. You once spent a couple of months stranded here with my father. Think of it, Elizabeth: I've been living on this island in strict exile for more than five years. Did you know that the Romans punished their political enemies with exile from Rome? Absence from Rome, you see, signified a kind of annihilation.

I can't say I miss DC. I never gave a damn for the power games that so obsessed my father (and still obsess you). But I am only twenty-six, and my unlived life stretches endlessly before me. Am I meant to stay here until I'm ready to join my father and Kay Zeldin in this island's earth? You've granted me an idyllic life, some would say. I enjoy infinite leisure and access to scholars and books and such small luxuries as can be procured at a distance—through your generosity, of course. (Never, my dear jailer, would I forget such a paramount fact.) But I find myself increasingly disturbed by the effeteness of this life. Certain aspects of my personality grow stronger and more dominant the longer I stay here. For instance: I'm being devoured by solipsism of the most narcissistic sort. Can't you, for godsake, give me some insignificant non-security-related job? I'm not your political enemy, Elizabeth, nor have I been at any time in the past. I haven't the faintest desire to usurp your power or regime. Nor do I complain about our arrangement vis-à-vis the Sedgewick Estate.

If it isn't a question of trust, then I must assume it's a matter of punishment. I presume the idea of trapping me here with the traces of my father all around me, to surround me with the guilt of his death and a constant reminder (as if I needed one) of his presence in my life, once appealed to you. Does it still? When shall I have been punished enough? You didn't say when you offered me the terms of this exile.

Elizabeth, I beg you. Consider a new arrangement. I'm not asking for total freedom. I would agree to any restrictions you might choose to place on me in other circumstances. Even a short stint at one of the other houses and limited access to social and cultural activities would make a vast difference to me. The fact is, I fear that if I don't have a change, I'll crack up.

Respectfully yours,

Alexandra

Washington, DC
5 January, 2096
My dear Alexandra,

The note of pathos in your plea was well achieved. Nevertheless, let me remind you of the alternative to what you call "exile." If you should choose to exchange the relative freedom of your island for a private cell, you have only to inform me and it will be done at once. Whatever you may think, punishment does not concern me. I've always found retribution to be a distraction that is often dangerous and at the very least a sapping of resources better spent. People do punish *themselves*, my dear, don't they—to the extent that they can ever be "punished." As for the matter of your trustworthiness, that is not—and probably never shall be—clear. Consider, Alexandra, the *facts* that I have to go on where you are concerned:

(1) You freely chose to cut yourself off from our women's world. You have not spoken to your mother in more than seven years, and you continue to refuse to see her and your grandmother. Now I can hardly cast the first stone when it comes to maternal relations, for I haven't seen or spoken to my own mother in more than thirty years. Nevertheless, taken with everything else (your father's overt attack on all career-line women, for instance) it is merely one more sign of your estrangement from the values most executive women share.

(2) I have no information by which to analyze your possible reasons for deserting your father as you did. In the Company we follow a general rule of thumb that defectors and renegades are never to be trusted. Sound rule, don't you agree? Although you did not precisely defect from your father, at the end you chose to take my terms rather than share exile with him. You may think it unfair of me to hold this against you since it was I who offered that choice to you, yet you must see that it suggests an intrinsic lack of loyalty in you. Need I remind you that in earlier times I stood by your father in his darkest hour? I did not "betray" him until *he* had first betrayed *me*.

(3) If you genuinely want this favor of me, it was maladroit of you to drag Zeldin into your letter. Yes, I can verify that she died on January 12, 2078. But as I've mentioned to you before, I don't appreciate your introducing her into our intercourse.

I'm glad the girl pleases you. I contracted with her for an extravagant sum precisely *because* of the nature of your sexual tastes. She knows what to expect. I wouldn't dream of sending you someone who didn't. I may not share your tastes, but I can sympathize with such a long drought for one as accustomed to sexual activity as you are. It's to be hoped you won't tire of her as quickly as you have of the others. (In other words, don't expect a replacement when you've finished with her.)

Elizabeth

Wednesday, 2/1/2096

Very well, I'll do it. In this book. With the full understanding that it may be read without my consent—for I know, Elizabeth, that the girl is your spy. Not that you especially needed to add her to the crew already surrounding me. But she freely penetrates my bedroom, doesn't she.

After all these years I must have acquired enough detachment to be able to poke around & see what I can see. How to explain to Elizabeth what I myself don't understand? She of course was being disingenuous in her letter. The reason she keeps me here is not concern for any treachery I might be capable of but that she fears what I am. I know her father killed himself. When she saw me turning my back on Rbt & thus—according to her—instigating *his* suicide, it rang bells long muffled & buried in her psyche. (It must have!) & then from what she had told me shortly before I made my decision to desert him, Kay Zeldin's murder-suicide (whatever is one to call such an event?) was certainly on her mind, & she associated his death with Zeldin's.

If ever I'm to find a way to escape this bleak, futureless existence, or—should escape prove to be impossible—to discover a way of coming to terms with it (& therefore with myself), I must discover who & what I am, as well as comprehend Elizabeth's attitude toward me. To convince Elizabeth that I'm trustworthy, I need to understand a multitude of things that I've blocked off.

Though I'm surrounded by people who either guard or serve me (usually both), I'm essentially devoid of close human contact and communication. Which is my own fault, I suppose. I could cultivate the tutors, for one thing. Even though they *are* paid. They aren't in the same category of employee as Sally, though they are paid to amuse me. (& spy on me.) Each of them engages passionately in work on research projects that give meaning to their lives—a far cry from Sally's life here. She's here only to amuse me, her sole interest the handsome recompense Elizabeth bestows upon her. In short, she's a parasite.

& so I begin this book with the clear purpose of understanding. Which first entails forcing myself to *remember*. It will be painful, yes. But every day I lived in my father's house I suffered such pain. Perhaps it will be easier for me now, given the distance of years & the fact that however vividly I remember, I am, physically at least, out of his reach, now & forever.

Where to start? I thought I needed to do this four years ago, when I requested a psychoanalyst of Elizabeth. [Knowing how Rbt would turn over in his grave at the very idea: the equivalent of throwing myself into the arms of my paternal grandfather, the final betrayal.] But the request horrified her. *We must preserve silence at all costs on your relationship with your father. I've done my utmost to protect your reputation, Alexandra. Don't be an idiot about this.* She never did tell me what she did with the med-tech who assisted her with my loquazene exam. I'd put nothing past her. Consider what she did to Wedgewood when it came time to hand him over to the human rights vultures. Anything to preserve the family secrets, right, Elizabeth? Maybe that's your real reason for jailing me here, maybe I'm a deep dark secret you want to keep under wraps. From yourself, even. What you really wanted to say in your letter is that you can't trust a taboo-breaker. It's nothing to do with my lack of loyalty to my father. But of course you can't say that since you pride yourself on your open mind. Proven, you no doubt believe, by your sending me Sally in spite of the flavor of my sexual vice.

But chattering at Elizabeth isn't the point of this book. The point is to unravel the past. (At twenty-six I can speak of a "past": but at what cost? Can I imagine speaking of a future? Can one think of an unending infinity of exile on this damned island as the/a future?) Where to start? With my birth? With the Blanket? With my father's tearing me out of my grandmother's (island) womb? With my becoming my father's lover? Or do I start before my own birth? After all, many things that happened before my birth directly influenced the shape my life took, though not to the extent that *he* liked to claim.

I know you better than anyone ever could. I know you better than you know yourself. Bullshit. & god how boring that repeated assertion became. *What a front you put up for the rest of the world, Persephone. But you are* my *secret.* Yes, that said it all, Rbt. That someone as naive as I was should fall into your hands…

Can you really blame me for my mistakes, Elizabeth? If you'd called me at any time during those years, I would have gone to you like a shot. The dreams I had about you. The fantasies. That you would sweep me away, that you would save me for myself... Did I think of it that way? Probably not. Except that for a while I thought I could still find the self I once was. And then I knew it was too late. After two years of that life of insanity, going tamely off to Sarah Lawrence and studying piano and child development? No more could I do such a thing now, even if you allowed it.

Fuck it. Here I am writing to *her*. This is for myself, this book, this accounting.

Yes, *accounting*. I want to render an accounting, to understand what has happened to me, to find what I am. You mistook me, Rbt, for I do have the guts for it. But then why look at me any more fully than you ever looked at anything in the whole damned world? Blind old man, you lived a fantasy that you dragged the rest of the world into.

I swear on my executive womanhood that I will never drag more than one person at a time into *my* fantasies. Alas poor Sally. But she's getting paid handsomely for it.

Thursday, 2/2/2096

I take a surprising amount of pleasure in simply staring at Sally. But now it's time to disturb the texture I've woven so deliberately between us. I shall explore a new pattern tonight. Slowly, slowly. I will not be caught by her. Is that what Elizabeth intends, sending me someone so cool, so visibly detached? Does the girl herself imagine she can snare me? But why else should Elizabeth send me girls at all but to trap me emotionally? Why should it matter to her? She's devious. Yet so am I, so am I. I had a *lot* of practice with Rbt.

Let them both be devoured by curiosity, wondering at my intent, my reactions, my interest. By the time I'm through with Sally she will give up even trying to comprehend. & Elizabeth will grow frustrated and—*perhaps*—realize that whatever it is she wants to know she will have to seek firsthand for herself.

Saturday, 2/4/2096

Last night I shook Sally's equilibrium. She's been with me for over a month & so far I'd required nothing more from her than Swedish massages, the care of my clothing, & small, trivial services. I haven't even required her to dress my hair, since Jenson shampoos and trims it twice a week like clockwork, & god knows it takes no more than a few swipes of the hairbrush to maintain. So it struck me as amusing to assign the girl all the housekeeping duties for my bedroom suite. I was fairly certain she'd never touched a robocleaner in her life & so was hardly surprised when this morning a bewildered Lavoisier came to me & wanted to know whether I really intended Sally to have such an important responsibility, given the fact that he would have to instruct the girl on even the simplest aspects of the robocleaner & its functions. The staff is used to my vagaries. They'll jabber for a time about this new whimsy of mine but will soon be taking it for granted.

As for the girl herself: start with the fact that though Elizabeth briefed her on what to expect from me, I've been nothing but civil (if cool). Then add the kind of lifestyle she is undoubtedly accustomed to & the sorts of services she specializes in. Result? One confused service-tech. Those lovely green eyes opening wide in surprise—she's been waiting, though not, I'd be willing to bet, for orders to do *housework*.

But I'm stalling. Today I'm to start the project. Do I muse stream-of-conscious? Or do I set myself specific questions with which to grapple? How to go about analyzing myself & my short life? The basic outlines are tediously obvious: I hate my mother, loved/hated my father, & was probably responsible for his suicide. I killed him—I wished him dead. So where do I go from there?

I can't seem to think. I'd rather read Nietzsche, truth to tell.

Wednesday, 2/8/2096

The damned fog seems to have settled down over the island permanently. The tutors are not only depressed from the dismal atmosphere, but are also upset at being cut off from the mainland. (Sylvia especially.) Little did they imagine a year's sabbatical on an island off the coast of Maine could be so deadening. Jameson of course makes a big production about how much work he's getting done poring over his epigraphic data. But then classics scholars are *supposed* to be oblivious to their surroundings.

But Sally, yes. The iron maiden now quivers like jelly at the very sight of me. Whatever *did* Elizabeth tell her? [Sally, if you should be reading this book for Elizabeth, I doubt you'll enjoy it, considering where you and I are headed. I'm tempted to wax pornographic just for that possibility.] Between Sally & my studies I've left no time for anything else. With unconscious intent, no doubt, since no one holds me to a schedule. I pay them; they are here for my amusement.

Rereading my letter to Elizabeth, it struck me how Elizabeth's & Rbt's political styles at least superficially conform to different historical styles. Rbt always prided himself on following Machiavelli above all other political theorists. Metternich, Treitschke, Mao, Schmidt, and Kissinger—the Big Five of Modern History—are all, according to Rbt, irrelevant to the post-Executive Transformation world. (& of course I tried on more than one occasion to tell him Machiavelli was irrelevant to the post-Blanket world, but each time, the very suggestion sent him into a rage.) His preferred method of dealing with enemies was excision. Either that or stripping them of their rank & fortunes (where possible). With his most powerful opponents, excision was easier than depriving them of power. While Elizabeth, on the other hand, doesn't stick at excision—after all, one can safely assume she arranged Wedgewood's—she prefers the old exile method. Rather like the methods of the *ancien regime* in France. Oh hell, what would Kay Zeldin, a *real* historian, have to say about all this? Her book on what happened between the onset of the Blanket & the Civil War was fascinating enough. (I bet it was Elizabeth who sent it to me: Rbt so furious at this anonymous "gift"—never having read it himself—or so he said—then wildly bingeing after doing so.)

What is it that Kay Zeldin has to do with me or, rather, with my "story"? My intuition tells me that she is a link between Elizabeth & me. I'd like to talk to Elizabeth about this, but there's no chance of that. Some of what the three of us share in common is obvious. & do we add Rosemary Sedgewick to the chain? Elizabeth, we *are* a chain: don't you see? But you don't like the hands that forged us, so you'll deny the connection.

Shit, how can I get anywhere when everything leads back to my trying to talk to that absent quondam mentor of mine? How different everything would have been if Elizabeth hadn't gone renegade. I'd have been utterly different myself. Was I really so sugar-&-spice nice, or was that only the customary self-protective veneer forced onto executive girls? [Do you know, Mama, Grandmother, why I won't have anything to do with you? It's for what you did to me, both of you. Worse than what *he* did, far worse. Between you, you crippled me, hobbled me, maimed me. While he only warped what was already diseased.]

I'm raving mindlessly, off the track. Is that why I wanted a shrink? To complain about my upbringing? But shrinks always take the side of the parents, always accept an environment as given. I'd have gotten no sympathy there.

Is everyone this lonely? Rbt denied his loneliness—only to find himself completely alone, without the illusions my existence provided him. *Is* that why he killed himself? Because he finally had to face his solitude, a solitude he'd spent a lifetime denying?

Loneliness is something I've known from the time he summoned me from Barbados to the Georgetown house. I shared his illusion for a little while after we first started playing together, but it didn't take long for me to figure out that basically nothing had changed, that I was still alone & would always be alone—only that now I'd be more finally alone, since before we started fucking I had naive ideas about Mama and Grandmother. After my eyes were opened, I could see the desperation of his illusion. [Elizabeth, you knew, didn't you. So how come you weren't clever enough to play it for all you could get? You tried, I suppose. But somehow you couldn't manage. No wonder *I* couldn't. You were (& are) so much smarter & stronger than I.]

Illusions, illusions…& what illusions am I weaving for myself now? I'm alone. & I appear to think that if I can get off this island I won't be alone. I want to believe that. I so long for that mysterious women's world I've never belonged to, a world now in the thick of everything Rbt considered important. Five women Cabinet officers… It must be killing George Booth. I laugh in your face, bastard. Where are you now, I wonder? Sunk in oblivion, certainly…

You're so perverse, Alexandra, gloating at another's obscurity when you yourself are lost in the fog of this godforsaken island wilderness. Gothic fantasy, indeed. A woman's home is her prison.

Meanwhile, Elizabeth's living in the Georgetown house, having appropriated it for her own use—since *this* Sedgewick will never have any need for it. But I don't care about that. I don't care about the damned estate. Did you think that would bother me, Elizabeth? Sure, it would have driven *him* wild, but I'm not *him*. It was never mine to play with in the first place, for all he made so much of making me his heir. Anyway, I can have my tutors & Sally & Nicole's cuisine & any object that can be shipped here without straining your fucking security arrangements. But you don't believe I don't want that power, do you. You're as bad as he is in the cynicism of your assumptions.

But let's get serious. I was born on Vashon Island, Mama always said. My chromosomes were immediately dealt with, wiping out all those ticking time bombs lurking in my genes. The image of those genetic diseases—running in which blood? Sedgewick blood? Raines blood? Dunn blood? & then all my vaccinations. Against small pox, tooth decay, & a host of other diseases I've never heard much of. The filter installed. & then the bliss (one assumes!) of being breastfed by Mama herself. On demand. Daniel, she says, was livid with jealousy.

But perhaps I should have started the account from conception? With the shocking fact that the last time my father ejaculated before fucking me was to conceive me? He particularly liked that fact. For some unexplained reason it made him feel more powerful than almost anything else could. Over & over & over this fact had to be remarked upon & discussed… & then from Vashon Island to the winery house, & from there to the Colorado house so that Mama could ski. & from there her memory of the legendary itinerary breaks down. A lot of time spent in the Georgetown house, with summers on Vashon Island. My first memory, though, is not of Mama, but of Marie. Marie was with Mama for a long, long time. She taught me French, & she tried to make my life easier vis-à-vis Daniel. I don't remember Rbt at all. Not a single memory of him until at age fifteen he sent for me. Once he dragged

out some photographs of me with him, to prove that he had paid me
some attention as a child. Hah. Any attention he chose to spare to his
children all went to Daniel. Shit, I couldn't win. Naughty or obedient
I lost that game. Mama claims I was always manipulative, that I was
always angling to draw attention away from Daniel onto myself. &
where's Daniel now? Probably permanently hooked up, never to stir
again. It's amazing he's still alive. But then being a Sedgewick he has
people to see to that for him.

Off the subject again, Alexandra. But in my own defense I was actually *trying* to think about childhood. Mama says I was strong-willed
& manipulative, Rbt that I was precocious, very intelligent. Grandmother that I was alternately sweet & wilful. (She *would* choose
those poles—by which she defined how to treat me from moment
to moment. Smothered in affection when "sweet," banished to my
room when wilful. "Control, little girl, you must learn to control your
mouth. No retorts, no comments, all that is required of you is respect
& deference. No one is interested in hearing your blather." If I talked
back after such a summation, off to my room with me. If I lowered
my eyes & said a nice controlled "understood," then I could sit with
Grandmother & after a while babble my grievances—provided they
were put in the correct tone of voice & as an attempt to amuse her—to
my heart's content. Mama was the same way, only not so quick to forgive. Talk about *cold*: she fairly froze the marrow in my bones when
she meant to cut me off. Maybe that's why I found Rbt's contemptuous moods so crushing? In some ways, it was Mama all over again.

Control, control, control. & then Rbt came along with his games violating everything I ever learned about control, while insisting that
outside of the games everything must go on as usual. It makes sense
to me *now*, but at the beginning I thought I'd go crazy with the mood
swings the whole business induced in me. I can remember so sharply,
so distinctly, that slap when I began screaming at him in the corridors
of that Security Central basement, out of my mind with wanting to
escape that horrible Wedgewood scene, & somehow what he said to me
then clicked as it never had before, even though he'd repeated it often
enough to me. I forbid you to lose control, he said, I will not have it,
this is reality not play, I will not assume responsibility for controlling

you outside of our games, you *will* control yourself." All this said so low, right into my ear, so that none of the creeps on hand could hear a word. Though god knows enough of them saw the slap to ensure a major buzz of gossip around the whole damned Company. Through my fury, fear, & humiliation, what he had been trying to tell me for all those months finally penetrated. & so then I tried & tried & tried to cut myself into pieces. To draw lines. To compartmentalize. But Rbt didn't help. When it came right down to it, he only pretended to himself to draw lines. Which, from what he's told me about Kay Zeldin, is where he went wrong with her all those many many years ago.

Oh hell. I can't take this. I've done enough for one day. As long as I make myself write more tomorrow, there's no need for marathon sessions with this book.

Monday, 2/20/2096

So much for my claiming to write here daily. But I just can't drag myself to this book when there's anything at all else to do. Or to think about. (Sally, for instance. Or the philosophy course I started last week with the morosest of the tutors.) The twentieth anniversary of the Blanket came & passed. To tell the truth, I find it hard to imagine this world before the Blanket, I even find it nearly impossible to imagine the world without that faint, nearly invisible, alien presence. It is said in the newspapers that two of Elizabeth's Cabinet officers have had personal contact with aliens... It is maddening how little seems to be known about them. Well, perhaps that will change now that Elizabeth has instituted a new Executive Department devoted exclusively to studying & relating to the aliens.

Last night Sally finally broke down in all-out hysterics. How divine it was, soothing her, calming her, caressing her into tentative security. Afterwards, when I gave her the fur-trimmed leather coat, she suspected a trick, suspected that I'd take it from her, that it was a cruel joke I was playing. Is she lulled? Superficially. The fear peeks out sometimes in the sidelong glances she gives me, her forest green eyes glinting like sun raining through translucent leaves in the woods in summer. She's quite beautiful—no wonder I spent her first few weeks here simply staring at her. Slowly, slowly. I must go slowly this time. Think of it as delayed gratification.

I've become obsessed with the fact that Elizabeth has not come to see me even once since dumping me here. Sometimes I think that if I could see her in the flesh we would work things out. But she wants no face-to-face contact with me. Why? I need to figure that out—if it's possible to do from a distance. If I can figure it out, I might be able to induce her to come to me & thence negotiate new terms with her. It *must* be possible. I *cannot* spend the rest of my life here, living this way. I *cannot*.

So, today I'll write about Elizabeth. Elizabeth & me, I mean. I think of my first acquaintance with this room, called the Small Study. That first year I hated this room over every other place in the house (with the exception of that bizarre room at the top of the house). Every afternoon, tea in this room with a man half-dead & horridly disagreeable. Sometimes he'd lie on that sofa, drunk, & demand things from me I barely understood. Mostly I didn't understand anything of him that first year. I'd sit by the fire & fantasize Elizabeth's being here, rescuing me from the tedium, the tyranny, the humiliations. Because she had once rescued me from him before she went renegade. & then the letters & packages she sent me (all of which stopped after Rbt's reinstatement & my appearing publicly at his side) sustained a wild hope in me that renegade or not, she would rescue me. And with all the speculation about what she was "up to," she became a romantic figure for me. What really fired my imagination was what we learned from the naval intelligence man returned by the terrorists to the Pentagon. For his debriefing, Rbt insisted upon what he called "deep interrogation," which elicited details that utterly enthralled me: Elizabeth being made to cease her on-the-spot torture of him by her companion, obviously a lover, threatening to leave her. Hazel was the name the naval intelligence officer revealed. Hazel. Later Rbt came up with the information that the secretary Elizabeth took with her was named Hazel Bell. He doubted the story, saying that Elizabeth would never make important decisions to please a service-tech lover. (Undoubtedly he thought the incident a bad example to everything he'd been trying to teach me about relations with service-tech sexual partners.) But I

believed the story & savored it, & went over & over & over it with the
greatest pleasure. And would say that name, over and over: *Hazel Bell.*
I don't quite know why it gave me so much pleasure. But I think it
must be considered an important factor in the shaping of my feelings
for Elizabeth.

She seemed everything to me—so confident, controlled, pleasure-
loving, competent—all at a time when I was floundering in bewilder-
ment & fear at my father's tearing me out of the womb & thrusting
me into his big, cold world. Elizabeth offered a link between the two
worlds. A link between my parents, too. Rbt listened to her where he
did not give Mama the time of day. Rbt *respected* Elizabeth, an attitude rare for him when it came to women. She'd stride right into that
house & take control, yet was never narrow & cold & contemptuous
the way Rbt was to the world around him. When it came to the staff,
for instance, he wanted as little to do with them as possible. He'd accept direct service from at most two or three persons per household—
including his valet—while Elizabeth generally saw to everything &
was fairly good-natured and persuasive in her approach to management. (Except that one time when she fired someone in my father's
house for neglecting me while I was under room arrest.)

Once Rbt got me involved with his work, I continually asked myself
what Elizabeth would do in my situation. To be honest, if she'd asked
me at any time to betray Rbt for her, I probably would have, except
during that one mad patch when I first started fucking him. I would
have joined her band of renegade women. (Ah, romance.) But once she
wrote me off as Rbt's creature, she never gave me a thought. Think
of it, all that time I was secretly cheering her on, tickled at each new
slap she delivered at the Executive as Rbt fumed. & when they discovered the location of her HQ & planned that commando raid on it,
I was beside myself trying to decide what, if anything, I could do to
save her from it. Elizabeth, you'll never know my sense of relief—&
ecstatic delight—at hearing the news of how your people repelled the
commando force (taking a third of it prisoner, too), shooting down the
air support that as a matter of last resort was to bomb you out if all
else failed… It was a humiliation for the Company that had Rbt in a
rage for days, berating & demoting the three executives who had been

given the honor of taking you out. He wanted you alive, did you guess that? Did you guess that they wouldn't try excising you until finally they decided that was the only way of stopping you?

But I'm doing it again. I've degenerated into talking to Elizabeth. I should be talking to myself. Isn't that the point of this book?

Sedgewick's Island, Maine
Friday, February 24, 2096

Dear Elizabeth,

I've been pondering the problem the Executive appears to be having with the human rights lawyer working with unionizers arrested in workplace incidents. All three of the dailies I take (the *Ex Times*, *The New York Times*, & *The Washington Post*) have given extensive coverage to her activities, & the *Ex Times* recently profiled her. Though the *Ex Times* urges you to have her debarred and charged with sedition and jailed, naturally you hesitate to do that, given her contacts with the aliens and her national standing as a leading human rights spokesperson. It would surely cast doubt on your claims to have created a government willing to accommodate dissent and eager to ease repression.

May I offer a suggestion that I think will suit what I can make out of your political style? I suggest you co-opt her into the Executive. Either by giving her a job with the Justice Dept., or—which there's a better chance of her accepting—making her a Federal Judge. Though the latter would generate resentment among executives (since executives have, after all, held a monopoly on judgeships since the Transformation), the controversy would be weatherable and ultimately preferable to battling this woman. From what I've learned of American History (which, you know, has become a passion with me in the last five years), usually this kind of cooptation succeeds beyond one's imaginings, although at the outset it does entail some risk for the establishment. Key here is the fact that institutions always win over individuals. Espin would soon feel certain invisible collegial pressures she'd be bound to respond to. But as it is now, she's clearly very clever in her understanding of how to manipulate the law. And in your game, Elizabeth, manipulation of the law is everything, since you've chosen law and subtle persuasion as your media of control. (I especially appreciate your new pop-culture movements—obviously someone's stroke of genius.)

Best wishes,

Alexandra

Saturday, 2/25/2096

It will be hard writing in this book today—though I feel I must, to get my mind back on track—because things are getting more & more interesting with Sally. Last night I took a bold step: I caressed her genitally, bringing her to orgasm several times while maintaining my rule forbidding her to touch or kiss me. We were in the Small Study on the rug by the fireplace, the first time I allowed her in there (where she'd no doubt like to penetrate in order to get her hands on what-ever I might have lying around to read for her reports to Elizabeth). I invited her to drink cognac with me & then asked her to undress. (I did not remove my own gown.) She's even more beautiful—what a flush!—coming than crying. I gave her a solid gold bracelet after-wards, which she handled curiously, as though she'd never touched gold before. It bewilders (&, of course, undercuts) her, my not allow-ing a so-called reciprocal sexual intimacy. But in order to keep her from thinking anything had changed, I added another rule to those I've already given her: that she must stay in my bedroom suite from eight until four every day, even when there's no task for her to attend to. (& here she was probably hoping I'd change my whimsical mind about making her do the cleaning in my suite: it being, perhaps, the keenest humiliation of all that she has to bear.) However, her only response to hearing the new rule was to lower her eyes & say "yes madam." She's a quick study—I doubt she'll try taking liberties with me no matter how felicitous our relations might occasionally be.

But let me think where I was in this project…I was musing over my hero-worship of Elizabeth. Yesterday morning in bed I kept wishing I could ask Elizabeth what it is she thinks I should have done—spent all those years shut up at the winery house? I had no reason to believe he'd ever lose that power over me, at least not while I was defying him. The only way I could possibly have dealt with him was to do as I did, for it gave me a slight measure of power over him as well as some slack. But I always knew my very survival depended on my playing his game, by his rules. The only alternative was to run away: but to where? To whom? If I'd run to her—& god knows I thought about it often enough—Elizabeth would have suspected me of spying for him. Sometimes I imagined contacting the Austrian ambassador & giving him a letter for Elizabeth. But then I'd think of how vulnerable that would render me to blackmail from the ambassador, not to mention anyone else who might get hold of the letter—even from Elizabeth, though that lay only in the back of my mind, for I always believed she would care for me as though I were her own. It was Elizabeth I wished were my mother, or at least my sister.

Rbt once told me that Elizabeth was three years younger than he.

I seem to be getting nowhere in examining that side of the equation. Perhaps it's time to look at the negative. To look at my relationship with Rbt.

That's about the last thing I want to do. But not today. I need to get drunk to take *him* on.

Sunday, 2/26/2096

It's a curious thing about Sally—how she's never attempted the slightest familiarity with me. I suspect this is due to Elizabeth's briefing her about my vices—& perhaps, too, to my not once in those first few weeks having laid a sexual finger on her. But now that I have, she apparently still does not feel free to call me by my first name, probably since I haven't specifically invited her to call me something other than "madam" or "Ms. Sedgewick." I shall keep it that way, even now. This experiment with Sally shall be as much for Elizabeth's benefit as my own. Is there possibly a strain of voyeurism in her sending a girl like Sally to spy on me?

Why why why *bother* with it? It just doesn't make any damned sense that I can think of! What should it matter about me personally—the stuff she can't get out of the gorillas or the tutors or the staff, I mean. Can it be she's actually thinking of letting me off this damned island, provided I pass some test she's concocted for determining whether she wants to let me go free? But if that's the case, why rebuff my request for a change of arrangements as harshly as she did in her letter?

Monday, 2/27/2096

I know when I first hated him. It was in October 2087, about two weeks after my seventeenth birthday, on the third occasion in my life that I tried to defy him. A few weeks after starting classes at Yale—seizing every occasion I could to stay overnight in the apartment he'd bought for us there—I first began avoiding sex with him & then outright insisted we stop for good. He appeared to accept my decision, in line with his eternal claim that my pleasure was the sole reason for our ever having sex. I remember that birthday his watching me in that way he had. When he wasn't sure of me, his watchfulness took on a cool, almost suspicious cast. Otherwise it probably appeared to outsiders as indulgent fondness—though never was it that—but no one ever suspected much less understood the nature of our relationship. Oh how excited I was at this other life I led apart from him! Staying alone in that apartment (alone except for staff, that is), I first tasted freedom. & I began to get ideas. Also, I met a few other executive women attending Yale & occasionally dined & frequently lunched with them. One of them introduced me to a charming girl named Darlene, who was at the time without a contract. So I conceived the idea of forming a contract with her. Maybe I had visions of living during the week in that apartment; I suppose I thought I could convince Rbt to let me give up the constant commuting.

At any rate, one night when were alone at dinner, I raised the subject, revealing to him I'd already moved the girl into the New Haven apartment. As I recall I brought up the subject for the explicit reason that I needed the correct legal formula for wording the contract & thought it would be easier to do it through him than to go to the family's attorneys myself (who would have required his approval, anyway). Easier? I must have been out of my mind. His face went into its dead-fish mode. In front of the butler & a service-tech he announced that if I brought a girl on contract into any of his residences he'd have her thrown into the street. *& is that clear, my dear?* I understood immedi-

ately that he was jealous. Naturally, I was furious. (I am, after all, my
father's daughter.)

I sat through the rest of dinner stony silent—as did he. I began to plot
how I could get my own back. (That's how I thought in those days. I
was a petty little bitch, alright.) When we were alone he said that the
TNC project was flailing, that I hadn't been keeping up with the work,
& that consequently we would be going into the office that evening
to review the current status of the project together. I couldn't protest
that I had too much school work since I never went to New Haven on
Thursdays, & he knew it. (How I regretted having the responsibility of that project—once school had started I'd found it increasingly
onerous & had finally taken to ignoring it.)

So in we went to the office. I always hated going there at night. The
building was pretty forbidding even by daylight, but at night…at
night the full complement of fluorescent lighting flooded the corridors & the guards made themselves more visible. That night as we
stepped into Rbt's private elevator I informed him that I'd be spending Christmas vacation on Barbados—with Mama & both grandparents. Did I have amnesia, that I didn't think of how he'd blocked me
that first spring I spent with him? At any rate, it hadn't occurred to me
that he would prevent my going to Barbados. I simply assumed he'd
fume & feel hurt (my revenge for his denying me Darlene). The only
reason I hadn't spent much time with my mother or grandparents that
summer had—I honestly thought then—been my wanting to please
him. It had always seemed to be my choice. But when I made this announcement, he stared at me for a long time & then said, "the hell you
will" in that tone of voice that sounded as final as a gavel slamming
following delivery of a verdict. I decided to leave it at that—to make
my arrangements without arguing about it.

Right.

He set me up at the conference table with the last few weeks' reports
on the TNC project & then went to his desk & made some calls. He
pitched his voice so low that I didn't hear what he said. Probably I
wasn't trying to hear, either. I preferred to know as little as possible
about what he did as Chief of Security. & then he sat at the table
with me, & for the next three hours we toiled over the project & what

needed to be done about it. Since he was pissed at me he frequently
hammered me with questions & lashed me with his most cutting criticism. I thought the session would never end. All I wanted was to get
away from him. At one point I said something about having been up
since five-thirty, working all day & attending four classes. That, of
course, only earned me a dose of his primest sarcasm.

We stopped when the phone interrupted. After Rbt hung up he said
we were going "downstairs." I thought he meant we were going down
to the garage—& thus home. But when we got into his elevator he
punched in one of the basement levels, not the garage. Because his
face had gone rock-hard and flat, I didn't dream of asking him why
we were going to a basement level.

A gorilla met us at the elevator & led us to a room in the south block.
That section of the building was cold & smelled. Of chemical of some
kind, & maybe of sweat and urine. Was this an illusion of mine? I
don't know, I may be projecting backwards. Still, I found the unre-
lieved concrete depressing, dismal, bleak. We went into a room with
a table & chairs; one of the walls was glass. We sat almost in the dark,
while the room we could see through the window was brightly lit. Rbt
told me to sit in a chair facing the window; he stood behind me, irritating me by resting his hands on my shoulders, occasionally kneading
them. By this time I was feeling so intimidated that I refrained from
asking him what we were doing in that room. I didn't want to know, I
just wanted to get out of there.

What happened next…even now I can hardly bear to think of it. Nor
can I describe it. I've thankfully forgotten most of the details (which I
recall, plagued me for weeks afterwards). The bald fact is that Rbt had
ordered Darlene picked up from the New Haven apartment & brought
to DC. While I watched, she was dragged into that brightly lit room
on the other side of the window & five gorillas beat & raped her. I
shouted & screamed at Rbt to order them to stop, but he clamped one
hand over my mouth while pinning me into the chair from behind
with the other. I dissolved into nearly hysterical crying. The realization of why he was doing it hit me like a sledgehammer. When after
what seemed an eternity he ordered the thing stopped, he took me
back upstairs to the office.

By the time we reached his office I had begun to recover—somewhat. Enough, at any rate, to turn on him the minute we were alone in his office. I hurled at him every abuse I could think of, calling him a bastard, railing at him for his sadism, telling him that I hated him. Big mistake. His response was to go to the phone & order another assault on that girl. How did he put it to me? I think he said something like *I see you learned nothing from the lab. We'll simply have to repeat the experiment until you're able to pass the quiz.* That was the metaphor he used. He added something caustic about my lack of control & how he refused to take the responsibility of controlling me, that I was old enough to control myself.

I burned with hatred. (It later occurred to me that the way I burned with rage when being forced to listen to him psych up his shock troops was nothing to the way I felt that night—which is when I realized the vastness of the difference between hatred & outrage.) But though I burned, at the same time I chilled down fast. (Hatred can be a cold burning, too.) I had to think about that girl down there & what she must be feeling & how it was only her connection with me that had landed her in such a nightmare.

There was this horrible silence in the room with us as he waited for me to take it all in.

I pulled myself together because I had to. I apologized, said how wrong I'd been. In short, I offered him total abjection. When he showed signs of softening, I went to him & put my arms around him. I kissed him. & then he was demanding declarations of love from me, declarations of sexual desire... He said he didn't want to share me with anyone. I told him everything he wanted to hear. & then I wheedled him into countermanding the order. "Wheedled"—yes, it was all of that & more. It was delicate. But of course we both knew that was the payoff. So he picked up the phone & ordered Darlene released—to be dumped in some remote area of DC. Needless to say, she'd never know who'd abducted & assaulted her or why. I didn't dare ask him for the further favor of returning Darlene to New Haven—I feared pressing his now mellowed mood. He fucked me on that long mahogany table. & then we went home. All the time a terrible hatred burned in me, while I played the role of passionate lover & dutiful daughter, sick with the most intense nausea. That's when I first really hated him. He never knew. No one knew. It was just another one of my deep, dark secrets.

Washington DC
27 February, 2096

Alexandra:

How the Executive chooses to handle Espin is none of your business. If, in the future, I receive from you any more such pieces of meddling, I will return unread any subsequent letters you should favor me with. I hope I make myself clear.

Elizabeth

P.S. As far as I'm concerned, you are the consummate amalgam (monstrous as that necessarily must be) of the worst character traits found in each of your respective parents. Should you get too bored with your current circumstances, there's always a cell waiting for you. I advise you to bear that in mind when you're reading the newspapers and playing hypothetical power games.

Thursday, 3/1/2096

What was it he jeered at me that forever cured me of tears? Oh yes, I have it verbatim in my memory, I can just hear the nasty drawl in his voice—*Poor little Alexandra, poor dear, she's hurt herself and now she's indulging the luxury of tears. A nice soft lusciously masochistic feeling, how sweet it is to lose control. The perfect belly-soft, slime-slick response. So there's just little Alexandra in the whole wide world, and not letting anyone or anybody else in, that'll show 'em.* And then, when I only glared at him, he added through his teeth, *All crying is a damned stupid ploy for going out of control.* And god knows one dare not go out of control except in designated situations... Nothing so infuriated him. *I refuse to take responsibility for controlling you. You, my dear, will control yourself!*

Yes, & so I do, & so I do.

I went into the Music Room & for the first time in more than five years opened the piano & stumbled sentimentally through some Beethoven. My fingers, though trembling, though uneven, remembered the pattern of notes… It sounded like shit, but it felt…comforting. For a while. Until frustration & disgust at my own ineptness made it impossible to continue the exercise. Ended up slamming the lid back over the keyboard (did I beat my fists on the keys first? I seem vaguely to recall doing that, only everything is a blur). Wine, I drank a great deal of wine in the late afternoon & evening. The Syrah slid easily enough down my throat. Still, I have no desire today to touch even a drop of alcohol. Elizabeth missed that: unless she counted his drunken binges one of his *less* obnoxious traits?

At some point I summoned Sally down to the Small Study where I was doing my drinking (right in his fucking footsteps, woman). I was lying on the sofa & had her (naked, of course) kneel beside the sofa on the rug, with her head on my breast while I fingered her labia. Got to thinking about Sally's probable relation to Elizabeth (Elizabeth not unnaturally being on my mind). Let my anger shift onto Sally, Elizabeth's paid spy-whore. "Do you want me to send you back to her?" I asked, probably not very nice in my tone of voice. "Whenever you've had enough, you're free to go. You've only to say the word." I'd been pretty rough with her before dinner, when my mood of self-pity had metamorphosed into self-hate and general rage. (Childish, I know. I can't seem to properly grow up.)

"No," she said, "I don't want to leave." & then she turned her head, & I felt her lips pressing through my gown against my breast.

A spear of pleasure-pain streaked through me. One of *those* moments. & with her, yet. I grabbed her hair & yanked her head back—to call attention to her transgression of the rules. To punish her I said, "Elizabeth must pay you exceedingly handsomely." The gifts I'd given her wouldn't have been enough to hold her through two miserable months (assuming she isn't a masochist) without the salary Elizabeth was paying her making it worth the pain & humiliation.

Her eyes, the color of steamed spinach, flinched from my gaze. "Yes," she whispered, "the pay is good."

I finished the wine in my glass & had her refill it. "If you're going to cry," I told her, "go away. I'm not in the mood for it." Actually, I haven't enjoyed her tears for a long time now.

Her long, graceful body (soft the way only the most parasitical service-techs' bodies are) poised for flight, yet she seemed indecisive. Like a deer frozen, waiting to determine the safest route for escape. "Do you want me to go?" she asked in that hoarse throaty voice she acquires at times of stress. I had the urge to shake her & yell at her to stop being such a worm. Sometimes that weakness gets to me, makes me want to prod it into outright defense. But of course she's beyond prodding. These days it doesn't take much to reduce her to a quivering, gelatinous mush.

I should send her away before I lose control of myself. What is it I'm doing with her, anyway? I wanted to pass the time. That's how I thought of it when she arrived the day before Christmas. But if she stays much longer...god knows what will happen. Can she be *that* greedy? Yes, of course she can. Some people will do anything for money.

Elizabeth. Damn her. I should have known about her savagery. She managed Rbt all those years, there's no way she could *not* be tough. As for what this means about her attitude toward me... No. I can't think about that now.

Oh christ that she muzzles me...it's an end to any hope, any hope at all. She doesn't care enough about me even to make it likely she'd give attention to any attempt I might make to explain myself. To her, Alexandra Sedgewick is only a remnant of an opponent she once had to overcome. *A monstrous amalgam.* But she hasn't talked to me in ten years! She doesn't know me!

But she doesn't care to know me.

A monstrous amalgam. As though I'm trapped in the tentacles of my parents' lives, beings, genes...as though I don't exist as a real self. Just a little leftover piece of Rbt. Alexandra Sedgewick never did exist. God knows there's no one even to remember *her*—only him. People will remember him, all right. & he's left me behind as his ghost. Some life. It's almost as good as being dead.

Monday, 3/5/2096

Yesterday Sally sent me into a rage. One of those states I so seldom fly—fall?—into: insensate, wild, unreasoning anger that blocks out all else. Typically, this obsessive state of mind dominates me until I have a chance to dissipate it. Rbt was the main object of my rages in the past, which I usually dissipated by finding ways of making him suffer. (Easy enough to do—though there was always a special price to pay for the pleasure.) Oddly enough, that's not how it worked this time. Oh, I did take it out on Sally, but doing so didn't dissipate my rage.

It all started with her faking orgasm. I'd been caressing her for a long time, but she proved elusive. Perversely, I insisted on continuing, though it should have been obvious after a certain point that we'd be getting no joy this time. & then she pulled this ridiculous stunt of trying to fake it. As though I wouldn't know what she was doing! Surely her other lovers haven't let her get away with *that* particular form of manipulation? I was so incensed that I grabbed her by the hair & slapped her. And she actually looked surprised! All I could think about was how I would punish her for the deception. I shouted at her demanding to know how stupid did she think me etc., & she turned fiery red & mumbled something about how sore she had been getting, about how she knew she would never come, that once she got sore & dry it was hopeless. Etc. etc. When her words penetrated my fog of rage, I understood immediately what she was saying. How could I not remember similar situations with Rbt—when I *did* fake it—successfully. No matter how familiar men are with women's bodies, they know next to nothing about the female body. Everything's guess-work for them. Familiarity helps, but approaching the female body as an object that can be scientifically understood leaves gaping chasms in what they choose to call "comprehension" or "understanding" of female sexuality. Rbt was no exception. How could he be? He could be a good guesser, yes. But that was all.

This bizarre identification was disorienting. There I was one moment, out of my mind with anger at her trying such a thing with me, & the next remembering my doing the same thing to Rbt, remembering how bored & irritated I'd get at his attentions at such times, wanting only to bring the whole tedious exercise to an end. & somehow Rbt never could grasp that it might be possible to be irritated on one occasion by the exact same thing that had produced ineffable pleasure on another. & I never knew how to make him see that. So there I was remembering the irritation finally driving me to put an end to it in the only way Rbt would accept…& realizing that Sally had felt the same. There's no doubt she felt little confidence in my reaction should she simply come right out & say that any further attempts would be futile… A terrible jarring, this juxtaposition. So I got to my feet & poured myself another glass of wine & sent Sally away. There was no point in being angry at her. All I could do was tell her not to try it again, that she needn't think I'd put up with that kind of insolence…

So now I have to wonder if she despises me. Why else would she think she could pull it off? Well if it should happen again, she had better ask me to stop instead of trying to dupe me. I might give her a hard time for it, but I certainly won't be anything near as hard on her as I'll be if she tries faking it again.

Oh hell. Elizabeth's paying her a fortune. Why bother trying to be decent to her? Girls like her deserve everything they get.

Sedgewick's Island, Maine
Tuesday, March 6, 2096

Dear Mama,

I won't blame you if you refuse, but I'd like it very much if you would come see me. I miss you terribly. I've been spending a lot of time lately going over the past, trying to understand what's become of me. In the process I've uncovered a great yearning for you. Please, Mama. Please come visit. I know I've been unforgivable. But he's dead now. And all that is—must be—past. I was so young, Mama. Please remember that as you judge me. If you can't forgive me, I'll understand— with infinite sadness. But I'm hoping your heart is large enough to give me another chance.

It's a sad commentary on the state of our relations that I don't even know where to send this. But I'm sure Grandfather will see to it that you get this.

Your loving

Alexandra

Thursday, 3/9/2096

The weather's cleared, the wind is high, & the sea & sky are glittering blue. I've taken to walking every afternoon along the edge of the water, circling the island. I'm trying to find if not peace, then some new source of hope. (The resignation that got me through the first five years seems to have deserted me.) When will she get my letter? It could be weeks. First it has to pass muster with Elizabeth's office. And then be sent to Grandfather. And he then must forward it to Mama. Will she even answer me? I responded so angrily when she made that single request to see me after Rbt's death that I never heard from her again. Or Grandmother, either. But Grandmother long ago lost the will to forgive me my infinite transgressions. She declared me ungrateful the last time I saw her: for Mama's sake rather than her own, I think.

Can anything come from rapprochement? I *must* try. It's all I have left.

I'm so testy lately the entire household is on edge. Except stolid icy disapproving Nicole: she knows she has me where she wants me; & except for the guards, of course—for though the estate pays their salaries, Elizabeth is their controller. I'm merely the object of their scrutiny & precautions, hardly their employer.

Which brings me around to Sally. Of course. Always to Sally. I'm beginning to worry that writing about her is my real reason for scribbling in this book. She's in the room with me now as I write. I've let her glimpse this book, I want her to take note of it—for I write in it only in this room, & it looks very different from all my reading notebooks, which I leave lying around open to inspection. Let her wonder, let her speculate...in her reports to Elizabeth?

Yesterday I took her walking with me. The guards of course followed us every step of the way, never letting us out of their sight. But I care little about privacy now. Nothing I do with Sally need be kept secret in the way that *all* sex games with Rbt had to be.

I walked on the outside, closest to the water, with my left arm around her waist, delighting in the feel of the wind on my face, the smell of the ocean, & above all the sunlight. The ocean, at least, makes life almost bearable here—I must be thankful Elizabeth allows it to me. Though god knows it's hard to think about it that way when life stretches so endlessly before me. When we came round onto the stretch of beach overhung by the cliff, I backed Sally against the cliff wall and stared into her dazzling eyes, which had turned a lovely blue green, the color of the sea on less brilliant days. "How can you be so greedy?" I demanded of her as I caressed her neck.

She gave me a worried look. "Have I done something wrong?" she asked in a throaty voice.

"To stay here when I treat you so badly," I said. "Only greed could be motivating you."

She lowered her eyes. "Yes, madam. I suppose I *am* greedy."

Her tone of voice left me oddly disturbed. Was it sadness? Or no, perhaps resignation would be a better way of describing it... At any rate, I was swept by an overwhelming desire to kiss her, something I had never done, so I put my lips to hers & did a little exploring. I found her pliant & her mouth deliciously warm & sweet, like moving into a patch of sunlight. How strange to find again the cave. But when I became aware that her arms were around me, her hands stroking my back, & her tongue in my mouth, I disengaged. I raised my hand to slap her, then stopped myself. My heart was racing ridiculously. I took a deep breath & said as calmly as I could, "You've violated my rules. You'll have to be punished." She said nothing, only implored me with her eyes, so compellingly I could hardly tear my gaze from them. But I strove to regain control of myself & at last indicated that we would resume the walk. I took her arm & felt it trembling. We walked without speaking until the tide crept too high for our booted comfort.

She sits now on the rug in front of the fireplace, staring at the flames, her face pensive & calm. She cannot be thinking about my abuse of her last night. So what is it she's thinking about? What could it be other than money? What Judith MacLaury all those years ago referred to as "delayed gratification" as she endured a life serving a master she detested...Judith managed it, somehow. I suppose for some, enduring me is no worse—& it is, after all, a relatively short-term thing. While Judith knew her bondage would go on for years before paying off.

I never pitied Judith. I certainly shall not pity Sally. She may be free of me whenever she chooses. While I shall never be free of this exile, ever.

Wednesday, 3/14/2096

It has been eight days since I sent the letter to Mama. Will she answer? But of course the damned thing's probably still sitting in Elizabeth's office. My correspondence is low priority. Who reads the letters, I wonder? Elizabeth herself? Or a trusted PA? What nonsense to waste my time on. I should instead think of what I should say if Mama *does* decide to see me. (Perhaps she'll come out of curiosity—to see the one residence Rbt never let her near.) *Can* I forgive her for raising me to be so vulnerable, so weak, so unprepared for the life I was thrust into? Her only notion was to make me feel as guilty as she could for living in semi-harmony with Rbt. For refusing to fight him. What the hell did she expect of me? My entire girlhood was designed to make me as docile as possible. Or at least sufficiently self-censored in my speech & deeds to make me appear to be docile. Not that she was ever around for most of it. My father was right when he accused her of dumping me on Grandmother. That's *exactly* what she did. Because he wasn't around to hold her more tightly to her contract. Contract! That's all I ever was to her: a means to an end. What counted was that juicy trust-fund that was to be hers upon my twenty-first birthday, provided I turned out reasonably acceptable. Well, thanks to my intercession she *got* her trustfund. Not that she has any idea he ever seriously intended to refuse it to her on grounds of non-compliance with the contract. She felt she earned it. Daniel, Rbt, myself: we were the bondage she had to endure for the sake of delayed gratification. Oh christ. At least he never leveled *that* at me, though now I can see it for myself, plain as day: it was all for the money—giving birth to me, raising me. It explains a lot. (*Girls are so* difficult *to raise!*) I must have understood this all along. That must be why I knew Rbt was more likely to love me than she. At least with him I could tell. There was nothing there for him to get out of it. He could be (& was) as honest as he pleased. *She* has always been a supreme manipulator. & she worked to teach me her ways. Touché, Elizabeth.

Monday, 3/19/2096

& now what? That things have come to this—it's so bad I've spent
the day running back & forth to the toilet, my bowels—no, my whole
body—in turmoil. I must *think*, must think *carefully* before setting
anything more into motion. (God knows I've done enough damage
already.) That I could have made this kind of mistake sickens me, horrifies me…& *frightens* me.

Part of it must be in some way connected with this godawful nerve-
wracking wait to hear from Mama. (*If* she even bothers to reply.) I
have to face it, I've been totally obsessed with thoughts of Sally's greed.
Going further & further, trying to find a limit to what she would take.
Last night she seemed almost to the point of breaking. Having just
knocked her to the floor, I shouted at her, "For godsake girl, what in
the *hell* is she paying you?" & that started the whole thing unraveling
before my horrified eyes.

My shouting this at her scared her out of her wits. She only gaped at
me, &, when realizing I meant her to answer, choked out, "A lot. She's
paying me a lot."

I ordered her to get up off the floor, then sat her down on the sofa
beside me. "How much?" I demanded, determined to know the exact
figure & the arrangements for payment & so on. I wanted to know
every last grimy detail. That's how wild I was.

"A lot," she repeated.

I slapped her hard. "Give me the numbers," I ordered.

The look of sheer panic on her face should have told me something.
When I raised my hand to slap her again, she cried out a figure. The
figure was ridiculously low, slightly less than what I used to pay Nicole in the days when I handled the estate's finances. (She probably
makes twice that now, all things considered.) "You expect me to believe that?" I scoffed, furious at her for lying to me.

"I'm sorry," she got out, her voice so hoarse I kept wondering if she'd
be able to form words with it. "I wanted to impress you." & then she
named a figure *half* of that she'd originally given!

I took her so small-boned, so delicate wrist in my hand—using one of Rbt's old tricks for helping to assess the truthfulness of responses. "You're lying to me, Sally, & I want to know why. Shall we see if I can make you tell me?" Her pulse speeded up even faster. It must have been 200 beats per minute.

She gasped for breath. "I can't tell you," she choked out. "No matter what," she added, bracing for another blow.

By this time my mind had begun to work (god knows it seems to go on idle whenever I'm with Sally). The most significant implication of her lie was that though she wanted to convince me Elizabeth was paying her, she hadn't the faintest notion of what a girl like her could be paid—even for non-extraordinary circumstances. Say, to serve my mother. But for *these* circumstances, the figure would be off the scale—a scale she seemed to have no notion of. Elizabeth was careless here—she attended to so many details to make the girl authentic, but she omitted the most obvious, even though she'd assured me she was paying the girl an extravagant amount. "Let's calm down," I said as non-threateningly as I could, & with my free hand stroked her face. The contact at first was difficult for her, but after a few quiet moments she steadied a bit, and her pulse slowed to perhaps 100 beats per minute. So. Now I had something to work with. "You've never done this kind of thing before, have you," I said, watching her face for any revealing tightening. Her pulse picked up somewhat.

"What do you mean?" she asked.

"You've never served an executive woman before, have you," I said very gently.

Her eyes dropped. "Yes I have," she whispered.

"You're lying," I said. "And you're a lousy liar. You can't even look into my eyes with that lie, can you."

"I did serve one, sort of, for a month," she blurted out. "It's not entirely a lie."

"But you're not a whore," I rapped out.

She swallowed. "No." She lifted her eyes. "You're going to send me away now, aren't you."

"Who are you & what are you doing here?" I demanded. She lowered her eyes. "Now listen to me, Sally—if that's really your name—I knew from the beginning that Elizabeth sent you here to keep an eye on me. I even told her I knew that when I wrote thanking her for such a thoughtful Christmas present." She looked up, startled. "You're a Company girl?"

She swallowed again. "Yes," she said, and her pulse leaped back into wildness.

"That's a lie," I said. "I bet you don't even know what the Company is, do you." She looked stricken. "Tell me the truth, Sally."

Her eyes squeezed close. Tears followed, then silent heaving sobs she could not control. After awhile I prompted her. Still she didn't look at me. "I might as well," she sobbed. "It's gone too far...I'm useless now... Everything's finished." She was crying so hard that she could hardly choke the words out.

There was a way I had of holding & stroking her that I never used with her at any other time than to comfort her, & this I used now. She responded to it because she unconsciously associated it with a temporary spell of tenderness she could count on lasting for hours & hours. (Oh the things my father taught me...) When I'd soothed her into quiet peaceful tears, I crooned to her, "Tell me everything, Sally, I need to understand."

Essentially she told me a tale of how Elizabeth was blackmailing her into spying on me. That if Elizabeth was satisfied—& there was no time-limit or real goal, for Elizabeth apparently wasn't looking for anything specific—then her lover, a service-tech who'd given assistance to an underground member of some terrorist group, would be released from prison & given a full pardon with the felony charges expunged from her record. Sally herself was an actor—she played the soaps, mainly (& I've checked this out with Nicole, who now seems to recognize her as someone who played a minor role in one of her favorite soaps for three years not too long ago). She'd been judged suitably talented, motivated, & attractive for pulling off the job. Elizabeth had personally briefed her on what I would like & had had her train with an executive woman for a month. From what I can make out, Elizabeth seems interested in getting an in-depth picture of my emotional & intellectual states, as intimate & detailed a portrait of me as possible. Since the guards & some of the help regularly report more superficial things to Elizabeth, I suppose it makes some sense… Though it still seems a little crazy. Why in the hell would Elizabeth want to know about me—especially considering how she's gone out of her way to profess total indifference to my existence here?

So what do I do about Sally? I writhe at the thought of all I've done to her. After she finished telling me her story—which I believe without reservation—I apologized & assured her I would try to find a solution to her problems. That she has suffered at my hands for love of another—I'm sick at my own cruelty. I can never make it up to her. But perhaps I can come up with some way for her to satisfy Elizabeth. In the meantime, we must keep from alerting Elizabeth's other eyes & ears in this house. Her restrictions are to be lifted—with the cover story being that I am suddenly infatuated with her. When this morning I ordered Penderel to restore the old arrangements for the cleaning of my suite, I could see the wheels turning in that repulsive old head of his… Think of it. The strength & courage & utter determination of that girl—who knows more about love than anyone I've ever met. Elizabeth is right: I *am* a monster.

Chapter Two

Sunday, March 11, 2096—Seattle

It's getting harder and harder to keep things straight with myself. Last night's party at Venn's... I've dutifully written a detailed description of who was there and what was said. But all the same, I have a terrible uneasiness about it, as I always do when I have to write about Venn's parties. A lot of the things I report are clear-cut. But where Venn is concerned... No, I have to be honest. That's the whole *point* of this diary.

It's just so hard to put into writing. I could say that I admire her tremendously. And I do. But her politics confuse me. I try to leave any evaluation of them to smarter heads than mine. I mean, what do *I* know about politics? But anyone can see that this situation can't go on forever, now that everything's changing. In all honesty, I never believed that Weatherall, Lise, and Mott would succeed in their crazy struggle against the old Executive. But since they did, I have to take their plan to oust the Co-op and take back the FZ seriously. How can anyone doubt, now, that Weatherall will succeed in accomplishing anything she sets out to do? She's changed everything, and Lise assures me there's more to come. The woman is simply unbeatable—lucky for us, I suppose, though not so lucky for Venn and her friends.

But to get back to Venn. I can write it here, what I can tell no one. Sometimes my keeping my feelings for her secret feels shameful. At least with Alice my shame was more a matter of knowing she was unattainable. But while Venn is unattainable (triply so—given that she has a lover, she is heterosexual, and she's too far above me to give me a thought), there's also this other problem: where my relations with her are concerned, I'm mostly dishonest. I write about her in my reports, constantly, without ever revealing my feelings. And of course I have to make everyone here believe Lise is the great passion of my life in order to give us a reason for continuing to meet at such frequent intervals. It's such a silly cover story that I wonder anyone still believes it. Oh yeah, it's the great tragedy of my life, being unable to live with my lover because of the personal tyranny of my lover's boss... But then people here don't take me all that seriously. (People anywhere, Anne: be honest.) They may suspect *Lise* of an ulterior motive, but not me. I'm too wide-open and guileless to be devious with them. I should, Lise sometimes says, feel very clever. But somehow, putting off a lie on others—others who are basically willing to take the people they meet at face value—doesn't seem very creditable, or clever, either. I know how smart some of the women around here are—how could I feel clever compared with them, just because I've been lying to them for years?

Venn always has an interesting mix of people at her parties—and being invited to join such people always makes me feel a little flattered. But to tell the truth, I'd rather not be around her lover like that, it makes him too real. I'd gathered from the other times I've been to her parties that Miguel is non-American, some kind of Hispanic. (Well that's obvious, isn't it.) But I didn't know any of his personal history until last night. I suppose it came out because of who was there—that woman from São Paolo, the two New Zealanders, the two women from the Free Zone in Asia, and the couple from Martinique—it was a more cosmopolitan and politically active bunch of people than usual.

I keep wondering about the things Miguel said about what happened in Cuba when Military took it over. Everyone's heard the stories about how horrible it was in Cuba under the Communists. And Miguel says he wasn't a party member, just "an ordinary university professor." (Are university professors ever ordinary?) He claims that at first he was determined to stay, to "fight in defense against the ideological campaign being waged against the values of the people of Cuba" as he put it. According to him, the reason Cuban professionals—academics especially—were offered lucrative positions (or sometimes two-year grants) at universities outside of Cuba was to lure the most articulate upholders of "Cuban values" out of Cuba and thus open positions in the professional structure for SIC-sponsored professionals who would be the vanguard for an American propaganda campaign. He kept talking about "Cuban values," which I know must mean the Communist party line. When I pointed out that even if what he said is true, at least the occupation forces had not violently purged Cuba, as many other occupation forces would have, he gave me an intense look and said that I was mistaken if I thought that blood had not been shed. He said that he had decided to leave because all those who spoke out against the occupation were losing their jobs and were sometimes even found dead. His wife, he said, had been imprisoned for refusing to teach a revised version of twentieth-century history to her secondary school students.

I kept my mouth shut because I didn't want to give myself away. But I can read between the lines on *that* little story. *I've* heard some of the lies they taught Cuban school children about the US. It was propaganda designed to make their first Commie dictator look like a hero and the US a persecuting monster. It's a cinch our government was never that stupid, or the CIA that inept (in their lies about the supposed Bay of Pigs invasion attempt or the supposed assassination attempts that Miguel was saying the occupation forces demand be suppressed). But Communists always have distorted history for their own ends, whether deliberately or because their ideology misguides them.

I guess the thing about Venn's parties that I find the oddest is that she usually has men at them—and not just Miguel. Also, she frequently has as many professionals as service-techs—not surprising, I suppose, since she herself is professional. But how is it that as a service-tech going to her parties I don't feel uncomfortable? Is it because this is the FZ? Or because I'm so hyper-aware of how I'll be writing everything down in my report afterwards?

Venn is so very different from *every*one I know—most of whom fall into two categories—anti-Executive and pro-Executive. All those women I recruit for Lise's media organization are of course pro, but discreetly so. (This *is* the FZ.) They make no bones about being anti-Co-op, though: every one of them belongs to organizations devoted to the downfall of the Co-op. But the Executive is so unpopular, so bad-mouthed around here that declaring yourself to be *for* it is unthinkable. Even the first few times I talked to these women they were kind of embarrassed about coming out with positive statements about the

Executive. It's strange the way things can be so different. That there can be this force-like thing that changes the way people feel, and all so intangible. It affects even me. One thing, though, is that the reorganization of the Executive has perked up a lot of people: there isn't the whole human rights thing to fight now. I always felt it emotionally obfuscated the picture. People got so worked up about human rights that they weren't willing to look at the system as a whole. Focusing on the abuses of individuals is one of the anti-Executive ideologues' main tricks.

What I don't want to face most of the time is that Venn *is* one of the main anti-Executive ideologues in the FZ. She has a lot of influence. Not only do people listen to her and repeat what she says, but she also makes decisions about what is to get published and herself writes books and essays. I'd never try to argue with her, that's for sure (even if I didn't have to keep my political opinions and objectives secret). She's so intelligent and so incredibly educated that she could probably run circles around almost anyone who tried to argue with her. She's always reading very detailed history, in order to make highly abstract patterns and of course ideological points. (History is something anyone can use crookedly.) Not that I'm saying her integrity is crooked: I don't believe that. She's gotten off on the wrong foot, that's all. Before the Blanket she specialized in Social Policy Studies. That tells you a lot right there about what kind of abilities she has. But she never achieved the final stage of tenure—for ideological reasons, she says. Also, according to her, they—at least in the past—trained more graduate students in Social Policy Studies than could be employed by the universities, with the understanding that a large percentage of the new PhDs would be steered into Security Services, the Dept. of Health, and Com & Tran, all of which hired PhDs in SPS as "policy projection analysts." (They still do, according to Lise.)

Now take this as an example of Venn's reasoning: she cites these facts as points showing how evil the Executive is, how the Executive has a "strangle-hold" over everything going on "in the academy" (as she likes to put it). But what she fails to acknowledge is that the whole point of having Social Policy Studies in the first place is a practical one: to train people to analyze the sorts of things the Executive needs to know in order to make the best policy decisions possible for the entire country. Instead, Venn is indignant about it, saying that apart from doing as she did around the time of the Blanket—teaching one-third time and editing for a publishing company two-thirds time—her only alternative would have been to work for one of those three Executive departments running data collection and extrapolation programs according to formulas supplied by supervisors. She said the reason they'd have hired her to do that would be that then she'd be no trouble to anyone, taking away the voice she had as a teacher and researcher, while not allowing her any decision-making responsibility whatsoever.

These people have developed a very complex but weirdly distorted view of reality, Venn included. I find it hard to understand how such intelligent people can do this, but I suppose their intelligence just makes them all the more ingenious in elaborating the details of their theory. What they can't see, after a while, is that they've started out with a distorted set of assumptions to begin with. (Because they're swallowed up in the details.) No matter how intelligent you are, if you accept certain things on faith you'll always go wrong. Their Number One premise is that the Executive is evil. And for some of them, that *any* form of government is wrong. Everything else follows from these premises. They have really closed and dogmatic minds when it comes to the Executive.

But Venn is wonderfully kind and well-meaning. That shines through her efficient exterior—it's in her eyes, and all the little things she notices. She never says condescending things. I guess that's what I've noticed the most. About condescension, I mean. I never realized how condescending most people are to others who are socially inferior to themselves. Maybe it's a bad thing, though, that I'm picking up on it now all the time? I'm afraid it's making me overly sensitive. I don't want to turn into one of those people constantly affronted, constantly having their dignity wounded. But take a simple little thing like the word "girl." I hadn't noticed it before I started living among these FZ people. But they *never* use the word girl except to refer to females (of any social class) below the age of fifteen or so. (Not that there are that many of them around.) People here refer to me as a woman. Now I'd gotten more or less in the habit of thinking of women as always being executive or professional! And the weird thing is that I hadn't even realized that until I heard people saying "women" all the time around here, and it struck my ear as odd. But the more I got to thinking about it—and the more used to it I became—the more it felt natural. And "girl" started to make me self-conscious. I remember once asking Lise how the "girls" were—Lacie and Ginger, I meant—and then feeling strange about it. I guess that's when I realized about this condescension thing. Then I began listening carefully to the way different people talked, and it was clear as day!

Why didn't I hear the difference before? I suppose because no one in my life ever referred to me as a woman. First of course my mother and father and teachers and schoolmates always said "girl." Well that's what I was. But as soon as I got out of school I started working as a secretary. And then I became one of the girls. It just never occurred to me. Until I started working for Venn, that is. There are so many subtle little things. It gets confusing. I sometimes don't know anymore what's right and what's wrong. And talking to Lise about it doesn't help. She gets that look in her eyes. Questioning my loyalty, maybe. And I can't talk to anyone else about this stuff.

I'm caught in the middle.

And then there are all those twentieth-century novels (and other books) Venn has stocked the Rainbow Press's library with. I don't look very much at the nonfiction (some of it is sort of interesting, though again sometimes boringly ideological), but the fiction…that's something else. What a bizarre world those twentieth-century people lived in! A lot of the books are about heterosexual relationships. Which can be a little difficult to take sometimes (though surprisingly many of such novels *are* readable). But there's a lot of stuff about women getting upset about language in them, too. Those are the really angry books. I can't take that much of *them*. It's all very puzzling. I wish I could talk to someone about these things. But I guess not being able to is what I get for leading a double life.

Wednesday, March 14, 2096—Seattle

Depressed. Irritable. Not in the mood for reading. And not willing to put myself out to be amusing to another person. So I guess I'm stuck with myself, here, alone. Why is the price of other people's

company so high? You have to be in good shape to have it; but when
you're in good shape you don't really need it. Thinking of how characters in books always get to pour out their woes to some understanding
soul who's genuinely interested in how they're feeling… Hunh. Guess
I don't have the right kind of friends.

Friends? Sometimes I feel that "friend" is the most absurd word
in the English language. Especially living here like this. How could I
claim to be a friend to any of the people I write about in my reports?
As for those I do the spying *for*… Do I have friends among Executive
people anymore? I see Lise about twice a month solely so that I can
pass her my reports. We make love in this apartment, never saying
anything that couldn't be overheard by a suspicious enemy, proceed-
ing as we do on the assumption that my apartment is bugged and that
it's an opportunity for us to bolster my cover. Which is crazy. It makes
me feel used. How can there be anything real between Lise and me
when mechanically, like clockwork, she comes to pick up my report
and have sex for the benefit of real or potential eavesdroppers? And
then when we do go out and walk it's mainly to talk about business.
Lise's job—I know that's what it is, it's so damned clear—is to make
sure I'm psychologically on base, still loyal, etc. etc. So that I can be
reeled in if I start to waver. But why bother to keep me here? I don't
have access to anything important. Lise insists I'm a "well-placed
mole." Hah. Venn hardly ever goes to Steering Committee meetings.
While I do—as almost anyone can. Hardly anything could be more
boring than Steering Committee meetings, as Venn likes to point out
when people chide her for not going.

The trouble is, these FZ people just like to hear themselves talk.
Everything around here is a subject for debate, an excuse for people
to get all puffed up with their ideas, forcing them on everybody else.
Take half the people today at the afternoon break. I was feeling a
little anxious. During my lunch hour I finished that novel I'd been
reading—one from Venn's collection—and was feeling strange about
it. Queasy, and maybe angry, too. I hardly slept last night because my
head was filled with its images and ugly language. What I really wanted at break was to talk to Venn about it. I'm sure she's read it. (She's
read almost every book in that collection. I've yet to mention something to her that I've been reading that she couldn't meaningfully

comment on.) In some ways it was a beautiful book and very compelling. On the other hand, I was sort of embarrassed to bring it up to her. I mean that's not the kind of thing you're supposed to talk about. But in so many ways Venn is different—she has so many books in that collection that I've glanced at that have to do with the subject (the twentieth century is like an alien culture, so primitive and wild and *blatant*, and of course hate-filled), that I'm pretty sure Venn has *thought* a lot about the subject whether she's ever *talked* about it with anyone else or not.

Well, break is probably not the right place for such a conversation. But still, I wonder how she can sit there and listen to all that tripe without telling them how absurd they are. If I were she I would. And I *wish* she would. It would be so much better if *she* were to talk instead of them. But she keeps a low-profile at break.

One time when I asked her about this she said that break is "for everyone." And that anyone who wants to talk should feel free to do so—which they wouldn't if she were always doing all the talking. And that furthermore she was a co-worker, not a professor with students. Well there I wanted to tell her she was wrong: because she's the boss, not a co-worker. Typesetters can't possibly compare to editors. And anyway she's so educated. I wish sometimes she *were* a professor and I a student.

Well I think we should boycott them, argued one of them. Well I think we should go farther than that and get the Water Co-op to turn off his water and drive him out of business, argued another. But then someone else said those measures were too strong-arm and that it would just be better to persuade someone else to open up a competing laundromat. How stupid to spend the whole break discussing what to do with someone's overcharging them for the use of washing machines and driers! Just because the laundromat people didn't lower their rates when the price of water dropped last year when the last of the big water clean-up projects were completed, the women living in that neighborhood are plotting against them, furious at their "greed."

Not that I think it's great for these people to be making a whopping profit (if piling up barter credits can be called "profit") now that water is so cheap (and who has their own washing machine, anyway?)—but to spend all that time going on and on and *on* about which methods are most ethical and effective for dealing with the situation seems absurd to me. I'd rather continue with the old way than have to endure these kinds of "discussions." And what did Venn say? Very little. She asked a few questions to bring out points (ironic points, *I* thought) that she felt were being neglected, but didn't offer any suggestions herself. But then everything gets done by committee around here. It's true what the anarchists have been saying all along: there are no leaders in the FZ.

But this book... Well, it's a real love story, between two women. Two very poor women. (We don't have people that poor anymore.) They're black women. And all through the book that's stressed. Which is, I guess, why I can't talk to Venn about the book...but is why I'd like to. Racism is such a delicate thing. What was it Mom said to me when I was little and curious about differences in skin color and hair and all the rest? *We don't talk about such things in a civilized society, Annie. In the past people were very ugly to one another. Which is why it's so impolite ever to refer out loud to somebody's race or ethnic background. Or even their religion, unless they volunteer it. Words are so dangerous that people have killed other people because of them. So be careful, Anne Lydia Hawthorne. For all our sakes.* It was something like that. Those kind of things stick in your head. Especially when spoken in that thundery kind of voice Mom would sometimes get into. And of course people never *do* talk about such things, not in polite company. The only exceptions I can think of were those men who raped me... and once some men coming out of a bar I was passing, when they saw me and the girl I was with walking arm-in-arm...and then that first time Weatherall spoke to me about infiltrating and how I could say I was attracted to the Co-op because some of its leaders were black.

What if I gave that book to someone else to read? But who? Not Lise! And anyway, giving it to someone else would be like talking about it. But why do I want to talk about it? I guess because those characters made such an impact on me. What a strange name, Shug. But then people used to like strange names in past centuries...

Sunday, March 18, 2096—Seattle

Lise just dropped me off and is on her way out of town. I wonder what will happen now? Could be nothing, and we'll just drag on as we've been doing for the last ten years.

Lise is angry with me about it. *That* I don't understand—why *she* should be angry. Her eyes have been guarded with me for ever so long, but today...today I could read nothing in them but a kind of cold withdrawal—though a watchful one. I wouldn't be surprised if she recommends an evaluation. I haven't been evaluated in a long time, so they wouldn't even need an excuse. I can't blame them for being cautious. People in my situation have been known to double.

It started the moment Lise arrived for her visit. We do everything by routine. First the sex. Then the meal at the executive women's club. Then the walk. And finally Lise drives off—unless she's planning on staying the night, in which case we go to the executive women's club from the start and stay there until morning. This time as she started going through the usual crap about having missed me, I asked if we couldn't take a walk. Muttered something about a headache (for the presumed bug) and how some air would help clear my head. Once we were out walking I said flat out, "Isn't there a way we can do without the sex charade? It's really starting to bother me that we do this performance twice a month for the sake of a microphone that might or might not be there."

Lise stopped dead in her tracks and stared at me—her eyes just about boring a hole in my face, they were that intense. Her face clenched, then got very still and rigid. "You'd better tell me all about her. And what you've told her about me."

Her voice was tremulous, which worries me: it probably means she thinks I'm in trouble. But I was also confused by her question, because I couldn't figure out who she was talking about. "Who do you mean, Lise? I never talk about you to anyone!"

She took my arm and started us walking again. "Who do you think I mean?" She sounded oddly close to tears. "Your new lover!"

I just gaped at her for a few seconds, she so took me by surprise. And then I said, "I don't know where you get that idea from, but I haven't had a lover since you, Lise. I knew I couldn't handle it, not

living this double life. It would tear me to pieces trying to love someone under these circumstances. So mainly I keep my distance. I have
casual encounters on occasion, but not often."

Lise stopped again to look at me. Her lips pursed, and I realized she
was angry. "Just when did you stop thinking of me as your lover?" she
asked in a frigid voice. It was at this point that I really felt the chill
coming from somewhere behind her eyes.

I decided to tell her the truth. (I suppose because I'm sick of keeping
it to myself.) "I guess it was when everything happened in that house.
You know. When Ms. Weatherall talked to me about everything."

"I don't understand. Why should you have stopped thinking of me
as your lover *then*? Because we asked you to infiltrate the Co-op?"

It was embarrassing to be talking about this stuff. I hadn't thought
about any of it for so long. It hurt me terribly for a long time, but now
I don't care. It really doesn't matter any more. "*You* know, Lise," I
said, hoping Lise would nod and say she did. But she didn't. So I tried
to explain. "I was pretty upset that you were asking me to leave you
only months after I'd gone renegade for you. Well...Ms. Weatherall
just pointed out the facts of life to me, and said that I was an adult and
was responsible for myself. That I couldn't hold you responsible for
making a major decision like going renegade. Well that was true, and
I knew it. And then she said that she knew you better than anyone else
did and that you had been in love with someone else for a long time,
even before you met me, and that you had always felt an obligation
to be kind to me, because I was in such bad shape after the rape. And
that it had gotten to be a habit, being kind to me, and an easy habit at
that. I saw that what she said was true. The fact of the matter is, I've
always chosen to be in love with women who are kind to me but don't
reciprocate the feeling. It's one of my worst faults. I know I was pretty
pathetic over Alice. And then you. So, after Ms. Weatherall said these
things to me, I could see that what she said was true. That I'd made
my bed and would have to lie in it. What choice did I have? I couldn't
go back. And I couldn't stay there. So I just learned to accept it."

Lise got very angry with me for all this. I suggested she find me a
new controller, someone I wouldn't have to have sex with. That there
must be easier ways to do this. And that besides, wasn't she a little too
busy now to be running out here to Seattle twice a month just to pick

up my reports? After that we didn't talk much, just went to the club, where I gave her the new report and she gave me the direction she had been instructed to pass along.

What I'd really like would be to be called home. But I didn't ask. Lise long ago made it clear that Mott is insistent I stay here.

Home! I don't even know what home would be now. Imagine if I'd stayed, if I hadn't gone renegade...I would have continued working for Alice. Unless, of course, I'd been purged simply for having been Lise's lover. Would I have gone with Alice to the Chief's office when Sedgewick took over again? What a strange thought! But if I went back now, would there even be a place for me? Who's there now to go to bat for me? Though Alice is apparently still working in the SIC— Weatherall hardly purged at all, Lise said—she wouldn't want me back. The idea of living the way I did all those years before meeting Lise—sharing cramped quarters with a whole bunch of girls, scarce water and tubefood, barely getting by from month to month. And no more longevity treatments. (Perhaps the best thing about living in the FZ is being able to have longevity treatments.)

I feel like an orphan.

Monday, March 19, 2096—Seattle

Ran into Venn in the Press's library today—I was returning *The Color Purple* and planning on finding another book, hopefully by the same author. Venn was there, sitting cross-legged on the floor, read-ing. She saw the book as I checked it back in and shelved it. She sort of half-smiled, then said something about what an "extraordinary" and "brave" book it was. Then she asked me if I'd appreciated it. (I'm glad she didn't ask me if I *enjoyed* it!) I blurted out something about how I hadn't been able to put it down or, once having finished, stop thinking about the characters, even though it was such a painful book to read and think about. I think I also said something about how aw-ful the twentieth century sounded, if such novels were anything to judge by. And about how people were certainly a lot cruder—they are in *all* the twentieth century novels I'd read. Venn got a little pink in the face and said "You mean because they brought things out into the open more than we do now. They didn't consider it bad manners then,

you know." "Yes, but that must be why there was so much violence?"
I asked. Venn disagreed that the violence had anything to do with
"speaking the truth." She half-argued—I couldn't tell whether it was
one of her "academic" arguments for the sake of arguing, or whether
she believed it—that not talking about things like racism just covered
them up. But whenever I think about the kinds of things people had
to put up with hearing others say about their racial and ethnic back-
grounds, I *know* Venn's argument is wrong. Because at least there isn't
that horrible rudeness now. I mean, there used to be *jokes* people ma-
liciously made on the subject. When I said something about this, Venn
said yes, the way they still joke about women's sexuality, but that even
if they didn't make those kinds of jokes and call women rude names
there'd still be the same underlying problems that women have to put
up with in most places. (Less here in the FZ, she implied.) Anyway,
Venn picked out a new novel for me that she said I'd probably like
since I "took" so strongly to the Walker. This book is by an author I've
never heard of. I wouldn't have found it by myself, except accidentally.
I'm going to start reading it tonight. It's so thin I can probably read
the whole book in one sitting.

Wednesday, March 21, 2096—Seattle

Lise called last night—most rare of occurrences. I am to ask to take
my vacation as soon as it can be arranged—so that I can "visit" her
in DC. I know what that means. (I'm not stupid.) Damned honeyed
conversation—just in case someone was bothering to tap my phone.
So I asked Marlene and Janice today if it would be convenient for me
to take the next two weeks off, and it's fine with them, they can cover
without me. I just won't take another book project. God how I wish
they'd just transfer me back to my old job. But that's not possible, is
it. Even if so many former renegade executives are in powerful positions now, my case isn't like theirs. I have a feeling being a renegade
service-tech is considered quite different from a renegade Weatherall.
Or a renegade Allison Bennett. Weatherall always did have it in for me.
And Alice—who oddly enough hasn't been booted out, even though
she and Weatherall have always been enemies—Alice wouldn't give
me the time of day now. It was her I walked out on, wasn't it. And I

know very well I can't count on Lise. Not now. What was it that made her so angry? It can't have been my saying out loud what we've both been thinking for months (no, years!), could it?

But even so, surely they'll be fair with me. I'll have hours of debriefing and then a loquazene exam. My old reports will all be trotted out. And then they'll decide whether to keep me in this position, and if they decide yes I'll return here and possibly they'll assign me a new controller. Or not. And if they decide not, then it will be a question of why not that likely determines what happens next.

Chapter Three

Time now to brace for reproaches, lectures, and accusations. Already I can hear them pouring out of her as she runs her eyes over this place, poking & prying into every room (Rbt meanwhile turning in his grave); & then, having decided which rug is the most fitting complement to her splendor, she will sink down onto it & demand that I order some exotic tea or other (which she will have brought with her) prepared.

& how will I respond to her barrage? Shall I be the meek, penitent daughter? The very thought of it makes me gag. I must find a way to patch things up with her enough for it to look convincing to Elizabeth. Perhaps a bribe offered in a suitably discreet manner?

I'm certain Elizabeth doesn't take Mama seriously as an opponent. I wonder if that's wise of her? According to Mama's note, Elizabeth has refused to see her every time she's requested an appointment. Can Elizabeth be so socially inaccessible that Mama hasn't been able to touch her in that sphere, either? Hard to believe—considering the social circles Mama moves in... Elizabeth did threaten to tell Grandfather about the incest if I tried to enlist his help. But she never delivered the same threat vis-à-vis Mama. It wouldn't do her any good if she did. After all, I think I might enjoy springing it on Mama myself. She was the one who started the damned Persephone crap. (As though incest was in the back of her mind all along.) I'd tell her all about it if I thought it would make her feel even slightly guilty, but I know better. Nothing could scratch a hide as tough as hers...

Last night Sally & I got pleasantly tight together, two bottles of Cabernet Sauvignon between us. It's rather strange with us, still. Sometimes her face takes on that wary look, as though some tone in my voice is triggering the fear lurking not far beneath the surface. (I can hardly blame her. Apart from which she may still feel vulnerable to me since I could at any time let Elizabeth know the game's up, & she knows *intimately* the worst side of me.) I don't suppose she'll ever comprehend how much I admire her for the strength of her love. How many people in this hell of an existence would ever consider sacrificing themselves as Sally has done? Dissociation is what one would expect. Instead, she has made a bargain with Elizabeth. A horrible ugly bargain. Yet never a hint of any of this in her demeanor—but then the girl's an actor.

I learned at an early age, I told Sally last night, that there's no choice but to make whatever compromise is necessary for survival. It's what they wanted me to learn. Executives have a finely developed drive to survive. (That's not strictly true, but I wasn't about to tell Sally about all the broken-down failures I saw working for Rbt.) At any rate, that each of us has done what has seemed necessary to do, however ugly & degraded, is something Sally & I have in common. Of course I never had the exaltation of acting out of pure, selfless love. I never will. That's something closed to me, forever closed to me. I mentioned something to her about how even if she cannot succeed in springing her lover from prison she will at least be able to leave this island, free. As I will never do. That struck her hard, as though she'd never before realized it. Perhaps this was the first time she saw me as something other than a monster?

There must be a way to help Sally out of her mess with Elizabeth. But what would satisfy Elizabeth? That's the question. What if Sally were to report that I'd fallen in love with her? Would that satisfy her? What *is* it that Elizabeth intends with Sally? (Is it possible Sally knows & isn't saying—still out of fear?)

So hard to keep my hands off her. I had to send her away before we'd finished the second bottle...

Thursday, 3/29/2096

This morning Sally reported to Elizabeth's office that I've declared myself to be in love with her. According to Sally, she reports via terminal with a direct com-link to Elizabeth's office twice a week. The others also use terminals similarly linked. Although I *mail* my letters to Elizabeth, Elizabeth's office doesn't bother with the pretence—the top gorilla here simply delivers print-outs of Elizabeth's letters to me personally. If I'd thought about it much I'd have realized their instant com must be in addition to any phone conversations they hold with Elizabeth's office.

Although my having made such a "declaration" will require constant, consistent acting, it also means the oddity of my treating Sally decently will seem perfectly explicable. When I asked Sally if this would be a strain, she reminded me that she's a pro, that this new role will be easier than the one she had to play with me. That working with me rather than against me changed everything. What worries me is the likelihood of Elizabeth's administering loquazene to Sally once Sally is taken off this job.

& so as Lavoisier set up for & carried in our lunch, we produced plenty of ostentatious hand-holding & billing & cooing. I'm not very good at such things, but I have no trouble putting expressions of desire for Sally into my eyes.

Mama arrives tomorrow. Am I ready? Of course not. I could never be ready. & I'll never forgive her for the basket of pomegranates.

Saturday, 3/31/2096

Mother & daughter: face to face. Hah. When has Mama ever really *faced* anyone? But she's here. The first few hours of her arrival went pretty much as I'd expected. I met her at the bottom of the stairs as she alighted from her little jet (needless to say Elizabeth's gorillas were all over the place, ready to foil any rescue attempt should we be crazy enough to try such a stunt), &—as though she'd last seen me a week or two ago—she offered me her cheek for a demure filial kiss, then noticed me. Yes, *noticed* me: an audible gasp of dismay, shock-widened eyes, flaring nostrils. "My dear Alexandra, how can you? The man's been dead for years! Why, why, *why* go on *mutilating* yourself like that?" Haven't had to be a well-controlled daughter for some time, but of course it all came back to me. I only shrugged a little, smiled sweetly, & excused myself with "You're referring to my hair? I'm sorry it distresses you, Mama. I'd forgotten all about it. It's just so much easier this way—I've kept on his valet, you see, & he has only to trim it twice a week for me." She made a Herculean effort to contain her horror. Suddenly she frowned & sniffed. "Your scent, dear. I suppose *he* chose it for you, too?" That was carrying it pretty far, I thought. "I like my scent, Mama," was all I said. As though I should go on living my life in reference to Rbt? For that's what she's asking when she hints that I should have rejected everything he had a hand in. As well try to have my genes exchanged.

Naturally she had to have a tour of the house. "Imagine his keeping it secret from me," she said at one point. At another point—while we were in the Piranesi Room, as I recall—she remarked on his "appallingly morbid taste." She wondered why I hadn't redone the house. "By mail?" I said sarcastically. "You could always have decorators in," she said. "I'm sure Elizabeth wouldn't begrudge you that." When I said nothing, she raised an eyebrow. "Or would she?" Considering where we were, I decided to let that opening pass. She's intending to stay for at least the weekend. Thus no rush.

I had a bad moment when she asked me didn't I have a girl. When I admitted that I did, she wanted to know why Penderel was serving us. So I've ordered Sally to serve us. Damn. If anyone will be able to spot peculiarity in my relations with Sally, it's Mama. But perhaps she will put down our strangeness to the perverseness of my sexual habits.

The evening was spent in bland gossip—Mama telling me all about people I barely have name-recognition of. Her life is one long, gaudy flutter. Even if she counts herself less endowed with worldly riches than she'd like, she's still got the wherewithal to do everything she wants. She was in Paris last week. I was in Paris only once in my life, with Rbt for a flying visit, most of which was spent attending horrid cocktail & dinner parties & conferences with power creeps. But I didn't mention that to *her*. She could never imagine what my life with Rbt was. Which means she'll never imagine/see/perceive what I've become. No, not Mama.

Sunday 4/1/2096

What a surprise Sally is turning out to be. She's been perfectly charming to Mama & acts to perfection the role of my lover. One particularly rapt expression I spied flitting over her face reminded me so

forcibly of her dramatic capacities that for a moment I was alarmed
into wondering if everything she'd told me was a massively conceived,
Byzantine lie. But recollecting the circumstances, I regained my rock-
bottom conviction about Sally's position vis-à-vis my situation with
Elizabeth. I could swear that if Mama weren't so wrapped up in that
revolting Pamela she's brought with her she'd be after Sally herself.

But apart from her adopting this role for Mama's benefit, Sally's astonished me &—I admit it—touched me with her supportiveness.
Though Sally may perceive that fooling Mama is necessary for sal-
vaging her arrangement with Elizabeth, giving aid & comfort to me
in private is hardly called for. She's discreet & skillful—nothing too
obvious. (For a service-tech she's really quite intelligent.) It strikes me
as poignant that she finds it uncomfortable to drop the use of formal
address when speaking to me, so that when we are alone she doesn't
call me anything, unless absolutely necessary, & then it's the usual formal address. Around Mama she lavishes stagy endearments upon me.
I've never heard her say my first name. I can hardly blame the girl for
being reluctant to use it. I recall only too clearly how hard it was for
me to switch from *Papa* to *Robert*. But more on *that* subject later.

Since this book is turning into such a confessional, I might as well
admit that I take advantage of Mama's presence to touch Sally. I try
not to push it, I've put her through so much. & when we're alone…
well, I put a lot of space between us. The truth is that I'd like to have
genuine reciprocal sex with her. But I won't. She with her lovely long
chestnut hair is devotedly in love with another. There can be nothing
between us.

Monday, 4/2/2096

What a bitch she is. Most of the time we were talking last night I kept
imagining saying to her that even if I'd had my choice between him
& her I might have taken him. Not that it's true, for she wouldn't have
so confined & constrained me the way he *had* to do. That wouldn't
have been her desire—after all, she spent most of her active maternal years attempting to free herself of us. Of me especially. But her
goddam self-righteousness makes me want to puke. Last night she was
in full dress, dividing her attentions between Rbt & Elizabeth. God

how it galls her that Elizabeth controls the estate. & naturally she had to put in time railing about Rbt's having "deprived" her of the two residences she claims she had coming to her. Oh, & she had plenty to say about Daniel—he apparently sees her occasionally, which thrills her. She still thinks he'll "pull himself together." & even if he doesn't have a shot at Rbt's estate, there's still Grandfather for her to hit on. But Grandfather *never* liked Daniel, even before Daniel started plugging in. Anyway, I've promised Mama to attempt to sign over to her the Paris apartment—I'll never use it, & it's not a rental property, never will be. ("You can count on it that that bitch has appropriated it as she has the Georgetown house," fumed Mama.) I doubt Elizabeth would object to my giving it to her—it's nothing in the larger scheme of things.

Once we worked through the bullshit, we got down to discussing the current political situation & my options—if any. Part of the bullshit was a long avowal by me that I withdrew from the women's world & more particularly from her because Rbt made it almost impossible for me not to. She hardly trusts me, but appears satisfied. (The Paris apartment helped, I'm sure. Can't keep myself from thinking of her hard green eyes going soft & misty at my casual suggestion that I would try to sign it over to her.)

I have to admit that I'm impressed at what she had to say about the political situation—it's hard not writing her off, she appears so flighty & fluttery & too self-indulgent to be in any way aware of anything outside her small circle of snobs. She bitterly acknowledges that Elizabeth's political acumen is quite, quite sharp. That Elizabeth's stock in executive circles is soaring—that there's no question of her falling from power, at least not in the foreseeable future. The bankers especially like her. Well, for one thing, the cities have stopped burning. But certain industrial elements are not quite so keen—nor, of course, do Military circles like her. Her purge & reorganization of the upper echelons of the Pentagon has provoked rancor in many potentially dangerous quarters. According to Mama, the surprise was that Elizabeth apparently enacted no excisions. (Who would notice Wedgewood, anyway?) Mama's opinion: my only hope is to join Elizabeth's team. None of the dissenting factions have been able to get so much as a single Cabinet position. (But I might have pointed out to her that none of the surviving dissenting factions would be likely to want to spring Sedgewick's daughter, either, unless out of a spirit of mischief. By the end he hadn't many friends left.)

At any rate, we left it at her trying to find a way to reach out to Elizabeth—discreetly, without annoying her. But since all communications go through Elizabeth's office, there can be no direct contact between us. The important thing is that Mama now sees it as in her interest to do what she can for me. This is a long-term strategy. Mama can work some influence at a distance. Indirect power should never be dismissed as useless.

I've warned her that going through Grandfather would catch Elizabeth's interest & antagonize her. Considering how little contact I've had with Grandfather, Mama had no choice but to accept that stricture.

Wednesday, 4/2/2096

Had the recurring dream last night. The torrential rain not stopping, inexorably washing away Rbt's grave near the holly bush, revealing their moldering corpses. All that I see of her body beyond its decay are those strange blue eyes staring at me, while Rbt's skeletal hand clutches her remains, gripping her even in death.

Every time I have this dream I remember the funeral, I relive those moments when, unable to keep myself indoors while they dug his grave, I went & stood gaping down into it as they shoveled, terrified they'd turn up her skeleton. It must be a skeleton by now. No, I mustn't think about it. All that's over now. Over & dead. Long dead.

Rbt turning in his grave? I can well imagine it. Indeed I can. I can imagine him defying even death should his rage grow sufficient. He would say I'm a failure, that I've betrayed everything he taught me. That if he had been me he wouldn't have been so passive, so accepting, so submissive. That there are ways. But that I haven't sought them out.

& he'd be right.

Thursday, 4/5/2096

This morning Sally came to me & told me Elizabeth had phoned her at seven a.m. This bald announcement sent a shockwave over me: for the first time I thought of Elizabeth—& everything she is—in real, physically proximate contact with Sally. & all I could do was wonder whether Elizabeth had had the girl. But Sally then went on to say that Elizabeth asked her to explore a new theory she was considering. I waited for Sally to elaborate, but embarrassed, she had to be prompted. "She seems to be wondering if maybe you are driven by a masculine persona," the girl finally said. "She suggested that your dropping all connections with women, cutting your hair like your father's, &—" but she halted at this point. I raised my eyebrows at her, but she stared down at the floor. I urged her to go on. Without looking up she said, "And, well, your non-reciprocal sexual relations with me, which, she said, is probably a simulation of your father's sexual practices."

I could, of course, read between the lines of what Elizabeth would *not* say to a service-tech: simulating how a fixed male executive would approach sex.

"Perhaps you'd like me to report we now have reciprocal sexual relations?" Sally ventured.

I asked Sally if they'd discussed anything else.

"Two other things. She wanted to know if I still considered you to be infatuated with me." Since I'd instructed her to report an infatuation, the question hardly surprised me, though it did disturb me, sitting there only a few feet from the girl, barred from touching her, put at arm's length by her polite *Madam*s & *Ms. Sedgewick*s. I wondered why she had come to me with the communication from Elizabeth at all. She could have simply not told me. I'd never have known. "And the other matter you discussed with her?" I queried.

"I asked Ms. Weatherall about my friend. About the limits of this 'job.'"

"And?"

Sally shrugged. "She was vague. As vague as she's always been on the subject."

I baldly put it to her: "Did you have sex with her during your recruitment & training?"

Her head jerked up, & those emerald eyes went wide with surprise. "How could I?" she said in a tone of confusion. "Oh, I see," she said, her eyes narrowing. "You mean did she demand *that* of me, too. No, she didn't."

"She's beautiful. & has a legendary reputation as a lover," I said.

This offended her. She didn't look at me, only waited for the next question—or for dismissal. I let her go, of course. If I were to make a move on her she would probably endure it & might even feel pleasure, but I'm fairly certain she'd only hate me the more for it, while lashing herself for days & nights afterwards. I know all about that.

She's beyond me, this service-tech—a person of enormous courage & integrity, a real person, not a role invented by someone else—even if Elizabeth attempted to make her that. No, she loves & is loved for the unique being she is. She's authentic. I have to respect that.

Saturday, 4/7/2096

I've been procrastinating writing the letter to Grandmother I promised Mama to get off at once. It's not the humiliation of making a mea culpa—that I can handle. (Some things simply don't bother me as they once might have.) No, it's the prospect of Grandmother's responding by paying me a visit. (I can't imagine Elizabeth forbidding it, since she didn't forbid Mama's visit.) The thought of having to look into her eyes…I haven't seen her in nine years. The last words we exchanged were bitter. & I wasn't looking into her eyes then, either. In fact, I *wanted* her to cut me off precisely because I was afraid she'd see everything in my face. Who knows me the way Grandmother does? Even if she hasn't seen me for nine years, she remains the ghost of my conscience (presuming such a thing as "conscience" exists for one such as I), haunting me in my darkest hours. I can't imagine pretending anything with her. & while I can imagine telling Mama about me & Rbt—& taking pleasure in doing so—it's another matter entirely with Grandmother. If I don't want Grandfather to know, the desire is ten times more fervent when it comes to Grandmother.

She was angry at me for avoiding Mama, but what else could I have done? I had to choose him. Rbt was the one who loved me, not her, even if his loving *was* twisted & cruel & crazy. While all Mama ever cared about was what she could get for herself. I have to give him credit for never trying to turn me against her, never trying to keep me from seeing her. But then he could afford to be generous. Once I went to him... But no, I can't think about that now. Grandmother. I must think about Grandmother. & make myself write to her.

Sedgewick's Vineyards
3/31/2096

Dear Ms. Sedgewick:

A week and a half ago I received notification from Mr. Sheridan that I was being let go by the Sedgewick Estate, beginning the first of April. Mr. Sheridan didn't give any reason for my termination. He just told me I had to go. (Zita was told nothing at all, and when I asked Mr. Sheridan about it he said she could stay or go as she liked.)

I'm writing, Madam, to ask you to reconsider. Or, if this wasn't your decision, to look into it for me. It's not fair, Madam, not fair at all. I've been running that winery at a profit since Mr. Sedgewick first hired me back in '68. And you know, Madam, that when I first came to the winery it was operating at a big loss. Mr. Sedgewick always said I ran the place to perfection. And seeing as how Mr. Sheridan fired me without cause, not one he's willing to name, anyway, it doesn't seem fair that after so many years of faithful and efficient service I'm being kicked out. And in case you don't realize this, Madam, according to Mr. Sheridan I'm not due for a pension unless I stay on the job another eleven years. But for a man of my age it's hard to find new positions. People get prejudiced about age. They don't seem to understand how important and valuable experience is.

All I'm asking, Madam, is for some fairness. I know Mr. Sedgewick wouldn't have treated me this way. He knew what I did for this place and treated me accordingly. Because he cared about how this place was run.

Yours truly,

Roger Barlow

Sedgewick's Island, Maine

Saturday, April 7, 2096

Dear Elizabeth:

I assume you're familiar with the letter Roger Barlow, longtime manager of Sedgewick's Vineyards and Winery, wrote me concerning his
termination. As he mentions in his letter, he's served the Estate long
and faithfully. On that account I request that you reconsider the decision to terminate him. It does seem rather rough to chuck him out at
eleven years short of having earned his pension when others will be
unwilling to hire a man let go at that age.

Alexandra

Washington, DC

10 April, 2096

Alexandra:

There isn't a chance in hell I'll agree to keeping Barlow on. Apart
from other considerations, doing so would taint me with complicity in
and tolerance for his excesses. He's made a tidy profit for the winery,
granted, but at a price. His management practices are not acceptable.
I can't afford such an association.

Instead, I've already contracted with a work collective advocating
experimental managerial and work methods and practices. Whether
these innovations prove financially profitable is frankly irrelevant to
me. If you wish, I'll have Sheridan send you copies of the collective's
proposal and the contract I've signed with them. In any case, the
matter is closed. As for Barlow, he's scum of the ilk I've taken some
trouble to cleanse Security of. He's not worth the trouble you'd incur
by attempting to push this.

Elizabeth

Wednesday, 4/11/2096

I wonder if I should have hinted in my letter to Elizabeth that Barlow probably knew (through Zita) about the incest? Would that have concerned her, I wonder?

But even if Barlow suspected, what could he accomplish now by blabbing? After all, he's just been terminated. (Bitter rejected retainer takes revenge.) & Rbt is dead. He knows no one important. & no newspaper would touch such a thing... Damn Elizabeth for her high-handedness. Not that I ever liked Barlow, or can feel very sympathetic towards him. (Elizabeth's intimations hardly surprise me—there was evidence enough before my eyes each time I stayed in that house for me to comprehend how things were there. Used to wonder how Zita could stomach marriage to slime like him.)

Political motives. That's what Elizabeth was referring to. She wants her hands clean. Is it possible she's feeling pressure? But if so, from *whom*? Why should it matter what sub-execs think of her? Anyway, how would they connect her with Sedgewick's Vineyards and Winery?

Things must have changed a great deal over the last five years for Elizabeth to be taking such things into account. I feel cut off by and lost in the mists of time, here on this so-remote island...

Monday, 4/16/2096

Yesterday so depressed I was drunk by 3 p.m. & determined to go on drinking until I either passed out or got sick. Now today I have that horrible crawling sort of depression that wraps around me after such bouts of excess (whether with alcohol or sex, it doesn't seem to matter). Drank not in the Small Study but in the Music Room. Stupidly trying to play first the piano & then the harpsichord & finally settling on the CD player. Sally came to me in the evening. I told her to get out unless she wanted me to abuse her. She gave me a long, steady look, then said, "Your shutting yourself away from everybody, me included, for so many days in a row is beginning to raise eyebrows. You'd better let me stay with you, at least for a while."

"You heard what I said," I retorted in my nastiest voice. "I'm drunk & refuse to take responsibility for the consequences if you stay. I'll interpret it as an invitation if you do." She left. Naturally.

Must have spent hours then brooding about that girl. Kept remembering that time I kissed her & she responded (for which I later punished her), pressing herself to me, her tongue moving in my mouth. What I would do now for her response... (No. I'm dead sober now. Dead responsible for my actions. I won't touch her.) But of course she still hoped then to move me. I know exactly why she responded to me. In that sense my interpretation of her response as opportunism wasn't far off. Oh to feel that response again... But it would be even more obviously bogus now. Just something meanly demanded by the monster that I am.

I've only to think of Rbt's mouth pressed against mine. A mouth with such teeth. To think of the traces of his teeth over my body, teeth that made themselves felt wherever his lips & tongue were busily deployed. & then to switch to thoughts of kissing Sally: one arrives at an obscenity. As disgusting as wishing to dribble slime over something pure & beautiful. Or like taking a knife to a Botticelli. I cannot wish myself on Sally. Not even I am that monstrous.

I once joked to Rbt about what he liked to call his "nibbling." My joke was to call him a vampire. He flashed back with something about how he might better be compared to Cronus, the Greek god who consumed all his children (but one, Jupiter), at birth. That such an analogy was apter than that of Pluto or the more banal generic vampire. I think I made some crack in return about Daniel being able to agree with him on that, & that sent him into a rage. But being Rbt, instead of letting his rage loose, he smiled & murmured that as far as he was concerned Daniel was not his offspring & he meant only me in his analogy, that it was his special pleasure to consume me & regurgitate me & reconsume me & on & on ad infinitum. All this made me sick, literally sick, & I had to press my hand over my mouth & run to the toilet. He followed to watch me vomit. When I finished, I told him I'd never forgive him for what he'd said. (I was shaking, it was a purely visceral response, my mind was hardly functioning at all.) I wanted to get away from him then, I was determined never again to give him any of the things he perpetually demanded of me. But he made me stay, he forced me to lie with him, he showed me myself & made me loathe myself so fiercely that in the morning what he had said hardly mattered to me any longer.

I am my father's invention, his creation. His creature shaped & formed to serve his needs & desires. What remains after his death is only a collection of shadow behaviors & feelings, the loose ends of a marionette's strings. All contrarieties were ruthlessly driven out of me, crushed, suppressed, until nothing but his creation remained. There's only the entity he named "Persephone" remaining. The name obviously to offer endless reminders to me lest I forget any of it. He knew what he was doing with me. Upon me he refined the theory & techniques of a lifetime. I was his masterpiece.

Persephone. Only Persephone truly existed. Alexandra Sedgewick was merely a name. To the world, Alexandra Sedgewick was a mere shadowy trace of Robert Sedgewick—only the entity perceived as Sedgewick's daughter. Even for those who knew me as something other than Sedgewick's daughter—Mama, Grandfather, Grandmother—I was not any more real. For Mama I was a troublesome millstone tied around her neck that, borne long enough, might win her a fat juicy reward. Think of all those times she'd "drop in" on us in Barbados; just off the plane she would already be bored, tediously saddled with this obligation of a thing called daughter. For Grandfather I was never anything but a sweet young thing, his little Rosebud. Faced with the real Alexandra Sedgewick—i.e., with Persephone—he'd never again look in my face, I can be sure of that. As for Grandmother...was I real for her, ever? I used to want to believe that, but it's so painfully clear in retrospect that she was only doing what she felt her daughter should have been doing—training a recalcitrant young girl to be an acceptably submissive executive woman. When I recall how she faintly expressed her disapproval of *Mama's* sexuality, the blood rushes in my ears as I imagine her acquaintance with Persephone...

Until Sally, there have been no others. What Sally sees when she looks at me is this monstrous reincarnation of Robert Sedgewick. I am becoming my father. Living in his house in seclusion on his island, abusing another human being as he abused me, drinking myself into

a stupor, even falling into the blackhole of unrequited sexual obsession—wanting a girl whose main wish is to be away from me, just
as he longed for Kay Zeldin, who I know with every fiber of my being always wanted desperately to be free of him… Being this crea-
ture/creation/invention of Robert Sedgewick…a creation without
its creator…what could be more useless? More forlorn? As I sit here
writing in this book the truth becomes increasingly, painfully, clear:
in any important sense of the word "I"—as an independent recogniz-
able subject in the world—"I" has never existed. Only the roles my
creators have invented for me. The tenuous, painful interiority that
lurks beneath the surface does not warrant the significant pronoun
"I." Never quite human, at least not socially, Alexandra Sedgewick
can only exist as a she/it. Never as an authentic self. Always another's
creature. And now not even that. The single human who cared that
this creature/entity, that this she/it exists, himself no longer exists.

Why does she/it go on? Only because this she/it thought there might
be life in some possible future. Life. What is *life*. Not being an entity
that exists only as a "she" & "her" in reports that are made about her/
it. If the truth is put quite bluntly, starkly, baldly, it must be acknowledged that no one on this earth would have anything to miss if the
entity ceased to exist. The one person who would have cared is dead.
(Dead because his creation failed him.)

That is enough to know. That & knowing that it will always be like
this, that nothing will change, ever. There was one chance, & that was
Elizabeth's sending a real person here. But she/it could not birth a
real person in response, even then, rather she/it chose instead to grow
more monstrous—a creation imitating its dead creator. She/it threw
away the only chance ever given it.

When this entry is finished she/it will hide this book where it will
not be found (for Sally's sake). & then she/it will find a sure no-fail
method of suicide, despite the lack of available weapons, despite the
eyes watching its every move. It must not fail. It will not fail. It has
gone on long enough.

Chapter Four

[i]

Emily handed her room key to the professional behind the desk. Smiling, the woman thanked her. "Such a lovely morning, Ms. Madden," she said in her dulcet, musically-accented voice. "I always do say that April is New Orleans' best month."

Emily returned the smile. "I have to admit that I wasn't entirely charmed when I visited here last August. I thought at the time that this must be the most oppressive climate in the entire country."

The woman clicked her tongue against her teeth. "Oh, August. "August is pretty terrible anywhere you go in the South, you know. Or the Midwest, for that matter."

A service-tech who had worked in the dining room the night before slinked through the lobby and winked at Emily as she passed. Emily squelched her grin at the cheekiness lest the service-tech misunderstand. Tightening her clasp on her briefcase, she glanced at the professional. The woman, leaning hard against her side of the desk and drumming her fingers on the marble desktop, half-whispered, "What do you think of that bizarre way they're making up their faces, Ms. Madden?"

The service-tech who had just passed through was sporting a chartreuse enamel oval patterned with white and yellow daisies over her cheeks, a butterfly on her forehead, a bee on her chin and—the *pièce de resistance*—a tiny ladybug on the tip of her nose. Emily grinned. "I find it amusing. Though I suppose the point is that certain people are making millions off the fad." Such comprehensive and often complicated face-painting must be a serious drain on service-tech purses. Emily suspected that a concerted campaign to push it had been strategized for perhaps two or three years before the fad had burst onto the pop-culture scene. From what Emily had read and heard about it, the fad had taken root after a glitzy mini-series on the "Can-Can Scene" (the name coined in the series) "in Toulouse-Lautrec's France." Soap opera stars had begun sporting green and pink and purple faces, a fashion that had grown more elaborate and spread to male service-tech fashion as well. Right on cue the department stores had been ready with the face paints, and soon a whole new service-tech occupation had sprung up—that of painting special designs (mostly using stencils) on top of the main base color spread in either ovals, rectangles, or hearts over service-tech faces...

The professional shook her head. "I've been having a terrible time with the girls about this. The more, ah, *popular* of them insist that our members prefer them to have their faces painted that way." She shrugged and rolled her eyes. "I've been privately sounding out our clients, to see if the face-painting annoys them."

"And?" Emily said, curious.

"I've been getting mixed responses. Some of them detest it. Say the stuff is greasy and conceals aesthetically pleasing faces. Others seem to like it." She sniffed. "They certainly all agree, however, that the gaudy flapper dresses the girls are wearing are attractive."

Emily was supposed to have been at the gallery by now. "Maple Street is a few blocks on the other side of St. Charles?" she said, to ease the conversation to an end.

The woman nodded. "Yes, Madam. Cross St. Charles, then walk two more blocks and you'll come across Maple Street." She beamed. "Some of the finest boutiques in the South are on Maple Street."

Emily made a courteous escape into the warm, humid air. As she stared around her at the dense green foliage lushly lining the sidewalk, the mild sun glittering in the deep azure sky seemed strong enough to create a suggestion of what steaming jungle would be like. She crossed the near side of St. Charles, then paused on the sidewalk to wait for one of the constant stream of streetcars to finish trundling past. According to the Blue Book, these streetcars were ancient things, though their numerousness and the vastness of the network branching throughout the city dated only from the early decades of the twenty-first century. The streetcar on the opposite track waited for her to pass—pedestrians supposedly had the right of way over streetcars, so the Blue Book maintained, though Emily doubted that would always be the case. Perhaps for executive pedestrians that might be true. But she would believe the practice extended to service-techs only if she saw proof of it with her own eyes.

Some of the azaleas blooming along the way had already begun to go brown. In Seattle they would just be coming into bloom and then would stay in flower through June. She crossed Hampson Street. Yes, there it was, Maple Street. To the left. On this side of the street. The discreet brass plaque set into the wrought-iron gate of the fence enclosing the house's yard announced *Collage Miscellany Studio and Gallery Associates.* Above the plaque, in a small glass case, a 4" x 5" card announced the imminent opening of the Stuart Banner exhibit. Emily hoped Betsy Avery had done what she had promised, for she, Emily, would have no time to solicit a decent attendance. She had no way of knowing what to expect from Betsy—she had met the woman only once and had talked briefly and to the point with her on the phone only four times since last August.

Emily rang the bell in the gate and watched the ornate front door through the fence railings. Almost at once the door opened and a tall, stocky, bearded man stepped out onto the porch. He glanced her way, then ducked back inside the doorway. The gate buzzed. Emily turned the shiny brass knob, and the gate swung open. The buzzing ceased before she had finished closing the gate, and when she looked again at the door she saw the man standing out on the porch, his arms folded across his chest. Emily strode up the walk, mounted the few shallow steps to the porch. "Good morning," she said. The man's unsmiling brown eyes met her gaze. "I'm Emily Madden." She held out her hand.

He shook her hand. "Stuart Banner."

Staring at the cunningly selective use of paint on his face—dark violet lines raying outward from the thick turquoise ovals circling his eyes, the startlingly lifelike small cockroach crawling out of his beard toward his left ear—it for the first time occurred to Emily that some people would use face paint to create protective masks as well as to articulate the otherwise (for whatever reason) inexpressible. "Everything on schedule?" she asked, just to say something. His eyes—hard to make out because the paint distracted so from them—both disturbed and attracted her.

"Of course, the schedule." Sarcasm. So when his hairy arm swept expansively, to indicate the first room off the entry hall, she waited to see if he would add an ironic bow and was relieved when he did not. "Apart from a few minor decisions, my end of it is nearly delivered."

Tingling with sexual warmth spiked with a faint dis-ease, Emily followed him into the large front room. The light-flooded space, stripped bare to pale wooden floor and white walls with pale, oak moldings, held about a dozen sculptures. After only a few seconds in the room, Emily became disoriented. Trying to make sense of it, she realized that her sense of imbalance must be caused by the unconventional spatial arrangement of the sculptures. Several seemingly unrelated pieces had been positioned too closely to one another, as though shoved randomly together to be put out of the way, while one piece in particular sat by itself isolated in the far corner, with its nearest neighbor seven feet distant. Emily turned to Stuart Banner and found him watching her. She said, "You have your reasons, I suppose?"

His face showed nothing. "You want me to change it?"

"It's your exhibit." She walked across the room to take a closer look at the piece crammed into the corner and tried to envision it positioned a few feet out into the room. The satiny smooth luster of the black paint stroking the wood drew her fingers, but she restrained herself from touching it. The piece—and she did not know how much this reaction had to do with its being pushed too far into the corner—evoked a sense of static, closed-circuited tension through the smoothness of the painted wood, the perfection of the joins between sections of the piece, and the lack of sharp corners, all of which taken separately offered a surface seemingly innocent of tension, while the curves overtly suggested movement. At the off-center heart of the sculpture, the one knot of arms not black but vividly, sharply, scarlet seemed almost dissociated from the rest of the piece, though it not only nested in an intricate tangle of tentacles but also grew out of the same piece of wood from which the tentacles had been formed and thus could in no way be physically separated from the rest of the piece.

Emily turned away from the piece and looked at its creator standing at almost the exact center of the room with his hands jammed into his jean pockets. The attitude in his pose made her acutely aware of the lines of his body straining against his tight service-tech clothing, of his pelvis thrust slightly forward, reminding her of the attitudes routinely struck by the service-techs working the dining room in the women's club six blocks away. Deliberate mockery? Or unconscious invitation? Surely given his dealings with Betsy Avery and whomever she might have introduced him to he must have learned the rudimentary facts about executive women. "The smoothness and luster of the painted wood is alluring to the touch," she said, holding his gaze.

He ignored her implied compliment about his technical expertise. "So go ahead and lay down the law about the set-up," he said. "Avery made it clear you would find it unacceptable."

"As I said before, the set-up is your business. Obviously you don't want advice. So I won't give any."

"It's your gallery," he said in the same stolid voice. "Where you hope to make a profit selling these here *commodities*."

"You want me to repeat what I've already said twice?" Emily kept her tone mild. He wanted to get a rise out of her, wanted her to assert her dominance.

"What about your profits, aren't you worried about that, Madam?"

Women artists never felt it necessary to stress their awareness of her status as he apparently did. If he had bothered to read his legal agreement with the Collage Miscellany he would know that she benefited financially only past a certain level of profit among the Miscellany collective as a whole, a level the Miscellany was unlikely to achieve in any ordinary year. And that her percentage of that take would be the same as each artist's percentage. But she wasn't about to point that out to him. He would then be likely to demand incredulously if she thought he was naive enough to think *her* so naive as to be managing Miscellany's shows and books without the profit motive to drive her. Emily glanced at her watch. She had an hour before she was to meet Celia for lunch on Magazine Street. "Since I don't have too much time this morning, I'd appreciate your showing me around the rest of the gallery and maybe letting me peek into the studios upstairs," she said.

He shrugged. "As you like, Ms. Madden." He moved to the door.

She almost asked him to call her Emily, but even as the words were on her tongue decided against it. He'd probably resent it. He needed to see her as a hard, money-minded bitch. Thus whatever overtures she made he'd find a way to interpret in line with that need.

[ii]

"Sorry it didn't work out last night," Celia said after they'd been seated and given menus. "Martha Greenglass called Dowsanto's bluff, so I ended up staying the night in Baton Rouge. Not surprisingly, they jailed her with everyone else who participated in the demonstration. And then yesterday at five they charged her with a felony." Celia's gaze flicked sideways at the executives sitting at the next table. "And then, to top it all off, at her arraignment this morning Martha informed me there was no way she would accept what she calls the 'concept' of bail."

Emily couldn't repress the chuckle that burbled up through her throat. "And did she attempt to give the court a lecture on the absurdity of government?" she queried, conjuring up a scene in which Martha stood before the bench explaining the principles and benefits of anarchy to a black-robed, authoritarian judge.

"It's not funny, Emily." Celia looked worried. "Apart from my, ah, *conceptual* differences with Martha, this whole thing could be explosive."

The waiter poured half-liter bottles of water into their crystal goblets. "What's the felony they've charged her with? Thank you."

"The State of Louisiana—as do several other states—has a statute prohibiting what they call 'external agitation.' It works such that anyone arrested while committing civil disobedience who is found to legally reside outside the county in which they are arrested is automatically subject to the felony charge of external agitation." Celia opened her napkin and folded it neatly in half, then smoothed it over her lap. "I've been involved for the last year in a national initiative urging state bar associations to get the statutes repealed." She grimaced. "We've gotten nowhere with our efforts. If anything, we've lost ground in the last year because of the mushrooming in the last three years of local actions."

They listened to the waiter's recital of the day's specials and gave him their order. When he had gone, Emily said, "And with Martha it's more complicated, isn't it."

Celia said, "The Marq'ssan will follow her lead."

Surely the local executives knew who they were up against. "Have you tried talking to the Dowsanto people?"

"Up until now I've been talking to a rep of the Baton Rouge plant. But I have an appointment with an official in the regional office— located here in New Orleans—at four this afternoon." Celia poured water into her glass. "Martha's made it clear to me that if they don't release her she'll request that the Marq'ssan 'liberate' the entire detention center."

"You don't sound too happy about that," Emily said. "You know," she added casually, "if I were you I'd contact the Secretary for Alien Relations. I'm sure she'd be very interested in Martha's case."

Celia sighed. "Yes, I know, that's on my list. Martha, though, would prefer to push this thing to the max." She shook her head. "As far as I'm concerned, getting her released is my first priority, above all political ends."

"Is it just coincidence that you happened to be on the scene when Martha went into this action?" Emily took a large swallow of water.

"I'm on retainer to the National Association for a Health-Neutral Workplace. When they decided to target this particular plant they sent me there because I already have a few local connections from my human-rights work days."

Probably Celia had had no idea of Martha's involvement... The waiter served plates of boiled shrimp and several small bowls of sauces. "I'm still amazed that the Executive is allowing unrestricted travel privileges to Free Zoners," Emily said. But then Elizabeth Weatherall was acutely canny. Having figured the angles, she had apparently decided that trying to keep Free Zoners like Martha Greenglass out would cause more damage than letting them go in and out of the country at will.

Celia frowned. "How much can someone like Martha Greenglass be restricted, anyway? It's not as though she has to travel by conventional means. And she has plenty of contacts scattered all over the continent who would gladly take care of her other needs. Lifting the restrictions merely made it easier for those not so intimately connected with the Marq'ssan."

"And gives the appearance that the Executive is granting concessions to the aliens and the Free Zone. As well as allowing them to trumpet their claims of being an 'open society.'"

Celia scowled. "Come off it, Em. Things have changed entirely. This is once again a law-abiding country. Civil rights mean something again. *I've* seen no signs that it *isn't* an open society."

And of course Celia was no longer a Free Zone resident, either. For herself, Emily found it hard to imagine ever considering a permanent return to San Diego. If any place could be called home now (and that point remained stubbornly moot), it was Seattle. In Seattle she ceased being an executive and managed to slough the onerous awareness of structures that now seemed intolerably perverse and confining. A certain consciousness she suffered everywhere else seldom arose in Seattle. Whatever the complex reasons for that, it was a simple fact of comfort that determined the desirability of escaping as often as possible to the Free Zone.

They ate for several minutes in silence, savoring the sweetness and juiciness of the shrimp, until Celia said, "So how's the Collage Miscellany holding up?"

Emily dabbed her lips with her napkin. "So far this year we've opened new galleries in three cities, adding thirty-seven more artists to the Miscellany. We're still operating on grant money, but we're starting to see a few more sales in the galleries we opened last year. One of our traveling exhibits has been doing particularly well. And apart from the sales, the stimulus of circulating the work of artists unknown outside their home regions has to be counted as significant."

Emily recalled last summer's workshop on the Olympic Peninsula sponsored by the Co-op; it had been useful for the twenty Collage Miscellany artists who had attended it. Stuart Banner, she thought, might have found it useful, too. He obviously understood and resented the art business; but if he had participated in that session he might have got a little farther than mere bitter resentment of the status quo. He seemed to have joined the Miscellany without having much idea of what it was about. Free studio space and exhibiting privileges had probably been as far as he'd looked, while assuming that if he were even moderately "successful" he'd be ripped off by the Miscellany's "management." Someone should talk to him, Emily thought as she finished the last shrimp on her plate. There should be some sort of mechanism for discussing such things with the artists before they joined... But then she personally had had little to do with setting this one up, and she'd assumed Janna would take care of all the local practical details. Janna, after all, had helped set up the Atlanta group and had been the one to make contact with the artists in New Orleans.

"Do you ever think of going back?" Celia asked.

Startled, Emily looked into Celia's eyes. "Going back? To San Diego, you mean?"

"Yes. To live there."

"No. The place would make me sick." The sickness Emily felt outside any of the Free Zones was magnified by ten times in San Diego.

"Not even to be near your family?"

"Especially not to be near my family." Emily wondered at Celia's asking her such a thing. Celia knew very well what her relations with Daddy were.

The waiter removed their plates. "It's hard for me to imagine never wanting to see my family again," Celia said. "And what about your mother, Em? Don't you miss her at all?"

"I never think about them. Either my father or my mother. When I accepted their trustfund I did so on the condition that they would make no demands on me. I meant it, Cee. I could no more stand seeing her than I could him."

Cee of course couldn't understand that. Oh, she could understand about not wanting to see Daddy again. Daddy was the Consummate Villain, the robber baron, the pirate, the black marketeer, the traitor to all Celia's most cherished values. But Mama... *That* Celia could have no inkling of. What kind of world Mama lived in. Celia, herself so tied up with her family, obviously found it incomprehensible that something other than Total Villainy (as in Daddy's case) could stand in the way of close family relations. But Mama was not Elena Salgado, not by a long stretch of the imagination. "To return to Martha's situation." Emily wanted to get Celia off the subject of family and roots. "Do the locals have any idea what might be at stake?"

Celia's eyes narrowed, and her brow beneath its thick low wave of glossy black hair furrowed. "I hinted delicately at it, first to the Baton Rouge Dowsanto executive I've been parleying with—he's offered to

drop charges if Martha agrees to leave the state—and then to the pros-
ecuting attorney handling the felony charge—a professional, who's
arranged a meeting for me tomorrow morning with his superior—an
executive." Celia bit her lip. "You do realize, Emily, that a private/
public dichotomy barely exists in places like Baton Rouge. The judge
assigned to Martha's case happens to be the son of the plant's managing director."

"Are you saying they don't seem very interested in the general
ramifications of the case?"

Celia nibbled one of the grapes garnishing her plate. "The
Dowsanto executive put it this way: 'I don't care if the Executive itself
tries to dictate to us on this. We're not letting outsiders instigate disor-
der in our plant.'" Celia grimaced. "They profess total indifference to
a larger frame of reference."

Emily vividly remembered her father's response when the
Executive began battling him. "It's a question of turf," she said.

"And Dowsanto—and here I mean the corporation, not just the
local plant—may be *wanting* this," Celia said. "I imagine they're
starting to get nervous about all the activism afoot. They're a prime
target. I bet they're hoping to push for a crackdown on activism and
maybe even a stand against the Marq'ssan."

Emily knew several executives who thought Elizabeth Weatherall's
tactics of dealing with the Marq'ssan a serious mistake. Some of
them claimed they'd rather take the consequences of opposing the
Marq'ssan. "Well then," Emily said, smiling at the look of irritation
on Celia's face, "the next few weeks could be very interesting."

"She knew what she was doing," Celia said suddenly.

"Who?"

"Martha Greenglass." Celia's eyes flashed. "She understood all
the ramifications before she even dropped into town. I think she has a
game plan all worked out in advance."

"When Martha decided to resign from her facilitating activities
for the Co-op, that should have told us something. I imagine she's going to give the Executive a lot of headaches."

"Not just the Executive," Celia grumbled.

Emily laughed. Whatever Celia said, she was probably enjoying
herself immensely. Celia hadn't had much faith in her projected suit

against Dowsanto in Federal Court, but with these new developments Martha would be giving her a lot to work with.

The waiter arrived with their entrées. To change the subject, Emily asked Celia to describe Baton Rouge, a place Emily had never visited, had never wanted to visit.

[iii]

After an hour and a half of frank and at times tense discussion, they began drifting off the subject Emily had deliberately raised— namely, how the Collage Miscellany functioned. Janna, it turned out, had talked about this to the two other women in the group, who were therefore reasonably well-informed but had had little communication with either of the men. The men, it seemed, had become a part of the gallery almost entirely by chance—having heard of it in a round- about way from someone they knew who worked in the San Antonio gallery and decided to apply on the premise that they had nothing to lose but the time the effort required. Neither of them had bothered to read the flimsies sent to them, except for the contract they had signed. They had understood that the gallery was to host the exhibits of art- ists from other parts of the country and that the Collage Miscellany would make a commission on any work of theirs it sold while in turn granting them free studio space and frequent opportunities to exhibit. Nothing else had much interested them. And the women... Yes, the women clearly found them a nuisance. In the course of the discussion, they had expressed concern that the men not be allowed to domi- nate the gallery and had said that they felt hassled by "the kind of environment men seem to spread like a miasma by their very pres- ence in a building." Through this portion of the discussion the men had gone on the defensive. Johnny Williams had made a derogatory crack about lesbian sexuality, which had in turn elicited a scathing remark from Lucille Alicarne about the sexually exploitative themes in Williams' work and a thinly veiled aside about his relationships with his models.

At least, Emily thought, the artists now know that the Collage Miscellany isn't run by executives like Betsy Avery and that the role of Betsy Avery and others like her is limited (though the Collage Miscellany did need the Betsy Averys, at least at this stage, for establishing a buying clientele). Emily pushed her chair back from the table and stood up. Johnny and Stuart apparently took this as a sign that the meeting was over, for they, too, got to their feet, Johnny in that quick, lithe way he had of moving, Stuart slowly and deliberately. "If any of you come up with questions you want me to answer, I'll be around tomorrow," Emily said. "And be sure to think about whether you know of any others who could use the remaining studio spaces. It's a shame to let them sit vacant."

"What do we do if we know somebody who could use the space?" Johnny asked.

Emily's eyes were again drawn into appreciation of the contrast offered in the bright phosphorescent salmon paint dappling his dark walnut skin. "First you propose the prospective artist to the other local members. And then you have him or her fill out papers for the Collage Miscellany."

The two men exchanged a look. Then Stuart looked back at Emily. "If we have to vote on it, you know what'll happen if the artist happens to be male, don't you."

Emily let her eyes travel around the circle of their faces. "First you try working these things out among yourselves. You're all intelligent adults. And then if you have an irreconcilable problem, I or somebody else from the Miscellany will act as facilitator." Emily met each artist's gaze in turn. "But before dragging somebody down here I'd hope you'd have the sense to talk it out very thoroughly and openly." Thick silence. After waiting a long, uncomfortable half-minute, Emily took her briefcase from the table and headed for the door. At the threshold she turned and said, "See you all tomorrow," and the others offered a jumble of muttered good-nights.

Emily walked alone to the front of the house and let herself out the door. On nights when she was feeling like this there was only one thing to do. Betsy Avery had told her about a place, over on Oak Street, less than a mile away. Depressing as such places could be, a kind of oblivion could be found in them, too…which sometimes, for all her efforts at heightened consciousness, she needed to seek.

Chapter Five

Sunday, April 15, 2096—Seattle

Feels as if I've been away from Seattle for two months instead of two weeks. DC is another world—no, another universe. Felt completely out of it. The dress and the make-up are all different from ours. The manners are different. They eat differently. They *talk* differently. Yes, above all the talk is different. It's almost as though they speak another language. One for which there's no dictionary to get help from, either.

And then there was the security review... I've no idea what I said under loquazene. Except for my babbling about Venn, that is. Which I discovered I'd done while coping with the surprise of getting personal attention from Mott herself, who surely has more important things to worry about than insignificant operatives like me. I suppose it's because Lise is involved. Lise is special now, being Weatherall's longtime protégée. And though Weatherall has no "official" position, it seems that she's the most important person in DC now.

Still, how extraordinary to be shown into Mott's posh office on the top floor of Security Central and be greeted by her, the Chief, with a smile and the offer of coffee. When she linked arms with me and led me to the sofa we then shared, I felt as though I'd been whirled backwards in time to those months when we all lived together in that house out in the boonies. Her attitude *seemed* friendly. But after some smalltalk she launched into the subject of my feelings for Venn, completely taking me off guard. No one else had even mentioned it to me, so I had no idea that I'd said anything about *that* while I was under. Between questions, Mott talked a lot about emotional conflict and torn loyalties. When I assured her that my feelings for Venn hadn't gotten in the way of my work for Security, she shifted the subject to Lise.

Now that I think about it, I have to wonder why it should matter to my performance of the job that I'm no longer "in love" with Lise. It's as though I hadn't been working loyally for Security long before I even *met* her.

But wait. I've just remembered another fragment of that conversation. Mott said something like, "We fully realize, dear, that with someone like you, emotional ties are of paramount importance. It's obvious that you never would have gone renegade if it hadn't been for the strength of your attachment to Allison."

That may have been the most important thing anyone said to me the whole time I was undergoing review. Sounds like they have me pigeon-holed—as someone who would go renegade for a lover.

Though they sent me back here—while the review pends—I see now how likely it is they'll recall me. How frustrating this is, to think they so little trust me. All because I went renegade with Lise! That's so unfair. Considering how I've kept my head all these years, having always to figure things out for myself when everyone around me is talking in that same ideological language of the enemy. Don't they understand how strong you have to be to do that, especially for someone like me who's not very well educated yet is constantly exposed to smart clever people with college degrees?

And then that evening with Lise. When I think about it, it makes me feel a little sick. I enjoyed seeing Mom and Dad, but after a while... And seeing the girls again, well, it all fell kind of flat, made me feel as though I had known them in a parallel universe. So going out to dinner with Lise struck me as a way to break the monotony.

I never was one for roaming any city at night by myself.

We went to her club, the most high-powered executive women's club in DC, the Diana. She used not to like such places. Really high-powered types were stopping at our table all through dinner to say hello to her. I could see how important Lise has become, even though she isn't officially in the Cabinet. I guess when it comes to power in such very high circles, certain things go unstated. Anyway, Lise didn't bring up the subject of the review or anything connected with it. Talked more about the old days, that kind of thing. And she kept putting her hand on my thigh, which she hadn't done for years. That seemed a little peculiar to me, but I guess I just brushed my awareness of it away and concentrated on the conversation and our surroundings. Most of the service-techs in that club were wearing short skimpy dresses and bizarre paint on their faces. Glitter and feathers in their hair. I could have sworn one of them had (paste?) sapphires and rubies set in her teeth. I felt drab, wearing the only non-FZ style evening wear I own, many years out of date.

We drank a lot, Lise and I. I wondered a little about that, because for years now Lise has been extremely circumspect (at least when I've been around her) with her consumption of wine.

After we finished eating, Lise said that we would have our coffee upstairs. I looked at her, not sure what she meant. I mean, I wasn't familiar with that club. She could have been talking about a lounge or bar or something like that. But I wasn't sure. Maybe because of her touching my thigh like that. Her face was smooth, and though her eyes still had that wary look in them, I couldn't read her face. What could I say? I didn't feel I could make the assumption she was talking about going to bed with me and thus come right out and say something gauche to make it clear how I'd feel about that. There was just enough ambiguity in the situation—and me already in this problematic security tangle—that I couldn't find a way to speak about it. So, as I've always done with Lise, I let her say where we were going and when. And I followed her lead.

I didn't like it when her personal amazons got into the elevator with us. I wondered how the other members of the Diana felt about the presence of amazons in their club. Before, because gorillas were exclusively male, security escorts were never allowed in because of the universal rule excluding males from executive women's clubs. But Weatherall's security practices have been extensively copied, and now a lot of women executives have female escorts.

We got out on a floor of private rooms—sleeping and bedding rooms. I knew it wasn't possible we'd find a bar or such on *that* floor. For some reason, my stomach—uncomfortably full of rich food and heavy burgundy (I really am not very used to eating meat swimming in rich sauces)—pitched and rolled. How ridiculous, I chided myself, this is Lise, whom I've known for years. When we get to the room and are out of ear-shot of her amazons, I'll tell her straight out.

And so when we were alone in the room she had taken (what were the amazons going to do? I wondered), I said at once, embarrassed and nervous, "I thought we had decided, Lise, that there would be no more sex between us."

She turned her back on me and went to the window, parted the draperies, and stared out into the night. "I want to *talk* with you, Anne. Where there's no danger of our being overheard." She turned to face me. "By *any*one."

I thought about this for a few seconds and concluded she must mean Security Central. That surprised me and intensified my uneasiness. "What could you have to say to me that—" I began, but Lise interrupted.

"Elizabeth and I have been quarreling," Lise said. "Because of what you told me that last time in Seattle."

Her eyes pinned me. Things were even weirder—and scarier—than I'd thought. My breath was coming fast enough to make my voice breathless when I said that I didn't understand.

"About what you told me Elizabeth said to you when recruiting you for your current operation."

The first thing that popped into my head was that Weatherall must be pissed at me for having caused trouble between her and Lise. Elizabeth Weatherall is not someone it's safe to have pissed at you. I think I stammered something about not knowing why any of that mattered now.

"It's clear to me that Elizabeth lied to you in order to break us up," Lise said. I had a feeling then of some anger in her; her voice had that edge in it. It's easy enough to miss, she hides her anger so well—most of the time, anyway. "There wasn't anyone else, Anne. That was a lie. Who could it possibly have been, anyway? Would I have asked you to go renegade with me if I'd been in love with someone else?"

I had to sit down, my legs were wobbling so badly. "Look, Lise, none of that matters now," I said. "That's more than ten years in the past. It's not worth your quarreling with Ms. Weatherall over."

There was a long silence, and Lise just stared at me. It must have been one of the worst silences in my life. She just stared at me. And then she said, "You're talking as though you still believe it. No wonder you don't give a damn about how *I* might feel."

I think I gaped at her for a while before gathering my wits together enough to say, "But Lise, you know I always cared—"

She cut me off and said something about how I'd made my indifference to her clear. All I could think about were those so very perfunctory meetings, for years and years. Saying "sweetheart" for any microphone that might be hidden. And then the business dinners at the club. And how when we spent the night at the club we seldom bothered to have sex.

I'm still not sure how it happened, but to cut a long story short, we spent the night together. With sex. And tears. And too much talk. Lise wanting me to say that I focused my attentions on Venn because Venn was "safe," there was no chance of anything happening with her, that in fact my deepest and "most mature" love still belonged to her, Lise.

I wish I understood.

My fingers are so cramped I have to stop. Description of family has to wait until tomorrow.

Thursday, April 19, 2096—Seattle

Contact with Mara today. I'm still not sure about her, so hesitate to take the penultimate step of introducing her to the print media group. I need to discuss this with my controller (whoever she may turn out to be) before making a recommendation. Sometimes I wonder at their having made *me* a controller. Weatherall made that decision, way back at the beginning: and I still don't understand why she placed such confidence in me. A service-tech like me, when most of my agents are professionals ideologically devoted to democracy and capitalism... It's curious. Most of them bear executives little love. Yet they work with *us*. Surely they must know who they're working for?

Take Mara: in her fifties, a civil engineer specializing in water quality control. A number of her colleagues have had to find other kinds of work because their jobs have been phased out over the last six years. Mara herself may have to go—because in most of the FZ now the ground water aquifers—as well as most lakes and streams—have been cleaned up. It's thought that the aliens either did this for the FZ or taught them how to do it. (According to Lise, Austria has a program to do the same, in full swing now—a deal Martha Greenglass worked out through Margot Ganshoff, no doubt.) Anyway, Mara's job's in danger. There would be other things she could do, of course, but she's feeling angry about it. "At my age——" she says, to explain why she doesn't want to have to think about a new occupation. Well, take that and her memories of what life was like before the Blanket, plus her dissatisfaction with the Co-op system (she really hates the Steering Committee crowd and the boycotts and work negotiations and the very idea of morality being dragged into intrinsically economic decisions—all that talk talk talk drives her even crazier than it does me), plus the change in the country since Weatherall took over (or, as Mara thinks of it, since they returned to democracy, restoring elections—and thus letting the people "oust" Wayne Stoddard, upon whom the blame for everything has now fallen)—taking all that together, you come up with a woman who has decided she wants democracy and free enterprise back. I don't think she connects her job situation with it at all. But I can tell she blames the Steering Committee crowd for costing her her job. Of course she wouldn't say any of that part of it out loud—it would sound terrible if she did, it would sound as if she were bemoaning the wonderful water situation we now enjoy, which is a windfall for everyone (except, it seems, water quality specialists).

I guess that bothers me a little, that Mara should resent our enjoying plentiful, inexpensive, safe water. Everyone's been buying dishes and cookware, because washing water is no longer a luxury. Also, the fact that she doesn't really understand how things work—her illusions about elections, for one thing—nags at me a little. Makes me uneasy. I wonder what it is she really wants and what it is she thinks will happen when the FZ falls (as I know it must) and returns to being a part of the US. Why doesn't she just move into the US proper? Why stay around here? When I asked her that, she said something about the problem with getting started all over again and talked a lot about credit and the standard of living. She doesn't pay rent now. And certain things are cheap here (while others are expensive). And then there's the problem of her age—she says. That it would be hard to get hired on "back there" as she calls it without someone exerting a little "pull" for her. Is that want she wants from working for us? An assured job, some extra credit?

But why am I getting so worked up about Mara? It shouldn't matter to my decision what her motives are, as long as they're not likely to lead her to betray the units I ultimately put her in contact with. Lise would probably tell me to go ahead and make the introduction. The little errands Mara's doing for us now may eventually grow too tedious to hold her. And she might begin to wonder if we ever intend to use her in her higher capacities...

Sunday, April 22, 2096—Seattle

Another one of Venn's parties last night. And Hazel was there. Got that little flutter in my stomach that afflicts me in the first moments whenever we meet—as one part of me wonders whether she's given me away or will do so at some time in the future... Awful to have these doubts rushing over me with Venn standing nearby.

She was vivacious. She and Venn spent part of the night in intellectual talk that I couldn't follow. Sometimes when I see Hazel I find it difficult to adjust to her having gotten a PhD and become a professional. Though since she dresses in the same old FZ styles she adopted after leaving Weatherall, it's not completely obvious that she's a professional. But her speech—anyone would spot her as a professional by the way she talks. (Though Hazel always did speak well—I knew she was really smart from the first time I met her that weird day in the mountains. And I suppose considering how crazy Weatherall was about her I had to know she was smart just because of that.)

There's a confidence in Hazel's voice these days. And her intensity has taken on a sharp edge. You can feel it as her attention suddenly zooms in on something. No, that's not quite right, because there's this sense that she's taking everything in. (Including me. But I suppose I'm a little sensitive about what she knows about the falseness of my position here.) Sometimes, too, she challenges people in the most unexpected ways. Sort of digs into something they've said (usually in passing, something you don't think could possibly be important and that up till then no one has even noticed), digs in and undermines. Cutting the ground out from under the poor person who was silly enough to have so carelessly given themselves away... Really makes me nervous, the way she does that. Keep waiting for her to pounce on me. Or to casually let slip the real reason I moved out of that household. Yet she doesn't. *Why* doesn't she? So that she can do the most damage when we can least afford it? I wish I understood her. I used to think I did.

I know she travels all over the US giving "seminars" on what she calls "the politics of reality." According to Lise, these "seminars" are really political rabble-rousing sessions given an educational veneer. Her degree is in some esoteric field that I gather exists only in the FZ. A cross between social psychology, philosophy, and political science, I think. When she tours, she's described as a psychologist. Lise once hinted that Hazel is considered a subversive and has an ever-thickening file with ODS. I've hinted that she would do well to be careful on her "seminar" trips (which are funded by a Co-op grant, yet), but she seems unconcerned. Given the kind of things they talked about last night, I see now that she may think herself beyond the reach of Security's authority.

The talk was mostly about what Martha Greenglass is up to in Baton Rouge, Louisiana. I should have had a NoteMaster recording everything; since I'm not an analyst, I don't know what's important and what isn't. The generally accepted "facts" (which I'm treating gingerly as yet, until I get confirmation or denial from Central) are that Martha, "organizing" (as FZ types like to call it) an action against a Dowsanto plant in Baton Rouge, ostensibly because of its negligence with hazards to employees' health, got herself arrested in a civil disobedience demonstration, knowing full well that she would probably be charged with a felony. It seems that Martha *wanted* this.

Someone pointed out that Martha expects to be treated with kid gloves when detained, and that every law enforcement officer anywhere in the US will know who she is and that she has the aliens backing her.

Anyway, Martha wanted to be charged with a felony. So that she could force a more critical confrontation than just the one between plant employees and management. On the one hand, she's eager to call attention to the external agitation statutes a lot of states have enacted since Weatherall began reforming ODS and Military. As well as to call attention to "criminally hazardous work environments" and thereby to encourage others to organize actions all over the country. On the other hand, she hopes to force the Executive either to go farther in its reforms or to "show its true face," as Mallory Waites puts it. (It's becoming clearer all the time that Mallory is something of a disciple of Martha's—may even be the next Martha Greenglass of the Co-op. Thus filling what some people say is a power vacuum in the Co-op since Martha resigned her position.) Martha is thumbing her nose at the Executive, that's clear. Everyone says she's going to have the Marq'ssan destructure the detention center she's being held in if the charges against her aren't dropped. ODS is keeping a low profile in all this, no one even brought them into the discussion last night. The local law enforcement people, though, are out for Martha's blood. My guess (and Venn's, too) is that the Executive will probably pressure the locals to cool it. In which case, Mallory says, Martha will up the ante. How? Mallory wouldn't say. Venn astutely pointed out that relations between locally involved executives and the Executive will be strained by all this. I could see she thought that a valuable by-product. In the meantime, Martha is refusing to "play the game" by refusing to apply for bail, refusing even to stand up in respect for the judge's authority, refusing to answer questions put to her, and so on.

An interesting sidetrack that the discussion took involved whether the Marq'ssan should destructure Dowsanto property if, after destructuring the detention center, Dowsanto proved "obdurate and obstructive." Venn said they'd have to be very careful, because if they put the workers out of their jobs, Martha's efforts would be wasted and that the same kind of resentment people have felt toward the Marq'ssan for the economic disaster the Blanket wreaked would again rise to the surface. Hazel argued that displaying any concern for that would allow Dowsanto to hold all those jobs hostage. And that while destructuring the plant might temporarily cause greater hardship and would probably increase anti-Marq'ssan sentiment, in the long run the effects might be quite different. So then Venn and Hazel got into a long discussion I couldn't follow about long-run and short-run consequences and Hazel started talking about "breaking the chains of the perception of the dominant reality as absolute" and all that metaphysical crap that drives a down-to-earth person like me wild. I don't know, I *think* Venn came a little toward Hazel's way of thinking. Though I can't be sure. They never come right out and say things in a simple, easy-to-comprehend way.

Hazel's argument thoroughly demonstrates what's wrong with her and Martha and others like them: they lack any responsible moral sense. And that's what makes the difference between their kind and Lise's kind. Executives can sometimes be cruel, cold, and calloused, but they'd *never* casually thrust so many people into misery, chaos, and violence (which would be inevitable were Martha and the aliens to destroy that plant), tearing down what little good already exists, and leaving people to fend for themselves in the aftermath. Until Lise explained to me about the executive system, I never fully appreciated how fortunate we are to have it. I can see, now, about the insoluble problems the commodification of leadership brought on. The masses still enjoy their "theater of politics" (as Lise calls it)—never realizing that's all it is, their polls, their immature kneejerk reactions, their unthinking emotional consumption of one-liners, and, finally, their elections. How in the world can we morally abandon important decisions to masses who either can't or won't take responsibility for keeping themselves sufficiently informed? To masses with attention spans of less than a minute? Things aren't that simple, no, though most citizens can only *see* them as simple. This is good, that is bad. (Martha in her own more sophisticated way is guilty of the same thing—Dowsanto is bad, so get rid of it!) Which is why the water supply was poisoned in the first place, for example. So people who can look at the large picture, who can see what is really at stake, must take responsibility. (People like Weatherall, who in spite of my personal feelings about her, is perhaps the best-suited person in the country to be making decisions.) While leaving the idiot masses to their theater. That's all they *really* want, anyway.

Venn and the others have absurd illusions, though. Even in DC the average person-in-the-street (Mom and Dad and their neighbors) hasn't the faintest idea of who Elizabeth Weatherall is. The best-informed professionals know who's officially in the Cabinet. But outside of that... And now I'm going out for my off-Sunday walk. To the park along the waterfront, I think. It's misting outside, but that will mean fewer people out on *their* Sunday afternoon strolls...

Wednesday, April 25, 2096—Seattle

Hazel's just been here. I'm still in a kind of a flutter. She didn't beat around the bush, didn't even bother with smalltalk. She said flat out that she had come to ask me to pass a message to Lise—to presumably be passed on to Weatherall. (Looking into those burning yellow eyes I had to wonder what she *really* feels now about having left Weatherall.) This message apparently originates with Martha's group. Hazel said rather vaguely that they knew she could get a message to Lise through me, and so asked her to talk to me. This makes me uncomfortable, but I suppose they *could* be thinking strictly of my personal relationship with Lise and not necessarily suspecting me of other activities... Basically, Hazel and the others want to press the Executive to explicitly involve themselves in the Baton Rouge situation. Reading between the lines, I think they're hoping they can force the Executive into negotiations that will result in certain large-scale concessions...holding the threat of unleashing "destructuring tactics" over the Executive's head... I can see straight off this is going to put Weatherall in a bind. She'll be getting it on all sides. It's just blackmail, I said to Hazel. She retorted with the argument that forcing workers into hazardous conditions solely for the sake of earning a living wage was even worse blackmail...

Lise won't be pleased. And the fact that it's Hazel who's acting as go-between won't help matters. I hope to god I don't get dragged into this any more than I already am. It's nerve-wracking, having Hazel coming here demanding I contact Lise. She knows I'll do it because of what she knows about me. And that is the most unequivocal blackmail of all. But of course we neither of us mentioned it.

Chapter Six

Monday, 4/23/2096

Don't know where "here" is. Only that I've been here six days and under close surveillance—lying immobile, in traction, with a broken back & numerous other skeletal fractures as my damaged bones & tissue are regenerated.

I've failed. I thought it impossible not to die going over that cliff onto the ice-water-washed rocks below. A fluke, that this body still somehow kept breathing, its heart somehow continued beating. A god-awful fluke.

There's no ocean anywhere within earshot of this room. That's all I know. For years had the sound of the ocean in my ears. When I stood on the edge of that cliff staring down into the swirling dawn-lit sea, it sang powerfully in my ears, and its beauty tightened around my throat, choking me breathless in its cruel, relentless grip. And yet that beauty did not suffice. Lying here in this chrome med-tech contraption, I can hardly remember what the ocean sounds like. Smells like. Or looks like. There is nothing here but the fact of my broken body. I suppose I must consider myself fortunate to be able to use the self-hypnotic pain formulas the physician informs me only executives have the discipline to take advantage of.

& today I saw Elizabeth. To think that for years I've longed to see her. & that seeing her… Fuck it. Seeing her has left me feeling more depressed & impotent, more abandoned, than at any time of my life. Just writing the words that I've seen her makes my stupid eyes well up with tears. [Yes, Rbt, damn you. It's a stupid indulgence. But that doesn't matter now. Nothing does.]

She came here in a kind of rage I don't think I'll ever be able to fathom the source of. Her braid has returned. She is still the most beautiful woman I've ever laid eyes on. & is even more powerful now in the way she carries herself. Elizabeth the Magnificent. But her harshness… God, the hardness in her face, the harshness in her voice, took my breath away. Literally. I could hardly reply to her questions. This is a side of her I've never seen. Cold & nasty, yes, but never like this. If eyes could annihilate, I would not still be breathing, my heart would have ceased for good, instead of simply stammering in its stupidly spastic beats. She believes I took a calculated risk with the cliff, that I calculated the odds to be favorable for my surviving. She opened her attaché case & flung this book down on the bed beside me. (That was as physically close as she got—mostly she stood at the foot of the bed glaring down at me.) "You were clever, Alexandra, but perhaps just a shade too clever in choosing to write in a book so closely resembling the original. I won't fall for the ploy a second time, I can assure you. Scribble to your heart's content, I'll never open your devious little book again." What was it she was saying to me? I've gone over & over it but come up with nothing beyond the obvious fact that she thinks I wrote in that book in order to work some devious manipulation on her. But at the time what overwhelmed me was the realization that they had found this book, that Elizabeth had read it & therefore knew about Sally. I felt sick. I had thought that concealing it in *that* room they'd never find it. I should have burned it.

"What has happened to Sally?"

Yes, I asked it—begging, nakedly begging.

If anything she looked even angrier. "Don't think I'll buy that line of shit twice, either." Oh, her sneer. I begged, pleaded, to be told what she had done about Sally, but she changed the subject. "I don't know what kind of block he put in your head that you could elude my loquazene examination, but it's clear that it's time I changed tactics with you." I could hardly look at her, her eyes were so cold. Stupidly I just lay there & gaped at her. I had my chance to talk to her & couldn't. "I'll let you return to the island where you can pretend to commit suicide to your heart's content—once you've divulged to me the transcript's location. I'm warning you, I can make your life a misery. I'm tired of your game-playing. Games with Felice Raines are one thing—I can handle her no matter who is pulling her strings. But I won't be a fool about the transcript. The only thing that's kept me from pushing this before now was your refraining from openly trying to blackmail me with it. But I warned you, Alexandra, about playing games using your observations about Kay Zeldin, didn't I. I won't have it, I won't put up with it." I could only stare at her—probably with my mouth hanging open. "I suggest you tell me now. Your life will be far more comfortable if you do."

"What transcript are you talking about?" I finally pulled my wits together enough to ask. The thought had come into my mind that if I knew what she wanted me to tell her I could bargain for Sally's sake. But Elizabeth scathed something at me so much like my father's worst efforts that I can't write it down here. (Maybe I will forget it if it's not written down.)

It's clear, now, what Elizabeth's interest in me has been—or almost clear. There's something she wants that she thinks I know the location of, that somehow Rbt programmed my unconscious to resist questioning on. This was why she sent me the girls. Now there will be no more girls, no more Sally. No more tutors, probably. I suppose she was hoping I might fall in love with one of them & be willing to do anything for their love.

But quite apart from the threat of this thing, Elizabeth hates me. Truly hates me in the most annihilating way imaginable. I kept thinking as she stood there glaring at me that she would be pleased by my death—once she learned from me what it is she thinks I know. If she got that information she might even have me excised. That's how much she hates me.

Oh Rbt, I can't bear this. Anything would have been better than this. I was a fool to turn to her, away from you. You were all I ever had.

Thursday, 4/26/2096

This room that I can see so little of seems crammed with med-tech but little else. I don't think there are any windows. I know the walls are starkly white, the lighting fluorescent, the floor that horrible thin chemically produced fiber of an ugly orange color. In short, there's nothing to look at but the med-techs who tend my body & occasionally one of Elizabeth's gorillas, who apparently have orders to periodically enter the room to verify my continued presence here. How awkward writing without the use of my left hand to steady the book. I try not to think about that hand, never knowing what kind of use I may ever expect from it again. "Totally reconstructed" the physician said. It took hours of micro-surgery. Plus tissue & bone regeneration in parts. A wonder my right hand escaped relatively unscathed (two fingers broken, lacerations, sprains, but nothing major—& this when the arm itself took considerable damage). It's been a long time since I imagined I could ever be a competent pianist. What does the permanent closure of that potential matter now?

But judging by everything Elizabeth said to me yesterday, I won't be anywhere near a piano again. Not unless she changes her mind about forcing something out of me that is simply not there.

This transcript must be what she & Rbt were talking about just before he killed himself. I was so distraught at learning that Rbt had killed *her*, that he had lied to me about this for years, lied to me about something so important to him, that everything those two were flinging at one another hardly penetrated. I'd do a memory regression session of that day, but I don't think I could bear it. That day was probably the most hellish in my life.

I suddenly have this terrible feeling that I understood nothing of what I saw & experienced the few years I was "out in the world." Not only where Rbt was concerned (& where he was concerned I always knew I understood only a fraction of what passed between us), but now I see that I was a naive fool about Elizabeth, too. God how that hurts. When I recall how I thought of her all those years, of how I fantasized joining her (my hero of a renegade), of how I savored those memories of her that I always held tightly to myself as a beautiful secret warmth… When probably her only reason for ever paying the slightest attention to me after Rbt summoned me to DC from Barbados must even then have involved some plan to use me against him.

Elizabeth, you've turned my entire history inside out. How will I ever find a self I can recognize?

Lying here, I've realized that I needn't have chosen the cliff at all. I could have simply dropped into a deep trance & made my heart stop. I know how to do it. Not that I'm thinking of doing that now. I'm miserable, yes, but not in the mood to die at this moment. How can I be less depressed than I was when I leaped from that cliff? But no. I'm not *less* depressed. I'm *differently* depressed. For I've seldom been as depressed as I've been lying in this bed absorbing the fact that she's probably planned my excision once she finds whatever it is she's looking for. I don't know why it is, but this makes me less desirous of ending the arid futility of my existence. The legal document I signed granting her power of attorney also wills everything to her. I imagine that neither Mama nor Grandfather would raise questions about it once she revealed the incest and threatened to expose it to the executive world if they did. They aren't like Rbt: neither of them could bear that kind of scandal.

All I have to amuse me now is this book. (Which is not very amusing.) Elizabeth does not allow me reading matter. Or music. And the med-techs make only the curtest, most laconic replies to my questions and otherwise do not speak. Ironic, isn't it, that I long now for that island existence I repudiated.

I can't tell her what I don't know. Will she return me to the island anyway? Or is this the beginning of a very unpleasant end? But this, too, is something I can't afford to think about.

I will close my eyes now & try to remember every note of that Beethoven concerto I once knew so intimately…If she thinks she can destroy me through boredom, she knows nothing of my inner resources.

Later (Thurs. evening)

She may not ever have felt affection or even goodwill toward me, but at least I had *his* love. Even at the price of filth I would feel his love surrounding me those times we lay close, my head on his chest, his arms around me, and I would know deep inside what love is. And this would come to me often when he would look at me, sometimes even in public—during meetings, for instance—his voice carving out a little corridor of privacy between us, almost palpable. & the others knew—he loved me deeply & intensely, they could *see* it, recognize it in him. So it *must* have been real, & strong. & he wouldn't have loved me if there weren't *something* there inside of me worthy of being loved. Because he *knew* me better than anyone has ever done. (But then I don't think anyone else has wanted to. Be honest, Alexandra. Did anyone but him ever try to learn who you were? Which suggests that no decent person would *want* to.)

Can it be his love that she hates me for? Did I somehow seem to steal it from her? For when I came into the picture it had been just the two of them for years & years.

No, I understand nothing. For *she* left *him*. He didn't turn to me until she had deserted him. He barely noticed my existence, except when I defied him. But if she suspected he would one day love me? I wish I understood. To be so hated by someone one has felt only adulation for... No. I can't bear thinking of it. I'll drop myself into sleep now. All I want is unconsciousness...

Wednesday, 5/2/2096

It has been two days since this last visit of Elizabeth's. One could say that her visits break the monotony, but... Fuck it. I've been too upset even to write in this book. Wallowing in the worst kind of misery. Like certain bad times with Rbt. Those times I'd lie on my bed & stare at the ceiling, listening to music, clutching my pillow, or lying on my stomach, pressing my fingers into my vagina as far as they would go. But such paltry comforts are inaccessible to me now. No music here. & in traction one doesn't have many choices about pillows or fingers.

It felt, the way she talked to me, it felt the way it did when Rbt flung rage-directed filth at me. She talks about things the way he did. Her sneer reminds me of his. My head is so full of her contempt now that I can't remember anything about his loving me; all I can recall are those times of cold contempt & icy rage. I keep remembering that time he beat me, which I hadn't thought about in years. She has taken every good, comforting thought/memory from me. She thinks I deserve to be miserable. That I'm a traitor to my womanhood. I hate women as he did. That is what she said to me. She played me selected bits of the recording she made of Sally's loquazene examination. About how Sally felt about the way I'd "sodomized" her. This, Elizabeth said, she would play to put an end to the "sham" I made of caring about Sally (which seems particularly to gripe Elizabeth). "You have as much respect for other human beings as your killer father had." I am a monster, she said. A menace to all other human beings. My very existence oppresses all other women. It was a pity I had ever been born. But what could one expect from people like Robert Sedgewick & Felice Raines. That on reflection, it was hardly surprising that a "spawn of such misfits" should want her own father to fuck her. That my "having a cunt" was a biological mistake, that I had the degraded mind of a male, that there was nothing beyond the accident of my sexual physiology that was remotely female in me. It spewed out of her, all of this, in a kind of hate-stream. I don't think I can find a way to make myself understand, I'm shaking as I write this, I can't think straight when I remember her words, so how can I think about any of it?

Mostly I said nothing. I was shaking the entire time she spoke to me. I couldn't look at her face because my stomach heaved every time I caught even a glimpse of her contempt. I lost control, though, when she started talking about what a monster I am. I cried out that he had loved me. Stupid, stupid, stupid Alexandra. I see now that this was the only thing I had to hang onto at that moment, that a terrifying chasm had opened at my feet, that I would be falling into that endless lightless vertigo if I couldn't manage to hang on to the single thing that might keep me from falling in. But she took that from me, too—that's when she started talking filth at me about him & me, about our incestuous relations, & then I couldn't remember that he'd loved me. It was like him going on at me, it wasn't even her anymore, so how could I hold on to him then?

She says she is having all the furniture ripped open, all the floors torn up, all the walls examined—the entire island house opened to the most minute scrutiny. That she would find it, that if I wanted to prevent the house from being seriously damaged I'd better tell her now where the transcript is. I think she likes sacking the house—because it, too, was his creation. That house, & me. (& it is, after all, where she sent Kay Zeldin to die.) I'm to understand that I will share the house's fate if she doesn't find it. Years, she's waited. The tutors & girls were supposed to get it out of me. Sally must have been her last hope.

Oh god I wish I knew what it was—& where it is. Presuming this thing still actually exists... I want to sleep now. I don't think I can bear being awake for much longer, not with all this so fresh in my mind. Maybe when I awaken some of it will have faded & I'll be able to bear myself better than I can now.

Thursday, 5/3/2096

Can't seem to get Sally & the bits Elizabeth played for me out of my head. & I know why. (I can't help but know why.) I always expected (& wanted?) Sally to be feeling such things during those few occasions I "sodomized" her. (What a revolting, objectionable, & inadequate term for Elizabeth—so holier-than-thou—to use. Does she expect me to believe she restrains herself from all but the most blandly straightforward sexual practices? She who is known for her voracious appetites, her unbridled lasciviousness?)

Now & then I close my eyes & go into a light trance; then I can see, hear, & almost feel Sally. It is after one of her carefully circumspect massages. My body is throbbing from her touch; she moves around the suite putting away the oil & sheets. I can sense the tension of her waiting to see whether I'll have her stay—her body so obviously self-conscious, though still remarkably poised & self-possessed, enough so to make it impossible for me to send her away at once. I stand near the windows working a wad of parsley in my mouth. She lingers in the doorway between the dressing room & the bedroom, having finished every small task she can think of to perform. In a few seconds she will speak, to ask me if she is to go or to stay. Her words on these occasions vary; I can never deduce from them whether she wishes to go or not. We each present blank, desireless visages to one another, we betray nothing, we keep all feelings locked deep inside, private, a secret meant to be inaccessible, perhaps even to our own selves... This time I don't make her ask. I request that she undress & leave her clothing in the dressing room. Minutes ago I was naked for her massage, which she administered fully clothed. Now I wear a dressing gown, & she will be naked under my hands—hands, unlike hers, free to do as & go where they will. I arrange her in a comfortable position in a chair with strategically placed pillows. At my request she closes her eyes. & then I

do the things I know will give her pleasure, without speaking. As I caress her & she grows more & more excited, I split into two, one part of
me standing aside watching this power I have to make her feel, though
she is Elizabeth's paid whore & possible spy who's interested only in
what she can get out of me, while another part of myself imagines
physically exactly what her sexual sensations must be…& when she is
coming I begin to come, too, & I press my vulva hard against the arm
of the chair, confident that the girl cannot know, confident that I, the
watching detached guardian, am in control… Was that the way Rbt
felt when having sex with me? For not only could he not have sexual
sensations, he could not even imagine what my body was experiencing. When I was coming his penis would slide into my vagina or anus.
But only for the purpose of making me feel—since he felt nothing. In
my vagina so that I'd go on coming, on & on & on. Or in my anus…for
other reasons. & when he gave me the dildo to strap on, to thrust into
him? What were his reasons then? (& what was it he felt then?)

I can't bear this. I've perverted my fantasy, I've let Rbt ruin my simple
pleasure with this absent girl as he would if he consciously could. He
would never not speak, he would never ask me to close my eyes. & I
would never inflict his filth on a girl. But it doesn't matter. Sally must
hate me.

Friday 5/4/2096

Would prefer to pass the tedious empty hours in sexual fantasy. That
or sleep. Since there's only my own thoughts… The med-techs, unfortunately, persist in refusing smalltalk & seem to be around less & less
often now that my healing has become routine. But I can only sleep
so much. (As it is, I yawn all the time I'm awake—so saturated am I
with carbon dioxide.) & every time I start fantasizing Sally, I end up
thinking about her. & about Elizabeth, about Rbt. & about myself, of
course. So then the fantasy evaporates. & that one fantasy is the only
one I have going. I'm so damned hooked on her. & now I can't even
get past imagining kissing her—probably because I'm so certain she
hates me.

Over & over & over certain words & phrases from Sally's loquazene
exam echo in my head. I keep wanting to make comparisons with

my own experience. In some ways I had it worse with Rbt, but in other ways not. I never spoke filth at Sally. & I've always felt that was the one insupportable thing with Rbt, his insistence on all that verbal abuse. On the other hand, Rbt didn't use anal sex as punishment, the way I did with Sally.

Oh shit. Face it, Alexandra. You wanted to shame her for exploiting you.

For all my infatuation with her, I sometimes hated her. & now I see that someone helplessly subjected to another person's hatred has to feel a great deal of pain. Look at how I reel under Elizabeth's hatred. (But did I ever hate Sally like that? No, I can't believe that I did.)

Maybe it seems over-reactive for Sally to mind so much, when Rbt *wanted* me to use the dildo on him. When he presented me with it & demanded I use it, I had to force myself to come up with the appropriate verbal abuse with which to apply it… I got such a weird feeling at times with all our role-switching. Trying to imagine what he felt, always wondering if it was ever the same as I felt when doing or being done to the same things. I could never believe it with him. Yet when I think about Sally being done to, I keep having this strong feeling that she, on the other hand, did feel the same things I felt. Even though it was different. & she a service-tech. (Rbt was always arguing that executives of cross-gender are more alike than cross-class people of the same gender. Even executive men who are supposed to be sexless— but then Rbt didn't believe any of that theory they have about fixed males. & he also maintained that sex is only minimally dependent upon pleasurable genital sensations, that it goes much much deeper.)

Oh, what's the point of trying to understand any of this. Sally's gone. & I've no future with anyone.

Sunday, 5/6/2096

This book wasn't under my pillow when I woke this morning. Did I move it in my sleep (doubtful, considering how still I have to lie to remain comfortable enough not to waken), or have my guards been reading it? I have to remember that for Elizabeth not to read it needn't necessarily mean she won't have someone reading it for her.

Nothing I write in this book can be of possible interest to anyone now living. Whoever you are who is reading this, I hope you're enjoying it. You might bear in mind that Elizabeth Weatherall disposes of people when they know too much for her comfort. This could be a costly voyeurism for you. Consider that, my friend. Ice water runs in her veins. Some of us have learned that the hard way.

Monday, 5/7/2096

A little while ago one of the guards brought in a print-out of a letter from Mama. Why does Elizabeth bother? Perhaps she's just being ironic with me. God knows. It's clear she doesn't intend to allow Mama any more visits to me; & as for the question of Grandmother visiting as Mama proposes, that would be totally out of the question.

Also, of course, I am permitted to appreciate the fact that Mama always & ever responds positively to bribery. Elizabeth must have allowed the transfer of the title of the Paris apartment to Mama, since Mama waxes so effusively on the subject in her letter. About how "charming" it is—none of Rbt's "hypermodern nonsense," straight Louis Quinze decor & furnishings. Mama of course considers this "lapse into taste" an accident & not to Rbt's credit. His being raised a professional & all that, it would have to be accident. Mama's snobbery is so colossal that I can't help but wonder what induced her to contract with Rbt in the first place. I suppose his being in the Executive had something to do with her reasons.

What will Elizabeth give her afterwards to keep her quiet? Apart from the threat of scandal, of course. She knows well the irresistible effects of carrots matched with sticks. If she gave Mama something truly magnificent she'd forever have Mama's devotion & allegiance... God, what depressing thoughts. I'd go to sleep again, but the physical therapist is due.

Wednesday, 5/9/2096

It took me years to appreciate Rbt's efforts to wean me from the horrible Clarice, my first whore/lover. He showed me the connections between sex & greed, made them impossible to miss. But that wasn't enough, not for Rbt. Showing me was only the first step. Every slightest attempt to pursue my simpler sensual appetites provoked him into repressive tactics that ultimately taught me to control my impulses where the slightest manifestation of that kind of wanting was concerned. The little incidents before Darlene (past which it's not possible to talk even of incidents, but only of unexpressed, surreptitious, iron-controlled longings) always included momentary snatches of kissing or flirtation. Or simply a meeting of eyes, in which one could read & likewise convey the promise of a little warmth & pleasure. Flirtation! Hard to believe I ever had a flirtatious exchange in my life, so controlled & inhibited am I now. Sometimes I think I've only fantasized those early encounters. As I fantasized being a part of my mother & Elizabeth's world. His cold remoteness, yes, & slaps. Hard slaps that usually left bruises for the world to see. Hair-pulling. & always a constant stream of filth for apprising me of the girls' interest in me: my credit. All any girl ever smiling at me or twining her arms around my neck & pressing her tongue against my teeth could possibly want from me is material largesse. How fatuous could I be to think they were in the least bit sexually attracted to me for myself. That when they looked into my eyes they could ever see anything but gold.

After a while, when I'd see them looking at me that way I'd feel nothing but anger. Fury. It's astounding that upon seeing Sally I wanted her. Not that that's all I felt. No, I knew Elizabeth must be paying the girl a fabulous salary for spying on me, while from me personally Sally would be expecting to rake in greater than usual profits of whoring since my demands were so exiguous. Never once did I allow myself to see Sally for the person she is. Instead I concentrated on my rage at what she represented. All those nasty comments, all that sarcasm, all those slaps... Hating her more & more for refusing to leave, taking her persistence as proof of a basic vile, even extraordinary, cupidity. Hating her for my even wanting her.

Hating her when it should have been myself I hated. No, that's not right, for I do hate myself. Myself & Rbt for making me like this. Maybe hating Sally for being like myself in accepting those slaps, in accepting the abuse, in playing every game I required of her—in some crazy way duplicating me & Rbt? Then Elizabeth is right, I might as well be Rbt. Slapping Sally for not playing the game by the rules I'd announced, as he so often did to me. Slapping her for "lying" to me. (His notions of truth-telling somehow eluded me even when I was trying hard to please him.) Slapping her for being me & making me be Rbt when I hate these games & wish to get free of them but can't because they're all there is of me. So who am "I," anyway, her or Rbt? But this is to ask who I am for my own self. Sally could say who I am. Rbt: could he say? He'd say I was Persephone. & who was she? Maybe he'd say I was & was not Kay. That I was & was not himself. All four of these things at once, he might say. Either I could satisfy by being these things—himself or Kay, that is—or simply not satisfy because of this lack (being not-him, or not-Kay) that reduced me to non-functionality, & then that's when he had to punish me, punish me for failing to be the only things that might be seen in me (that or the lack of those things)...

I'm so confused. But Sally's outside this system of phantoms & mirages. Not a question of lack in her, she's a full presence even though I blindfolded myself to that for as long as I could. A full presence. A real person.

Where now I am only lack. I am lack because there's no one to take me for some other one. He's no longer there to take me for Kay or himself. Lack. An infinite state of invisibility. Which is why Elizabeth takes me for him. (Or sometimes she does.) She's said so. Maybe that's my answer. That I can at least exist for Elizabeth by letting that phantom take me over completely. But even those times I know she is taking me for him it doesn't quite feel as though I'm there. Not like when Rbt took me for Kay or himself.

No. Even when she takes me for him, even then I feel non-existing.

But I did feel existing with Sally, I know I did.

Because I was him then? Is that why?

I can't go on with this. I can't bear thinking. I'm such a damned coward.

Thursday, 5/10/2096

Relief that I'm through with the physical therapist for the day—she qualifies, I'm sure, to be one of Wedgewood's people, given her psychological make-up. She certainly fits that special profile that fuck-er favored.

...Rereading Mama's letter for the zillionth time (what else besides this book & my thoughts is there to occupy myself with?), I realize again how bitter I am that she never gave me love. & how absurd, how pathetic that I trot that out. How shameful. Lying here thinking about that kind of deprivation. Feeling sorry for myself. Days & days & days of feeling the despicable emotion of self-pity. Yet there it is. Love is something executives are apparently supposed not to need—we're taught how illusory & self-interested & self-delusive it is. Executives are supposed to know better than to get anywhere near such a cynical word—except when being properly cynical while using it.

Love. Love. Love. Never from Mama. Only from the service-techs she employed to take care of me. As Rbt liked to point out. Heavy em-phasis on the word "paid." Paid. Paid love. For a little girl. Did the little girl know it was paid for? Probably. The little girl learned early that only her brother was worthy of "real" love (i.e., that not requir-ing payment). Everything for Daniel. Little girls are inferior, they have to learn to control themselves. Otherwise they'll spend all their time in their rooms, by themselves... Guess I must not have properly controlled myself. Isn't that the lesson in all this? Alexandra sent to her island with only paid keepers for company. Keepers who are there only for the money. To make sure she doesn't leave. To spy on her. To seek out her secrets.

The first thing my father did after seeing me for the first time in a decade was to confine me to quarters. A dismal horrid room, & I knew none of the service-techs, & they certainly didn't guess it could be lucrative to pretend love for me, who on her first night in the house was in heavy disgrace with their employer. Only Elizabeth sometimes came to see me. & once even disobeyed his orders by taking me out to the Diana—promising me that on my sixteenth birthday I would be made a member. Promising me everything, promising me the moon. I thought because of the way she looked at me, because of the way she stroked my hair, because of the way her voice caressed me, I thought she was promising me love.

But then she vanished. & there was just Rbt. So finally someone loved me. Suddenly it happened, for he had decided I was like him. He was the only one who *could* love me. *Don't you see, Persephone, that I am the only one who has ever loved you, the only one who* can *love you for yourself?* Did he really say that to me, or am I making it up? It *sounds* like the sort of thing Rbt would say. I'm so confused now, I worry that I could be making it up.

Comes into my mind just now that dream I had sometime in those first few massively confused months after his death. Where I'm practicing shooting, in the practice range. On the island. & then, without even knowing I'm going to do it, I turn & point the gun at Rbt—& shoot him in the heart, & he dies. I take off the mufflers & hand them & the Colt I shot Rbt with to Blake. But then I feel a hand on my ass. I whirl & find it's Lamont. He grabs me & tries to force me to the floor. Blake does nothing to help me. But just as I hit the floor, just as Lamont is reaching to rip my tunic off me, Rbt gets up—momentarily alive—& shoots Lamont. Then he crumples to the floor & is again dead. A horrible dream. I understood what it meant, of course. & now that I'm in this mess with Elizabeth…I see why I've thought of it again. He could have blackmailed her if he'd stayed alive. *He* would have known what she wanted, & everything would have been different… (But would I prefer it that way, to what has been? Imagine five years tied to him, with nothing else to occupy him, no men to command, no country to run… The very thought makes me shudder with horror.)

Rbt said to me, again & again, that he had long known that only someone his twin could love him & that this did not bother him. His twin. Like Kay. He said Kay was his twin. Or like me. & that that was how it had to be. & that he would never delude himself it could be otherwise.

I've run out of twins. But could *I* love someone my twin? I don't see how. (& if Kay was his twin, & if I was his twin, & only twins could love, why then did Kay want to escape him, as I wanted to escape him?)

Confused, confused. Always I've been confused. Rbt claimed that everything could be understood coldly, clearly, rationally, that confusion was only mental inadequacy, emotional indulgence. Sloppiness. Lack of discipline. My mind perfectly capable, according to him, only problem laziness & occasional hysteria… Have to stop now. I'm lost, lost.

Saturday, 5/12/2096

Today one of the med-techs let me know (subtly, of course) how disgusting she finds having to handle my bedpans—I hate even to think about it, my usual diarrhea is at its worst. Lying here for hours seems not to stultify my bowels. At any rate, I have a strong desire to recompense these people stuck with me, but it's not likely Elizabeth would allow it. At least not as long as I'm here—it would smack too much of bribery to a suspicious mind like hers.

Hard to be disciplined enough not to let myself dwell on what a hell this situation is. Have to avoid thinking about what my body is going through, what I might face when I've finished "healing." Have to avoid thinking about physical therapy when I'm not undergoing it. Have to avoid thinking about how much I crave parsley. Have to avoid thinking about what Elizabeth has planned for me next. What does that leave me with? This book. The past. Sexual fantasy. (Not even the food—for that comes from tubes & is hardly even noticeable on the palate.) Sexual fantasy? But that seems inevitably to lead me back to the past. How can I think about Sally now without thinking about all that? & I seem incapable of in any way touching on sex without Sally's presence in my thoughts.

Sally. Has her lover been freed? Or has she returned to her career, having needlessly undergone—oh my god. No. I hadn't realized it. My damned sentimental delusions about Elizabeth, or simply a desire not to see—but it's obvious, now that I consider it. Oh hell. This is one thought I can't bear. Elizabeth is, after all, too cold-blooded for there even to be a possibility... She's like Rbt. She would never take any kind of chance, not if she didn't have to. She wouldn't balk at excision. No wonder she didn't bed Sally. She knew even then. Whatever it is that is driving her—whatever it is she is desperate to keep quiet—she would *never* allow a possible witness loose on the world.

No. No. No. I can't

Monday, 5/14/2096

Elizabeth came today. I've just stopped shaking enough to write. Her anger is wild. Or maybe she wants me to think that. How else account for her seeming to fly out of control so far as to slap me? Elizabeth's strength & size descending—literally—on me made me feel small & powerless, hanging in traction as I am. No, it must have been deliberate, calculated. To unnerve me. Or to intensify my fear of her anger. (Which was already considerable.) Elizabeth is far too controlled to go out of control with me; her control is legendary.

Need to try to remember the things she said. Harsh remarks directed at what I'd been writing in this book (I was correct in my conjecture that someone reads it for her). Told me that as I blather on about not being loved I should consider the "fact" that I'd never loved anyone, that I was a self-centered bastard that showed my brother Daniel to advantage.

She said that if I wanted to know what she was going to do with me when I finished healing I should consider the contents of the transcript I was keeping from her, that I should know from that that I would regret not cooperating with her. But what seemed most to infuriate her was my saying in this book that she is like Rbt & that ordering excisions came easily to her. It was when we were talking about that that she slapped me. She leaped half-way across the room at me, as if making a preemptive strike against some deadly opponent packing something large & concealed. What I write in this book incenses her, she thinks I write it all for her benefit.

I'd have to be more determined & stronger than would seem humanly possible to play that kind of game in this situation. I'm only trying to get by, trying to survive an intolerable situation. (As on the island—little did I realize how delightful that situation might seem in other more extreme circumstances.) What is it she imagines I can do, anyway? Her physically attacking me demonstrates well enough the true nature of our relationship.

& when I asked her pointblank what Sally's fate is to be, she refused to say. She asserts that Sally is none of my business & only a red herring I persist in dragging across the trail for devious reasons she has no intention of taking the trouble to decipher. Her performance has done little to reassure me about Sally. Though Elizabeth will undoubtedly react even more extremely at my writing it, by this point I'd have to say Elizabeth fits Wedgewood's profile even better than the physical therapist does. She is no one I recognize. I can't even find Rbt in her now. Just this sheer wall of hating. No wonder Rbt was desperate by the end to excise her. He probably knew her better than anyone has ever done.

Chapter Seven

[i]

The guard stared at Hazel's plastic and frowned—presumably because of the designation **FREE ZONE** prominently embossed on its surface. Still, the lemon color elicited the usual deference in voice and gesture. *These physical objects that are fetishes of social hierarchy serve as symbols for their worship: how else take a small rectangle of cheap plastic seriously?* The guard swiped the card through the reader and stared for a few seconds at the screen. He looked again at her, and she saw a new expression in his eyes. Carefully he handed the card back to her and indicated she could pass.

Every time she traveled in government-dominated territory anxiety that past sins and associations might finally catch her up dogged her. Some of the anxiety resulted from the contrast between the presence of government-dominated structures and the lack of such things—in this case, "security measures"—in the Free Zone. One did not have to undergo routine identification procedures in the Free Zone. One did not carry plastic in the Free Zone unless one wished to do business with multinational corporations or government-associated companies. And one did not receive special treatment for meeting international definitions of professional-ness in the Free Zone, either. So naturally ingress-egress controls at government-dominated airports induced anxiety in her. These procedures invaded and distorted her sense of reality: forcing an acknowledgment of this other construction of reality that she would prefer not to exist. The guard's taking her card, categorizing her by class, and swiping the card through a data reader epitomized a reality she abominated.

And yet on occasion she submitted herself to such structures— and clung to the resulting disorientation. When such procedures began to feel "normal" and quotidian, then she would know she must be succumbing to insidious (because intangible) forces working against her. Accordingly, Hazel sought to keep her forays into this alien reality as brief as possible. Adjusting herself to others' constructions of reality came all too easily to her. Boundary fluidity, Hazel named her susceptibility. Fluidity, flexibility, responsiveness could all too easily be interpreted as "weakness." At one time she had heard such qualities characterized as "softness." Hard not to judge herself by *their* terms, even now.

Hazel strode into the airport's new terminal. A few yards past the guard's booth, a thin, dark-haired woman approached. "You *are* Dr. Bell?" the woman asked hesitantly.

Like Hazel herself, this woman wore a green scarf around her neck. "Mary Amato?" Hazel held out her hand.

The woman looked doubtfully at Hazel's hand but, after a moment's hesitation, extended her own in an unexpectedly firm shake.

Hazel smiled. "Please, call me Hazel." Being called "doctor" worked to bring about these "seminars," but the tendency of people to want to construct things out of the "doctor" created problems.

After picking up her small overnight bag from the Baggage Security Service, Hazel informed Mary that the grant paying her travel expenses would also pay for the rental of a mass-auto two-seater so that they wouldn't have to spend a lot of time coping with transit hassles. As sometimes happened in these situations, Mary expressed embarrassment that her group couldn't pay Hazel more than a nominal honorarium scraped up among them. The embarrassment vanished, fortunately, in the business of claiming the vehicle Hazel had reserved.

When they had squeezed themselves into the two-seater and input their destination, Hazel asked Mary to point out changes made over the last few years in Boston and to describe what the "Sectoring System" had been like and how it had worked. The subject absorbed them, since many physical remnants of the System had not yet been eradicated from the streets. At one point Hazel wondered aloud whether these traces remained as grim reminders to make the residents of Boston more appreciative of the current regime, or whether they remained because the government was unwilling to spend the money for completely dismantling and removing them. Mary exchanged a look with her. Mutely, she shook her head. Hazel did not press the matter.

When they came to an extraordinarily wide street—two lanes in each direction for mass-auto as well as a lane each way for free-wheelers, separated by waist-high concrete dividers—lined on each side by rubble-strewn vacant lots with the only viable buildings in sight perhaps a quarter of a mile away on each side, Hazel looked at Mary and said, "What in the hell happened here? This can't still be from bombing during the war, can it?"

Mary swallowed nervously. "No. At first some of the buildings around here were burned by the Boston Collective and other terrorist groups. Later, the cops decided to level everything around and clear the area. You see how wide this street is?" Hazel nodded. "Well they decided to make a street here that could handle all the traffic in the area—everything around here dumps onto this street, so that at Galveston Square—about a mile up, you'll see it, they never did pull it down—they had a major security checkpoint set up. All traffic coming in or going out of this sector into the next had to pass through that checkpoint—which meant they needed a road big enough to hold the traffic." Mary shook her head. "But this road was still always full-up, and the wait was really long at Galveston Square. Even the mass transit vehicles had to detour to stop there. And of course they didn't run the subway then at all. So if you were going in or out you'd have these incredible waits." She shrugged. "I and almost everyone I know eventually gave up trying to get out on the weekends. It was just too damned much of a hassle."

After such a description, Hazel recognized Galveston Square without Mary's having to say a word. Their vehicle cruised unhindered past the various open gates that along with massive concrete barriers and electric fences guarded their lane. Studying the concrete and steel guardpost as they passed it, Hazel saw that the cameras and spotlights attached to the roof had not been removed. Other structures on the roof suggested frames and dollies for weapons of the sort Liz had had on the roof of her house in the Free Zone. In spite of these remaining traces, Hazel spotted only a solitary armed guard, presumably detailed to protect the structure from vandalism.

She shivered. "Why haven't they dismantled that thing?"

Mary avoided her eyes. "I just want to forget those days," she said. "I hardly even go this way anymore, since some of the old streets have been opened up again and the subway is running."

Their vehicle had entered a residential section in which apartment blocks overshadowed long strings of row-houses obviously, given their naked facades, made of the gray super-fab material common before the Blanket. Hazel was surprised to see about a dozen children playing in the street. Since she had no idea what safety-devices—if any—existed in non-Free Zone mass-auto vehicles, she took manual control. "Interesting to see so many children here. Is it possible that the Executive eased up locally in its Birth Limitation policies? I wonder what *that's* all about. Does anyone know?"

Hazel snatched a look at Mary and found her staring at her. Quickly she returned her attention to the street. After about half a minute Mary said, "You know, Hazel, the whole reason the Clerical Workers' Association was able to have you at all is because of the educational nature of the seminar. We're a social support group, not a political organization. I hope you understand that?"

Hazel obeyed a signal from the processor to turn right. She didn't know whether to take Mary's statement as a pro-forma protest—an interpretation Hazel tended to favor, since she had assumed the invitation from this organization had been informed and coded—or whether the tenor of her remarks were alarming Mary. "Education always has a political orientation," Hazel said. "Whether you explicitly admit to it or not. The politics of learning are inescapable."

"All of us have clauses in our contracts prohibiting any unionizing activities," Mary said flatly. "Each of us could be vulnerable to summary termination if the management decides they can make a case for that kind of activity."

"Yes, I know. But I'm not unionizing. You won't hear *me* talking about unions. Or dues. Or election of officers. Or any other sort of organizational structuring." Hazel turned her head and smiled at her grim-faced interlocutor. "I'm a psychologist, Mary. Not a politician."

Returning her attention to her driving, Hazel wondered just how this group had come to invite her to conduct the seminar. The way would not be smooth this weekend, she could see that already.

[ii]

So far, so good. She had gotten them to shove the furniture to the perimeter of the room and sit on the floor with her. Hazel thought the nylon carpet patterned with interlocking aqua and brown diamonds ugly, but she noted that it was newish-looking and clean. Judging by its lounge, this particular company dorm was a cut above most. Hazel had only hazy memories of the few unpleasant weeks she had spent in a dorm when she'd first moved to DC after the war—and sharper memories of her sense of relief when she'd finally been able to move into her own studio apartment.

Most levels of clerical service-techs could not afford studio apartments; their choice generally lay between living in dorms (for those who needed their own private space) or sharing an apartment with either family members or workmates or a lover. In Denver Hazel had lived in her parents' apartment. But when she had moved to DC, her salary had been raised sufficiently to allow her a tiny place of her own in a run-down building in a seedy neighborhood with streets she avoided after dark. Though not all fifteen women participating in the seminar lived in this dorm—Mary Amato, for one, lived in a shared apartment two blocks away—Hazel took care not to reveal her feelings about dorms. This one might not be as horrendous as the one she had stayed in eleven years ago. And no matter what its condition, people living in this dorm wouldn't appreciate an outsider's dismay at their "plight."

Hazel began by making a brief statement describing the format of the seminar, stressing that she wanted discussion with them rather than to lecture and encouraging them to ask questions or raise issues when they thought it relevant. This tack carried the risk of dissipation into gossip, but Hazel felt confident that she could create the necessary context needed to make such excursions relevant.

A woman with straggling thin brown hair pushed behind her ears, who spoke in an aggressive tone of voice, took Hazel at her word. "I have a question," she said. Her brown eyes glittered through narrowed lids—sardonically, Hazel thought. "I'd like to know why you excluded men from this thing."

Hazel glanced at the questioner's name-tag. "If we had men here, what we talk about would be different. And the women in the group would hold back. Whether they mean to or not, men *always* dominate the discussion in these situations. It's one of the games we all play, mostly unconsciously." Hazel paused, then went on. "I want to avoid as many of those kinds of behavioral structures as I can in these discussions. At some point it might be possible to have a mixed group, but only after certain things have been worked out." Hazel considered describing the evolution of mixed-gender discussion modes in the Free Zone, but decided it was too soon. She could see that most of them hadn't a clue to what she meant. The woman neither commented on Hazel's response nor posed another question. She only smirked, as though her worst suspicions about Hazel had been confirmed.

Hazel removed her yellow plastic card from her tunic pouch and tossed it in front of her. The card bounced and came to rest three feet from her, face up. She glanced around the circle and saw puzzlement on most faces and shades of longing, envy, and hostility on others. "Let's talk about that physical object I just flipped into the circle." Hazel waited to see if anyone would speak. After about half a minute she said, "Nothing to say about it? Then let's start with the most basic facts. What is it?"

"It's yellow plastic," a small, compact woman said impatiently.

"Suppose I were someone who'd lived on an otherwise unpopulated island in the South Pacific all my life," Hazel said to her. "And I asked you what this thing is. What kind of answer would you give beyond 'yellow plastic'?"

The woman flushed. "I don't know. It would be complicated, wouldn't it, because the person wouldn't even know what credit is."

"I know what *I'd* say," the sardonic-eyed woman said. "I'd say it's a thing that makes the owner of it a privileged character. It's something that gives you things you want. It probably means the person who owns it can use it to go out as often as she'd like, can travel, can buy food that doesn't come out of a tube." Her smile mocked Hazel. "It means the person who carries it has it easy."

"Because it's yellow?" Hazel asked.

"What else?" the woman snapped back.

"Okay," Hazel said. "That's one aspect of what this piece of plastic is. You're talking about how it can be used—that is, one of its functions, and what that use can mean to the person who carries it. We'll come back to that in just a minute, but first let's pay closer attention to it as a thing per se. We can pretend it's orange or blue for a while, if you like. Though we will eventually get back to its being yellow, since the color of plastic is not insignificant. But for now, let's forget the color of the plastic and look at it as a generic thing. As an object in and of itself, without reference to its credit power." They were looking puzzled again. Hazel leaned forward and retrieved the card. Turning it around and around, she said, "Tell me about the reality of this thing. Would you say it's real? As a thing?"

"Real?" a round-faced woman with short gray hair and narrow glasses with pink frames said. "How can it not be real? You're holding it in your hand. You can feel it; we can see it. Of course it's real."

"You mean it's real in the sense that it would be real whether it had my name and number embossed on it, whether it was white or red or green?" Hazel asked.

"Of course!"

"Just as a piece of plastic," Hazel said. Several voices murmured assent. "Then what's the connection between this thing as a real physical object absent the markings that make it significant to you and the whole constellation of associations going through your heads when you look at it and see that it's yellow plastic?"

Hazel waited for about half a minute, but no one spoke. "Okay, let's go back to our outsider who doesn't know what plastic is. So you show her the piece of plastic. And try to explain that there's more to its reality than the fact that it can be handled and seen physically."

After a few seconds Mary Amato said, "You mean the way there's a difference between wedding rings and other rings?"

"Ah," Hazel said, "let's switch to rings as an example. To wedding rings. What makes a wedding ring more than a piece of metal that can fit around your finger?"

"It's a symbol," Mary said. "Wedding rings are a symbol that people wear."

"Would you say the symbolic aspect of it is as real as its being a piece of metal that you can handle?" Hazel asked.

Mary's eyes narrowed. "Sure. I mean, everyone knows what it means. I guess I don't know what you mean by *real*."

"Are the meanings of symbols real, even though you can't touch them with your fingers or *see* them?"

"Oh!" Mary's face lit up. "Oh! *I* see what you mean! You're talking about how plastic is a symbol that we use, and that the way we use it is real in a different way from the plastic itself! But that someone who didn't know what plastic is a symbol for wouldn't have any way of understanding that there's more to it than the thing itself. Is that it?"

Hazel smiled. "Then if this thing we're talking about isn't available to touch and see with our eyes, physically—I mean all the things that the plastic *means*—how can we talk about this thing—we could call this thing a set of abstractions—how can we talk about this set of abstractions that carry over from the card as being real? I can't see it or touch it. Can you?"

"I can touch the things plastic obtains," the cynic said.

Hazel's smile widened into a grin. "Maybe so, but that's not what we're talking about. We're talking about whatever it is that turns the piece of plastic into the thing that can buy other physical objects. It surely isn't the plastic itself. Anyone could make a piece of plastic that looks like this if they really wanted to. The International Bank mass-produces these pieces of plastic for perhaps a thousandth of what an average tube of food costs. So it's not the plastic." Hazel held the woman's gaze. "You see what I'm getting at."

"Yes, I think so. You're talking about the system."

"*The* system?" Hazel raised her eyebrows. "That's a little too broad, although we could get there in a few giant leaps if we wanted to. No, I'm talking about *a* system. A set of structures, we could say. Or we could call this a structure in itself. This thing that makes the card *work* as a *real thing*." Hazel reached for the liter bottle of water she (like the rest of them) had been supplied with and twisted the cap off the bottle. She continued: "Let's switch tracks for a minute. For the vast majority of people living in the Free Zones, plastic doesn't exist. It doesn't mean anything. You go shopping, and most places don't accept plastic. They use another system there. Some places accept plastic, and some people still carry plastic. But most don't. Because they'd rather not. You could say that in most cases in the Free Zones, plastic doesn't work. The *idea* of it doesn't work. Whatever makes plastic work, whatever gives it the power of purchase in countries that have governments, doesn't work—isn't acknowledged—in the Free Zone. So by comparison, to come back to Boston, what makes plastic work *here?*"

This question drew more of them into the discussion, and Hazel saw that at least a few of them were beginning to have a fuzzy notion of what she might be talking around, even if they couldn't quite grasp it yet. But this way of talking was new to them and demanded their *thinking* in a way none of them had apparently ever tried before. Those who didn't make the necessary imaginative leap would grow bored and frustrated. But those who did make the leap might find their entire world changed—if, that is, she could stimulate them far enough to make the strain of the effort worth it to them personally. Challenging *them* challenged *her* beyond anything she knew.

[iii]

On the second day, during the first hour in the morning—designated the "Coffee and Donuts Hour"—before the session was formally scheduled to begin, a woman who hadn't spoken much the previous day settled near Hazel, clutching a steaming mug of the stuff they called coffee. Hazel had identified Denise as the youngest in the group, perhaps as much as seven or eight years younger than the average age of those attending the seminar. She wore pink and lavender face enamel—obviously to enhance her blonde hair, delicate features, and light blue eyes. Her clothing so closely matched the face enamel that it seemed likely that either the paint or the clothing had been selected to match. "What you were saying last night about your experiences living in that house with executive women," Denise said softly.

Hazel recalled that Denise had been enthralled at that particular set of personal revelations—far more so than any of the other women, who had been variously curious and repelled. At first they had refused to believe Hazel's assertion that most executive women were lesbians. "But on vid," they had objected. After discussing the question of the soaps' reliability for accurate depictions of social reality in general and executives in particular, Hazel had suggested they study the only real-life view of executives available to them—news conferences, which though carefully staged and scripted would reveal subtle things, such as the body language used by executives of both sexes when sharing the same live-vid screen.

Some of the women had drawn fresh insight and made a few of the connections Hazel had been trying to suggest to them when she had used the eating-arrangement issue as an example. Perhaps Denise had been puzzling about it and now wanted to discuss it before the group reconstituted itself for the morning session? "Yes?" Hazel said, and bit into the sugary, greasy confection she had accepted against her better judgment.

"I was wondering how you go about meeting those kind of women." Denise's eyes shone with excitement. "Executives, I mean." Hazel experienced the sinking sensation of dismay as she realized the point of Denise's interest. "Because I'd like to meet women like that."

"Would you," Hazel said. Nothing, nothing at all had gotten through to Denise. It *couldn't* have. "You mean you wouldn't mind being treated like that? As an inferior not worthy of sharing the same table with executives?"

"It wouldn't matter about *eating* with them. I don't care about things like that. Who'd want to eat with a whole crowd of executives like that, anyway? It would make me feel funny." She slanted a sly look at Hazel. "*I'll* never be a professional, I'll never be anything but a service-tech. Which is fine with me. But the pay is better when you work for executives, isn't it. It isn't like working at Safeco." She frowned. "I've never even seen a single executive woman at Safeco since I've been working there. I mean, how did *you* get to work for them?"

Hazel sighed. That was the problem with being categorized on the lecture/seminar circuit as a self-help specialist. She could, of course, tell Denise that all she'd have to do would be to hang around Boston's executive women's clubs. And Denise would then go away thinking the "self-help seminar" had been worth the small fee she had paid to attend it.

Some help *that* would be.

[iv]

"No," Hazel said, shaking her head, "'lifestyle' isn't it, for when it comes to lifestyle the service-tech-executive gap isn't as wide as you might think, given that service-techs share with executives certain basic assumptions that have more power in shaping lives than the perceived *differences* between them. Some of the shared assumptions are what make the whole plastic system work, for instance. When we think about *differences*, it might be useful to see to what extent we tend to express things in terms of opposition. Executive versus non-executive. Good versus evil. Rich versus poor. Hard-working versus lazy. Terrorism versus national security... By thinking of differences only in terms of oppositions, we limit our options to either this or to that, thus forcing ourselves to stick to the same old assumptions that are more significant a part of the problem than the oppositions themselves..."

[v]

"But it's hopeless reaching for the sky—and I think that's what you're telling us to do," Sharon—one of those whose minds had been visibly responding—objected to the ambitiousness of the change Hazel was urging on them. "What is needed is better pay, better working conditions, better living conditions. These are the things we might conceivably get by bettering ourselves. What you're talking about isn't even *imaginable*, much less *likely*."

The group had by this time shrunk to four plus Hazel. The others, Hazel guessed, did not want to throw away the little free time they had left of the weekend by spending their afternoon cooped up in this room talking about the incomprehensible.

She had twenty minutes before she had to leave for the airport. "The sort of things I'm talking about," Hazel said, trying to imagine what was going through Sharon's mind, "can be small or large. You can individually rebel in small ways, individually work to break down certain structures of the reality around you, to create for yourself. It's possible. Though that must be the hardest thing in the world for anyone to try to do. Thus though I call it *small-scale*, I don't mean it's the easiest way to go. Because you'd constantly be going against the grain, fighting everything around you, all the time. Who's strong enough to do that for more than the first short period while one is sustained by an enthusiastic burst of energy?" Hazel glanced at the others. "But there are other possibilities than going it alone," she said quietly.

After a few seconds' silence, Mary Amato said, "You mean like moving to the Free Zone."

Hazel half-smiled. "That's one possibility, certainly. It's the one I took. I moved out of the executive world and into another world, a world in the process of changing and reworking and dismantling old structures."

"And you are saying there are other possibilities?" Sharon's tone was skeptical.

"Sure. There are always other possibilities. The ones people explored before there were Free Zones." She smiled. "The aliens didn't create the Free Zones out of nothing. They simply made it possible for them to exist and to go on existing. But the actual *creation*—which is on-going—of the Free Zones is the imaginative, effortful, and disciplined making of the world by humans, mostly women. Groups of people trying to maintain their own constructions of reality in conflict with the dominant construction of reality have existed in this country for a long, long time. Maybe for as long as there have been humans living on this continent, and I'm not talking only about Caucasians. Such groups have saved the sanity of a lot of people throughout history. Have made life bearable. Even if their fates haven't been to triumph over the dominant reality."

"You're talking about organizing now," Mary said sharply.

Hazel shrugged. "It depends on what you mean by organizing. I can see how some people would think it worthwhile and a first step to organize all clerical workers, for instance, into a union. Though many people would pay a high price for its accomplishment, eventually certain things would improve. And then later the union might be dissipated, or the executives might find a way to make the union irrelevant because of new management or production techniques…and then the whole process would have to start all over again. And in the meantime you'd still be living in more or less of a police state, slave to a piece of plastic…" Hazel glanced at her watch. "I have to be leaving."

"We've only started getting to the point of being able to really talk about things," Brigitte said regretfully. "What do we do now?"

Hazel grinned. "You think about things. And if you're interested in stuff to read to help you think about things, you try some of the books and articles on the reading list I handed out at the beginning.

Or you can write to me care of either the University or the Co-op—both addresses are on the handout." Hazel's gaze met each of theirs in turn. "And," she added softly, "if you're really serious, you can come to see me in the Pacific Northwest Free Zone."

Brigitte leaned forward. "None of us could ever afford to do that. That's a pipe-dream."

Hazel shook her head. "No it isn't. I'd help you find a way to get there if you really wanted to come. I can promise you that."

They looked at one another, as though for guidance on what they should be thinking about this offer. It was too much all at once, Hazel thought. And she had to leave them now.

[vi]

At the airport, after the guard slid her card through the reader, he said, "I'm going to have to ask you to wait, Ms. Bell."

Hazel's heartbeat accelerated, and her body first flushed with heat and then shivered with cold as the guard picked up the phone and announced that he was holding her for whomever was on the other end of the phone line. "What is the problem?" Hazel said, managing to keep her voice steady.

He shook his head. "There's a notation here that you are wanted, Madam."

"I have a plane to catch," Hazel said, knowing the statement to be both obvious and useless. Besides, Hazel thought in confusion, whether or not she made her plane (she did have some extra time to spare, since the traffic had been lighter than she had allowed for) might pale in significance before whatever they were "holding" her for. Suppose ODS had decided to detain her on the basis of that file Anne was always alluding to. Suppose Martha's activities had led to the open declaration of hostility against Free Zone activists and to the decision to "crack down," whatever the Marq'ssan-produced consequences might be...

A woman dressed in what Hazel took for a uniform (though the colors mauve and gray rather argued that it was *not* a uniform) entered the security-control area through a service door set into the wall. "This is Hazel Bell?" the woman asked the guard. When the guard confirmed Hazel's identity, the woman turned to Hazel. "You're earlier than I expected, or I would have been out here waiting for you. Sorry for the delay. But I have this to deliver to you." She flourished the purple envelope she held in her left hand. "If you'll sign my book, I can deliver this purple to you and we can both be on our way."

Hazel sagged into rag-doll limpness as relief washed over her. But as she signed the messenger's e-book, she thought how odd it was for her to be receiving a purple, and her anxiety returned. The messenger handed her the envelope, and the guard handed back her plastic and buzzed the gate open. Hazel tucked the envelope and her plastic into her bag, then passed the green light and walked through the narrow corridor out into the junction of concourses. She glanced at her ticket flimsy and consulted the neon markers that labeled the concourses. Mechanically she trudged down the concourse until she reached the appropriate gate.

Only after sinking down into a plastic bucket seat did Hazel take the purple envelope out of her bag. It bore no return address, only her name, printed in Times-Roman twelve-point type. She slid her finger under the flap, not sure she wanted to know its contents. The letterhead consisted only of an address in a government building in DC. Her mouth dried. Perhaps it *was* ODS. Perhaps it had to do with Martha's challenge. Perhaps... But with those people one never knew...

Summoning up her courage, she read the text of the message.

Hazel—Because of your message to me via Anne Hawthorne, I thought you might be interested to know I'm willing to involve myself personally in the imbroglio Martha Greenglass has been stirring up. On Friday two Cabinet officers spoke at length on the phone with Baton Rouge's District Attorney as well as with Dowsanto's South Central Regional Director and persuaded them to drop all charges against Greenglass should she agree to (a) leave Baton Rouge and (b) cease and desist in her campaign to incite opposition to Dowsanto management by employees and the communities in which Dowsanto plants are sited. Greenglass refused.

In view of the fact that you are closely associated with both Greenglass and the Free Zone Co-op leadership, and in view of our past successes in negotiating together during the years I was based in the Free Zone, I think, Hazel, that you and I might profitably meet to discuss this situation. If you agree to undertake the role of

Greenglass's rep, then I will make time in my ever-full schedule to attend to this matter personally. If you don't care for the idea, however,
I will leave the matter in the hands of the two Cabinet officers already
involved.

Margaret Canfield, my personal assistant, can be reached by phone
between the hours of 8 a.m. and 5:30 p.m. EDT at (1199) 7777-4477.
I've instructed her to make all the necessary arrangements for you
should you choose to take up my offer.

All best,

Liz

Hazel stared at the signature. *Damn her arrogance.* But she reread
the message with care, and her first impulse—to throw the purple
pages into the nearest waste-receptacle—receded. It would be egocentric of her to reject the offer out of hand simply because Liz's arrogance enraged her and, to be honest, because coping with Liz and
Liz's world would demand more of her than she could easily afford to
give. It might be that after discussion of the pros and the cons and the
politics, Martha and her allies would conclude there was nothing to be
gained by having personal access to the most powerful person in the
Executive. But it would still have to be considered seriously.

Her flight was called, and Hazel tucked the letter into her briefcase and obeyed the instruction to queue to board. One single advantage to the situation occurred to her: she knew how Liz operated, how
she thought, how she strategized, better than anyone else in the Free
Zone. The advantages would not *all* be on Liz's side. This thought
almost comforted Hazel even as it churned up eddies in her mind that
whispered insidiously to her about responsibility.

Hazel boarded the plane and found her seat beside a lawyerly-
looking professional who was already toiling diligently over an electronic notebook. Pleased to know she wouldn't be bothered with
demands for conversation, after belting in Hazel leaned back in her
seat and closed her eyes. Tired as she was after the intensity of the
weekend, she wanted time alone to think before talking to the others.

Chapter Eight

Sunday, May 6, 2096—Seattle

This time when Hazel showed up I insisted we go down to the cafe on the corner. Once we were outdoors I explained that I didn't know if my apartment was bugged and didn't want to take the risk. Hazel laughed at me and said I was paranoid. And then when she saw that the cafe belongs to the Capitol Hill Neighborhood Co-op, she laughed again and said I was being corrupted and subverted by living in the FZ. This infuriated me, but I didn't give her the satisfaction of seeing that it did. I remarked that belonging to one's neighborhood co-op was convenient for anyone obliged to live in this damned city. "Oh yes, *very* convenient," she retorted, smiling as though that proved her point.

Once we had gotten our respective pots of tea, Hazel handed me a purple addressed to her and told me to read it. I refused, saying that I could see it was a purple, which meant it was for her eyes only and she should know me well enough by now to know I wouldn't violate security regulations. But then she said she'd read it *out loud* to me—right there in the cafe where anyone could hear!—if I didn't read it for myself. And that furthermore the letter was her possession now, hers to do with as she chose, and that more than a dozen people had read it since she'd gotten it last Sunday. Her casualness about the whole thing burned me up, but I decided I'd better read it. I didn't want the contents broadcast to the whole damned room.

When I finished reading it, Hazel said that she had been discussing it with "the others" and that *if and only if* "satisfactory terms" could be worked out would she be willing to meet with Weatherall. Then she went on to say that she had decided that it would be best if I were to act as a liaison in "parleys" between her and Weatherall's office. I could hardly believe my ears. I pointed out that Weatherall was being incredibly generous in making the offer at all and that *they* were the ones with the problem, because it was Greenglass who was in jail and wanted to be released. Hazel just gave me a scornful look and began laying down her conditions. That the meeting take place in the FZ. That two additional "negotiators" participate in any face-to-face meetings. And that the only electronic devices admissible to face-to-face meetings be a single jammer and NoteMaster apiece. I sarcastically said I'd pass the message on but that she was a fool if she thought that just because she'd walked out on Weatherall all those years ago she could get away with treating the most powerful person on the continent with such insolence. Hazel said there were reasons for all her conditions and that I was mistaken if I thought either she or Weatherall would be dragging their past personal relationship into the matter. She said that she, Hazel, had discussed these things "thoroughly" with "the others" (whom she refused to name) and that Weatherall's reason for "involving herself" lay in the seriousness of the situation. That if I thought about it I'd understand how critical this situation was becoming to Weatherall's own survival.

Hazel has me over a barrel, and we both know it. So I tamely agreed to send the message. I'm hoping Weatherall will insist on setting up a more direct contact. I know some people think it's a wonderful thing to get as close to the very powerful as they can. But such closeness means nothing but trouble for people like me. The fact is, I'd be all too likely to find myself bearing the brunt of her frustrations in this. And judging by the attitude Hazel displayed this afternoon, I've no doubt Weatherall's going to be frustrated. Hazel has no sense of propriety whatsoever. She thinks she can make up new rules as she goes, can dump all the social graces that make life bearable and do as she damned well pleases. Well, she can do it, all right—at least as long as she stays in her own little world. But what about the rest of us?

Her wilfulness will eventually alienate everyone who ever liked her. She drives even Co-op type people crazy with the little things she does and says that make them uncomfortable. Someday she may have no friends left at all. And then what?

Saturday May 12, 2096—Seattle

I hate having to be in the middle of this damned "parleying" as Hazel persists in calling it. Not only is there a stalemate because Weatherall insists on DC and Hazel on the FZ, but Weatherall wants no other persons in on their meeting. As instructed, I told Hazel that Weatherall would agree to the limitation of electronics—though it went hard against the grain for Weatherall not to have a terminal at her fingertips, as Hazel should already know (this was actually a specified part of the message, that Hazel knew this about Weatherall)—she'd agree to *that* condition if Hazel agreed to meet in DC and to have no other parties present during any face-to-face meetings. Hazel refuses. Or rather, she offers a counter-deal on one of the points of contention. She'll agree to meet in another place—provided three things: that it isn't DC, it isn't in a government building, and she, Hazel, has veto power over physical situations Weatherall names or sets up, in return for Weatherall's concession on the electronics. But she's adamant on having two persons with her during face-to-face meetings... God how I hate this, all this running out to use public com booths and getting cryptic phone calls from Lise tipping me off to call Canfield. Shit. I knew Hazel would exact a price for her silence all these years.

And tonight, Lise. I'm feeling so, well, *pressured* by her now. The last time, our first meeting since DC, she came on very intense and demonstratively affectionate, even when we were alone. Calling me "Annie" the way she used to. It's not that it's unpleasant, exactly. Just that I don't feel that way about her now. It puts me on the spot, sort of. Because if I don't respond warmly enough it looks as though I'm sulking or being ugly. But when I force myself to be warm, then I feel like a phony. And that's a shitty feeling, knowing you're giving the other person a false impression. I mean, I *like* Lise, that's not in question. But to let her think there's a chance for us to be the way we used to be? It's just another deception.

How ironic, isn't it. The only person I'm not deceiving in any way is Hazel. And right now I'm pissed as hell at her. What does that say about the state of my life?

It doesn't bear thinking about.

Sunday May 13, 2096—Seattle

Lise left not five minutes ago.

The axe has fallen. I'm to tell the Rainbow Press I'll be leaving at the end of the month. Mott has decided to assign me to the Office of Information. Lise hasn't decided yet how exactly she'll use me (the decision about my transfer was just made on Friday). But since Lise essentially acts as something like a liaison between Security and Com & Tran (only more powerful, with initiatory powers and such, and total access to Weatherall, which counts for a lot), I suppose I'll be assigned to some kind of media project, since I know nothing at all about technical electronics.

Leaving this place comes as a shock, even though I knew it was a possibility. To uproot myself and move elsewhere. To leave Venn... To return to the real world. I'll have to get myself back up to date, which won't be easy after all this time away. Funny how flat I feel. After all, this is what I've wanted for a long time. Maybe it's because it means I in some way failed the review—otherwise why remove me from this position? When I think of all the agents I handle... Who will take them over? And who will be able to keep up with the ones I've been bringing along? When I mentioned Mara to Lise she told me to go ahead and make the recommendation to bring her in, and then after that's done I can arrange to introduce her to the person who will be replacing me, and this new controller will take her through the remaining steps.

In the meantime, I have a new assignment that will call for my making reports on data-disks since Lise is going to be wanting them as soon as I can get them out. The drop is to be in the john in the Capitol Hill branch of the Seattle Public Library, in the crack between the towel-wipe dispenser and the wall. I'm to call a Seattle number some station person monitors and announce I have a package to deliver and then drop the disk at the library on the way home from work that night. I hate doing that kind of thing. But it won't be for long—because I won't *be* here that much longer.

Wednesday, May 16, 2096—Seattle

When I relayed Weatherall's latest offer for compromise to Hazel (namely, that half their face-to-faces be with "advisors," half be "completely private," and that the advisors be named in advance), Hazel said she'd have to think about it. Then she dropped her bombshell—that Martha is considering making a deadline she won't announce to us, a deadline that if passed would lead to the Marq'ssan springing her—and wrecking the jail in the process. (I imagine they have that jail well guarded, but it's a fact that it doesn't *matter* how heavily armed a place is, the Marq'ssan can still destroy it. The Argentines and the Russians have learned that the hard way.) I don't think Hazel realizes what a mistake she's making if she thinks she can manipulate Weatherall—or any of the Executive for that matter—by brute force. When I asked her how Martha can *choose* to stay in jail (pointing out that it had been almost a month now since Martha had been arrested) and how she can hold Martha hostage like that to fussing about stupid details blocking her meeting with Weatherall, Hazel started talking about how Martha knew it wasn't for long and how she was getting exemplary treatment and how the longer Martha stayed in jail the more difficult psychologically it would be for the Executive, knowing as they must that the days before the Marq'ssan struck were trickling away like sand in an hourglass.

Hazel must be enjoying all this. It must be a real power trip to have Weatherall's office dealing with her like this. I wonder if she has any inkling at all of what thin ice she's skating on. Even Weatherall's patience is limited. And Hazel has been rocking the boat for some time now. If things come to a definite rupture between the Executive and the FZ, Hazel—as well as the FZ—will have a lot to lose. Because this time the Executive might decide to declare all-out war on the FZ as they never have before—especially since the Marq'ssan don't seem to be paying this FZ that much attention anymore. It hasn't escaped our notice that everything the Marq'ssan have been doing lately has been concentrated in other parts of the world...

Friday, May 18, 2096—Seattle

Two things today. First, had a long talk with Venn about my leaving. She said—and I think she really meant it, too—that if I found I
didn't want to live in DC (I had told her on Monday that I was moving there to be with Lise, since I had to tell her something) I could
always find a job back with the Rainbow Press and that if necessary
the Press would help pay the expenses for my return. (She *must* be
serious to have offered *that*.) She frankly doubts I'll be able to "stand"
living outside the FZ. When I told her I'd been born and raised in
DC, she said that was no guarantee that I'd like living there now. I
mumbled something about how difficult it had been living apart from
Lise, about how Lise had found me a good job and that I'd thought
long and hard about this. That it had been visiting my parents and old
friends in DC that had really tipped the balance.

What a liar I am.

The second thing...Lord. I wouldn't like to be in Canfield's shoes
when she tells Weatherall who it is Hazel intends to have as "advisors." I know from Lise that Weatherall considers Celia Espin to be
a prime pain in the ass (and finds her personally irritating to boot).
I can't remember on which occasions they've met. But I remember
Lise talking about how Weatherall becomes extremely formal and
high-horse when talking to Espin...looking down from Olympus, as
it were. Lise told me about it because it so flabbergasted her (it being a
side of Weatherall she had never seen before). The other person Hazel
wants to take into their meetings is Emily Madden. I hadn't realized
that Hazel and Martha were that tight with Emily. But then Emily is
a special friend of Espin's. And Emily is tight with one of the aliens,
too. I can hardly wait to hear from Canfield. This may be the point at
which the "parleying" breaks down.

Chapter Nine

[i]

They kick off their court shoes. Collapsing onto the daybed, they lean their heads back against the wall. Slowly, slowly, Celia lets the icy gin she sips from one of the rose-tinted liqueur glasses that have been in Jodie's family for generations slide down her throat, tracing a fiery trail down her esophagus that chills after it's passed.

Their almost identical jackets (lawyerly beige linen appropriate to this frequently insupportable climate) hang over the backs of two of the dining table chairs. "My great-great-grandmother crocheted that entire tablecloth herself," Jodie says, apparently noticing Celia eyeing the yards and yards of lace draping the oblong expanse that takes up nearly the entire dining room. Jodie smiles sidelong. "Covetous colleagues have offered me filthy lucre for it. But I'll never be parted from it."

Celia thinks of some of the things she and her mother would never have parted with, either, that disappeared from their house when she herself was forcibly disappeared... "Exquisite," she says. And finishes the gin in her glass.

"And eighteen matching napkins, too," Jodie says. "They made families *big* back then. That table could be expanded. And *was*. Out into this room. Thirty grandchildren the woman who crocheted that lace had. Can you imagine?"

It sounds like a fantasy, thirty grandchildren. Thirty first-cousins. A fantasy passed down mother to daughter to daughter to daughter... But a photo of the woman posing with her daughters graces the wall opposite, each woman in the photo a different shade of brown, though all hold their heads at the exact same angle. Celia gets up to fetch the gin bottle from the freezer. No shop talk tonight.

[ii]

Baton Rouge, again. Another visit to this single client remaining in detention. *Do you appreciate my efforts, Martha? No matter if you don't. I'd still do it. Something's happening here that's important.*

Celia braces herself to submit to the goddamned fucking strip-search. Fiercely ironic, she tells herself she should be grateful that because she is an "officer of the court" she needn't go through the body-cavity search as well. Real trust and faith, Celia thinks, but as always down here in this strange territory not her own she keeps her irony to herself. The Louisiana Bar Association thought the strip-search not unreasonable. You can never tell how someone might try to use you, by slipping something into your clothing. No need though for the body-cavity search, hah-hah, you'd know if someone planted something there, wouldn't you...

Celia doesn't exactly appreciate her Louisiana colleagues' humor. And she knows she would only humiliate herself if she attempted to explain why strip-searches are such a trauma for her. *A trauma? Isn't that an exaggeration, Celia? You go through it each time because you must. If it were a trauma you wouldn't be able to do it, would you. And you're going into the strip-search situation as a lawyer. There's no resemblance to those old days. Everything's changed, for defense attorneys, for detainees.*

[iii]

"No, sir," she assures Philip Guidry, Mr. District Attorney himself, "I do not condone my client's making threats. I'm merely passing a message from her to you. She has not been specific with me about the details because she knows I would apprise the Court of them should I learn of them."

His small brown eyes narrow in his coarse-featured, rubicund face. According to Jodie, Guidry drinks a bottle of wine with lunch, every working day. "He thinks drinking a stiff cup of espresso afterwards sobers him up," Jodie added with a straight face. Celia sniffed and said she knew of judges in San Diego like that. These executives aren't as funny as Jodie liked to think.

"Ms. Espin, I don't think you appreciate the gravity of this situation. I understand that the Rules and Procedures Committee of the

Bar Association of the Sovereign State of Louisiana are questioning the wisdom of allowing outsiders to be so easily granted standing before the State Bar. Your client's belligerence will certainly not inspire confidence among my colleagues in the integrity of our out-of-state colleagues."

Jodie also said that Guidry was among those trying to bring about a synthesis between the Modernized Updated Interstate Statutes and the Napoleonic Code, in order to make Louisiana once again unique and to "celebrate the state's extraordinary cultural and legal heritage." But the traditionalists appear to be thwarted not only by political opposition but by the near impossibility of formulating such a synthesis. Jodie has heard rumors that certain Tulane Law School faculty have been working on such a project for decades.

[iv]

She hates arguing with Emily; any kind of friction between them makes her stomach churn acid. But this time there is no help for it. "I refuse to be dragged any further into Martha's machinations," she says into her handset. "And I won't under any circumstances act as a representative for her anarchism to Weatherall or anyone else."

The very *idea* of seeing Weatherall again makes her seethe. That haughty, insincere bitch forced her to put limits on certain of her human rights projects as a condition of the Government's funding the torture recovery clinics. The whole thing left such a bad taste in her mouth that she is determined never to do business with the woman again. That damned sham of a press conference nauseated her. While she and her mother, newly elected President Sellwyn, and Secretary of Health Rogers posed for the media, Weatherall trumpeted the "humanitarian concerns" of the new administration. Though Mama talked sensibly about what the clinics would do and tried to say a few words about their being long-term projects, not band-aids, Rogers claimed the lion's share of attention, nattering on about how the new administration would soon have the nation "back on its feet"...

"But Cee." Emily's slow, warm voice thickens into its most persuasive tones. "Hazel proposed you because you are Martha's legal counsel. And one of the issues being discussed is Martha's release. Which is why it would make sense for you to be there."

"Martha's threats to incite the Marq'ssan are implicating me. I want no part of it, especially since we're beginning to build a really beautiful case for the suit we're bringing against Dowsanto in Federal Court. There's a chance we'll win it, Em. Which would mean a hell of a lot more than anything Martha Greenglass can extort from the Executive!"

Emily's sigh comes through the handset loud and clear. "I think you're wrong, Cee. But you're going to be stubborn about this, aren't you."

Celia hates it when Emily calls her stubborn.

"Okay," Emily finally says. "But at least think about it some. Will you do that?"

Celia rolls her eyes. "Sure, I'll think about it. But tell Hazel I don't want to be present while she's trying to extort concessions from Weatherall. That kind of thing isn't my idea of honorable negotiation."

When they disconnect, their friendship is still intact. But Celia knows: on certain things, they will never agree.

[v]

The windows of Judge Partee's chambers look out over the Mississippi River. Somewhere down there squats the Dowsanto plant where the pickets still doggedly march along the fence perimeter and back and forth before its gates. The workers aren't, however, blocking traffic. No one is ready for another round of civil disobedience. Or rather they're saving themselves for what might be required for possible developments in Martha's case.

"Mr. Guidry has relayed to me the gist of your conversation with him, Ms. Espin." Judge Partee's manner is cold. Out of the corner of her eye Celia sees a repressed smirk tugging at Guidry's glistening, pallid lips. Maggot lips, Celia thinks, only half-listening to Partee review the course of her conversation informing Guidry of Martha's intentions should she not be released by the unannounced deadline.

Celia speaks as firmly and unequivocally as she can. "I wish to be quite plain that I have advised my client against either making or carrying out her threat, and that I do not condone such violations of the law."

"How will she implement this threat?" Partee asks. "And what are your opinions about this deadline?"

Celia shrugs. "I'm sorry, Your Honor, but my client hasn't told me anything more than I've told you. She knows where I stand on this. As for *how* she would implement her threat—she will ask the Marq'ssan to do it, and they will."

Partee's pale blue eyes are furious. Stiffly he leans forward. "And how will she manage to ask them if she's kept incommunicado?"

Celia is certain he won't like her answer. "They probably visit her in her cell. Or else communicate with her through some high-tech device."

"She and her belongings have been thoroughly searched," Guidry says.

Partee clasps his pudgy, red-haired hands on the desk blotter. Celia notices for the first time that he wears a gold pinky ring set with diamonds. "You will write up an affidavit and leave it with my bailiff, Counselor. And then I advise you to seriously consider dropping your client. You are jeopardizing your career by representing someone who obliges you to deliver threats of serious felonies. For you, personally, there is a question of ethics at stake here. And I doubt if you would find a colleague who would fault a decision to drop such a client."

Celia is dismissed and leaves the two executive men together. Martha is pulling her into deeper and deeper waters, treacherous with riptides. What of her suit against Dowsanto? What of her drive for the constitutional amendment guaranteeing human rights? What of her push to get the external agitation statute repealed? Maybe she'd better give up on accomplishing anything in this state. If the Marq'ssan really do destructure that detention facility, her name here will be mud.

[vi]

Stepping out of the chemical shower and patting her too-hot body dry (it would never dry on its own, not in this humidity), Celia happens to glance at the white streak of scar tissue on her thigh. And the old uneasy feeling creeps over her as she wonders again how it came to be there. To acquire a scar and not know its origin... She knows only that it had been there when she woke from the stupor. Try as she might, she has never managed to recover even a fragment of a memory that could account for it. Once, intensively searching her memory to find it, she made herself sick for a month. But even then she failed.

Whenever the scar draws her attention to the fact that even the outside of her body is so secretive and obfuscatory, she is driven into an anxiety close to despair. Had it been something too horrible to remember? Or something done to her when she hadn't been conscious? Or something so minor she hadn't noticed because far worse things had been claiming her attention?

Celia dresses. When the crisp linen suit covers the scar, it becomes nothing more than a mark on her body.

[vii]

The Deputy Warden, rail thin, offers his hand. Celia controls her face so that he will not notice her distaste for his loose, wet clasp. He sits back down behind his desk. "What can I do for you ma'am?" He smiles, one professional to another, southern male to non-southern female.

"I'm concerned, Deputy Warden, at your having placed my client, Martha Greenglass, in isolation." He watches her without speaking. "She's broken no rules and has displayed no signs of violence or potential violence."

"She's disrupting the tranquility and stability of the facility, Ms. Espin," the Deputy Warden says mildly. "Some of the inmates have started to get agitated." He shrugs his sharp, bony shoulders. "I guess we should have expected this from a pro like Greenglass. She's a professional agitator. At the rate she's been going, she'd be inciting a riot in no time."

Celia knows there are no legal arguments she can invoke until the isolation has stretched into thirty consecutive days. And it's damned clear Martha won't be in isolation that long because the isolation itself will probably tip the balance. As long as Martha had contact with the other prisoners she felt she was accomplishing something. Now she has no reason to wait.

"'Privacy rooms.'" The Deputy Warden sneers. "Now what in hell are *privacy rooms*? I never heard of such a thing. But it's an idea Greenglass has put into their heads. The rumor is they may decide to try a hunger-strike and work-stoppage on us. In a situation like that, things could get violent fast. And then, Counselor, we'd have to resort to drugs. I'll tell you what. If you can get your client to agree to keep her mouth shut, we'll let her return to the general population."

Celia knows there's no point in trying to talk to him or the Warden about the Marq'ssan. The Warden's idea of handling Martha would be to have armed guards in her cell ready to shoot at anything that moved. She'd do better to call Hazel and have her call Weatherall.

Celia senses the crisis approaching. She knows time is running out before everything goes completely out of control. Damn Martha's arrogance... And damn these stupid blind fools for their parochialism.

[viii]

Perhaps it is the lighting, perhaps a particular expression on Jodie's face, perhaps the angle of her vision...but for a few seconds Celia marks a strong resemblance between Jodie and Jo Josepha, of whom Celia has not thought for a long, long time. "I'm remembering a lawyer I met at a human rights meeting in Ecuador," Celia says, suddenly finding the pinkish dusk light achingly beautiful in the way it lays slats of color onto the clean white walls, the way it stains the lace tablecloth a deep rich orange, the way it flickers in Jodie's half-closed eyes as her strong, muscular throat swallows gin. "Her name was Jo Josepha," Celia adds. It's barely possible Jodie might have known her. Not many lawyers had fought that particular fight so early on. But Jodie had.

"She was among those the ODS slaughtered," Jodie says, shifting to fold her legs beneath her. "I met her a couple of times. Never really talked to her, just an occasional meeting of eyes, that sort of thing. I didn't think she'd be my cup of tea. The Boston Collective aren't my kind of people."

Yet Jodie had done her best for some of the people in the local version of the Boston Collective. "I met her just once," Celia says. "A couple of months before they murdered her. I talked to her for a couple of hours. She was more like us than you might think."

"She was a fool to have gotten mixed up with that kind of group," Jodie says. "She could have accomplished a lot more if she'd stayed straight."

Straight... And what good had she, Celia, accomplished by staying straight? Well, she's still alive... By accident? Maybe. But the distinction counts for something now that things have changed. If Jo Josepha had lived, where would she be today? Not practicing law, obviously.

It's Celia's turn to get the next round of gin. But she'll wait a few more minutes, until the color leeches away and the room fades into darkness. New Orleans does have nice sunsets.

[ix]

This executive, according to Martha, was supposedly chosen to be the Secretary of Alien Relations because she has a doctorate in anthropology and experience working in Eastern European embassies. "It's really a shame," Justine Steadman tells Celia, "that Greenglass has decided to get pushy. We've had a steady improvement of relations over the last five years that had made me quite hopeful about the prospects of future alien-human relations."

"That's what you see this as?" Celia asks—out of curiosity more than anything else. "As an alien-human conflict along species lines?" She finds it impossible to conceive of this crisis in that way. After all, who knows better than Celia (other than Martha herself!) that Martha is running this show?

"Oh, but definitely," Steadman says, nodding vigorously. Steadman is visibly energetic in all her movements: her hands sweep through the air to dramatize her speech, her pen taps on the arm of her chair, her foot jiggles as though eager to be pulling its owner out of her chair and onto her feet: Justine Steadman in no way resembles any other executive Celia has met or seen. "It's true Greenglass has a penchant for confrontation: long before the aliens made their presence felt she was routinely getting herself arrested for civil disobedience. But then she was directed by a harmless, rather dull-witted group, one of the leaders of which was her lover. Now, however, Martha has superior tactical direction backed by technological prowess. I think we can safely assume the aliens are on the move."

Frowning, Steadman leans over the arm of her chair toward Celia. "If we understood their ulterior motives, the trajectory of their strategy would be clear to us. As it is, their attacks have the appearance of discrete, random events." Steadman's eyes flame with intense interest.

"But just because we can't yet *perceive* the pattern doesn't mean there isn't one. Martha Greenglass of course has one conception of what she is doing. But she's probably no more privileged than the rest of us in having an idea of what the aliens ultimately intend. *We* of course would like to know what they intend so that we can have a chance of resisting." She bites her lip, and her eyes—their gaze never moving from Celia's—narrow. "What we need is information, Celia. Hard, solid information. The aliens keep an extremely low profile and severely limit access to themselves. Except when it comes to Martha Greenglass and a few others like her. And frankly, Greenglass isn't very bright, is she. She lets herself be used. What we *need*, Celia, is someone on the inside. Do you see?"

This frenetically babbling woman wants Celia to help her recruit an informant? Is that what this is all about? But they are supposed to be discussing how to diffuse the situation! This woman is off the wall if she thinks it is the Marq'ssan manipulating the Free Zoners! Celia *knows*...but for a few seconds doubts flicker chilling shadows over the surface of her mind, as she wonders if perhaps she has been taken in, if perhaps the aliens were sneaky and deceptive and only presenting to the humans they meet the images those people wished to see... "Justine," Celia says. "If something isn't done soon, the Marq'ssan *will* destroy that jail, *will* free Martha Greenglass. With serious ramifications for the current administration. There's still time to prevent such a fiasco from occurring. At the very least Martha must be released from isolation!"

But Steadman shrugs with weary fatalism. She tells Celia that she cannot make the locals see reason, that the Executive is reluctant to interfere in any authoritarian way, that persuasion and negotiation are the only tools they have to work with.

Celia wonders why Justine Steadman isn't attempting to use these tools on the local executives. An individual with an *idée fixe*, she thinks, is useless in the real world.

[x]

Celia struggles out of the bridge dream to respond to her name. "Celia, wake up!" the voice hisses in an urgent whisper.

Celia pries her eyelids open. After a few seconds' effort, she focuses enough to see Martha and Sorben kneeling beside her bed. "Martha!" Celia cries out, abruptly wide awake.

"Sshh," Martha whispers, "you don't want to wake Jodie, do you?"

"What the hell are you *doing*?" Celia demands in a whisper, but she knows. They have done it, and it's too late to stop. The worst has happened.

"Do you want to come back to the Free Zone with us tonight?" Martha's tone is urgent. "They'll be after a scapegoat now."

Oh yes, Martha knows, Celia thought bitterly. Martha knows they will do their best to punish her for Martha's crimes. "No," Celia replies. "There's still the small matter of the reason I came to Louisiana in the first place." Celia glares at Martha, whom she can hardly make out in the gray dawn light. "Small for you, that is," she adds, to make sure Martha gets the point.

"I'll be back myself," Martha avows.

Celia looks at Sorben. "You shouldn't have done it, Sorben. It will be counterproductive."

"That's debatable," Sorben says softly. "We've held off applying visible pressure for a long time. We needed to make that kind of statement."

Celia shakes her head. But they can't debate the matter now. Someone will be knocking at her door very soon. And she knows she needs time to prepare for them, to marshal all the thinking she has done in the past two weeks on what the implications and ramifications of this action might be. She will shower and dress. Then she will make some phone calls, as many as she can before they arrive. They will find her waiting for them when they come, waiting and prepared.

Chapter Ten

Tuesday, 5/15/2096

My eyes & ears are uncomfortable from the light. My nose bleeds while my skin tightens, pulls, scales… & my hair: oily, it flops constantly into my eyes, uncomfortably long, itchy, oppressive. As for the rest of my body—I don't allow myself to pay attention. Only these minor irritations can be allowed into my consciousness. Plaguing—but not overwhelming—me.

Sometimes I think my eyes burn because of the harsh fluorescent lights. Which is nonsense, scientifically speaking. Sure, I can have the lights off. Losing that faint ringing in my ears, I fall into silence, into lightlessness, into the seeming-void. But I only request that the lights be off when I'm ready to sleep, which means that I do all my brooding and thinking under their ugly glare. Imagine how much worse it would be to let my mind loose in the dark! Anger, pain, self-pity would follow…and then, finally, madness. I comprehend the series sufficiently that I strive again & again to break it before it swallows me up.

Thursday, 5/17/2096

A few minutes ago I ripped out the last two pages I'd written in this book. & then carefully, laboriously, tore them into bits—using my teeth. Ashamed of such gutless tripe, ashamed at the flood of self-pity I allowed to overcome me. Ashamed at my cowardice.

No wonder Rbt's dominating my dreams. Each night his intense eyes compel me, watch me, & ultimately scorn me. He's angry at me for my self-indulgent despair. Angry at me for failing to fight back.

Friday, 5/18/2096

Woke this morning with a madrigal in my head. How wonderful to remember something beautiful. (Not *every*thing in my life has been ugly.) I remember my success teaching Rbt to appreciate Renaissance madrigals. Or at least Gesualdo's madrigals. At first he wouldn't listen to any of my madrigal recordings, saying pre-Baroque music bored him. So then one night at dinner I told him the story of Gesualdo's life. He ate it up: how could he resist feeling an affinity with a dark Renaissance prince, a man said to be an enigma to all of his time, whose bold & intense, violent & poignant music was so strange, so original that no one could ever mistake it for that of another composer? Rbt grew excited at hearing about Gesualdo's obsession, about his murdering his beautiful young wife and her lover—supposedly *in flagrante*—as well as an infant son the prince decided resembled his wife's lover. After dinner Rbt demanded I play all the Gesualdo I had. We spent that evening and the next listening to Gesualdo with our cognac. Such strange, bizarre, yet always beautiful music...Rbt wished to know more about Gesualdo's life, he wanted *facts*, he wanted to see Gesualdo's portrait...& in this way I lured him into listening to madrigals—or rather, *some* madrigals. He didn't ever really like Monteverdi. But he learned to enjoy de Lassus & a few others. Some parts of our life together were good. Those are the parts I need to remember now.

Sunday, 5/20/2096

What is the point? Collapsed today during PT—as usual lathered in cold sweat, suffering vile nausea & dizziness & tremoring muscles, but this time I *did* pass out. Damned if that bitch didn't insist—once I'd come around—that we keep on. I refused. Dug in my heels. Went on strike. So she poured out a litany of all the ill-effects I'd suffer for the rest of my life if I didn't push myself harder than I've been doing. But, to repeat, what is the point? There's no future for me, why worry now about this wreck of a body?

Monday, 5/21/2096

Had a fright today. One of the med-techs brought in an enormous hypodermic this morning. It being Monday, I not unnaturally had the idea it had something to do with a visit from Elizabeth. My mind connected the two things, & I concluded the injection was loquazene. But when unconsciousness did not immediately follow the injection, I knew I must be mistaken & demanded of the med-tech what it was she had stuck me with. Her answer: a megadose of vitamins.

Because of my collapse, I suppose.

later, Monday night

My mind's been running around in circles all day. The circles growing wider & wider & plunging deeper & deeper. I cannot remain inert. If I'm to continue alive, I must act, even if in a small way. No point otherwise. (Rbt, this is no heroic act, but it is *something*, it is a refusal of total passivity, though on the face of it, it may seem the opposite.) So I've formed my strategy. A few minutes from now just before dropping into sleep I will give myself a strong powerful suggestion: that I will not be able to stay awake as long as I'm not given acceptable reading matter. I am going on a sleep strike. I may be wakened, but nothing will be able to keep me awake for more than a minute. I may get tired of sleeping (& *they* will get tired of shaking me awake), but sleeping will not be as stressful to me as lying awake in this living hell. That fact alone will make the suggestion doubly powerful. Not even drugs, my voyeuristic friends, will force me to wakefulness. My body will know how to handle your invasions—& my mind will know how to ignore them.

Saturday, 5/26/2096

So enthralled with spending this day reading that I couldn't be bothered to record my small triumph. Yesterday they capitulated. I'm sure they tried everything, for giving in to me must be gall on the backs of their tongues. I requested everything of Nietzsche's. Of all my studies in those last months, the Nietzsche alone really interested me. (Nothing but his incomparable writing could compete with my *other* interest at that time). Nietzsche cannot be read in a vacuum, cannot be read as an arid intellectual exercise divorced from one's own existence.

& when Nietzsche writes about passion, I can't help but listen & ponder my own self & what I know about passion in the world beyond these four walls. I will quote Nietzsche in this book, for the pleasure of repeating his words, & in case they decide to take the books away. (We all know why this book will be the last of me to go.)

"All passions have a phase when they are merely disastrous, when they drag down their victim with the weight of stupidity—& a later, very much later phase when they wed the spirit, when they 'spiritualize' themselves. Formerly, in view of the element of stupidity in passion, war was declared on passion itself, its destruction was plotted...

"The church fights passion with excision in every sense: its practice, its 'cure,' is *castratism*. It never asks, 'How can we spiritualize, beautify, deify a craving?' It has at all times laid the stress of discipline on extirpation (of sensuality, of pride, of the lust to rule, of avarice, of vengefulness). But an attack on the roots of passion means an attack on the roots of life: the practice of the church is *hostile to life*.

"The same means in the fight against a craving—castration, extirpation—is instinctively chosen by those who are too weak-willed, too degenerate, to be able to impose moderation on themselves; by those who are so constituted that they require...some kind of definitive declaration of hostility, a *cleft* between themselves and the passion. Radical means are indispensable for the degenerate; the weakness of the will—or, to speak more definitely, the inability *not* to respond to a stimulus—is itself merely another form of degeneration. The radical hostility, the deadly hostility against sensuality, is always a symptom to reflect on: it entitles us to suppositions concerning the total state of one who is excessive in this manner."

I know what Rbt would say about this passage: *Eccolo!* There we have it: *castratism*, in its own special updated form. He would be thinking most of all of his father the crazy shrink. This, he would say, should have tipped everyone off to where Freudianism was leading us...

But what about Rbt himself? His hostility to my sexual interest in girls—jealousy, one would say, thus dismissing the matter. But I'm not so clear about that. As though he, too, imbibed the poison with his cohorts. He, the castrated. (Rbt, you know you were, for all you liked to pretend otherwise.) But more difficult to touch upon is the question of his perversions, especially in the way pleasure had to be so closely defined & confined—because of his anxiety about control. This is something I can't quite grasp. But I *feel*, when I read that one sentence especially about attacking the very roots of life, I *feel* that Rbt's practice of sexuality (or, to be more accurate his imposition of limits upon *my* practice of sexuality, as engaged in with him as well as his forbidding my interest in anyone else) did just that. If he were here & privy to my thoughts he would say that I'm talking about my guilt over breaking the incest taboo. According to him any bad feelings I had were due to that. How can one know about such things?

But now, to go further, to myself: what that passage says about me. Could I ever claim to have gotten past that first phase of "stupidity?" I don't think so, for I surely never achieved a spiritualization. I, the uncontrolled degenerate Nietzsche scorns. Only in this case I am a degenerate who does not voluntarily curb herself or moralize to extremes to curb herself... It is only the Sallys who manage to achieve that second phase. This is, indeed, what I can respect & admire in other human beings. It is the best we seem to be capable of.

No wonder the dualism of madonna/whore continues to proliferate in our world! This particular dualistic image in certain respects reflects this very matter—of passion either spiritualized or degraded. But of course that dualism offered a falsely simplistic picture. It has been only a means of doing the very thing Nietzsche is condemning in this passage—of fighting passion, of dragging sensuality down into the gutter, of separating mind & body (which reminds me again of Rbt).

Tonight my mind is working again. I feel alive. So I will resume the PT tomorrow. It will be hell after so many days of total physical inactivity. But for the moment I want to go on. My sense of triumph will fade, but I will still have food for my mind to chew on.

Sunday, 6/2/2096

It is six-forty. If I woke on the island at this hour I'd be out walking on the beach—perhaps. Because it would probably be a fine spring

morning. Instead I'm here…indoors. All right. But still, I'm awake at
this hour & called the med-tech to turn on the lights for me because I
woke with an eagerness I haven't felt for so very long…an eagerness
to take up where I left off last night. So I will read & sip water & jot
notes in this book.

In one brief section Nietzsche turns his sharp eye from the spiritualization of sensuality to what he calls the spiritualization of hostility.
I'm not certain I can agree to call it a spiritualization. It reminds me
too much of Rbt's making all dissidents into an enemy that had to
be exterminated: "Almost every party understands how it is in the
interest of its own self-preservation that the opposition should not
lose all strength; the same is true of power politics. A new creation in
particular—the new *Reich*, for example—needs enemies more than
friends: in opposition alone does it *feel* itself necessary, in opposition
alone does it *become* necessary."

This is spiritualization? But why elevate it so (for he calls the spiritualization of sensuality *love*) when it is such a niggling petty ugly thing?
Yes, enemies direct one's poison outward. & Rbt would certainly agree
that as long as there was a plausible threatening enemy that could be
hated & killed he would be in demand. (Or at least until the price got
too high to be paid any longer—it was more a matter of that price,
Elizabeth, than your own brilliant luster that ensured your success.)

No, I cannot agree with his putting *this* example—i.e., of power politics—in the same class with what he goes on to describe as the creation within each of us of "internal enemies," "internal opposition,"
the things that make us grow, that keep us from stagnating. You see,
I wonder if Rbt had any such internal opposition left inside him. He
made everything so clear, so black-&-white definitive, that without
those *external* enemies to drive him, & without, it seems, *me* (or Elizabeth or Kay), he could find nothing else inside himself *but* stagnation,
but death… Was it this, perhaps, that drove him to fear "being alone"
as he called it? Could that be what he meant? Did he himself perceive
a chasm within, a chasm he knew would swallow him up the minute
he was forced to turn inward & face it?

It is easy to spin theories like this. Rbt is dead & can no longer speak for himself. & my knowledge of him is fractured, biased, incomplete. Though god knows I knew a lot more of him than I ever wanted to.

later, Sunday night

I've done my stint of PT, with dire threats of more to come tomorrow. No one so much as mentions my mini-rebellion to me. They pretend nothing has happened, nothing has changed.

I've been musing on what Nietzsche calls "the outrage of a revolt against life." I'm perplexed about this, about his talking about the value of life. Except for his conclusions, that is, which fill my heart with elation. His repeated theme of affirmation must, of course, be the culmination of such a discussion. "A condemnation of life by the living remains in the end a mere symptom of a certain kind of life: the question whether it is justified or unjustified is not even raised thereby. One would require a position *outside* of life, and yet have to know it as well as one, as many, as all who have lived it, in order to be permitted even to touch the problem of the *value* of life: reasons enough to comprehend that this problem is for us an unapproachable problem. When we speak of values, we speak with the inspiration, with the way of looking at things, which is part of life: life itself forces us to posit values…"

I can only think of this in a context that I don't think Nietzsche intended. Take for instance the difference between Rbt's & Wedgewood's view about the intrinsic value of life, about the morality of excision. Rbt insisted to me when I dragged him into such discussions (always after dinner on occasions when he was mellowed by cognac & deep self-satisfaction) that his "surgical excisions" were no reflection on his morality, on his value of life. He asserted that it was a practical matter, that greater harm would be done by refraining from such atrocities (he never used that word, of course—& I only used it in the privacy of my head) than by committing them. That he did not think about life as value. That people got themselves into tangled messes thinking that way. That he was a "naturalist" when it came to the question of life. That some people survived & others did not, & it was silly talking about morality in such terms. Wedgewood, on the other hand, seemed to have the bizarre notion that his way put a higher value on life than any other way. He believed that some people are not fit for life, that their very *existence* besmirches the whole concept of what is human.

What would Nietzsche say? Suppose I were allowed to have Nietzsche, Rbt, & Wedgewood all sitting around the same table & were able to direct them to discuss the subject... I myself would like to believe that Nietzsche would class the male executive view of the world in the same camp (from the same stream, even) as Platonism & Christianity, the two forces in the world he most detested & that he labeled most decadent (to use his harshest word of condemnation).

To affirm life...to spiritualize passion... I once would have said that of all people I've ever met Elizabeth came closest to such Nietzschean heights. But I have my doubts now. & where those doubts come from (these are serious things, not small petty spitefulnesses due to my dire situation) bear some thinking about. Perhaps I will essay such a task tomorrow.

But now, to sleep. I'm blissfully worn out, mind as well as body.

Monday, 5/28/2096

I find myself still thinking about Rbt & Wedgewood's valuations of human life. Remembering so much... *too* much. Could see immediately, that first time when Rbt was so rough with me to force me to watch to listen to see to smell—yes, most especially to smell—he had me stand right in that room with them...I could tell that what they were doing to that prisoner—literally destroying him, bit by bit—I could *see* that the process of destroying another person, for Wedgewood, somehow assured him of a sense of his own worth, of his own *humanity*—incredible as this may on the surface seem. For by reducing another human being—Wedgewood's declared "enemy"—to a howling creature locked away in his own experience of horror and humiliation so monumental that it opened a crevasse between himself and everyone else in that room (except, perhaps, for me, only I did try to dissociate myself from him, out of self-defense, I *strove* not to identify myself with his state & half-failed, too, even after Rbt made me return), a crevasse miles & miles from Wedgewood, who by comparison felt himself godlike, untouched, his mask intact. Wedgewood obviously saw this howling whimpering pleading cowering man as not-man, as subhuman, as animal. As not in any way like himself.

Another of those damned dualisms again: animal/human, & one that makes no sense to me at all, has never made any sense. Nature (the world?) is a unity in which difference between species runs a continuum, a spectrum, a gamut: how then talk about it as a dualism between humans & animals? This must be the religious streak in us at work—as Nietzsche might say.

While Rbt...no, I don't think Rbt would disqualify the tortured prisoner even in the most dire extremity from humanity. Or at least I don't *think* so. What he insisted to me in a wholly other context was how animalistic, primitive, base, & degraded was the natural human condition (I don't think he bought that dualism, either), that beneath the surface, when the masks are peeled off, we are *all* like that: naked, howling beasts. That possession of the masks—i.e., "civilization"—is a luxury, a privilege, a *prize* rewarding survival. His worldview was infinitely more cynical than Wedgewood's, who believed that the masks of civilization were in themselves the point that justified his atrocities. He didn't think of survival the way Rbt did, of that I'm certain. Rbt claimed that the reason we fought enemies was to preserve the prize—the masks of civilization, the privilege of determining civilization. (Survival in his view not requiring justification but being, merely, instinctual.)

Certainly in those sexual episodes of ours that he directed he took pains to make me experience a range of sensations along the pleasure-pain spectrum, variously modulated by such emotional states as humiliation, shame, pride, wild elation, to "educate my palate" as he liked to put it. He insisted that I taste everything on his menu, that we see which tastes I would "develop raging appetites for." By this means I was also to learn & understand about those things so heavily masked, which most people hide from themselves. & thus were engendered those times of the most wretched self-hatred, the worst loathing for myself & everyone around me... *This*, he said, *is what it is to be human. Underneath everything we're all like that. Give up the habit of lying to yourself, Persephone. I despise self-deception.*

& so what is this thing, humanity?

Surely it is obvious it is simply the most elementary bonds connecting us all? Why force the word into being a value judgment, good or bad, either about an individual or about the species as a whole?

That poor man howling for mercy. Infants screaming for the breast. & even Daniel, plugging in. How can it not be seen?

Or Sally's eyes pleading with me.

I saw, yes, but did I see clearly & far enough?

& Rbt's eyes: begging me to change my mind, imploring me not to abandon him to himself.

No, I don't yet see far enough or clearly enough.

Will I ever?

Tuesday, 5/29/2096

The most astonishing thing: this morning Chief Gorilla Phyllis came in & handed me a safe-box, which she said was coded to my thumb-print. I opened it & found copies of yesterday's & today's *Executive Times*! As well as a note requesting that I keep the papers in the box when any med-techs are in the room & that when I'm finished I re-turn the locked box to Phyllis. I'm not a fool, Elizabeth: I've always been careful with the *E.T.*, having learned such elementary things at my grandmother's knee.

At first I wondered if there were some special item I was supposed to come upon—something nasty. But I searched both papers thorough-ly—glancing at every headline on every page—before I let myself *read* them. I found nothing that struck me as significant. Is Eliza-beth trying to send me some kind of message? Both papers are largely concerned with an action taken by the aliens against a Baton Rouge detention facility. Which is in its own way quite extraordinary, con-sidering that there have been no alien actions in this country since Elizabeth's coup. The articles make clear that the entire thing was engineered & provoked by Martha Greenglass, who was arrested by local authorities for external agitation—a felony charge. Stupid of the local authorities, of course, who should simply have deported her back to the Free Zone & declared her *persona non grata*. Why *jail* her for godsake? It should have been clear enough what she was up to. & then when she delivered the threat of doing precisely what she in the end did do—that, too, should have been enough to make those idiots see what they were playing into...

Two facts in particular strike me as significant. First, not all prisoners chose to go to the Free Zone when given the choice of going there or staying in Louisiana & taking their chances with re-imprisonment. The editorial in today's paper suggests we should simply ship the contents of our jails off to the Free Zone, thus finally dealing with the problem once & for all. All this is meant to be satirical, of course. Sentencing convicted criminals (especially felons) to life in the Free Zone to let the anarchists live with the fruits of their ideology.

The second fact that strikes me is that that lawyer, Espin, was involved in the affair—was, in fact, Greenglass's legal counsel. Espin is now being held as an accessory before the fact. She naively warned both the District Attorney as well as the Superior Court Judge to whose docket Greenglass's case had already been assigned.

Elizabeth, your purge did not go far enough, do you see that now? You'll have to overhaul the local levels if you're really interested in reform. If you don't, you're going to be up against them in escalating conflicts & friction until finally this problem breaks you. You do see that, I suppose?

If the judiciary scapegoats Espin, they could alienate a significant portion of the legal profession. & that could in turn create a whole new set of problems for Elizabeth's administration...

The editorialists in today's paper of course present themselves as fair but tough, imaginative yet practical: "We urge the Executive to make up its mind as to whether to negotiate a permanent settlement with the aliens and anarchists or to declare all-out war on them. The time for wishy-washy avoidance of the subject is past: the country can no longer afford the resumption of these disruptions. The very future and security of the country is at stake. Failure to act now, failure of nerve and imagination, could result in chaos and anarchy of the worst sort."

Hunh. They want to make it so cut & dried—perhaps craftily trying to force Elizabeth off the fence, to make her jump in either one direction or another. But rather than jumping, I should say it's a question

of formulating an effective policy for dealing with external agitation, as well as coming to terms with the fact that hostile forces oper-
ate on this continent against us. For one thing, if we *did* have a real
policy for defusing external agitation, it wouldn't matter *how* many
Martha Greenglasses were roaming the country. Second, close watch
should be kept on all Free Zone leaders traveling around the country—so that they can be deported (*not* jailed) when their presence
grows too threatening—i.e., when they're on the verge of directing a
destructive strike against us. Surely Elizabeth's propaganda machine
(which I've admired for years now) must be able to find ways of making Greenglass & her sort unattractive, silly, boring, irrelevant, etc. to
the constituency she's trying to develop? Surely they must have some
satirists among them who would know how to construct local amuse-
ments at the anarchists' expense?

Better to try that first than to roll out our heaviest artillery when it is
obviously overkill to do so—*clumsy* overkill that likely lends Greenglass
more legitimacy than would otherwise be the case...

Wednesday, 5/30/2096

Another newspaper today, too. In *this* paper I had the ineffable pleasure
of beholding Mama—on the society page, of course, at the opening
of an event being held in six different European cities simultaneously,
called "The Festival of the Roccoco: A Celebration." In the picture she
is wearing evening clothes—& something on her face, a strange construction of sterling silver (according to the caption, anyway), pearls,
Venetian glass, and colored silks, some of which flowed in streamers
from the temple-pieces of the contraption. Not a mask, exactly, for it
bared a considerable amount of her face... I wonder she's not afraid
to be wearing glass like that, so close to her eyes. The others in the
picture were wearing similar constructions. It will probably pass, this
fad. Mama seems to seize all the most outré fashions without ever
waiting to see if they'll make it into more general circulation. I bet
this one won't.

If I'd seen that picture of Mama in the batch of papers sent yesterday,
I'd have assumed it bore the clue to the significance of Elizabeth's letting me have these papers to read... But I'm inclined to think Mama's

being in today's paper purely accidental. Though Elizabeth *could* rig up such a thing for my benefit, I don't believe she would. Unless…oh my god—it's just occurred to me that these could be dummy versions of the paper made up solely for my consumption. & that not a word in them is true…

No, that's an excessive idea. There would be no point, since there's nothing special in them. No, this is simply a whim of Elizabeth's, designed, perhaps, to provoke me into worrying about her purpose… In which case you must find yourself disappointed, Elizabeth. Because I refuse to consider the matter any longer.

Thursday, 5/31/2096

No *E.T.* today. Thus the pattern's broken. A mystery perhaps destined to go unsolved. Well, that's all right. There are a lot of those in one's lifetime, even in a lifetime as short as mine has been.

& I'm back to the Nietzsche. For a while he takes off on the subject of cause-effect. But then he suddenly switches to something—another "error"—he considers related—what he calls "the error of free will." He insists that the "doctrine of the will" was invented by priests of ancient communities "essentially for the purpose of punishment"— i.e., "to impute guilt." "Men were considered 'free' so that they might be judged and punished—so that they might become *guilty*: consequently, every act had to be considered as willed, and the origin of every act had to be considered as lying within the consciousness…"

Of course I couldn't help thinking of all that Rbt said to me over the years about guilt. & about Rbt's convoluted way of framing our incestuous relationship & its origins in such a way that I always *had* to feel guilt for it. In spite of his harping about how I *shouldn't* feel guilty, his major point was that I *did* feel guilty—perhaps because I *was* in some way guilty. He always insisted I assume the majority of the responsibility for our sexual relationship, pointing out that he gained less pleasure from it than I did, & that furthermore I had "started" it. Yes, I went to him that night & "started" it—technically, at least. But don't the origins of such a thing go back much further, isn't it all more complicated than that? Well then, he'd say, we'll go back to the beginning.

To my drunken declaration of sexual attraction to him... Oh shit. Not again. I'm trying to use Nietzsche to exonerate my own guilt.

Nietzsche would have "will" to be something invented in order to give certain individuals power over others. A political power over "truth," over "responsibility," over "blame." Maybe the reason people are so reluctant to act, so reluctant to take responsibility for themselves & decision-making is this brainwashing about will? & guilt? Did I *will* that Rbt fuck me? I don't think so. What I *wanted* was something else... That night I first went to his bed I wasn't *wanting* any of it. Because that night that wasn't why I went.

But of course I could never tell Rbt that...he would have been furious to hear me say such a thing. In fact, now that I think about it, if I had said anything out loud about other reasons for the incest than sexual appetite, he would have been more angry with me than he'd ever have been about any other thing I could have done or said...I knew that, though I never thought about it. But then I suppose I always weighed such costs unconsciously, so that I wouldn't have to confront certain "facts" of my existence...& so how to think about this relationship & its origins & motivations? Nietzsche brings me confusion rather than clarity, I'm afraid. At least when it comes to Rbt & myself.

Friday, 6/1/2096

This afternoon a visit from Elizabeth. A visit like none of the other visits. & now I am truly baffled.

Oh, she wasn't warm—no, I wouldn't say that. But she treated me as... a person. She had a chair brought in for herself. She sat at the side of the bed. Her eyes, though cold, did not annihilate me. She spoke no filth. & she never offered me the slightest sign of menace or violence.

It is time, she said, to be thinking of my leaving here. Apparently I will be permanently released from traction quite soon. I will need to sleep in a special apparatus, I will need to continue the PT, & there will be new frames & devices for assisting the healing process...but all this can be arranged so that I can return to the island. (Is she playing with me, is she mocking me by getting my hopes up?) A physician will come to the island once a week to examine my progress. There is to be a med-tech & physical therapist on the island to work with me, to see to my healing. No prison, no solitary confinement. No torture. No excision.

Do I believe this?

Speaking of torture and excision. I gather what I had written about Rbt & Wedgewood & their valuations of human life interested Elizabeth. She said she wanted to tell me *her* sense of such things. That she could not stomach my constantly accusing her of being someone who uses excision, my assuming that she would "stoop to torture." That she had thoroughly reformed Security Services & had done her best with Military (though she had less faith in her having completely cleaned such degenerates out), so that none of those methods would ever be used as long as she & her people were running things…& then she made a point of saying that she considered that the atrocious methods Rbt & Wedgewood used degraded humanity as a whole. That she was surprised that I would espouse human rights when in fact my sexual practices were an extension of these other practices, that my treatment of Sally made that quite clear…

What could I reply? I don't pretend to understand anything about it. At one point, though, when she was talking about her abhorrence of torture, I raised the subject of Kay Zeldin. (How could I not?) This deeply angered her, but she kept her anger leashed. No, no, she said, I was a fool to believe my father's lies, he may have come to believe that canard, but he knew very well that if it had been left up to him Kay Zeldin would have been handed over to Wedgewood. That her death had had nothing to do with her incarceration under Elizabeth's supervision, that Rbt had wanted Kay dead at the outset, had in fact demanded it, but that she, Elizabeth, had held out. And that Rbt had killed Kay because he feared he would not be able to control her.

At the time all this sounded very well & good, but I've just remembered something: Elizabeth threatened to do to me whatever it is she did to Kay. Why, Elizabeth, if it was so terrible, can you claim never to have been responsible for what you call the degradation of humanity?

Perhaps I'm a fool to have written that last paragraph. I'd never, for instance, have told Rbt what I was thinking just off the top of my head. & there's no doubt Elizabeth will be reading this page... But no, I shall return to Nietzsche, to refocus my mind. All I can do otherwise is speculate—fruitlessly—on Elizabeth's intentions toward me. Such speculation would be a self-defeating waste of time.

Chapter Eleven

[i]

"Have you heard?" Martin smirked with triumph. "Astrea's putting in an appearance."

"How do you know that?" Emily asked. Astrea was becoming quite the social butterfly. Of course Astrea did like Martin. Unlike most of the other Marq'ssan, one could *always* tell with Astrea whom she especially liked or disliked.

Martin's smirk turned into a gaping, toothy grin. "When she dropped by the studio last weekend and I invited her, she accepted on the spot."

"She dropped by *here? Alone?*"

"Uh-huh. Just to see me, Em."

"That's interesting," Emily said uncertainly. What did it *mean*? By her friendship with Emily alone, Astrea personally involved herself with humans to an unusual extent. Sorben and Martha's relationship was much more of an alliance than a friendship. But Emily's relationship with Astrea was—Emily believed and Astrea had once stated—unique.

What struck Emily as strange about Astrea's recent sociability had more to do with something Emily had never quite articulated to herself, a feeling she had about Astrea's attitude toward humans, an attitude vastly different from that held by all the other Marq'ssan Emily had ever met or heard about. It wasn't that Astrea exactly *despised* humans, but perhaps more that she lacked a certain tolerance for and willingness to forgive certain human weaknesses. Also, Astrea frequently had what Emily thought of as personality conflicts with humans. Perhaps the other Marq'ssan often felt this way about humans, but unlike Astrea they never revealed so much as a hint of it.

On the other hand, Astrea also had a gift for demonstrating her delight and pleasure and liking, again seeming far from other Marq'ssan in her freely-offered expressiveness. At times Emily had felt tempted to take this expressiveness, both negative and positive, as a human characteristic...to try to see Astrea as more like herself, to make it easier to comprehend and relate to a being so utterly different and other than herself. But something always happened—Astrea would make a comment or a perfectly foreign gesture—and the illusion would shatter. And of course Emily had other reasons for knowing and being aware of the profound difference between Astrea's consciousness and her own. Yet among those same reasons for heightening Emily's sense of that difference lay the reason for thinking that some day, perhaps, the differences might diminish.

"So," Martin said, crossing his arms over his chest. "I thought you were staying around town this week. That you'd be at the conference. Where've you been off to this time?"

The conference. Emily had forgotten all about the conference being held in Seattle this week, exploring distinctions between public and private art; she had especially wanted to attend it. She sighed. "I've been in Baton Rouge, Louisiana. Trying to help Celia Espin. I thought my biggest problem would be raising bail money" —Emily, expecting an outrageous bail to be set, had even braced herself to go to her father for the money—"but it's not clear whether there will even *be* a release on bail." Martin's eyebrows soared. "In the first place, no one will say where they're keeping her, on the grounds that if it's known, the Marq'ssan will repeat what they did for Martha. When her lawyer filed a writ of habeas corpus, Celia was produced in court—and then whisked away before I had a chance to talk to her. In the second place, they claim that Celia would just jump bail if she's released, and given the seriousness of the string of felonies they're saying they might charge her with being an accessory to—and that's in addition to a conspiracy charge—it's likely the judge won't set bail at all. So, until they decide what to charge her with, they're holding her as a material witness. And they can do that for a long time." Emily sighed. "But what's really going on, what they told Jodie, Celia's lawyer, is that if Martha Greenglass turns herself in and 'submits to justice,' then Celia will be released without being charged with anything."

"That's blackmail!"

Emily agreed. "In short, they're holding Celia hostage."

"The bastards."

"Feel a cartoon coming on?" Emily inquired, pleased at the idea of plastering appropriately satirical cartoons all over Baton Rouge.

"And what does Martha Greenglass say?" Martin asked.

"I haven't talked to her since I've been back. I suppose we're going to have to locate Celia and rescue her. Those bastards are capable of holding her indefinitely. Though of course Celia won't *want* to be rescued." Emily got up from the floor and went to the table on which Martin had set out the party's refreshments. Yes, he had provided tomato juice and tabasco and the other ingredients for her usual.

"Are you sure about that?" Martin asked. "A few days in jail can change anyone's outlook on the legal system."

Emily shook a few drops of tabasco into her juice. According to the label on the bottle, it came from Louisiana. Celia said that Louisiana people laced their tubefood with it. "It's not as though Celia doesn't know what jail is like," Emily said. "Though I suppose she might have illusions now about the so-called reformed legal system and about acting on principle."

"You sound fed up."

"Do you want something to drink?" Emily asked him.

"Water."

She carried a bottle of water and her juice back to where Martin sat on the floor. "I get tired of waiting for Celia's disillusionment. I thought it had come that time when the deal over the torture clinics was worked out. But no, it turned out she had no trouble drawing a distinction between the Executive and the legal system. Even though it's supposedly the Executive that *reformed* the legal system in the first place. It's not as though the people running things now aren't the same people who were running things before."

"She got pretty bent out of shape about not being able to prosecute any but the most flagrant cases," Martin said.

Emily took a long swallow of the thick, spicy juice. "I think she's given up on pursuing any of them. The public wants to forget the whole sorry mess, so she doesn't have much popular support any more.

But she's still hoping to get the human rights amendment passed."
Emily shook her head. "For all the good a thing like that would do."

"She's a believer," Martin said.

"Yeah. That she is." Almost exactly as Emily's mother was a "believer" in the Catholic Faith. Emily chuckled. "I've tried explaining about faith and believers in various theological and other ideological systems to Astrea, but she just can't grasp the concept of faith. Celia's stubborn adherence to her faith baffles her." Emily bit her lip. "In fact, I think you could say that Astrea is often, well, *impatient* with Celia." Which did not, of course, make Celia like Astrea any better.

A knock sounded on the door. Martin's gaze met Emily's, and he reached over and slid his hand along her thigh. "Do you think you might be interested in staying after?" he asked, half-smiling.

The sexual current running between them spiked so powerfully that Emily would have liked to have had sex right then and there. "Too bad you're having this party," she said, pitching her voice low in her throat. A flurry of knocks rained on the door, and a voice called Martin's name. "Let's see how it goes," she said. How could she predict how she'd feel five or six or seven hours later?

Martin levered himself to his feet and went to the door. Three people spilled into the room, none of whom Emily knew. The party had begun.

[ii]

Two hours into the party Emily spotted Astrea across the room leaning casually against the wall listening to a wildly gesticulating public artist from Portland. "Public art" was another concept that puzzled Astrea. A couple of years back Emily had taken her on a tour of some of the most famous "public art" in the world, hoping that seeing such work *in situ* would help explain the concept to the Marq'ssan. But Astrea's detailed questions afterwards about the economics, politics, sociology, and aesthetics of public art had made it clear that Astrea found all categories of the arts baffling. Though Marq'ssan had what Emily thought of as a strong aesthetic sense, they apparently did not produce objects or performances as discrete expressions of that sense. After years of talking with Astrea and thinking about this, Emily had developed a vague notion that the lack of commodities (for no culture on Marqeuei had developed an objective exchange system), the lack of religion (the Marq'ssan had, to the best of their knowledge of their own history, never invented gods), and the lack of what Emily loosely called structures of differentiation, accounted for the Marq'ssan not producing anything that could be identified as art. Still, the more she learned about the Marq'ssan, the more she wondered if this too weren't a mistake, if certain equivalences did exist that a human might dimly recognize but that a Marq'ssan, unable to grasp the concept of "art," might never imagine could fit the human concept.

Emily exited the conversation she had been engaged in and drifted through the body-packed room toward Astrea. "You see"—Emily could hear Lynn's soprano above all other voices—"there are two schools of thought on what public art should be. One school argues that it should be an expression of its surroundings and everyday viewers. For instance, that if a city commissions it, it should reflect the character, spirit, or ideals of that city and its inhabitants."

Emily sidled up to Astrea and leaned against the wall beside her. "Of course there's plenty of room for argument among those who agree to that since it then becomes a matter of deciding which particular voice determines what the spirit or character or ideals of the city are. Or, say, a corporation can commission such art. The controversy narrows at that point, of course, since the corporation itself can then define the nature of the expression. On the other hand, the other school of thought holds that public art should be a means for the artist to provoke and challenge and even educate viewers, to change the way they see their world, to help them to see the environment the work is situated in quite differently."

Emily slid into a light trance, careful not to go too deep. Then, when she had achieved the optimal state of looseness, she extended her awareness to perception of the heat signatures of the bodies around her. Adding what she thought of as "dimensional depth"—for seeing the colors of the heat patterns of the bodies and objects around her was a sort of two-dimensional vision lacking the textures that allowed one to perceive fields—she extended her perception outward until she could perceive, sharply and distinctly, Astrea's field. Lynn's field, she noticed, was pulled in tight, even though her body language expressed an outward flow of energy. As Emily studied Astrea's field and noted again its immense difference from the fields of all humans within Emily's range of perception, the Marq'ssan moved physically closer to her, so close that their fields touched. Emily extended her field toward Astrea until they had merged in that peculiar way that Emily could perceive only as a faint tingling, but which Astrea had assured her could be extremely pleasurable for a Marq'ssan. As soon as their fields merged, Astrea turned her face to Emily's, smiled, and linked arms with her. Astrea made this physical gesture for Emily just as Emily extended her field for Astrea, since neither of them could share the same sensations using the mechanisms appropriate to their species. Astrea's skin, like the rest of her synthesized human facade, acted as a mediator between Astrea's body and the alien earth atmosphere (as well as served to make Astrea look human). For Astrea, sensations experienced through touch were what Emily thought of as only intellectually comprehended and noted, rather than emotionally *felt*.

Aware of Lynn staring at her, Emily made an effort to handle conversation and continue what Astrea called "field management" at the same time. (Astrea had assured her that with practice it would become easier.) "You're wasting your time on her," Emily said, smiling at Lynn. "She doesn't understand the concept of art, much less of public art. It's gibberish to her."

Lynn frowned. "Oh come on, Emily. Don't put her down. She was just telling me some of the pieces she's been to look at. She's better informed than most humans would be on the subject."

"Yes and parrots can be made to repeat scientific terms." Emily grinned. "That doesn't mean they understand what they're saying."

"Emily's right," Astrea said. "It's hopeless. I've tried for years. Emily's taken me to galleries and museums all over the world. She's taken me to films, videos, plays, concerts, dance performances..." She shrugged. "I'm hopeless."

Lynn's lips tightened. "Right," she said. Obviously she thought they were putting her on, making a joke at her expense. She looked down at her empty glass. "I think I need another drink. My throat is parched."

Emily watched Lynn push her way through the crowd, seeking a better conversational situation.

"It's too much for me tonight," Astrea said into Emily's ear. "Let's leave. I don't think I can take it. She wore me out."

Already? Emily wondered. But then the dozens of people crowded into the room were noshing and imbibing without restraint. Astrea could stand only so much of watching humans consume food and drink.

Emily found Martin. Touching his arm, she told him they were leaving. "Come see me sometime," he said into her ear as she bent forward and kissed his cheek.

Outside, Astrea said, "Let's go to an ocean beach, Em." Astrea loved the ocean as she loved all things wet.

And so they spent the night on a beach listening to the surf, watching the moonlit waves roll in, and following the stars and the moon in their journey across the sky. They talked now and then, and the rest of the time were silent, sitting close and savoring the world around them. And all of the time their fields were merged, their hands touching.

[iii]

"It seems peaceful enough here," Emily said. The discrete twitters and trills of the birds piping in the park below would not have been so sharp and clear if it weren't truly peaceful in the surrounding neighborhood. Sitting on this balcony, one would never guess that a mob of media-people lurked out on the street in front of Martha and Hazel's house.

Hazel held out the platter of scrambled eggs. "Have some eggs."

Emily took the platter and added a spoonful to a plate already loaded with steamed zucchini, fried potatoes, and fruit. "So they weren't satisfied with your press conference, Martha?"

Martha viciously stabbed a chunk of potato. "That and the vid special—which, after all, is universally accessible—aren't what those types are interested in. They don't care about the issues involved—although in cases like this they pay lip-service to the issue, for otherwise they'd have no reason to be dogging me. No, they want to play me up as notorious, to create me as one of their public-enemy-number-one media-villains." She snorted. "I wouldn't be surprised if there's someone out there in the woods with a telephoto lens snapping pictures of us right this minute."

Hazel grinned. "I can see it now. The caption will read, 'The Free Zone Conspirators plotting the downfall of the Empire over breakfast.'"

They laughed, but Emily said, "That's not so far off. I brought back a couple of newspapers from Baton Rouge and New Orleans with me. I'll show them to you later. On the front page of the Baton Rouge paper there's a photo of people marching around the site of the destructured jail. They're carrying signs demanding that the site be *exorcized*." Martha and Hazel stared at her as though they didn't believe her. "Oh yes," Emily said. "Exorcism. They're Catholics, you know. And they seem to be firmly convinced—as various other religious groups are—that the Marq'ssan are devils, and that they destructure buildings using the powers of black magic."

"I heard some of that when I was in jail," Martha said thoughtfully. "There were a couple of warders who crossed themselves every time they came near me. I knew a lot of people there hated me. But I didn't realize—" She shook her head.

"Martha has a real fan club down there," Emily told Hazel. "The entire legal system of the state of Louisiana, for starters."

Martha put down her fork and leaned back in her chair. "What I find most baffling is the difference in reaction between the executives down there and the executives we dealt with when we were breaking the banana and coffee cartels. I mean, they're both corporate, both executive." Martha swallowed coffee. "You can bet the same kind of people are calling the shots at Dowsanto as do in the banana and coffee industries. Threatened with the loss of corporate property, the cartels decided not to burn the boats and warehouses of independent growers and shippers because doing so would open them to the risk of losing everything, and so they looked for other ways to maintain their stranglehold. But why is it that when we come up against governments, the same reasoning doesn't hold?"

"Something different's involved when governments get into the picture," Hazel said. "The calculus for winning and losing changes. Perceptions change. The stakes change. How else explain some of the stupid wars that individuals running governments have gotten into with the end result that they personally lost money on them?" Hazel ate a bite of fried potato, and the conversation dropped into a some-what gloomy silence.

"I take it you've had nothing positive from Elizabeth Weatherall," Emily said at last.

Hazel frowned. "No word at all since the action."

"She's playing games," Martha said.

Emily fingered her juice glass. "It doesn't make sense."

"I don't agree entirely with Martha's view," Hazel said, her golden gaze moving from Martha's face to Emily's. "Martha thinks the silence is a ploy to draw us out. But I think she's planning some kind of retalia-tory measure and intends to contact us *after* such a counter-action."

"Have you made an overture to her since the action?"

"No."

"And in the meantime," Emily said, "they have the President is-suing scathing statements about the Free Zone's lawlessness and their conspiracy with the aliens to destroy the Free World As We Know It."

"You don't think," Hazel said, her voice suddenly troubled, "You don't think they're planning on making *war* against us, do you?"

"Weatherall's not *that* big a fool," Martha said. "Come on, Hazel, you know her better than any of us. She knows the Marq'ssan could destroy the entire military establishment in her country in less than a month if they wanted to! She's not going to call our bluff just be-cause some provincials got her into a contest she didn't want in the first place."

"How do you know she didn't want a contest?" Emily asked. "How do you know she doesn't feel a need for that kind of a challenge?"

Martha said, "But why? She's made it clear all along that she thought the benefits of amicable relations would outweigh the disad-vantages. Why change now?"

"Maybe she needs an external enemy."

Hazel, who had been staring out at the park, jerked her head around to stare at Emily. "Maybe we haven't been paying enough at-tention to their internal politics," she said softly.

Martha snorted. "I refuse to expend my energies on watching ex-ecutives playing games with themselves and the public."

"All I know," Emily said, "is that after the Blanket when every-thing was so chaotic, most executives perceived the outbreak of World

War III as a stroke of luck. As a means of pulling everything back together again. And some people whose memories aren't good think it was the outbreak of war that ended the Civil War. They don't seem to remember that the Civil War ended *before* Russia invaded western Europe."

"Hello," a familiar voice said from behind Emily. She glanced over her shoulder and saw Sorben standing in the doorway. "Because of the crowd out there I let myself in. I'm sure they didn't even notice."

Not if Sorben had camouflaged herself, Emily thought, watching the Marq'ssan pull a chair to the table and sit down between herself and Martha. As usually happened these days when she saw Marq'ssan, she had a terrible desire to slip into field perception: she had a strong urge to look at Marq'ssan fields every chance she got, partly out of curiosity, partly out of the queer pleasure (aesthetic? emotional?) she got from seeing Marq'ssan fields. Also, from the few times she had snatched glimpses of their fields, she had found that Astrea's differed from the fields of the other Marq'ssan almost as much as Marq'ssan fields differed from human fields. But because she had not yet learned to manage such perception while fully attending to everything else going on around her she shied away from trying it except in large gatherings. Though Sorben would not be able to tell from her field what she was doing, Emily worried that something unusual in her behavior or appearance might make Sorben wonder about her, which might induce her to scan her, in which case she'd discover the slight change Astrea had made in her brain stem.

As Martha and Hazel brought Sorben up to date, Emily mused on what Sorben's gaze must be taking in…but no, Emily reminded herself, they don't use *vision* to perceive fields, they have other senses more finely developed, in fact they don't quite *see* at all, at least not in the sense that humans see. Emily always felt a little disoriented when remembering in the presence of Marq'ssan that all that human-seeming tissue bore no functional resemblance whatsoever to human tissue. As for the gestures, the facial expressions, the responsiveness of their eyes…all that had to be deliberately assumed and learned. Of course Sorben probably did it all as naturally—as unthinkingly—as a human did. Sorben had been living on this planet for longer than she, Emily, had.

"Oh my god!" Hazel said, pressing her hands to her cheeks. "I've just realized something!"

Everyone stared at her. "What is it?" Martha said.

Hazel bit her lip. "I've just realized that Liz is the first of the people running governments that we've had to deal with who understands certain things about the Marq'ssan."

"What do you mean?" Emily asked. Disquiet seeped through her mind and chilled her body. She had always tended to think that Elizabeth's knowledge of the Marq'ssan had been beneficial rather than harmful, since Elizabeth's lack of paranoia made it more likely she'd not engage in panic strikes against the Marq'ssan.

"Suppose she decided to challenge us by retaliating for the jail destructuring by bombing some site in the Free Zone, thereby causing deaths?" Hazel's eyes bored into Emily's. "I can just imagine her telling us there will be more casualties if we destructure any government or executive property in retribution. She'd know we wouldn't risk her taking more life."

"Oh fuck," Martha said, half under her breath. "I can just see her reasoning that way. I used to wonder when some government was going to realize that and blackmail us with it." She tossed her napkin onto the table and started stacking their plates.

"Unless she's willing to make random raids outside the Free Zone," Sorben said softly, "her blackmail *can't* work." She nodded at them when they stared at her; her silvery eyes remained calm, unperturbed. "We wouldn't find it difficult to protect the Free Zone from outside attack if we had to. Presuming the attack came by air." She frowned. "If it were made stealthily on the ground, that would be another matter... But we *can* protect the Free Zone from the most obvious military attacks—though it *would* consume a lot of our attention and energy to do so."

Martha's hand, reaching for Hazel's juice glass, arrested. "Do you think we should be worrying about such an attack? Is it likely?"

Hazel raised her hands, then let them fall. "I don't know. This is all just speculation. But I do know she's going to use every scrap of knowledge she acquired while living in the Free Zone to try to subjugate us."

"I think," Emily said into the silence, "that we need some talk with her. To try to get a little more information on where she's standing."

Martha finished collecting the flatware. "I disagree. She's the one who's keeping silent. The ball's in her court."

"That's a silly way to talk," Emily said. That was the way her father talked, using the idiotic metaphors the military boys liked. When Martha began to protest, Emily interrupted. "No, listen. Let *me* talk to her. In person. Face to face. I'm a member of her club, you know." She smiled wryly. "For various reasons I keep up my executive connections. They *can* be useful at times. And I think this is one of them."

"Don't go as an envoy from us."

As if. Emily leaned back in her chair and smiled. "Believe me, I'll make it crystal clear I'm acting as a free agent. Elizabeth will be a little annoyed, but she won't be entirely skeptical, since she knows people in the Free Zone often act independently."

"Yes," Hazel said, "but I did name you as one of the advisors I wanted in on the meetings with her."

"I'll let her deduce that we've had a falling out. Because Celia is in jail, no one who didn't know me intimately would be surprised at my blaming Martha for Celia's plight."

After further discussion they agreed that Emily should seek out Elizabeth on the pretext of asking her to use her influence to get Celia released. Emily wasn't thrilled about having to deal with Elizabeth, but she needed to do *something*. The only other possibility was to go with Astrea to Louisiana and search for Celia. But she preferred to hold that as a last resort—mostly because Celia would prefer it that way herself.

Chapter Twelve

Tuesday, May 29, 2096—Seattle

Marlene and Janice treated me to lunch today at the place around the corner from the Press. The weather was glorious (*all* the mountains out), so we sat on the back terrace and drank wine with our meal—taking an hour and a half (which they told me they'd make up the time for—including mine—on Saturday morning). They said they wanted me to know how much they'd enjoyed working with me, that they'll miss me. All this made me feel so warm inside. But now as I pack my books I'm remembering how often I dipped into *Rainbow Times* data files to steal material (especially reporters' confidential notes) I knew would interest either Lise or Mott.

Thank god the Company is paying my moving expenses. Shipping all these books and furniture and my kitchen equipment and dishes will be expensive. I'll have to leave my plants behind—am giving them to Marlene and Janice.

And this apartment. How I've loved living in it. I'll miss the walled-in patio, where I've read so many books... And my walks. I'll miss those especially. And Venn's collection of books: I'll miss those, too.

And of course Venn herself.

But it's foolish to dwell on the sadness of parting from the familiar and loved. I should look forward, instead, to life among the sane again. Where I won't have to tell lies.

Friday. I fly to DC on Friday. I still can't believe it, it's happening so fast.

Wednesday, May 30, 2096—Seattle

Just caught the full coverage of Martha Greenglass's press conference (which was held on Monday), broadcast on a vid station operating out of Chicago. Of course FZ stations didn't carry it—instead they carried personal interviews with Martha and endless discussions by various parties representing the infinity of political factions in this town on Sunday's "action." The press conference had some revealing moments. A network reporter asked Martha if the way the Marq'ssan bailed her out of every adverse situation gave her a "god complex."

Martha laughed at the question. And then she said that that was an interesting way to look at it, and that she thought the question raised an important point—namely that most people are constrained by fears that bind them in ways they don't even realize, that in one sense her being so privileged as to be able to feel confidence in the Marq'ssan "bailing her out" allowed her to act more boldly than she would otherwise have done. She thought this a good thing. (Of course she would think that: since it allows her to do as she damned well pleases!)

All the stuff I'm passing to the station to be sent to DC is material for a massive public awareness campaign for educating people about the aliens and the FZ. There are to be special issues in magazines and vid documentaries doing a history of the Marq'ssan since the Blanket. People know so little about them, Lise says, that they tend to treat them as though they're just another Hollywood production. This is because of the low profile they keep. It's amazing, but apart from those first few speeches they made on board their starship, there's absolutely *nothing* on digital media (except for a few pix the FZ has now and then printed in their newspapers) of the Marq'ssan. Which means all the visuals in documentaries will mostly be pans of the sites they've destroyed and interviews with people who have met them or seen them. (Lise says they might interview me.) Anyway, this blitz media campaign is a rush operation. They want to get it out within the next month or two. I can see already that my new job will be hectic.

One more day of work here. And then the day after that I leave. I still can't believe it. Almost everything I own is packed and ready for the movers, who are supposed to come tomorrow evening. I'm excited, but I have a sort of hollow feeling, too. Probably because I know so little about where I'm going and what I'm going to be doing. Guess I've gotten pretty set in my ways...

Thursday, May 31, 2096—Seattle

The movers have been and gone. (I'm keeping my safe-boxes and am carrying them in my personal luggage. Who knows what happens to stuff that gets moved across the country?) Feeling weepy. Probably from having drunk too much wine this afternoon at the party they gave for me. What a bash—the whole Press turned out. Venn gave me a long, tight hug, and I couldn't help crying a little. "Some day you'll come back to us, I can feel it in my bones," she said in my ear. And then she kissed me on the cheek. I wanted to change my mind then and there.

But of course that's silly. It's just not knowing my destination, not having a place ready to move into, not knowing what my job will be. Who wouldn't be feeling a little low about that? The thing is not to worry, to leave it all to Lise. I'm lucky to have someone to handle all my arrangements the way Lise does. Who else has someone arranging jobs for them and paying their moving expenses? There's nothing to worry about. Relax, Anne. And just think of it: I'll be going *home*. I'll be back in the normal, real, sane world. No more nattering on about whether or not someone's garbage pick-up should be discontinued, no more discussing the fair price of peaches to death... Just normal everyday life.

Saturday, June 2, 2096—DC

I'm staying at Lise's for now. Downstairs there's a dinner par-ty of super-VIPs going on—*three* Cabinet officers (Mott, Schuyler, and Steadman) and the CEOs of United Print Media Associates and Norton-Bush Communications Inc. Lise had me come downstairs to meet Schuyler apart from the others. Lise had told me she wanted to introduce me since I may be dealing with her and will certainly be dealing with Schuyler's people. I sort of wondered why Lise would bother. I'm such a minor player. But the way Lise talked and acted, she made it clear to Schuyler that we're lovers. She had her arm around my waist the entire time I was in the room. And she said a few embar-rassing things about how we'd had to live apart for the last five years and how wonderful it was for us to be together again. I don't know why she did that. But I could see Schuyler sort of pegging me, and she was very polite and affable and all that (as she wouldn't have been if Lise hadn't brought our personal relationship into it). I don't know what to do about Lise's going on like that. I hope she won't be making a habit of it.

But that's all a part of my uneasiness about staying here. Or should I say living here? Because it may be a couple of months that I live in this house. And what a house: Lise apparently *owns* it—a house in *Georgetown*. Somehow, living in the FZ, I hadn't taken it in when Lise told me about it two years ago. But now that I'm back in DC, the significance of it has hit me full force. Lise has a staff of people to run it, plus Julia Conover, her own executive PA (who's managing the dinner party). I'm to meet with Julia on Monday for more details of what Lise has planned for me. Apparently my permanent assignment won't be in DC at all, but somewhere in Pennsylvania where they're doing most of the production work for a new twelve-hour-a-week soap that's premiering in the fall. It's to be set in post-World War II (the First Cold War) Europe. My job will have something to do with handling the actors. Lise says that Mott thinks my best work has been the recruiting and running of agents in the FZ. Lise thinks that the same qualities that made me good at that will make me good at handling the actors, a very tricky and important job, according to Lise. Actually it sounds kind of interesting. So *different* from what I'm used to. Glamorous, even. Imagine, one of the actors will be Jennie Vale, whom I was madly in love with all through that soap she starred in back in the '80s.

But in the meantime I need to stay in DC a while since Lise thinks I should read the articles in their draft versions and watch the documentaries as they are being made in order to correct false statements and impressions and so on, given my personal knowledge of the aliens. I'm to be an "accuracy critic," she said. Though I'm also to say what I think about how the audience will respond to various things, since media people need all the input on that that they can get. They have focus groups already selected and ready for trial-runs, but Lise says that as long as I'm doing the one kind of critique I can do the other kind, too.

I wish, though, I could get my own apartment. Lise says I won't be staying in DC long enough to make the trouble worthwhile. The last time I lived in DC I lived with my parents—so that they could have the rent I could pay them, since back then we were all three of us thinking about scraping together the credit for longevity treatments for both of them. But all that time I was in the FZ pulling in that extra salary... No, no, they said, they were too old now to be thinking of merely prolonging their lives, and what was the point anyway since their retirement pay wouldn't be sufficient for allowing them to *do* something with their free time? I have to try to convince them that they shouldn't think that way, that I can help them out.

I couldn't live with them now, though. Not after so many years by myself in my own spacious apartment. Lise says it's absurd for me to "waste my credit" paying rent, that her house is large and comfortable and quiet and I'll enjoy the luxury of being waited on by her staff. But I do want my own place. I think I'll at least check into the possibilities for some short-term kind of rental. As long as I'm living here it will seem to everyone that I *am* Lise's live-in lover. And the more people who think that, the harder it will be to get Lise to see things differently. I have my own room (or should I say room*s*? Since this bedroom has not only a bath with a Jacuzzi but a sitting room as well), and Lise gives me plenty of space. (She's hardly here at all. Don't know where she was last night—when Julia met me here after the car brought me from the airport she said Lise wouldn't be in until very late. And I gather Lise didn't get home until eight or nine this morning.) I don't feel terribly pressed upon—yet. And I know Lise won't be in DC much. But this *is* her house...and when all my things arrive, I'll want to get settled. I have to make Lise understand that.

I think I'll read in bed for a while and then try to sleep. I'm going to visit Mom and Dad tomorrow.

Sunday, June 3, 2096—DC

What a day. (The aspirin dot has finally eased my headache some, at least.) One damned thing after another. First, the shock of what things cost here. Well, I knew everything would be pricey—this is, after all, DC. Yesterday when I ordered that plant from the florist for Mom and Dad it struck me as pretty expensive, but then I figured that that must be because I was having it delivered. But today, wanting to

take them some fruit and flowers, I couldn't *believe* the price of the
fruit—they were charging the equivalent of half a week's pay for a
reasonable selection of non-exotic fruit. And the flowers were just as
high. This was in one of those ordinary little produce stands you see
every few blocks in Georgetown. Well, I thought, it's because of the
neighborhood. So I decided to wait until I got out to the suburbs.

The trip seemed to take forever. And I kept thinking people were
staring at me because of my clothes being so different. When I finally
got out to the suburbs, there was only one store that had fresh fruit.
(And no cut flowers at all.) And the fruit in that store was even *more*
expensive (and slightly battered looking, too—definitely not of the
same quality). I bought some, but it went against the grain to pay such
an exorbitant price. Why should it be *that* expensive here? Because of
supply and demand? Can the density of executives here make demand
that excessive? I guess it's lucky I won't be living in DC for long. Who
could afford to (except executives, of course)?

Mom and Dad carried on too much about the plant and the fruit.
And then I couldn't answer any of their questions about what I'm going to be doing. Mom had gotten a lot of take-out stuff the way she
always does when she has Sunday Dinner (it was something of a shock
to remember that they never cook—no *dishes* even, except disposable
stuff—and that take-out's the only kind of stuff they eat other than
tubefood: I guess I must have been assuming that their standard of
living had risen with the recovery of the economy after Weatherall's
takeover), and it was pretty awful. A super-greasy and sweet barbecue platter, rubbery dry biscuits with margarine, and various kinds
of salads heavy on an awful synthetic-tasting mayonnaise... I tried
to pretend I liked it, since they went to some expense and trouble
with it, and there's nothing worse than someone being snobbish with
people who can't afford to eat better. But the worst part came when
they turned on vid to watch a "presidential address" about the "crisis
with the aliens and the Free Zone." Hearing Mom and Dad talk so
seriously about "what the President should do" etc., I kept thinking of
how someone on Lise's staff had probably written that speech. Of how
absurd it was to hear people talking seriously about the President and
what the people want and opinion polls and all that. I felt like such
a creep for sitting there and listening to it. Tried not to say anything

condescending. They did of course ask my opinion, not only because they believe everybody should "get involved" as a matter of "good citizenship," but also because of my having lived in the FZ for so long. I hardly knew what to say.

There's no doubt about it—I could *never* live with them now, not even for a few weeks or months. I'd be feeling false all the time, and going between the suburbs and DC I'd get schizoid. No, either I live alone, or I stay here with Lise.

Tuesday June 5, 2096—DC

Yesterday I acquired an expensive wardrobe. Of a certain kind of service-tech elegance—all the best materials, and a lot of it flashy. An executive, Pauline Richardson, whisked me off—with explicit instructions from Lise, she said. It was no good protesting to her, she said, she was only following orders. All the time we kept piling up this stuff (a lot of which will be altered to fit perfectly, which will take a few weeks), I was trying to keep a tally of how much we were spending (though of course a lot of things didn't have prices on them and who knows how much extensive alterations cost? I have to go back to some of the shops for special fittings, too), and as the total mounted, I got into a terrible state of anxiety. Lise says she's paying for all of it. But I can't let her do that. That's not the kind of relationship I want to have with her. (Or anyone.) Oh this awful weight dragging at my heart. When I tried to talk to her about it this morning, I almost started crying. She's so blithe about it. Just brushes it all away. Said something about how it wasn't my fault I'd spent all those years in the FZ where I didn't need to be well-dressed, and how my current and next assignments make it essential that I be well dressed (especially the job running the actors, she said), and that how I look matters very much to her reputation. This last point upset me more than anything else. I asked her how that could be, and she said that how her lover dressed was as important as how her PA dressed. I think I shouted at her (we were in the car—in the back of her limousine—riding to the office this morning, the first chance I'd gotten to talk to her since she hadn't come in until after midnight last night) that there was no reason for anyone to know we were lovers. And so then she got all upset and hurt and said why wouldn't I give her another chance, why was I being so cold to her, that I would see that what I felt for Venn wasn't "genuine mature love."

Which meant we arrived at the office—my first day on the job, too—in an emotional mess. She took me around herself to meet "everybody" (i.e., all the executives and professionals working in the DC branch of the Office of Information) and introduced me to my new boss in DC, Sara Monaghan, a professional whose main qualification seems to be a masters in communications (she has her diploma hung on the wall of her cubicle, so incredibly tacky). So I started today doing odd jobs, since my most important task here will only sporadically occupy me, at least at first.

Right off this afternoon Monaghan gave me a thorough dressing-down in front of the other two service-techs working under her. All I'd done was suggest a more efficient way for doing something—I mean, it was obvious, and I even asked Rosie and Tina about it first, and they (who've been doing it Monaghan's way since they first started working for her) agreed that the way I suggested was more efficient. We had about a five- or ten-minute chat about it, among ourselves, discussing the optimal way of doing the procedure. So then I went into Monaghan's cubicle and gave her our suggestions for how to streamline it. She got furious at me and insisted she and I go out into the main office the three of us share and "get certain things straight." She accused me of trying to play on the fact that I was "Bennett's girl" (she actually called me that) and of manipulating my co-workers and trying to stir up trouble. She said that she was my boss because she was better qualified than I, that I'd better not think my "sexual in" with Bennett could cut any ice with her. God it was humiliating. The upshot is that I'm to do exactly what I'm told and keep my "superior ideas" to myself. Rosie and Tina gave me the cold shoulder after that. Every time I have to ask them for something (since I don't know where anything is or how they do things, that's pretty often) they make me feel as though I'm stupid for having to ask. It's going to be uphill for a while, trying to win their trust.

Thursday, June 7, 2096—DC

Another fine dinner eaten alone. The staff have instructions to take "good care" of me when Lise is out, which is almost always. I haven't seen her since Wednesday morning when we drove in to the office together. This morning I went in her car alone—I'd prefer to get to work on my own when Lise isn't here, but that's just one more thing I have to take up with Lise once I get a chance to really talk to her.

I feel so incredibly awful. Maybe it's culture shock? I don't have the right social sense anymore. I'm so used to FZ manners and mores. And being known as Lise's "girl," I don't really have a chance at work. I'm beginning to realize it's not just my being known as Lise's girl but the more general problem of hetero-hostility for my sexual preference. I'd forgotten about that. Monaghan of course is hetero, but so are Rosie and Tina. I didn't even think twice about it until this morning one of them made some weird kind of crack that the other one giggled at. It took me a few seconds to pick up on it. I don't have as thick a skin as I used to, I guess.

And then that office. It has no windows at all. What it does have is fluorescent lights and muzak, horrible stuff that keeps playing all day in the most irritating way. The general (i.e., non-executive) cafeteria has only tubefood and horrible dried out sandwiches on inedible bread. I'm going to start taking my lunch—I spoke to the cook about it this evening, and she said she'd be happy to make box lunches for me, that since Lise is so seldom around she doesn't have much to do beyond feeding the rest of the staff.

And now, because I'm so wiped out after such a damned awful day, I'll go to sleep, even though it's only eight-thirty...

Friday, June 8, 2096—DC

I'm fed up with this new job, new boss, new co-workers. (Not to mention all the security crap one must go through as a matter of routine, as well as the damned excessive paperwork.) Today when I talked to Monaghan about coming to work early on Monday and leaving a little late and sacrificing my lunch break so that I could make up the time I'd lose going to the appointment with the rental agent, she gave me a cold look and said, "Personal business? The only kind of personal

business employees may simply take off for is medically-related personal illness. Is this appointment medically related?" When I said it
wasn't, she informed me I couldn't have the time off. When I assured
her I could make up the work (there isn't enough work for the three
of us) she said something snippety about how she had no intention of
granting special privileges to me just because I was "Bennett's girl."
Her saying that and staring pointedly at my watch (which Lise gave
me long before we went renegade), as though to imply Lise is keeping me, made me seethe. I stormed out of her office without saying
a word. I can't remember being that angry in years. Later she called
me back in and insisted I apologize to her for my "insubordinate conduct"—threatening to write a memorandum to be placed in my file if
I didn't. So of course I apologized.

So what to do about finding a place? The rental agent is all booked
up weekends and evenings for several weeks. I tried calling other
agents, but it was the same story there, too. So I guess if I want to see
an agent I'll have to make an appointment and then call in sick that
day. And to hell with Monaghan if she doesn't believe I'm sick.

It must gall her that my clothes are of so much better quality than
hers. I suppose a lot of this must be jealousy? Or maybe insecurity?
And Rosie and Tina ignore me (sometimes whispering—making me
paranoid, because I don't know if they're whispering about *me*). I ate
my box lunch (a delicious cabbage salad and a turkey and avocado
sandwich) by myself, trying to read, but all the time aware of people
staring at me (while avoiding me). Thank god I don't have to work
weekends. Now that *would* be depressing.

Sunday, June 10, 2096—DC

Took a long walk this morning and read the *NY Times*. The President on vid this evening, challenging the aliens to stop their "cowardly hiding behind the skirts of anarchist women." Never referred to
the FZ as such in this speech, which I guess means that the Executive
has decided to retreat from their acknowledgement of the FZ. (Or am
I jumping to conclusions?) More "challenges": that the aliens come
right out and speak to him and the American People, that they make
reparations for all the damage they've done throughout the world,

that they show their faces, that they drop their cowardly secrecy. A lot of taunts, in effect, to try to provoke the Marq'ssan into revealing more of themselves...or else mere propaganda for influencing public opinion. And as usual, the President excoriated the aliens for violating the decencies of law and order, for flouting their lawlessness before the world community. A speech reeking of frustration.

In short, nothing new.

Tuesday, June 12, 2096—DC

Lise got back today, so Julia buzzed me and asked me to come to Lise's office when I finished for the day. I did so, bracing myself for talking seriously to Lise about all the things that have been bothering me. But first she had to finish up her appointments. Then she had to sign a few things. Finally, she whisked me out of the office and down into the car, saying we had to run home and change because we were going to the Diana for "a drink and a snack to tide us over" and then to a symphony concert, with supper out after. In the car, she had to take a phone call, so we were almost home by the time she had explained our plans for the evening. She was in a gay, excited mood, calling me Annie and sweetheart every other sentence, her eyes sparkling, promising we'd have a wonderful time, saying she knew I must have missed the cultural life DC has to offer. (I was so provoked by something in her attitude—I guess it was the imputation that I'd become a terrible stick-in-the-mud provincial—that I nearly pointed out that in Seattle I went to symphony concerts a minimum of twice a month and plays and other things, too. But of course I didn't. Seattle's a backwater.) When we got home she came with me into my room and picked out one of the flashiest (and lowest cut) dresses Pauline had selected for me. I remember feeling uneasy when I first tried it on (it bares my legs *above* my knees and shows cleavage, which makes me feel *very* strange), and when I put it on and realized I'd be going out in public in it, I debated taking it off. But then Lise came in and oohed and ah-hed and kissed me...so I ended up wearing the damned thing. It is the latest style, that's true. Almost all the service-techs I saw at the Diana were dressed in equally racy clothes. Lise half-seriously suggested I consider getting my face painted. When I pointed out that not many people at the Office of Information had their faces painted, she pooh-poohed that, saying I shouldn't go by *that*.

We had about forty-five minutes at the club, so I thought I'd try to talk seriously. But what happened was I'd get a few sentences out and then some executive would interrupt, just to say hi to Lise or to exchange gossip or to ask a favor. Eventually, though, I got almost everything said. By that time Lise had that wary look in her eyes, and her gayness only reappeared when people stopped by our table. First she tried to write off what I was saying about everyone calling me her girl as my being upset by their hetero-hostility. She said she hadn't hesitated about assigning me to Monaghan because I'd worked so easily with heteros in Seattle and had liked my boss even though she was a hetero and a professional. I pointed out that *they* weren't hetero-hostile. And that besides, this was more to do with everyone knowing I was *her* lover (as opposed to just knowing I was lesbian) and with my wearing expensive clothes and living in her house and getting special attention from her. That I had the feeling that people in that office considered me to be kept, and that I found this humiliating. Lise didn't like my saying this. "I don't understand what you're so upset about. If it's Monaghan, I'll have Julia talk to her." No, no, I said, don't for godsake do that. That's all I need is more hostility. Lise then informed me very coldly that Julia was "the soul of tact" and that there was no reason for me to think Julia would turn Monaghan against me. Then I said that Monaghan was already against me and described the two confrontations we'd already had... Lise dismissed these, saying that I'd had a cushy job in the FZ because there had been no executives running things, that things were run more tightly here and that I shouldn't complain about that. This upset me, too—it simply isn't true that my job at the Press was cushy. All the editors were often complimentary to the three of us for our high level of productivity. I *know* we got a hell of a lot of work done. And some of it had to do with the methods of interdependence in our work projects—making sure none of us were indispensable to any single task or project. So that we could shift things around whenever we had to. We were *good*, the three of us. Not like Monaghan's stupid circus of an office.

We had to cut the discussion off to go to the concert—and by this time I could tell that Lise was pretty put out with me for spoiling her evening. But once we got to the concert she turned on again. We sat with Ginger and Lisa Mott, and Ginger fell all over herself telling me how thrilled she was to see me. I arranged to meet her on Saturday afternoon. After the concert, the four of us had supper at some fancy Georgetown restaurant where only executives go. And when we got home, Lise made love to me. Afterwards, before she fell asleep (I spent the night in her bed), she said something to me about how everyone knew the only reason I had gone renegade was for love of her, and that rather than that being something to be ashamed of I should be glad to have it known—because then people would "understand" about my years away from the Company. I think she was trying to tell me something important, but I'm not sure. She isn't being very clear about certain things. If I'm terribly confused about the cliques and factions and social behaviors going on in the Office of Information, I'm doubly confused by what's going on between Lise and me. The only thing I know is that I haven't convinced her that it would be better if I lived somewhere else than in her house.

Sunday June 17, 2096—DC

Just back from a wonderful weekend at a Cape Cod resort. I'm feeling *so* much better about everything. It turned out Lise could take some time for herself this weekend, which she did. I called up Ginger and put her off till next week, and then Lise and I just took off for the Cape. Wonderful weather, too, and we had our own little cottage on the beach, with *no* interruptions. Talked for hours. I feel that I'm finally beginning to understand certain things.

Poor Lise, she's been having a terrible time of it. Weatherall has pushed a lot of responsibility onto her—which Lise would like to gradually ease off. But apparently things are not so rosy any more for Weatherall—there are a lot of pressures on her now, and it's a battle for her just to stay in power. And all this stuff with the FZ and the aliens is a threat of crisis proportions. Lise says the work she does for Weatherall is critical and they both know it, and that Weatherall is depending on her.

I guess seeing her only twice a month on those weekends blinded me to what was going on with Lise. I admitted to her that I'd felt taken advantage of and used, though I didn't *mind* that exactly since it was for patriotic reasons, but that what I'd minded was feeling that Lise was putting those things above our personal relationship. And of course we *were* using our personal relationship to facilitate my cover. Lise reminded me of what she is really like—I suppose I've been pretty superficial in my view of things. I always did know what kind of person Lise was—that it's difficult for her to form attachments, but that once she does they're "forever." And so it was a terrible shock for her that weekend when I told her that we should stop pretending we love one another.

She has mixed feelings about my taking the soap assignment. But she says that even if we can't have an ordinary day-to-day existence together, our relationship means more to her than I can guess. Weatherall has little time for her, and she never was that close to Mott (who spends most of her free time home with Ginger—Mott being something of a "homebody" type, an anomaly for someone on the Executive I'd think; also Mott is thinking of having a *child*. But this is super-confidential). And though she sees scores of people socially, she doesn't feel close to any of them. Which is why, she says, she especially needs me now.

If I continue to find Monaghan awful, Lise will switch me to another job in another office. But I can tell she thinks it's my fault; she asked me to try to be "more accommodating," to "adapt" myself to "new circumstances." She promises to try to spend more time with me, though she warns that this crisis may completely absorb her. And she's urged me to go out in the evenings—to the theater and symphony and so on—she'll pay for all such expenses, she says. That she wants me to "get the most out of DC."

Sometimes Lise can be so sweet, and god knows she's terribly vulnerable. How can I not love her?

Chapter Thirteen

Tuesday, 6/5/2096

For days it's been nothing but tests & PT that left me so worn out I didn't even think of opening this book. I now have two PT sessions a day. This afternoon the physician informed me that my bone tissue is in "splendid shape." He also said that I've lost twenty-five pounds—& that I will be leaving at the convenience of Ms. Weatherall.

The examinations required my leaving this room. Not that I saw much. A blank sort of corridor. Rooms along it full of med-tech equipment. The usual female gorillas. Inside one of the rooms was a mirror, & I caught sight of my now unrecognizable face. Of course I knew about the reconstructive surgery. But I'd no idea that my firm, sharp Sedgewick jaw & my high-bridged Sedgewick nose are gone forever. My face is now heart-shaped (my hair so shaggy-long I could hardly see what that face looks like). The new nose is aquiline, very thin & long. I have this strange feeling that if Rbt could see me he'd disown me the way he disowned Daniel. That I looked like him reinforced his belief in our "twin-ness." I certainly look nothing like myself now, nothing like the person inside. It is an artificial facade, artfully created. No one seeing me would know me. A very disturbing thought.

Wednesday, 6/6/2096

Been pondering for some time, now, Nietzsche's virulent misogyny that flashes out unexpectedly, as if the banked fire had suddenly received a breath of oxygen and flared up in irresistible response. This morning it came to me: in Nietzsche's day women were allowed to be nothing but whores. & so it is *that* kind of creature he is so disturbed & revolted by, the very embodiment of manipulation, deviousness, & coy servility & all that goes with it. Not women themselves, but that

particular kind of social & emotional construction. In short, whoredom. He also inveighs against feminists. I tried imagining what a
"feminist" version of Clarice might be & realized I probably couldn't
have stomached it (as Nietzsche apparently couldn't, either)—strident,
demanding, even more self-centered, subtly seductive while pretending not to be: isn't that what "feminism" would have made of such a
creature as Clarice? A leech demanding to be called a noble creature,
denying its own parasitism on the blood of others?

Wouldn't Nietzsche, looking at men & women of all classes today, be
forced to concede that it is not a matter of biological sexual distinction
but rather something we see in males as well as in females? Males as
well as females now employ manipulative arts, though still it's mainly women who sink so low as to use their bodies, their sexuality for
their devious ends—for it is generally females only who have so little
self-respect that they don't hesitate to sell their bodies—I mean their
sexual selves (since many males do in fact sell their bodies in other
ways—but without the same sort of loss of self that selling oneself
sexually incurs)... In fact, isn't it a mixture of this deviousness & un-
derhandedness combined with an apparent driving desire to please
that Nietzsche determines to be the basis for all corruption? It is the
desire to please (the identification with one "stronger"—i.e., in a position of dominance to one's self) that leads to parasitism—& to the
mentality of devious manipulation. That is, if one is always trying to
please another, then acquiring/achieving/doing anything else must
always be done with an eye toward that entity one wishes to please.
But looking at it this way, the open whore (Clarice, par example) seems
almost clean in her way of living. After all, it was all understood. Except that it wasn't clean. Because there she was trying to dupe me into
believing she loved me—not only because I would then give her more
than she was already getting, but because she sensed me slipping out
of her clutches.

Rbt in fact reduced *all* attentions from service-techs to the level of
whoredom. Those who cared for me in my infancy and childhood,
for instance. He could hardly bear to have them around, even to serve
at table. (He pretended either that they weren't there or that they
were automatons.) He saw any personal expression from them as de-

graded—since, as he reasoned, they undoubtedly were being pleasant etc. simply to reap material rewards above & beyond what they were already getting. He never thought of professionals that way. *They,* he believed, have a code and take pride in their professional identity that overrides all else. & so consequently he thought of them as doing what they did to serve that identity—such that any material gain they reaped was a supplement to more important rewards. I don't think it occurred to him that ordinary everyday service-techs, like everyone else, need to experience the same social reassurances as to their humanity & their place in the world that smalltalk & other acknowledgments of their personal identity & humanity offer... In addition to believing this about those who served us, he also believed this about the service-techs working for Security, whether under SIC aegis or in ODS. He thought this of his own gorillas, for instance, though he did acknowledge that there is such a thing as "camaraderie," which was important in certain basic emotional ways that made "the boys" more likely to respond under fire as he wished. With "the boys" he insisted that ideology was relatively unimportant, that what mattered was pay, & perks, & respect for sexual expressions of power.

Which makes me wonder. Clearly Rbt understood their sexual psychology, which is the sexual psychology of most of the masses. Among them now, as used to be the case for the entire population, male sexuality is taken as an expression of as well as a metaphor for power. But with the most important males being fixed, and with some of the very most powerful people now being women, one must question this identification (even if "the boys" don't). Executive males grow up in a world in which for the masses that identification is as strong as ever. The phallic metaphor still reigns dominant, & rape is still the ultimate metaphor for domination. "The boys" (particularly ODS types), I've no doubt at all, still think of their (erect!) penises & their sex drives in that particular atavistic way. That being so, the question arises as to how fixed males who grew up with that mass conception everywhere around them psychologically reconcile this gap, this disparity, between themselves and this mass conception. (I suppose one might also wonder how we executive women likewise resist the heterosexual atmosphere of sub-exec culture?) As executives, fixed males exercise very real power that is denied to sub-exec males. Whatever "the boys" might have been thinking they were doing, in the larger scheme of things they had no real power. They were Rbt's tools. They were following orders. Their targets were selected by their superiors. That they experienced a momentary *feeling* of power by killing torturing raping is beside the point... Imagine what Nietzsche would have to say about fools like them!

Where was I...oh yes, the executive males & their inability to express power in that secondary way—i.e., through whatever surge of power males are supposed to feel when they ejaculate. This is something I'll never have a clue about—not only because I as a female don't experience such a thing, but because Rbt of course could not experience that form of pleasure & thus I never got so much as a whiff of the experience, even second-hand. Unless the mere fact that their castration is not functional but strictly in terms of sensation makes a critical difference to them? Is it possible that Rbt could accept being fixed & not feel "castrated"—which is another sexual term that is always used as a power metaphor, this time, like "impotence," to denote *lack* of power—solely because he could still *functionally* use his penis? & that perhaps exercising that function did something for him psychologically? So that really the old identification in some way persists for executive males, though with the added factor of very real control.

I know the theory in its most simplistic statement: all that malarkey about channeling the drives, which Rbt said his father helped propound, & the resulting "freedom" from the fog of passion & freedom from manipulation by the object of desire... In practice, this has proven to be not quite how it works, at least for some men, who *still* become obsessed with "objects of desire" & so on.

One begins to sympathize a little with those shrinks who thought that fixing males would free them from the tentacles of so much nonsense. My entanglement & confusion during just this little foray into the subject is proof enough of how bizarre sexuality is. Trying to talk about it, attempting to *think* on the subject, immediately plunges one into a quagmire in which one doubts one's very senses, one's perceptions, one's own experiences.

Thursday 6/7/2096

I'm to leave early next week: so says Elizabeth. She tells me she's brought me some clothing, which she's given to the med-techs. This visit—her last, & thus probably the last time I shall ever talk to her vis-à-vis, since she has said she will not be visiting me on the island—was the longest yet.

It amused her to talk about some of the things I've been writing in this book. She says my view of human nature in general & sexuality in particular is "cynical to the point of paranoia"—& that this is Rbt's doing. That apparently he managed to make me think of things in his own peculiar way, whatever the differences I think I perceive between my own opinions & attitudes & values & his. I have "an obsession" about the fact that service-techs are paid for the services they render. That as my grandmother & mother no doubt taught me (but that Rbt untaught me as he "perverted" me) there is no shame in the concept of service or rendering service, no matter what those services might be. As an example she gave the med-techs, pointing out that people would be without medical care & would thus die if it were not for such service. & then she asked me what I thought of Laurie. I gave her a blank look, but she said, "I know all about it. Though you've studiously avoided mentioning her in your diary, the amazons—whom I think you should stop calling 'female gorillas'—monitor your room, & of course they know the two of you chat whenever you're alone together. How do you account for her affection, Alexandra?"

Before taking her up on this I asked Elizabeth what had been said to the med-techs to make them so hostile to me & whether she had given orders that they not speak to me except when necessary. Elizabeth laughed and said in a nasty, malicious tone of voice that the amazons had merely "warned" the staff that my sexual orientation was sadistic & that my greatest source of pleasure was assaulting & raping service-tech women. She laughed with contempt. When I didn't say anything, she prodded, "But my dear you haven't answered my question. Maybe you think she's simply a closet masochist—in which case she must be quite disappointed—or else she decided that hung up in traction you were harmless & might be inclined to give her a nice fat juicy tip when you left? How else explain simple human kindness—from good lord! a service-tech?"

I said that she'd misunderstood what she'd read & that since I was writing only for myself I had felt no need to make things clear enough for an outsider to read & understand.

Is it possible, Elizabeth said, that I really didn't believe sexual pleasure could be anything but power games? I pointed out that I hadn't said that at all, that I had written only about whores. Why should that kind of service be thought any different from any other kind? Elizabeth wanted to know. In short, she got me too confused to be able to think clearly enough to answer.

& then she went further. She said that through what I had written about myself & Rbt it was her understanding that my incest with him was motivated on my part not by overwhelming sexual desire but by the need or desire to manipulate him. To please him. And that in fact my doing so fit the definition of what I called "whoredom."

This was the last thing in the world I wanted to discuss with Elizabeth. I said that I wasn't claiming anything.

"So then why did you let a man you hate fuck you?" Elizabeth wasn't interested in the complexity of the thing, only in hurting me as far as she is able. That is why she reads this book. Looking for clues for how to cause me pain. As part of her general campaign against me—to find her damned transcript, I suppose. [Unless, Elizabeth, it is you who are the sadist? But I won't give you the satisfaction, my captor, of seeing our conversation discussed any further in this book.]

I used to think when I was a child that part of the privilege of adulthood was privacy. Like my dreams of living in the women's world, that was just one more pathetic instance of my naiveté.

Sunday 6/10/2096

Laurie said good-bye this evening. Her days off are Mondays & Tuesdays; she has been told she would be starting a new assignment on Wednesday. Talked to me seriously about how I must "keep up with the PT" etc.—& around the subject of my suiciding, saying wasn't I glad after all, I was still alive, she knew I must be or I wouldn't have had the kind of recovery I'd had, that in these cases attitude is so essential. The girl hasn't the faintest idea of anything involved. Wonder what she imagines is the reason for my isolation & tight security? I wasn't about to endanger her by telling her anything on the subject [yes, Elizabeth, there's no doubt in my mind the girl (& all the others, too) will be examined under loquazene to make sure she hasn't picked anything up].

With such a confirmation of my going I can't help but wonder what it is that will be done with me. I'm preparing myself for various contingencies. I find I can achieve a deep trance—all the way to the bottom of third stage (which makes me think that if I wanted to I could get into fourth stage, too—something I've never tried) with the subvocalization of a single syllable. Third stage would be sufficiently deep for carrying out instant suicide. Or for evading many (though not all) drugs and other forms of stimulation. This is the best I can do for myself. That & making sure of my determination not to hesitate to do what I need to do should certain circumstances arise.

Friday 6/15/2096

Depression has kept me from writing in this book. The bleakest, starkest depression yet. But a depression with a sharp touch of anger in it, too. Anger fuels me. I can write that now since I have a reasonably secure place for keeping this book. (Though they may find it—I wouldn't be surprised if they did. Still, everything is such a mess, such chaos, that the chaos itself assists me in keeping this book secure.)

I had better start from the time of my departure from wherever it was they were keeping me. Long before dawn on Monday they came in and had me dress. (My trousers don't fit. Uncomfortably riding my hips because of my weight loss.) Then they administered a sedative— for they wanted me unconscious while taking me out of that place. I came to on the plane—on Rbt's jet—just as we were preparing to land. God it was beautiful—the sun rising out of the sea, & the island so green & lush below.

Moving about is still slow & painful. The accompanying physician, physical therapist, & med-tech helped me off the plane while the amazons, their weapons in hand, watched. They had a wheelchair for me at the bottom of the stairs. At first I thought I'd try walking (some crazy idea in my head about coming home), but I was too weak and ended up collapsing into the chair. Rather than letting the med-tech push me, I had them show me how to use the controls & led the way to the house.

The house looked no different from the outside, so I had no warning. I got out of the chair & walked (sweating profusely) up the stairs & into the entrance hall. The first thing I noticed was that the Cezanne was no longer hanging in the entrance hall. & that the Aubusson wasn't on the floor. I called Penderel (wanting to ask him why he'd removed these things). But there was no answer. So I went further into the house. & the next thing I noticed was the Long Drawing Room. The beautiful gorgeous Long Drawing Room…sacked. That's the only word for it. Not only were the carpets gone, but every floorboard had been removed (stacks of them lay piled around with nails sticking out of them), the paintings had been stripped from the walls, the vases were gone (in fact, I might as well say now that every piece of art in the house is gone), and the furniture had been ripped open, shreds of the stuffing hanging out though most of it littered the godawful remains of the floor. The only things intact in that room were the chandeliers, the draperies, & the solid wood furniture. Oh, & the ceilings & walls—which cannot be said for every other room in the house. God was I sick. Just sick. Unable to control myself, I leaned against the wall (forgetting all warnings about the kind of posture it is important that I maintain) & bawled like a baby.

After that…well, most of the house is like that. I haven't seen it all, I couldn't. None of the staff remain. The kitchen is the room in the best shape. (They knew I had no access to the kitchen or other service areas: I suppose that's the rationale.) Oh, & Elizabeth had left me a note, the bitch. Telling me that I wasn't "to worry" about the art work or the carpets, that she had had them removed & they were safe & sound & undamaged. Hah.

The room I am most afraid to know about is the Music Room. So I haven't gone in there yet & have told the med-tech not to, since I don't want her to tell me what has been damaged. Not all the floors are ruined. & things like my clothing have survived. The kitchen is full of preserved & frozen food, which we will live off for a while. & then, if we survive & go on like this, we will have to switch to tube-food…though there is the garden (what little was put in this year). If I were stronger, I would work the garden myself. No one of course will do things like that at my orders now. The physical therapist has quarters with the amazons in the place the gorillas always stayed in. (All the male gorillas seem to have been removed.) The physician left after checking me out. The med-tech stays with me, helping me get around, helping me bathe, giving me vitamins, therapeutic massages, etc. She is very cold, of course. It is clear she will be most happy to leave here as soon as the physician decides I can survive on my own.

Survive. Living in the midst of unholy wanton destruction. No wonder Elizabeth smiled at me whenever she talked about my returning here. Well, she did say that first time she talked to me that she would rip this house apart. & so she did it. She certainly did do it.

Tuesday, 6/19/2096

Finally, today, I was able to move into the Small Study—got it cleaned up enough to make it habitable. It's been such hard work. Nice not to sleep in the kitchen. I'd have been sleeping upstairs as the med-tech does in one of the service-tech rooms—which are, of course, untouched—only I can't manage the stairs without the most horrendous effort, & the very idea of going to the top of the house every night, just to sleep… The transcript must be very bulky. Because by examining what was spared & what was wrecked I'm beginning to get an idea of its probable size (though certain things, I've realized, were wrecked for sheer spite: most of the damage done to the Long Drawing Room, for instance). I wonder if it *is* on this island. Certainly Elizabeth has thoroughly checked every other residence Rbt owned… Does the thing still exist? That's the question. If it does, it's my ticket to freedom.

I'm coming to the conclusion that I'm going to have to examine myself under self-hypnosis to search for clues Rbt may have left me. I suppose he must have left me a clue? No, not necessarily. I'm sure he didn't see himself dying before me. He really thought he would live forever.

Sedgewick's Island
Thursday, 21 June, 2096

Elizabeth:

Since all arrangements for food deliveries to the main house have
been discontinued, I find it necessary to request their resumption.
Previously deliveries were made twice a week. I gather from the amazons that they are currently receiving deliveries twice a week. Since
the estate is presumably paying for the amazons' deliveries, it would
probably be most convenient all around if I simply have Phyllis ap-
pend my order to theirs. If this is amenable to you I'll work out the
arrangements with Phyllis myself.

Alexandra

Thursday, 6/21/2096

Last night after Kitty went upstairs I found a tracer in the binding
of this book. I immediately removed it & buried it in the binding of
a book in the library (the room I'm currently working to clean up).
What kind of game is Elizabeth playing, anyway?

Kitty feels sorry for me. She doesn't like me, & she's most definitely
afraid of me (& she's hetero to boot), but I think she's a little shocked
at what I—not yet fully recovered—have had to come home to. I
haven't asked her to help me with the clean-up, but she's too uncomfortable not to do so. So I accept her help, but send her for frequent
walks on the beach & apologize profusely for the inhospitable state of
my home.

Today I spoke to Amazon-in-Chief Phyllis & got her to send a letter
off to Elizabeth requesting semi-weekly food deliveries. Her answer
to this will give me some indication of the extent of her malice & the
shape of things to come. What a superhuman effort it took, keeping
my anger out of the letter. My first draft dripped with sarcasm &
ended "devotedly yours." To have to be polite to the woman who has
ravaged, sacked, & looted my' home makes me gag. But control will
out. (Isn't that what superior breeding is?) It's the one resource I have

now that can get me through. & get through I will—if only to spite that bitch.

Saturday, 6/23/2096

Last night I began my preparatory explorations. I can see with my own eyes that Elizabeth has gone through this house, top-to-bottom, & found nothing. My merely picking over ground she's already sifted would be futile. So, I've decided before doing anything physical to search my memories & intuition for clues Rbt may have dropped, for small subliminal things I may have picked up without realizing it.

I began by having a chat with Rbt—for the first time daring to confront, directly, his presence in my unconscious. Attained second stage trance, then visualized climbing the stairs to the top of the house & going to that room. When I unlocked the door (my god what a physical rush of sensation, my head swam, the sense of plunging was frightening as my hand pushed open that door), I found Rbt lying on the bed staring up at the ceiling. When I closed the door he turned his head & looked at me. (A terrible moment: I was afraid of how he might look at me, what he might say.) "So," he said, "after all this time you've finally realized who will help you & who will hurt you." (Obviously I feel guilty, obviously some part of me has been thinking Rbt would now be saying to me *I told you so*.) "She & I are at war," I announced. He smiled in that awful teeth-baring way that always made me shiver. "You always were, only you were too damned stubborn to realize it. All those stupid ideas about women sticking together. Really, Persephone, I taught you better than that."

I sat in the straight chair, a few feet from the bed. He told me that Elizabeth is at war with me as a continuation of her war with him. That it was *him* Elizabeth was battling, that she didn't really see me except as an extension of him. I didn't argue. Rbt never did understand certain things. Instead I said I wanted to fight Elizabeth, that my best weapon would be the transcript. Would he tell me what the transcript is & where he hid it? His response: I would know exactly what the transcript was if I made myself remember—through precise real-time memory regression—that last scene between the three of us. I flinched from that & accused him of wanting to make me go through it to punish me for betraying him. Giving me that awful smile again, he said no, my understanding how mistaken I was was punishment enough, that the answer lay in the words spoken between him & Elizabeth. When I asked him where it was, he only said that it's on the island & that if I thought about it I would know where.

So my unconscious firmly believes the transcript is on the island. Which is no guarantee that it is. But as for the other thing, about what the transcript is of, my unconscious is telling me that it knows. & that that scene is how it came to know about it. When I came out of the trance, I thought back to that scene. But I soon realized that I remember little but the statement I made to Rbt about leaving him, the statement I made to Elizabeth accepting her offer, & then of course Rbt's final words to me & his collapse from the cyanide he released from the capsule in his molar.

I don't want to relive that scene in real-time, excruciating detail. The thought of it makes me break into a cold sweat. But if that's the only way I'm to get more clues for how I can go about fighting Elizabeth, then I must do it. Only not just yet. When I've gotten my house in better order, & when I've gotten stronger, then I'll do it. By then my anger will have grown so hard & large & icy that I will be driven to it by fanatic zeal. Though it's hard to see myself in a fanatical role, I'm sufficiently furious that I can feel this purpose taking me over. I will not be Elizabeth's victim. It is *she* who has betrayed *me*. & I'll make her regret it—one way or another.

Monday 6/25/2096

Have been thinking it all out. Must be prepared to seize even the smallest opportunity. Tomorrow I will begin keeping track of the routine movements of everyone else on this island, as best I can, to sniff out their patterns. (They're probably going to be careless about things since in five years I've never once given any indication of being interested in escape.) I must find out where they keep their com-linked computer. (Oh that I had any mechanical skill at all—that I could rig something up with *my* terminal, which has been com-disabled since I arrived on this island.) Next I must see what kind of craft—air as well as water—are here. & see how well they guard such craft. & I must work harder to strengthen myself physically.

My objective in attempting escape must be making contact with Mama or Grandfather. I've thought & thought about it, & I think I can get Grandfather to help me, at least at first. Later, if Elizabeth should carry out her threat, he may decide to abandon me. But if she does, I'll then have a public existence. (& so will be able to nullify Elizabeth's power of attorney & have legal counsel at my elbow, ready to do battle for me.) She has no legal pretext for holding me. I have broken no laws. People may wonder about my role in Rbt's work, but there is no way of linking me to the abuses he ordered. I don't think Elizabeth would try to pursue me from that angle, since it would mean washing dirty linen in public she'd damned well prefer to keep private. Whatever she did, she'd have to approach it very carefully, because she herself could be too easily tainted.

If, of course, I get hold of the transcript, everything changes. But I can't count on finding it.

Grandfather will wonder why I allowed Elizabeth to hold me here virtually incommunicado, why I ever signed the power of attorney.

& then of course there's always the faint possibility of corrupting one of the amazons. Faint, but not unthinkable. In any case, I will make sure they continue thinking they can be as lax & careless as they like. I will mope a great deal, I think. Sort of wander around in my wheelchair, gloomy, depressed, restless, but ultimately inert. They will get used to seeing me roaming the island & will think nothing of it.

Disciplined, systematic, vigilant: I *will* outwit her. She's too contemptuous for her own good.

Chapter Fourteen

[i]

Margot Ganshoff was so Old School in her personal style and manner. Tea, served by her, required delicately painted, paper-thin china. And yet Emily knew for a fact that Margot picked up girls in the dance club on the top floor of the Diana two or three nights a week when she was resident in DC. She watched Margot pour out Formosa Oolong from the engraved silver pot and reflected that the Austrian probably lived in as many different worlds as she herself did.

Margot threw Emily a grumpy look. "If it weren't for this latest madness, I'd be in the Pacific Northwest now. No one ought to live in this place in the summer months. Elizabeth and Martha have damned rotten timing."

Emily accepted the cup of tea Margot handed her. Leave it to Margot to characterize the timing of an incident as "rotten" solely because she herself felt personally (and somewhat trivially) inconvenienced by it. "It's true that DC is unpleasant in the summer," she said. "And in general, the pollution in most executive cities is getting so bad that I'm thinking of investing in a portable respirator."

"It's no joke," Margot said. "Though don't put it off on the executive system." She smiled tightly. "In Austria things are not so bad." Her smile faded. "But then you don't remember what it was like before the Blanket in the high-industrial areas. Which I don't suppose San Diego ever was." She bit her lip. "And way back then we sometimes *did* wear respirators. Long before you were born, of course. In the old days before that unspeakable catastrophe in the Middle East and the subsequent drop in oil production made internal combustion engines too expensive to run." She took a sip of tea, then continued. "Normally it's not so bad. But when the temperature soars and a stationary front settles in, the stuff just sits there, refusing to move, piling up in ever greater concentration."

"Every breath I take out in the open air—which I'm trying to keep to a minimum," Emily said, "—feels as though it's searing my lungs."

"It probably is. Try to stay inside the buildings with the best air-filters. And of course drink plenty of water."

Emily took another sip of tea. "You should demand hardship pay for living here."

Margot put down her cup and leaned back and let the chair mold around her body. "As it happens, I do draw hardship pay. They know I'd rather have stayed in Seattle or returned to Vienna." Her eyes glinted. "But it seems I'm quite appreciated now." A little smile played around the corners of her mouth. "Everyone marvels that they made me First Secretary here." She snorted. "Which isn't the whole story. The only reason I'm not Ambassador is that if I were I wouldn't be able to make as many trips to Seattle as I need to." Emily scented complacency in Margot's self-mocking smile and tone. "The Ambassador takes his orders from me. Isn't that amusing, dear? Our distinguished old baron taking orders from a woman?"

"Is that so odd?" Emily asked, curious about Margot's air of weary triumph.

Margot gestured expansively. "Twenty years ago..." Her smile reappeared. "Twenty years ago it would have been unthinkable. That and the level of input I have in helping to formulate Austria's foreign policy. You see, what I worked out with the Marq'ssan and with Elizabeth Weatherall has made me damned near indispensable."

Emily finished the tea in her cup and leaned back in her chair. "As indispensable as Elizabeth is to the US Executive?" she said.

Margot's eyes narrowed. "*Is* Elizabeth indispensable?"

"That's what I was wondering."

Margot scrutinized Emily as closely as Emily had been scrutinizing her. "I wouldn't say she's indispensable," Margot finally said. "Right now..."

Emily finished what Margot had begun: "Right now she's inside a pressure cooker wanting to know if there's a safe way to let off steam."

Margot inclined her head. "That's essentially my assessment of the situation, too. At the moment she appears to be on a course that will force her into a head-on collision with Martha Greenglass and the Marq'ssan."

"Which, ultimately, she can't win," Emily said softly.

Margot's gaze met Emily's. "A head-on collision, no. No one could. But Elizabeth has other problems making it even less likely."

"And time isn't on the side of those opposing the Marq'ssan and their friends, either," Emily said.

"Nothing about what the Marq'ssan want and whether they can get us there is clear to *me*. But what is happening now with Elizabeth's Executive and Martha and the Marq'ssan *is*."

"Have you told Elizabeth so?"

Margot folded her hands and rested them high on her chest, just below her chin. "Jane Seely called the Ambassador into her office last Friday to inform him that the State Department thinks it high time for those in the international community who claim to uphold the principles of justice to take a stand against those who deliberately sabotage said principles." Frowning, Margot touched a control in the arm of her chair, and whining, the chair's leg-rest lifted until Margot's ankles were level with her knees. "Elizabeth's PA put me off when I called her office yesterday. I'm giving her one more chance, and then I'm going for a visit to Seattle."

"Taking care, of course," Emily said, "to let Elizabeth's office know where you can be reached?"

"Just so."

"I was hoping to see her myself," Emily said. "Does this mean she no longer hangs at the Diana?"

"Haven't seen her there in weeks," Margot said. "Don't even know if she's been in town. She knows how to make herself damned near invisible when she wants to."

Emily grinned. "I know her home address, though. And I know Allison Bennett's home address. And Lisa Mott's." A wave of gloom rolled over her. "I'll do what I have to to find her—for Celia's sake."

Margot rolled her eyes. "Ah yes. I remember reading that the locals grabbed her as soon as the Marq'ssan brought down that detention facility. There's little love lost on her at the Executive level, you can be certain. She's been a thorn in their flesh since the very beginning of Elizabeth's takeover."

"Maybe so, but I don't think the American Bar Association will be too pleased. Celia has *some* friends."

"You and Astrea are more to the point than a largely professional association," Margot said. "And you know it."

Emily got to her feet. "If only *she* knew it. I'll be going, Margot, so you can be getting back to work."

Margot disentangled herself from her chair. "How long are you going to be in DC?"

"As long as it takes me to see Elizabeth."

"A long time then," Margot said. "Maybe we should dine before I head off to Seattle."

Stepping out into the hot muggy air that made her eyes smart, it occurred to Emily that Elizabeth Weatherall owed her a favor that went back a long time. Ten years, in fact. Maybe it was time to remind Elizabeth of that.

Emily drove her rented two-seater back to the Diana. Sometimes favors owed could be as motivating a stimulus as blackmail. Not everything Daddy had taught her had to be jettisoned. And this *was* after all Elizabeth Weatherall she was dealing with.

[ii]

Emily peered through the peephole, then unlocked and opened the door. She asked Lisa Mott to come in, and they hugged, more lightly than in times past. "It's good to see you, Emily," Lisa said before giving way to a coughing fit. Emily fetched her a glass of water and asked her if she'd like some juice. Lisa shook her head. "No, don't bother, water is the best thing for this damned pollution. Helps our filters along." She took a lace handkerchief from her tunic pouch and wiped her eyes and blew her nose. "I don't have long," she said, sinking down into one of the two armchairs the relatively spartan room afforded. "I'm meeting Allison Bennett at the Symphony and have to go home, change, and pick up Ginger first."

Emily poured herself a glass of water and took the other armchair. "Basically, what I want to know is whether Elizabeth Weatherall is in town."

Lisa gave her an ironic look. "You requested that I come here in person simply for the sake of asking a question that could have been put over the phone?"

"I said *basically*." Emily watched Lisa's face. "Let's at least start with that."

Lisa bit her lip. "No. Elizabeth is out of town. I don't know where. She checks in with her office several times a day. That's all I know."

Emily stared incredulously at her. "You're Chief of Security and you don't know where Elizabeth Weatherall is? You seriously expect me to believe that?"

Lisa looked irritated. "She has her own security team handling her protection. And she doesn't *like* being subject to anyone else's surveillance. You think I'm going to cross her on a matter like that?"

Emily thought for a few seconds, then said, "Does she do this often?"

"What, go out of town without telling anyone where?"
Emily nodded.

"No. Not often. She's been doing it a lot lately. But it's highly unusual. She usually *wants* us to be able to reach her at any time."

Emily took a long drink of water. "Will you do me a favor, Lisa?"
Lisa raised her eyebrows.

"Will you contact me when you've knowledge that Elizabeth's back in town?"

"Why don't you leave a message with her office?"

"I'd rather do it this other way."

Lisa frowned into her water glass. After about half a minute she said, "I don't like the sound of this." She raised her gaze to Emily's face and searched Emily's eyes. "Explain," she said.

"I can't believe you don't trust me," Emily said. Lisa's eyes barely flickered. "All right." Emily sighed. "I have something I want to discuss with her. I know that if I leave a certain message for her she will probably agree to see me. And I don't care to leave the message until I know she'll be given it at once."

"Why don't you ask me to get you access?"

Emily shook her head. "She'd probably refuse. Because she will immediately realize I want to talk to her about Celia Espin."

"I imagine she'd see you if you just asked her PA for an appointment. After all, wasn't it true that you and Hazel Bell were going to be meeting with her—until, that is, Greenglass and the aliens blew this whole thing skyhigh?"

"I want to be sure she'll see me," Emily said. She half-smiled at Lisa. "I suppose you've forgotten she objected to both Celia and me as 'advisors' to Hazel?"

Lisa finished the water in her glass. "If the Free Zone leadership really want to do some negotiating with Elizabeth herself, your best bet would be Hazel alone. Because in the mood she's in now..." Lisa set her empty glass on the table between their chairs. "It's her old thing about Hazel, I think, that makes her willing to talk at all."

"She *said* that?"

"Of course not. This is Allison's theory." Lisa lowered her gaze and smoothed the hem of her russet silk tunic over her knees. "I can tell you this much: I send her the reports collected on Hazel's doings when she comes into the States." She looked up. "Just a listing of the places she's been and who she's seen. There's a tag on her plastic, you know, that identifies her as someone to be handled with care." Lisa shrugged. "The tag specifies that in case of trouble—which given the kinds of things she's getting into, isn't all that wild a possibility—my office is to be specially and immediately notified... Obviously she wants to make sure that in any, ah, trouble, Hazel will be treated well. What does that sound like to you?"

"I don't understand why you're telling me all of this, Lisa." It was such obvious ammunition to use against Elizabeth.

Lisa looked away. "I'm sure you can figure it out for yourself." She stood up. "I have to get out of here. God knows I've probably said too much already."

Emily saw Lisa to the door and watched her stride down the corridor to the bank of elevators. What had Lisa been trying to tell her? And why speak in riddles? Why not come right out and say whatever she had wanted Emily to know? Emily closed and locked the door and went into the bathroom and started a bath running. She did her best thinking in the bath.

[iii]

The insect-like stridulation of her handset dragged Emily out of an absurd dream in which the tentacles of a piece of Stuart Banner's sculpture had not only come to life but begun growing—growing to such a length that they penetrated the other studios in the building... Emily jerked herself awake as she fumbled open her handset. "Yes," she said thickly. "Hello."

"Emily, did I wake you?"

Emily struggled to identify the voice. "Oh, Lisa. Good morning. What time is it?"

"Seven-thirty, dear. I thought you'd like to know that Elizabeth returned to town last night."

"Oh," Emily said and came fully awake. "Yes, I'm glad you called to tell me." She could make an early attack then. "Have you let her know I'm going to try to see her?"

"No. I'd rather keep out of this, frankly."

So. She *would* be able to make a surprise attack. "Then I won't mention to her that you passed the news of her return on to me," Emily said, fairly certain Lisa wanted this reassurance.

"*D'accord*," Lisa said. "Well, I've got a full day ahead of me. Good luck."

"Thanks," Emily said. "I'll probably need it." She closed the handset and found that though the person lying beside her had her eyes closed, she was awake. Debra, wasn't it? "Do you mind if I open the drapes? Or is it too soon for you to be able to face light?" Emily lightly touched Debra's pastel-patterned shoulder.

Debra slitted her eyes and smiled lazily. "I don't mind. As long as there's glass between me and it."

Emily opened the control panel in the headboard and located the appropriate switch. At once the draperies swished open, and light flooded the room. Coffee next, she thought. Or no, a call to Margaret Canfield, who might be in her office already—judging by remarks Hazel had once made about Elizabeth's ability to inspire guilt feelings in the people working for her who did not keep the kind of hours Elizabeth herself kept.

"It's hazy out there," Debra said. "Every damned morning it's hazy." She stretched and yawned and wrapped her limbs around Emily. She tilted her head back to look into Emily's face. "But now that we have natural daylight, you can more fully appreciate my wonderful dye job." She threw back the covers and flung her arms and legs wide to show off her naked body.

"So it *is* dye," Emily said, touching the tinted skin and finding it as soft as the rest of her. "I was wondering how it could be so smooth and not smear. I was almost beginning to think it was a tattoo."

"Ugh, a tattoo? Then you'd be stuck with the same pattern forever. Tattoos are so past. Didn't you know? Anyway," she said, "this face- and body-painting thing is only a fad. Probably no one will be doing it a year from now."

"How long does the dye last?" Emily traced the pattern that curved down and around Debra's breasts and rippled over her ribs, a mosaic of subtly shifting tints and design flowing continuously from forehead to feet.

"About two weeks. I've had six different dye jobs so far."

"You're not worried about damaging your skin?"

"It's perfectly safe," Debra said. "Safer than wearing fixative, which is what *some* girls do. To keep the paint dry and set." She stroked Emily's belly. "The fixative stops the skin from breathing and clogs up the pores. Dye doesn't do that."

Emily groaned as Debra's fingers reached her pubic hair. "Before we get too involved, I have to make a phone call," she said, half-reminding herself.

"Are you sure you don't want to wait?"

"I'll be distracted if I don't do it first." Emily went to the desk to get her NoteMaster from her briefcase. She looked up the number Hazel had given her, went back to the bed, sat down, and tapped in the number. A female voice answered, repeating the number Emily had called. "Margaret Canfield, please," Emily said. The voice admitted to being Margaret Canfield. "This is Emily Madden, Margaret. I'd like you to give Elizabeth a verbatim message from me." Canfield told her to go ahead, that the call was being recorded. Emily drew a deep breath. "I'm interested to know, Elizabeth, whether your passion for

Louise Bourgeois art and sables is as strong today as it was ten years ago. You can contact me at the Diana, where I'm staying."

"That's the full message?"

"Yes."

"I'll see to it that Elizabeth hears the message as soon as she's free."

Emily thanked her and hung up. She wouldn't be surprised if she heard from Elizabeth within the hour. But she slipped back into bed and returned her attention to Debra.

[iv]

The pieces of the puzzle fell into place while Emily sat in the midst of a five-video installation piece set up in one of the oldest of the Collage Miscellany galleries. She had no idea why this insight about Lisa should come to her as she leaped from one to another of the various levels of meaning implicit in the piece. Perhaps her mind had been ruminating subconsciously on what Lisa had said to her, perhaps the connection between this piece and Hazel had struck resonances only subliminally perceptible to her. Moving from one "dining room" to another she could not help but be aware that Sylvia had worked out, explicitly, the details of Hazel's example from her own life of how differently reality can be constructed. *Somehow we must get Hazel here to see this.* To the four constructions Hazel's seminar had suggested to her, Sylvia had added a fifth, that of the six DC Collage Miscellany artists dining together.

Emily's moment of insight came while she was watching the video of the artists' drunken repartee. The writer in the group was battling the two performance artists over a semantic point. *But she wants a confrontation with the Marq'ssan no more than Margot does! Lisa wants Elizabeth to be persuaded against the course she's apparently decided to take. She may even feel, as Margot does, that fighting the Marq'ssan is a no-win situation!*

For a moment Emily doubted the conclusion she had leaped to. But thinking over the many and varied aspects of Lisa she had come to know through the years, she realized how convoluted and complex a person she was, and that this was something she had known about Lisa for a long time without ever having spelled it out for herself. Lisa had surprised her, for instance, with the fierceness with which she had shaken down Security after Elizabeth's coup. She hadn't believed that Lisa would be tough enough to pull it off—but had then had to admit that four years of waging successful renegade war with Elizabeth against Sedgewick and Booth had been sufficient to guarantee her "toughness." And what, after all, Emily had asked herself at the time, did she really know about that side of Lisa Mott? *Celia* had had no trouble believing Lisa to be tough: Celia's only doubts had been about Lisa's integrity when up against what Celia had called "Mott's own kind." Perhaps Lisa could see where the policy Elizabeth might be preparing to follow might lead, and seeing it felt the need to oppose it... Oppose it, yes, but without joining forces with Emily or Hazel or Martha. Lisa had made it clear that she would do nothing that might be interpreted as "conspiring" against Elizabeth. Emily got up from her chair and wandered out of the installation. Lisa might possibly give them more useful information than hints that Elizabeth still regretted the loss of an old lover, but Emily would not count on it.

[v]

The guards at the gate of Elizabeth's house as well as those standing sentry on her doorstep—all of them women—wore stylishly tailored mauve and gray uniforms—and respirator cannulae in their nostrils and oxygen canisters on their backs. The woman who drove Emily's two-seater away also wore mauve and gray. Thus when Emily saw the woman who opened the front door, the first thing she noticed was that she, too, wore mauve and gray. Livery, she thought to herself. Elizabeth has dressed all her service-techs in *livery*.

"How are you, Emily?" the woman said as she closed the door.

Emily took a second look. "Lacie! You're still with her?" Lacie had lost about thirty-five pounds since Emily had last seen her.

Lacie grinned. "Yeah. I may not be crazy about DC, but I've always liked working for Liz. So...here I am!" She swept her arm around the foyer. "I love this house. But let me take you back to her sitting room, she's expecting you."

Emily followed Lacie through halls crammed with art—old and celebrated work that could probably pay for this huge Georgetown house itself several times over, ranging from oils by Vermeer and Hals to at least two by Goya; a Turner and a Millais, a pair of Manets and several Picassos, Klimts, and Kandinskys. At the end of one of the halls Lacie opened a pair of tall doors and gestured her in. Emily did not at first see Elizabeth. Sunlight, filtered by brilliant green leaves and ferns, poured into the room through the floor-to-ceiling windows lining two and a half of its walls. It seemed enormous, an impression probably exaggerated by the lack of furniture. The room's thin delicate rectangles of rugs, small islands scattered over the warm gleaming parquet, held only cushions and small tables.

"Does that answer your question?" Elizabeth said.

Emily's gaze followed the voice and found Elizabeth—her green silk gown blending almost perfectly into the foliage on the other side of the glass—standing near the windows, her arm outstretched, her long index finger pointing. Emily's gaze moved along the trajectory Elizabeth indicated and came to rest on the Louise Bourgeois sculpture, positioned on a small table near the windows opposite Elizabeth.

"That's its usual place," Elizabeth said, dropping her arm. She moved toward Emily. "I'd wear the sable for you, but it's a bit warm for it, don't you think?" She bent and brushed her cheek against Emily's. "It's lovely to see you, dear. I promise you I'd never be so churlish as to forget your generosity to a fleeing renegade." She linked her right arm with Emily's left, then clasped Emily's upper arm with her left hand.

"I hope you don't mind my informality?" Elizabeth said before Emily could think of a response. "I find clothing more and more chafing the older I get. If you'd like, I can lend you a gown. You're about Allison's size, aren't you? She keeps a whole closet-full here. You'd be much more comfortable, you know."

Emily demurred, wondering at Elizabeth's prattle. She had never known Elizabeth to be so garrulous.

"If you change your mind, let me know. Unless you object, I thought we'd eat in here. It's light quite late at this time of year. And anyway I detest sitting in the dining room, I only do it when I must. Which is all too often these days."

Nervousness? *Elizabeth?* Gazing up into Elizabeth's face, puzzling over the extraordinary amount of color in Elizabeth's eyes—a blue that shaded into green—it appeared to her that Elizabeth's pupils were far more contracted than the amount of light in the room warranted. "I've never experienced such terrible pollution," she said, uncomfortable in the silence as she and Elizabeth stood with their arms still linked. "What makes it so bad here?"

Elizabeth drew Emily to a low table that had been laid with two place settings of linen, china, silver, and crystal. Emily sat where Elizabeth indicated and noticed that her own place-setting included wine glasses. "There's a great debate raging about which circumstances contribute most to the pollution," Elizabeth said, taking Emily's water goblet and pouring from a crystal water decanter in which floated a slice of lemon. "But the most basic problem—apart, of course, from the weather—is a bad site south along the Potomac that has been leaking." Elizabeth set Emily's goblet down and picked up her own. "Apparently it was all supposed to be neatly and safely contained for centuries to come." Elizabeth placed the decanter on the rug beside her. "Believe me, we've discussed the damned thing often enough in Cabinet meetings. Enderby—he's my Secretary of Energy & Environment—wants to re-contain it and try again. Which would be the cheapest thing in the short-run we could do. But Rossellini—Science & Tech—favors a new, more costly method. One he claims would have a better chance of permanently containing the stuff. And in the meantime we're all breathing the damned poison." Elizabeth eyed Emily over the rim of her glass. "I'd not be in DC now—nor any of the Cabinet, for that matter—if it weren't for this damned alien crisis."

Lacie wheeled in a serving cart, sparing Emily the necessity of answering. "Just serve us the soup, Lacie, and we'll help ourselves to the rest—if you have everything on that cart already?"

Lacie set an ice-frothed bowl of pale green soup garnished with thin slices of cucumber, baby dill, and sour cream before Emily. "Everything but the coffee and dessert, Liz." She brought a half-bottle of white Bordeaux to the table and poured some into one of Emily's wine glasses. Emily glanced speculatively at Elizabeth. Lacie set the wine bottle down near Emily and said that she had already opened the other bottle, which was chilling in a thermowrap on the cart.

"Thanks, Lacie." Elizabeth smiled warmly at her.

Lacie went quietly out, closing the doors after her. For the first time Emily noticed the two Renoirs hanging side by side on the wall near the doors. "From the little I've seen of this house, you certainly have a stunning art collection," Emily said as she dipped her spoon into the soup.

Elizabeth glanced over at the Renoirs and gave Emily an oddly sharp look. "As a matter of fact, I don't personally own most of the art in this house."

Who would lend so much valuable art to an *individual?* Emily wondered. "But of course," Emily said with a smile. "Artwork cannot *really* be possessed. One may *hold* it for a while..." Emily watched Elizabeth, curious to see how she would respond. In her experience, executives typically responded to that assertion with hostility.

"Mere semantics." Elizabeth swallowed a sip of her soup. "It's long been established that possession is nine-tenths of the law."

Emily grinned. "Yes, a good demonstration of law's origins in the jungle."

Elizabeth stared at her. "I suppose that means you've become an anarchist?"

"This cucumber soup is delicious."

Elizabeth rather self-consciously stared down at her soup and took another spoonful. She swallowed and looked again at Emily. "You risked your own safety for me by accepting and keeping my possessions safe, Emily. I will always appreciate that. But you do realize there are limits to the favors I can grant."

Emily took her first sip of the wine. "Celia's being stubborn. Martha and Hazel are being stubborn. And apparently many executives are being stubborn."

Elizabeth's mouth tightened. "You're going to have to be a little more explicit."

Emily dabbed her lips with her napkin. "The favor is simply this: to have Celia Espin released from detention and all charges or potential charges against her dropped."

Elizabeth's lips twisted. "You call that *simple?*"

"No," Emily said, "I didn't call that simple. I said that that one request is what the favor would—simply—consist of."

"I might as well tell you straight off that as soon as they arrested Espin I applied pressure to accomplish just that," Elizabeth said. "But now...as time passes, the nature of the problem changes."

"You can't have applied much pressure," Emily said.

Elizabeth flashed her a sardonic smile. "Oh but my dear, remember how your father dug in his heels when the Executive first tried to get him to behave? While we've managed to get Dowsanto to agree, the local DA's office has so far proven intractable. Not that we couldn't eventually prevail, but we'd incur significant losses in the process."

Emily put down her spoon. Her appetite seemed to have vanished. "Let me put it this way, Elizabeth. The only reason the Marq'ssan haven't done something about Celia is Celia's stubbornness and illusions about the law. After a time I will simply disregard her wishes and act. But be warned that you might lose more than that one detention facility you've already lost."

Elizabeth drank more water. "Do you want the next course now?"

Emily glanced over at Elizabeth's bowl and saw that Elizabeth had hardly touched her soup. She shook her head. "Don't rush on my account. I don't seem to be very hungry."

"Perhaps we should wait and eat the rest of the meal later. It's an entirely cold meal."

"As you like." If they could thrash this out in the next few minutes, she could escape earlier than she had hoped.

"I have a suggestion to make." Elizabeth half-smiled, and Emily raised her eyebrows. "Let's go upstairs and sit in my Jacuzzi. We can sweat out all the damned pollution and relax at the same time."

Emily laughed uncertainly. "You're serious?"

"Yes, I know, executives don't sit in Jacuzzis together." Elizabeth's eyes glittered. "But you're not exactly a respecter of taboos, are you."

Emily frowned. "Because I live in the Free Zone?"

"Because you take men as sexual partners," Elizabeth said, staring very hard now at Emily.

Emily's throat tightened. "You've had Lisa spying on me?" So. Lisa had rushed to tell her about Hazel yet had neglected to mention that she had given Elizabeth material with which she might conceivably manage to blackmail her.

"Years ago," Elizabeth said. "Before I even thought of going renegade. I simply assume that you still take male sexual partners."

"What makes you think I'd care whether that got out?"

"I imagine you'd mind being ostracized, since you do still live in the executive world when it suits you to." She got to her feet in one swift, fluid movement. "But I'm not in the least interested in blackmailing you." She stared down at Emily. "And to prove it I'm willing to share something similar about myself with you." A little smile flickered around the edges of her mouth. "But only if you come into the Jacuzzi with me."

Emily got to her feet. If Elizabeth had intended to knock her off balance, she had succeeded. What in the hell was going on here? And why the diversion? What did Elizabeth think she could persuade or coerce her to? "All right, Elizabeth," she said, "I'll play." Out of curiosity more than anything, Emily thought, though her level of uneasiness, rising steadily since her arrival, had now reached record proportions. With Elizabeth behaving so strangely she felt out of her depth. Following Elizabeth out of the room, she tried to feel it out. But the terrain, so unfamiliar, offered her no clues, intuitive or otherwise.

[vi]

Emily hung her clothing in the closet that held Allison's gowns and chose from it a garment of deep plum. Why, she wondered curiously, would Allison keep her gowns in Elizabeth's dressing room rather than in a closet in another bedroom? At a guess this house must have at least ten bedrooms. Perhaps they regularly took Jacuzzis together? It would be unusual, but then Elizabeth made her own rules. Emily draped the gown over her arm and went into the bathroom. Elizabeth, already stretched out in the tub, openly watched Emily toss the gown onto a stool and approach. Emily crouched and let herself down into the water. *It's as though she's daring me.* Had they entered some sort of competition? Should she deliver a stinging put-down, to warn Elizabeth to back off from whatever game she was playing?

"You've put on a little weight since that day you sported in the mountain stream," Elizabeth said, her voice carrying easily above the churning roar of the whirlpool.

"What an eye and memory for detail."

Elizabeth half-turned and reached over her shoulder. The noise of the whirlpool abated, and the reduced force of the jets barely frothed the water. "Sorry," Elizabeth said, smiling, "I didn't catch what you said?"

Emily slid far enough down to rest her head on the foam rubber niche tucked under the rim of the tub. "I was simply marveling at your eye and memory for detail."

"I didn't mean to suggest I thought the extra weight unattractive."

Emily lifted her head so that she could see Elizabeth's face. "Tell me, Elizabeth. Is it your contention that my accepting your invitation to join you in your Jacuzzi is in its turn an invitation for insult? Or do you feel free to insult me because you think I'll allow you to blackmail me?"

"Insult wasn't intended," Elizabeth said. "You're being overly sensitive, dear."

Should she get out of the tub now? "Perhaps you're going to tell me you talk to other executive women that way?" Emily said sarcastically.

"But we're different," Elizabeth said. "Obviously you don't care about the unwritten rules any more than I do."

Emily sat up; stretching out her arms she braced her hands against the sides of the tub. "The reason I said 'other executive women' is because they're probably the only group of people someone like you is likely to treat with the respect everyone deserves to be treated with. I frankly find your attitude toward service-tech women deplorable. But then I generally don't go around telling other people how to behave. It's not my way. Unless that behavior directly affects me—as in this case."

"Are you trying to claim you've given up girls?"

"I enjoy sex; of course I haven't given up sleeping with women. Or men. But that doesn't mean I have to play the games you play." She thought of how Debra, like too many others before her, felt so bowled over (probably without knowing why) by the way in which Emily treated her that she had insisted that Emily not pay for their time together. And even now, tonight, Debra was hoping to come to her after finishing her shift in one of the lounges.

"And lord do you play!" Elizabeth said, apparently missing the point. "You're the dilettante of dilettantes, running from one city to another playing your art game, strewing sex like rose petals along the way of your path. Imagine my astonishment when I heard you were to be one of Hazel's party! How did she manage to drag in someone who does nothing but play?"

"Oh I just don't know." Emily was irritated in spite of herself. "I must not have been paying attention when she invited me in."

Elizabeth smiled knowingly. "You're doing it again. Trying to hold on to both roles, both worlds. To keep all the perks and privileges of being an executive and none of the responsibilities. While playing around with subversives, pretending—probably to yourself even—to be on their side."

"Now that you have me neatly packaged and labeled," Emily said ironically, "perhaps we can get down to business?" She should insist they get out of the tub and dress. How could they talk seriously sitting together in the raw, especially after all the crap Elizabeth had introduced into the conversation?

"I had no intention of making you hostile," Elizabeth said. "I apologize, Emily. You just got my dander up. Nor had I any intention of insulting you, packaging you, or labeling you."

"Perhaps we'd have a more reasonable discussion if we were fully clothed," Emily said, looking around for the soap.

"But I wanted to offer you something to make clear that I'm not interested in threatening you."

"I'm tired of this, Elizabeth."

"I've botched it. And made you impatient besides." She bit her lip. "I've had an executive lover for years, Emily. How's that for breaking the rules?"

As though she were bragging, Emily thought. Why the hell else would she be telling me such a thing? "Do you think that matters to me?" Emily said.

"An executive woman lover," Elizabeth said. "Until recently."

"Such constancy," Emily said sarcastically. "I didn't know you had it in you."

"You don't know me very well."

"No more than you know me."

After a pause, Elizabeth said, "Women like us are rare, Emily. I'm realizing it more all the time." She sighed. "There's hardly anyone who isn't after me in some way or another. Factions who'd like to topple me. Plenty of people who hate my guts for the way I cleaned them out of the Executive. And now there's a rising hostility among the men against the women. It was something I hadn't planned for. Lisa

Mott started a training program for amazons. So now every executive woman wants amazons instead of gorillas. The men get upset when they see us running around with women bodyguards. They're paranoid. They even bring the sex issue into Executive meetings—where they still, of course, outnumber us. If I don't give the impression of reacting as a man would—and the damned bastards are starting to forget how much they lost through Sedgewick's tactics—if they think I'm being at all *soft*, they'll have an excuse to dump me. Oh, I still have the banks with me. But the others are as howling wolves. And then, with all this crap Greenglass has stirred up, I've realized how I haven't even *touched* the local level, not really. That's what the whole Espin affair has taught me. Just how little control I have, even with all my vast power."

Elizabeth's eyes, Emily noticed, matched the aqua-colored porcelain of the tub. "Let me explain to you," Emily said, "why I can't offer you sympathy, Elizabeth."

Elizabeth's mouth twisted. "Oh, that's easy enough to figure out for myself," she said bitterly. "Since you've never been in a position of responsibility and have in fact chosen the more romantic position of opposing anyone at all responsible while championing the *underdogs*, you can't possibly have the remotest idea of the kind of pressure I'm under." Elizabeth brushed a stray blonde hair out of her eyes. "You young women, those of you who were born with everything, you're the worst. Easy enough for you to turn up your nose at my achievement. Easy enough for you to decide you don't want power. It's always been yours for the taking, right from the start. That and being born into a system that works." Elizabeth shook her head. "I bet you complain a lot about the executive system. About the women's code. But if you had any idea how much easier your life is for it—"

Elizabeth's eyes filled with tears, and she swallowed; Emily was taken aback at this show of emotion. "I was born *before* the Executive Transformation, Emily. I was twenty-one when it officially 'took place.'" Elizabeth sniffed. "But it didn't happen all at once, the way it sounds—that date was merely the finalization, the formalization of changes that had been in train since before I was born. Fixing. Have you ever thought about what a shock it was when the first males had themselves fixed?" Elizabeth swallowed again. "I was there, Emily. I saw it. I saw what happened, though I was too young to understand. My father got himself fixed when I was eleven." She stared hard at Emily. "You say your mother lives in a weird heterosexual set-up. Well let me tell you, Emily, my parents were *married*, and were fully sexual when my father got fixed. Not only got fixed, but underwent aversion therapy. So that he'd never want to touch my mother again. Can you imagine what it was like for *her*? Do you wonder why I hate men so? Apparently he did it because he was told that he'd stop getting promotions if he didn't. He was a diplomat. We were living in Paris at the time. He flew back to the States and did it. And then saw a therapist in Paris.

"I was there that first year after he did it. And then they sent me off to school. To Crowder's. The headmistress was an executive woman. She understood what was going on, what changes were coming down. She conducted the sex education classes herself—needless to say, none of the teachers at the school had any idea of what was happening. My second year there we heard of two scandals, one involving two executive women—wives of men who'd been fixed—having an affair. The other scandal involved some other 'wife' being caught with a male professional. All hell broke loose. You'd better believe we discussed it at Crowder's. The women involved in those scandals lost everything. I mean *everything*. We were paying attention, Emily. And the headmistress made sure we understood. Another thing became clear, too—a tendency of such women to alcoholism." Elizabeth laughed. "Do you think any of us would ever want to look at a man, given what we'd seen for ourselves? My father's obnoxiousness to my mother..." Elizabeth exhaled a long, shaky sigh. "You have no idea how things were back then. You have no idea why we have these unwritten rules." She laughed shortly. "The biggest losers are the women not only of my mother's generation but of my generation as well who can't handle having sex with girls." Elizabeth barked another of those short laughs. "Not that whole-hearted loving is anything but an exercise in futility and self-delusion."

Elizabeth fell silent. Emily remained motionless, unable to think of anything appropriate to say. Elizabeth lifted her gaze and half-smiled at Emily. "Ah, how terribly bitter and negative of me, you're thinking. Believe it or not, there was a time when I believed in devoting myself to people rather than to doing things. But there's never much return. It's too much trouble for the people one loves. Or else they simply take it for granted without ever returning the love. I've seen other women destroyed by their persistence in thinking their purpose in life is to share their love." Elizabeth laughed again. "But why am I saying this to you? Love isn't one of your concerns, either. In fact, you're not cast in any of the old molds, are you." She reached for the soap. "Here I am ranting on and on at you. Boring you to death no doubt. I'm sure you've had enough of this Jacuzzi. Let's wash and get out."

Emily soaped and rinsed, climbed out of the tub, and took a towel from the nearest rack. "You're trying to excuse yourself for having constructed a situation in which you believe you have no way out but the one you've chosen to take," Emily said.

Elizabeth submersed to rinse. She switched off the motor, then lifted herself out of the tub, giving Emily an eyeful of just how powerfully muscled her body was. "It's funny," she said, "I can't remember ever telling anyone all that. Only one person knows all that about me, and that's because she went through it with me. An old friend who went to Crowder's with me." She patted herself dry. "That must mean I trust you, Emily." Elizabeth, still sitting on the floor, smiled up at her. "Don't you think so?"

Emily debated dressing in her own clothing. Elizabeth was behaving so unpredictably that Emily could easily imagine wanting to get away quickly and without hindrance. Yet what if she could find a way to get through to Elizabeth, given the kind of mood she was in? Slipping into the gown, she said, "I have no idea how you feel about me, Elizabeth. It sounds to me as though you're both resentful of and defensive toward me. For reasons obscure to me."

Elizabeth tossed her braid over her shoulder, rose to her feet, and picked up the gown she had been wearing earlier. "That should be easy enough to understand," she said as she pulled it over her head. "You've so clearly turned up your nose at what I've had to fight so hard for. Perhaps precisely because you had all the advantages to start with." Elizabeth looked at Emily. "You've had choices I never had. Career-line or a maternity contract were my only choices. And as a career-line executive woman starting from the bottom—" She shook her head. "You simply cannot imagine, Emily. I could have chosen to

be down-trodden, acquiescent, and overly-dependent on the usual social life. But I took the other road, the road of ambition. And I have no
regrets about that." She smiled and moved to take Emily's arm. "My
appetite has returned. Let's go downstairs and dine, shall we?"

Emily allowed Elizabeth to take her arm. She would try. Elizabeth
was demanding something of her and demanding it in such a way
as to render her intensely uncomfortable. But still, since she could
not see walking away from this rare opportunity, however delusive it
might be, she would try.

[vii]

"This poached salmon is delicious—and the herbed mayonnaise
perfect," Emily said before sipping the chardonnay Elizabeth had insisted she drink with the entrée.

"I agree." Elizabeth ate another bite with obvious relish.
"Unfortunately I don't have time these days to get into the kitchen
myself. But the cook I have—a French Canadian who trained with a
first-class chef—is always competent and sometimes inspired."

"You've talked a lot tonight about pressures and choices and so on,"
Emily said, intent on getting their conversation on course. "I'd like to
offer you a different perspective than the one you're working from."

Elizabeth sighed. "Of course. You want to tell me why I should
back down from a confrontation with Martha Greenglass."

"I'm not identical with Martha." Emily dipped a bite of salmon
into the mayonnaise. "And I don't consider our interests identical, either. I'm speaking only for myself. I want you to be clear on that."

Elizabeth dabbed her napkin to her lips. "But Hazel seems quite
sure you're on their team."

"And Hazel isn't identical with Martha, either," Emily said, watching Elizabeth's face for signs of what Lisa had hinted at. "You're the
one who uses the word *team*. We may from time to time work cooperatively, we may talk a great deal to one another, but that doesn't mean
our perspectives are the same. I don't think you appreciate the level of
diversity that exists in the Free Zone."

Elizabeth flashed a sardonic smile at Emily. "You know, Emily,
there was a time when I believed that. About what you call their diversity. But I'm not sure I believe in that diversity any more. Except

as a sort of veneer they plaster over everything in order to convince themselves that they are "freer" than they would be in the executive system. The truth is, they're entirely monolithic in practical terms—namely, they never let differences divide them enough to keep from effectively opposing the Executive. But within the Free Zone—and now, presumably, as they attack the Executive head-on..." Elizabeth drank from her water goblet.

Emily swallowed a bite of fish. "That's what you think they're doing? Attacking the Executive?"

"Greenglass knew exactly what was going to happen when she showed up in Baton Rouge. She planned the whole thing down to the smallest detail."

Elizabeth ate another bite of salmon, and Emily realized that they had gotten off the subject. "You do know, Elizabeth, that the Marq'ssan could be using their destructuring powers to be ridding you of that leaking pollution site instead of destroying executive property." Emily ate a bite of tender peas flecked with slivered mint leaves.

Elizabeth stared at her without speaking. After about half a minute she said, "At what price?"

"You don't think accomplishing such feats would give you a better seat on the tiger you're riding? Maybe you're looking so fixedly at one side of the equation that you can't see the other side at all."

"Beware of she who speaks in too many metaphors," Elizabeth said, reaching for her glass. Emily watched her drink and guessed that she was stalling. Elizabeth set her glass down, picked up her fork, and prepared another bite. "By the tiger you mean, of course, the people who allowed me to depose Sedgewick and Booth." She lifted the bite of fish to her mouth.

"You think only of executives as maintaining or threatening your power," Emily said. "You don't see anyone else as carrying weight. Isn't that true?"

"They're my power base. I freely admit it. And so it must be in countries in the executive-system. Just as it would be the mullahs in Islam, the Party in the PRC. I think that's self-evident, don't you?"

"So by that view the people you call anarchists could only serve to erode your power base."

Elizabeth snorted. "They sure as hell won't enhance it."

Emily took a long swallow of wine. "Let me ask you this, Elizabeth. Are you satisfied with what you've gotten? Do you feel secure? Are you able to accomplish what you set out to do? Or do you feel squeezed and constrained to do the bidding of powerful interests both within and outside what you consider your power base?"

Elizabeth finished swallowing the last bite on her plate. "You're referring to my grousing about the pressure I'm under."

"You've already admitted you haven't been able to get the local executives in Baton Rouge to release Celia."

Elizabeth moved back a little from the table and drew her knees up to her chest. "Believe me, I intend to begin tackling the local level. But it will take time. I've only been running the Executive for five years. I'm pleased with what I've so far accomplished. Who would have believed I could reform both Military and Security as I've done? And so I will manage to reform at the local level, too."

"But the Marq'ssan aren't going to go away. Nor is Martha Greenglass." Emily fingered the stem of her wine glass. "Have you forgotten certain facts about the Marq'ssan? That they could, if they chose, wipe out all Military property in this country in a month's time? That they could shut down this country with another Blanket? That they could destroy all the dozens of satellites you've spent so many re-sources on getting back into orbit? That they could destroy your major industries? That they—"

"Enough, Emily. You've made your point." Elizabeth didn't *quite* snarl the words.

"Or they could help you clean up this country's ground water aquifers," Emily said softly. "As we've done in the Free Zones, or as is currently being done in Austria, Ecuador, and New Zealand."

"The price," Elizabeth said. "The price is too high."

"Talk to Margot Ganshoff."

"Austria is a propaganda show-piece designed to lull every other government on Earth. The aliens are damned savvy when it comes to human psychology."

"Well," Emily said, "then I guess you'll have to be prepared to lose everything again. Because if you try confrontation with the Marq'ssan you'll lose. And you'll lose your power base at the same time. Your supporters aren't going to be very happy with you if their precious economy gets wrecked."

"I've had reports," Elizabeth said angrily, "showing that the Austrians are being squeezed. It's only a matter of time until Austria turns into a Free Zone. And then where will Margot Ganshoff be? She'll have brought it on herself."

"I wonder, what I should tell Hazel. She's going to want to know if I think it worthwhile for her to talk to you."

Elizabeth stared at her. After about a minute of intense silence she said, "I thought you said you were speaking only for yourself."

"That's true," Emily said. "And my main concern at this moment is for Celia Espin. But naturally I'll discuss this conversation with Hazel. You see she's not at all sure that this is a time for talking to you or any of your people. Since you now seem to favor confrontation rather than negotiation."

"Negotiation," Elizabeth said tartly, "presupposes an equal need or desire on both sides to resolve a conflict."

"Yes." Emily smiled. "And the need is greater on your side than on ours."

Elizabeth pressed her lips together, got to her feet, and cleared their dishes from the table. "Dessert will have to be fetched from the kitchen," she said.

"I'll pass on the dessert," Emily said, also rising to her feet. "I think I'll go upstairs and change. We've just about covered everything, haven't we." Emily moved toward the double doors.

Elizabeth stretched out her hand and touched Emily's sleeve. "It's early yet. Interested in going out somewhere?"

"No, Elizabeth, I don't think so."

Elizabeth edged closer. "I'll think about what you've said. Are you going to be in DC much longer, if I should want to talk again?"

"No. It looks as though I can be more effectively placed elsewhere."

Elizabeth's eyes glinted. "I will do everything I can to get Celia Espin released, Emily. I can promise you that. I'm fully aware of how much I owe you."

"Then my visit wasn't entirely wasted." Emily moved to open the door, but stopped when Elizabeth, who moved with her, touched her face. She turned her head and looked directly up into Elizabeth's eyes.

Elizabeth inched closer. "Emily, I——"

"No, Elizabeth," Emily said, aware of her face burning. Could she be misunderstanding Elizabeth's look and touch?

Elizabeth's hand dropped. "Why not? Because we're both executives?" Emily could see Elizabeth's lips trembling. "Or because of my age?"

Emily swallowed. "I don't feel anything sexual for you, Elizabeth. It's nothing to do with your age—which god knows doesn't show—or with your being an executive."

"How do you know you won't unless you try? Or do you only try sure things?"

"It probably has something to do with what I know of how you think of your sexual partners," Emily said—only because Elizabeth seemed to want to press the issue.

Elizabeth's mouth twisted. "You know nothing about that. And as I've already mentioned, I've had an executive lover for years." When Emily put her hand on the doorknob, Elizabeth rushed on, "I thought you were more adventurous than that."

"Let it be, Elizabeth." Emily yanked open the door. "Just let it be." She glanced over her shoulder as she stepped into the hall and saw that Elizabeth had flushed scarlet. Trembling, Emily set off for the staircase at a half-run. Her desire to get out of Elizabeth's house drove everything else out of her head. She hoped Elizabeth would not follow her upstairs. They had already had enough awkward and strange exchanges this evening to last them for years.

Chapter Fifteen

[i]

This set of jailers—small-town cops with strange accents—have decided to let her read the local newspaper. Celia eagerly takes it when the guard slides it between the iron, paint-flecked bars, carefully averting her eyes from the dirt under fingernails overrun by their cuticles. She murmurs something polite and listens to his receding footsteps echo through the otherwise empty lock-up. Last night and this morning there had been a bit of excitement: a loudly obscene drunk had been brought in, charged with public intoxication because of his obstreperousness. The paper is thin, but then it's local. She unfolds the few flimsy sheets. *The Teche News*, the letterhead proudly proclaims, St. Martinville, LA. So that's where she is now? In St. Martinville? But where *is* St. Martinville? *Where? In Louisiana, stupid.*

The paper offers no national news. Nor even Baton Rouge or New Orleans news, for that matter. The first page carries three stories. The story accorded the dubious honor of claiming the headline involves a debate over whether the public library should close at five or at five-thirty on Saturdays. It seems the librarian, a respected professional aged eighty-three ("Miss Juliette") insists that if the town's inhabitants want the library to stay open that late on Saturdays, an extra part-time service-tech clerk must be hired to stay late and lock up since the only part-time service-tech assisting Miss Juliette already worked as many hours as the library's budget allowed. The other stories consist of a description of the birthday party of a local notable's daughter and an interview with the parish priest concerning the space crisis at the cemetery.

The rest of *The Teche News* (twelve pages in all) boasts mainly advertisements, legal notices, a list of police arrests and citations for the previous week's misdemeanors, chatty columns of gossip, and three letters to the editor (two of which concerned the controversy about the library's Saturday closing time). Celia, of course, reads every word of the paper, neglecting not even the lost and found column. She's never been so bored in her life as she is sitting in these hot, humid, back-country mildewed-walled, cockroach-, stinkbug-, and fly-infested jails. Even *The Teche News* is preferable to life without print.

[ii]

The air-conditioning dries the sweat on her skin, and Celia shivers. They have brought her to Baton Rouge so that she can have a visit from her legal counsel. But she and Jodie are allowed to talk only in the presence of guards, presumably in case they pass information to one another about any plans the Marq'ssan may have. The guard opens a door and tells Celia to enter. Inside, Jodie sits at a table. Her gaze goes to Celia's, and in that first moment of recognition Celia can see Jodie's relief rapidly succeeded by a searching look of critical inspection. Celia understands—she herself has looked at clients in precisely that way, many many times.

Celia smiles. "Thanks so much for the cotton shirts," she says. "You have no idea what a difference they've made." Washing one out in the chemical shower she is allowed once daily, she then has the other to wear. Given the conditions in her cells, a shower an hour would still have left her stinking and feeling filthy; yet she has a keen appreciation for how good it is to be able to clean herself once a day while in detention, how wonderful to have real clothing to wear, however crumpled, stained, and sweat-laden it may be.

Celia sits across from Jodie. Two guards stand against the wall near the door, bored. Jodie flips on the NoteMaster and takes a yellow pad out of her attaché case. First she tells Celia about the "quiet investigation" the American Bar Association has begun conducting. Then she tells Celia that Dowsanto has promised not to press charges, which means the list of possible felony counts against her has shrunk (though not vanished entirely). And finally she tells Celia that Emily has been active on her behalf, having been twice to Baton Rouge, as well as Washington, DC, to "see people," and that Emily says there are major plans under way and that Celia had better not be a fool about it, either. Jodie smiles as she relays this last bit. "I like Emily," she says. "She's different from anyone I've ever known, but she has an amusing wit. I think she may be a little pissed-off at you, Celia."

Celia rolls her eyes. "Can't you press the issue a little harder to force Guidry to formally file charges?"

"This is basically a hostage situation," Jodie says.

"There's nothing legal about holding hostages."

"Yeah well I said that to Guidry, and he just snarled at me about your paying for this terrible outrage against the People of the Sovereign State of Louisiana."

"How long can he go without filing?"

"You're a material witness. It's discretionary with the court."

"Can't you appeal over Partee's head?"

"I'm trying, Cee. Give me time."

Celia nods, satisfied. She understands well how slowly things sometimes move. That's the way of the law.

[iii]

Given the choice of having the ceiling light on or off, Celia has chosen to have it on. The presence of a kind of cockroach previously unknown to Celia—enormous black, hard-shelled creatures that scuttle with sinister speed—makes her stomach heave. She knows they swarm over the concrete at night; several times now when she has had to get up in the night to use the toilet she has *felt* them—discovering one as she slipped into her shoe, hearing and feeling them crunching under her shoes with a sound that sends shivers up her spine (in the morning discovering only a stain on the floor—demonstrating that they are not susceptible to perishing by accident).

But staring up at the ceiling, trying not to be suspicious of every sensation on her skin (once fleas have taken up residence on one's body one's imagination tends to leap rampant), she finds herself unable to stop thinking about the look on a certain guard's face. On her arrival this morning he hung around in the narrow corridor outside the cell, leaning against the wall staring past the bars at her: "making conversation." *Ain't had a female in here since that shoplifting case last winter. And they say you a lawyer. Never had one like you in here.* At "dinner" offering to let her have some tabasco sauce for her bowl of tepid tubefood. His fingers touching hers as he passed the bottle through the bars to her… Celia, shivering, wondering if he could see or even smell her fear of men like him, tried to speak with lawyerly authority, all the time desperately hoping he'd stay on the other side of the bars—and he the only one in the entire police station. Just the two of us here, he said, just you and me.

Insomniac, Celia realizes that whoever is directing her peregrinations can't be too worried about security around her. The only time they bother to pay attention is in the larger jails and while transporting her from one place to another.

The days have begun to blur; Celia's starting to feel lost in time. Lost in this other world. The prisoner's world, she knows, is always another place and time. Yet…in these backwater jails, in these places where people speak in accents and idioms she can scarcely decipher, the guards variously address her as "Miss Espin" or "ma'am" (though that one guard looks at her in that way), she is in places she has never heard of…caught, as it were, in a time- or place-warp. The routine familiar, yet the *feel* of it not.

She composes statements in her head. Statements for Guidry and Partee. Statements for Emily. And a piece of her mind for Martha, too.

And then that question lurking, always there beneath the surface whether she speaks it within the safety of her mind or not: what she would do if/when the Marq'ssan broke her, too, out… If they destroyed the jail she inhabited, what would she do, cling to the guard? Or, on being returned home, would she fly back to Baton Rouge to throw herself into the arms of Guidry and Partee? Such thoughts sound like nonsense to her. How to find a reasonable course of action among such absurdities? *You've made a fool of me, Martha Greenglass. You've made a joke of The Law, an asinine joke, damn you.*

Patience. She needs to hold tight to her patience and wait for Jodie to extricate her by legal means—and then go after those bastards Partee and Guidry. Or perhaps Hazel would succeed in manipulating Weatherall into dealing with them. Either way, only those two solutions could work. Anything else would make a mess and mockery of her life and values and principles. And Martha Greenglass, damn her, should respect that.

[iv]

This time when the van door opens and Celia, handcuffed and ankle-chained, clumsily gets herself out, the fact that she's again at the now-familiar Baton Rouge loading dock registers—but only dully, brushing up against but not impacting the massive indifference she's steeped in. The sudden evaporation of sweat followed by gooseflesh makes a greater impression on her than the prospect of seeing Jodie (if, indeed, that is the purpose of her being brought here). As she trudges through the corridors, faint wisps of memory come and go in her thoughts, traces of the stupid hopefulness she felt most of the other times she has walked through these corridors. How many times has she been here now? Celia can't be bothered to attempt a count. It seems she's been doing the same things over and over and over again. She's been back to some of the same jails several times now. Everything routine. Ad infinitum…literally, it seems.

Jodie stretches her hand across the table and takes hold of Celia's. "I've brought you more clothing," she says, indicating a transparent plastic sack that appears to hold a shirt and underwear.

Celia forces herself to make the effort to nod. Then she stares down at the humidity-swollen sticky wooden table her hands and forearms rest on. The humidity gets to everything. No wonder every bedpad she's slept on has smelled like mildew. No wonder the smell of mold (when the smell of urine mixed with chemical isn't stronger) is always in her nostrils. No wonder metal bars and concrete walls cannot hold their flaking coats of paint. Everything is decrepit, moldering, decaying. Ad infinitum the process of death and decay goes on in this place where even the outdoors smells fetid.

"Celia," Jodie's voice calls her back. Effortfully she lifts her eyes to Jodie's face. "Celia, don't you want to hear the news?"

Why bother? But Celia plays the game. "What news?"

"A group of New Orleans attorneys have an appointment with Partee next week."

"Wonderful," Celia says.

"The other news isn't good," Jodie says and runs her hand—the one not still sweatily grasping Celia's—over her cheek, through her hair. "I'm afraid the American Bar Association is turning your situation into an occasion for reigniting the attorney-client relationship controversy. Which means they won't be doing anything. Not with the kind of furor they've gotten into."

Celia tries to think, to make the connections Jodie alludes to. "You mean," Celia says, feeling too worn out to properly make the effort, "they're taking the position that I shouldn't have continued to represent Martha? Or do they think that an attorney is responsible for crimes committed by her client while the client is in the relationship with the attorney? I don't think I understand, Jodie."

"I guess some people are thinking you let yourself be used by your client. That you let yourself be used to deliver a terrorist threat."

Celia sighs. "And what did they think I was supposed to do? Not warn Guidry or Partee? If I hadn't warned them then I would have been culpable of having foreknowledge of the intention to commit a felony."

"Yes," Jodie says unhappily, "it's a double-bind."

"What about the due process angle?" Celia tries to summon some faith in the only possibility remaining.

Jodie swallows hard and takes her hand from Celia's to reach for one of the half-liter bottles of water sitting on the table. "Well the problem is that they're classifying the Marq'ssan involvement as terrorist. And you know those special conditions governing terrorist situations. Due process is relaxed under those conditions. But those of us who are going to talk to Partee will be working on that angle, trying to insist on an exemption for you, considering your peripheral involvement in the felonies they want to charge Martha with."

"You won't get anywhere with Partee," Celia says.

"Then if we get nowhere with him we'll begin tackling his colleagues," Jodie says, all too doggedly. She twists the cap off the bottle.

Celia reaches for a bottle, also. Her brain is mush; her body decaying, moldering, stinking with the rot afflicting everything around her. And in a few minutes she will be back in the van, retreating again into nowhere, nowhere at all.

Chapter Sixteen

Monday, 6/25/2096

Must get a grip on myself. Somehow I will figure out what's going on & come to terms with it. Somehow I will manage to go on with what I've started, whether or not she's here. I will *not* let myself be taken over. You think you've really got me now, Elizabeth, don't you. For a moment there today when I was standing frozen, taking in the *fact* of her, my anger spurted out in such fiery rage that if Elizabeth had been present I would have tried my damnedest to kill her with my bare hands—a manifestly laughable proposition, but I wouldn't have paid any attention to that, not in the state of rage I was in as I stood there staring at that girl, gaping in shock.

"What in the hell are you doing here?" I finally yelled at her. Clearly she didn't expect this kind of reception—which must mean that Elizabeth had prepared her for something entirely different. My rage must have been apparent, for she backed away from me, beads of sweat popping out on her suddenly dead-white face, & she stammered something about having been sent & that the letter was supposed to explain... I snapped at her to give me the letter, but she just continued backing away. I tried to get hold of myself then. To reassure her. I suppose she believed I was going to hurt her—though if she'd only thought about it she would have realized that in the kind of physical shape I'm in she's much stronger now than I. I coaxed her the way I've seen Nicole coaxing one of the island's suspicious cats to take food from her hand. Finally she worked up the courage to hand me the letter. When I took it she immediately scooted away. Such confidence that girl has in me. As though she's forgotten all those weeks we were allies, when I never touched her for any reason.

Elizabeth's letter explained little. "I've no idea what to do with this girl," she wrote. "And you so obviously need a service-tech. Besides, I couldn't in good conscience see you continuing to entertain such vile suspicions of me. So here she is, the girl of your dreams..." That's about all she said in her letter, except to give her permission to my ordering food through the amazons.

Christ. Obviously the girl is to resume spying on me. Told her to settle herself in one of the rooms at the top of the house. That she's to do as she pleases, that if she wishes to she can stay in the amazons' quarters rather than in the house. She refused, saying she would prefer to stay here. That she wanted to help me, she could see I needed help. This is probably on orders from Elizabeth. Every small hesitant smile she offers me works another twist of the knife. Damn that bitch, she has to know exactly how painful even seeing the girl is, much less having her living here with me. Staring my most abysmal failure right in the face, day & night without mitigation. & offering me temptation, as Elizabeth well knows, to be more monstrous to the girl than I've already been.

& now I must worry about Sally figuring out the things I'm doing— my making observations & jotting them down, my emotional state, everything. All to be transmitted straight to Elizabeth.

Sally wandering from room to room, that look of shock on her face. Probably takes this as a direct warning of what will happen if she screws up this time—no doubt Elizabeth's put it to Sally as "I'm giving you another chance, girl. Don't fuck up this time. Or it will be your own rather than your lover's future at stake." I'm sure the scene went something like that. Caging the girl with me like this. It makes me sick. I'm going to try to talk her into moving over to the amazons' quarters. Letting her know she can tell Elizabeth I ordered her out of the house. Yes, that would be best, I think.

So now the two of them are up on the top floor together, Kitty & Sally. I can just imagine the kind of tête-à-tête they're having. Though Sally will have to be careful not to say anything about Elizabeth. They will talk mainly about me. About what kind of person I am. Damn you, Elizabeth. But you'll pay. I promise you that much. Because this time I've got Rbt on my side.

Wednesday, 6/27/2096

Yes, just as I thought, the two of them stick together. All kinds of so-
licitous crap. (Killing me with kindness. *Just* their style.)

Spent most of the morning trying to figure out how the machine that's
programmed to tend the lawns works, but finally gave up. If I don't
figure it out the grass will be waist-high by the end of the summer.
Let the damned island go back to nature, one part of me says. Who
gives a damn anyway? But then I recall my pact with Rbt, & another
voice in my head takes his part.

We've agreed that I will do the cooking & they will attempt to keep
some of the garden going. Kitty is still thrilled about the plentitude
of safe water for bathing, etc., &, taking that together with eating
something other than tubefood, thinks this an island paradise (albeit
a ransacked one).

Last night after we finished dining (in the little walled-in herb garden
Nicole had had put in behind her office—including table & chairs,
making me realize she probably spent a lot of her free time there),
Sally came to me in the library. Alone. When it turned out that she had
no particular reason for seeing me, I spoke harshly to her. & of course
she disappeared in no time. I will make a point of being so unpleasant
to her when she approaches me by herself that she will soon stop doing so. Sally is bait for Elizabeth's trap. I must never forget that.

6/24/2096

Alexandra, dear, I'm at my mother's now, & talking with her I've realized you still haven't written her. Whyever not, dear? I have a clear
memory of your promising to do so. You seemed so eager to make
your peace with her.

But for that matter I'm wondering why I haven't heard from you myself. Apart from your arranging for the Paris apartment to be put into
my name, I've heard nothing from you since my visit. Knowing of your
isolation and how you've been feeling about it lately, it worries me,
dear. After everything said between us... You do see how disturbing
for me your silence must be? Write, Alexandra, write! Remember how

we agreed that keeping the lines of communication open is important. Write to me, if not to your grandmother.

Lovingly,

Mama

Washington, DC
June 28, 2096

Alexandra:

Write her something that will put her off, preferably something that will make her unlikely to give you another thought for the next year or two.

E.

Thursday, 6/28/2096

I must think of some kind of concession to wring out of Elizabeth for answering Mama *at all*—& I certainly won't write something that will offend her in order to make life easier for Elizabeth. Perhaps Elizabeth realizes that if Mama begins worrying about me she will go to Grandfather? The thought doesn't displease me—except, of course, if Elizabeth decides to make a preemptive strike & contact Grandfather herself, in which case I might never establish communication with him. (Though would he be likely to take her word for anything she might tell him? No, but there are probably tapes of the loquazene examination she made of me.) So I must be careful not to provoke Mama to that kind of precipitate action. I will formulate some sort of response to Mama that Elizabeth will decide is better than silence. A response that will say that I'm eager to see her, but that I've been a little depressed lately & so hadn't been able to make myself do much more than eat & sleep.

It gives me a slight sense of power, knowing that not everything is going as smoothly as Elizabeth would like. How lovely not feeling so totally helpless. No wonder thoughts of revenge are so sweet.

Saturday, 6/30/2096

Gave Phyllis my reply to Mama. My guess is that Elizabeth will hold onto it while she tries to get me to write something more in the line of what she demanded of me. & then when I refuse she'll decide this is better than nothing. Or no, maybe not. After all, along with Mama's letter I sent Grandmother a little note asking her to visit, which I in-directly allude to in the note—& surely Elizabeth won't pass *that* on. I know she will simply destroy the note to Grandmother. & I'm sure she'll catch the allusion, subtle as I made it. I must think today about what I want from Elizabeth that she might allow me. A gardener? A whole work-crew? The restoration of the house? No, too grandiose. She wants me to be as uncomfortable as possible. The idea being to make me susceptible to giving her my cooperation in exchange for having things return to what they were, as though she would do that now, anyway. Though of course after a while people do start thinking the things they so desperately wish would be true *could* be true…& how long before I fall prey to that syndrome?

Last night another visit from Sally. Her persistence is a tribute to the strength of whatever it is Elizabeth has told her. I rolled my eyes and said, "All right, Sally. I'm getting a little tired of this, every damned night. What is it this time? As you can see, I'm still here, where you knew I'd be. What is it, do you have to report to Phyllis that you've seen me every night at this time?"

She opened the door & made a show of looking up & down the hall to make sure nobody was listening. (The girl is probably wearing a transmitter herself. How stupid do they think I am?) Then she closed the door again & inched toward me where I lay on my mattress. "I thought we should talk," she said in a loud whisper.

I sat up and got comfortable against the wall. "All right. I'm sorry you're in this fix, you're sorry you're in this fix. We're both sorry you're in this fix. That says it all. Now just run along upstairs & take your misery to Kitty. She's used to being around misery. Med-techs always are."

That stopped her for a few seconds, seeing herself as a burdensome pest. Then she shook her head. "No," she said, "it's not that. That's not what I wanted to say. I thought you'd want to know everything *she* said to me. After you..." She hesitated. "It was awful," she said in a rush. "I couldn't believe you'd done that. They didn't know if they could even keep you alive until the emergency team got here. I kept thinking how if I hadn't let you scare me away—"

I had to remind myself how easily actors can emote. I told her that she & I would talk about nothing but practical matters like eating, gardening, cleaning, that sort of thing, & that anything to do with her time here before was forbidden, that I wasn't interested in hearing anything she had to tell me about Elizabeth.

"I thought we had to work together, that we were going to help one another?" Her eyes—a very dark green now—still awash with tears, fairly pleaded. & then she took a few more steps & was right there in front of me, kneeling down at the side of the mattress. All I could think to do was to unleash a flood of obscenity on her & warn her that if she didn't get out she'd hear much worse about herself & that that was the only kind of talk I had to share with her. That drove her away. & now perhaps she is convinced & will stay away from me.

Still, it was a close-run thing. She was almost touching me. It's hard, looking at her, to always be reminding myself she's Elizabeth's weapon. & her distress at her situation makes her performance all the more poignant. Performance, all performance. Don't ever forget that. She's Elizabeth's creature. She may be in over her head & trapped herself, but my giving in to her won't help her any more than it would help me. So must just close my eyes to any needs she herself may possibly have...

Washington, DC
July 2, 2096

Alexandra:

Since your response to Felice falls outside the parameters of the acceptable, I will myself write a brief pungent note to her in your name for you. After which you'll have a great deal to thank me for, since I doubt you'll be troubled with any further correspondence from blood relatives you so thoroughly detest.

E.

Monday 7/2/2096

Well, that takes care of that—unless Mama gets suspicious. Which I rather doubt. Of course she stoops to forgery. Why didn't I realize she would? Damn her & her arrogance in putting these things down on paper—obviously she thinks she will be able to retrieve this note in which she admits her own misdoing. I will save this & any future notes from her & add it to everything else when I get off this island. Somehow I will get word to Mama. (I know: I'll stick a note in a bottle. Isn't that how people marooned on islands traditionally contact the outside world? Hahaha—probably it would wash up at the docks the amazons so vigilantly guard.)

The fantasies I've been entertaining of what I could extort from Elizabeth in return for my cooperation in writing to Mama… Absolutely pathetic. No, the only thing is to find the goddam transcript & threaten her with it. Though I'll have to be extremely careful in how I go about doing it. If I find it I'll hide pieces of it in innumerable places all over the island. Or should I leave pieces of it around for the amazons to read? I wonder if they have the same mentality gorillas have? Or is it possible their loyalty could be shaken? (That I must explore, thoroughly, at length.) Or perhaps one of them might be likely to join me as a partner in blackmailing Elizabeth? I could throw in a bribe. Imagine the kind of mind-blowing bribe I could offer a service-tech with even the ordinary amount of greed… But all this presupposes my finding the transcript.

Thursday, 7/5/2096

I'm beside myself from yesterday's Great Discovery. With this sudden wonderful boost in my spirits I almost feel ready to believe I can survive anything. I feel almost capable of taking on anyone, anything, any situation.

It started with the physician's visit. Physician & physical therapist & med-tech all conferred among themselves, & then I was advised I should begin using the Jacuzzi upstairs in my suite (the Jacuzzi Elizabeth had installed for me at the outset of my exile—which, I now wryly recall, I took as a sign of goodwill). I objected—since I've made a point of not going upstairs at all since that first tour of inspection and I am, after all, now walking unaided. But Kitty had told the physical therapist that the bathroom in my suite was intact & the Jacuzzi untouched. The physical therapist accused me of being lazy—of not wanting to climb the stairs etc. I said I had no intention of passing through the bedroom & dressing room & thus seeing the carnage every damned day. That I'd rather live with the pain and stiffness than deal with trauma that is daily renewed. But they ganged up on me & delivered an ultimatum: essentially that the med-tech & physical therapist would clear out if I didn't agree to take Jacuzzis at least once a day. Apart from the rather obvious fact that without the PT I'd likely not finish the healing process "as good as new," I realized that without Kitty there I'd be stranded alone with Sally. It was that more than the lack of proper healing that weighed most heavily with me. So I caved.

Thus it was that I went upstairs at around five-thirty yesterday evening—the plan was for me to take the Jacuzzi & then go downstairs to the library for one of Kitty's therapeutic massages. & then prepare dinner (for which I'd already done most of the work). So I closed my eyes to the wreck of my bedroom & dressing room & spent a sweaty half hour in the tub, reading a murder mystery. (Been too tired to manage Nietzsche—there's so damned much work to be done in this house. & somehow I can't seem to keep myself from trying to clear up at least some of the mess.) Then I climbed out, dressed, & braced myself for passing through the looted mess. I was coming out of my bedroom into the hall, walking with my eyes lowered to the floor, trying to see as little as possible, when I heard it: the sound of hesitant notes being clumsily plonked out on the Bechstein. At first I thought it must be a CD, but of course no one would record trial-&-error attempts at picking out what was obviously a pop tune. I stood leaning against the wall, listening, one part of me wild with joy, the other part not believing, thinking it a cruel hoax. The image I'd conjured of the Bechstein's probable state of destruction was so strong that it seemed a physical impossibility for me to be hearing it. At any rate, I couldn't help myself, I had to see. Or at least go to the door of the Music Room & determine if that was where the sound was coming from.

It was.

I found Sally sitting at the keyboard using one finger to pick out the tune. I made my eyes move around the room—& discovered everything almost exactly as it had been. None of the furniture had been ripped open. The paintings—even the Renaissance & Old Masters— were propped against the walls, the harpsichord & all the antique instruments were intact. I could hardly believe it. I stumbled to the end of the Bechstein and lay my head on the beautiful satiny top & threw my arms around its curves. I was beside myself. & then Sally noticed me & of course stopped playing & stammered out an apology about how Kitty had said that for some reason I never came into this room etc. etc. I straightened up & grinned at her & laughed & cried my joy—which she immediately took up herself, & there we were whirling around the room together—I put on full-volume Lully's *Te Deum*, the one he was beating time to with his big heavy stick when he drove it through his foot—& I at once knew that that *Te Deum* was exactly what I needed to express my wild excess of emotion, to hear those voices soar & trumpets blare their paean to power—savoring the very vibrations set up through the room, trying to explain to Sally (what Rbt had known at once) about Lully's writing this *Te Deum* presumably as adoration of God but in reality as adoration of Louis XIV's "absolute power" (Rbt laughing smugly at previous centuries' notions of power & luxury as compared with modern versions thereof)—pointing out to Sally those voices seemingly delirious with adoration caressing—you'd swear even singing voices can caress, the way that music was written—every *laudat*, especially the *laudat exercitum* phrase, worshipping power itself as well as exalting the king's victory & conquest & triumph…this the mood of my joy, this power-fed, ever power-hungry music, supposedly religious. (Now afterwards that I've settled down I realize that unconsciously I knew very well that Beethoven's ecstatic joy, for instance, would be inappropriate to me: given the feelings in my heart now, given my thirst for vengeance—the Ninth Symphony could only make me weep.) I doubt Sally had any notion of what I was trying to tell her. Yet in my babbling wildness I couldn't resist trying.

After throwing myself into the *Te Deum*, I finished preparing dinner, & Sally & Kitty & I dined in the Music Room & got exceedingly drunk together, all three of us. (Intaking alcohol for the first time since returning to the island.) Now twenty-four hours later I have to wonder why Elizabeth left me that room. Why she spared me that particular blow. But no. There's no thinking about this, at least not yet. I'm still too emotional. I think I'll go out for a midnight stroll, which will upset the amazons. They won't be expecting me to be going out for midnight walks around the island…which they'll feel obliged to monitor carefully.

Chapter Seventeen

Saturday June 23, 2096—DC

Lise and I quarreled last night. We were supposed to join some other couples for dinner and go dancing afterwards. As I was dressing she came into my room with a gift-wrapped box that she put into my hands and asked me to open at once. Turned out to be expensive jewelry. What would someone like me do with a diamond bracelet? It was crazy. So I tried tactfully to tell her I didn't want it and that I didn't want any more expensive gifts from her. That it made me uncomfortable and embarrassed me. In response, Lise went through another of her big rejection reactions (blushing, her eyes watering, her lips quivering, her voice tremulous) and asked me why. Why did it embarrass me, she liked giving me things and now after all these years she could finally afford to. I said that it bothered me that I couldn't give her such things in return. I thought she'd get the message then, but no, she talked about how much I'd enjoyed her gifts before we ever went renegade. Then she brought up all my objections about living with her so that she could point out that I had been happy to live with her in Colorado during the war. So I said that if she couldn't see the differences now she was being deliberately obtuse. She stormed out of my room, leaving me completely up in the air about whether we were still going out. So after a while I went to her room and found her sitting on the floor with her back against the wall and her knees tucked under her chin, staring down at the rug. She and Weatherall were hardly speaking now, Lise said, and it was all because Weatherall had "a shitty attitude" about *me*, that she wouldn't even apologize about the lies she'd told me about Lise all those years ago, that she was jealous because she had lost Hazel and never found anyone else.

We talked for a long time, and Lise agreed to take back the brace-let and not give me any more expensive gifts, to "respect" my "feel-ings about it." But actually she refuses to talk honestly about this. We ended up eating something here and then meeting the group we were to have eaten with at the bar. I hadn't realized that most of the high-ranking executive women who were part of Lise's and Weatherall's clique are in couple relationships. Most of the other service-tech women are more like me than Ginger's type. Though of course there are a few of that type, but they don't fit in very well. Most of the time they don't know what anybody's talking about.

Tomorrow I have to go out to the suburbs to visit Mom and Dad. Since I know I won't be in DC that long, I'd better see them as often as I can before I'm off to Pennsylvania. It's hard, though. Going to see them is like riding the subway into another (alternate) reality. Hard to believe we live in the same world.

Monday, June 25, 2096—DC

Couldn't manage to get any of it down last night, & now it seems like a dream, distant, remote, totally unreal, impossible. Didn't know what I had in me, I guess.

It happened on the way back from the suburbs. I had a raging headache. My eyes were burning terribly—the air is so much worse the further south you go, and Mom and Dad's house doesn't have an air-filter system. The subway car was sparsely populated and thus very quiet except for the coughing, which there was a lot of. It was around eight at night. A fairly drunk professional male sat down two seats ahead of me next to a young woman and started hassling her—the usual obnoxious crap you can expect from drunk men. She too shy to tell him to fuck off. Obviously intimidated, definitely embarrassed. I got upset, listening to his crap. Kept wondering if I should do some-thing, tell him something. Everybody else in the car pretended noth-ing was going on, even though the bastard was so loud everyone had to have heard him. Maybe it was the memory of that time in Seattle on the #7 bus when a big strapping drunk sat down next to a woman and started pawing her and talking filth to her. I remember that night so clearly. The woman was young, maybe nineteen or twenty, and Asian, and wearing a sports visor over her long, flowing hair. She hunched in on herself and moved right up against the window to try to get away from him, just like the woman on the subway did, and first asked him in a loud whisper to please leave her alone and then, when he didn't, tried to get up and move to another seat. But he wouldn't let her out into the aisle, saying he knew that wasn't what she wanted, and that was when the woman sitting across the aisle told him to sit somewhere else. He scowled at her and sort of growled and told her to mind her "own fucking business." Then the woman sitting behind him leaned forward and said loudly into his ear that he was an asshole and not welcome in that part of the bus. And when he turned around to face her, an older woman a couple of seats back, with a loud piercing voice that reminded me of Great Aunt Edna's, which Dad used to say sounded just like a crow's, started scolding him, telling him he ought to be ashamed of himself for behaving like a bully and an idiot. Pretty soon there was such a chorus of passengers reading him the riot act that the drunk turned brick red. His belligerence just deflated and he went sort of limp, and soon *he* was hunching his shoulders like a turtle—and ended up getting off at the next stop, just to get away from all those women criticizing his behavior.

I'd just about made up my mind to say something when he put his arm around her and shoved his face up close to hers. The woman kept saying—I could barely make it out, she spoke so softly—"please" to him. A terrible rage built up in me, and suddenly there I was standing over him and telling him to leave her alone, to move to another seat. First he ignored me—but I repeated myself, louder, getting more and more angry about it. Then he turned and looked at me, snarled it was none of my business, and called me a "nigger bitch." Then it was *I* who was embarrassed. But angry, too. When he again put his face up against hers, I grabbed his collar and yanked on it. I was pretty sure a drunk professional wouldn't be carrying a knife. And I knew it was likely that in a hand-to-hand fight I was better prepared than he— after all, I work out with an amazon three times a week. So when he reached out to shove me away, I used his shoving motion (he was aiming straight for my breasts, the bastard) to pull him flying out of his seat. He staggered into a pole, knocked his head, and collapsed onto the floor. Out cold! Part of me could hardly believe it. But part of me was terrified that I'd seriously injured him. I knelt down to see if he was breathing, and the train stopped. The young woman scurried out of the car, and almost everyone else, too. Then a transit cop boarded and found me crouched down beside this guy. I suppose I had a guilty expression on my face, I was so scared at having knocked him out.

To make a long story short, the guy came to and insisted that I'd attacked him without provocation. So they arrested *me* for assault and battery! It was my word against his. Whose word would a cop take in such a situation? It was a foregone conclusion. If I'd had my Security badge with me I might have been able to make them believe me. But I didn't. So when they finally allowed me to make a phone call I called home. Lise wasn't there, but Elly said she'd track her down and if she couldn't find her she'd try calling Julia and Mott. In the end it was Mott who got me released and the charges dropped. It infuriates me that they refused to charge the drunk. Said he hadn't broken any law. So Mott brought me home and had a drink with me, and then Lise arrived and I had to go through the whole story yet again. She said she didn't blame me for wanting to light into that guy, but that really it wasn't my business since I didn't know the woman involved, and that I shouldn't be so eager to interfere in such situations. Also that I'd better be careful not to get "cocky" about my self-defense training.

But I keep thinking about how in Seattle there would have been people backing me up—though no, it never would have gotten to that point in the first place, and certainly not to the point of violence, because they would have started in on that guy the minute he started in on the woman. Public criticism and ridicule usually make that type slink away with their tails between their legs.

I think I hate DC.

Lise is insisting I learn how to drive the free-wheeling two-seater. Making a big deal about how I shouldn't have to deal with public transport when there are cars at my disposal. That for all I knew that guy could have been armed and seriously hurt me.

But then Lise almost never goes anywhere without her own personal amazon now. And hardly ever stirs except in her chauffeur-driven car at that. Felt odd going to work today, so dull and ordinary, after experiencing an intense scene like that.

Tuesday, June 27, 2096—DC

I've escaped Monaghan's supervision. *Yes!* From now on they'll be wanting me to screen the stuff they're working on for the documentaries on the Marq'ssan and read drafts and look at photos and stuff and give my opinions at meetings about it all. Today I didn't do a whole lot—was shown around, given a desk, and instructed on how to write my comments and reports etc. (More paperwork.) These people are a lot less hyper than Monaghan. Involved in their work the way Monaghan isn't. And they don't seem to mind my relationship to Lise. I may still have to spend some time in Monaghan's office, but it won't be so bad now that my time spent there will be so reduced.

Got an invitation to join some of the service-tech women among the group Lise and I were out with last Friday—just the service-techs getting together on their own after work tomorrow night. I said I'd go. Considering how limited my social life has been since moving here, this may be promising.

Lise is out of town again, until Friday probably. So I have some time to myself…reading a junky novel Ginger lent me (claiming it was "enthralling"—but I'm afraid I don't think so. Not that I'll tell her that. Skimming through it pretty fast, so I'll at least know what it's about when I return it).

Thursday, June 28, 2096—DC

It's late—after eleven. But I'm a little too hyper to go to sleep yet. First there was all the trouble at work—when I realized they were going to make Fenton's hysteria the centerpiece of the first segment of the documentary, I tried to take up the subject first with the producer (a professional named Enright, who asked me if I was saying Fenton was a liar) and then with the executive in charge of the project, Hadley Creech. Creech rebuked me for going over Enright's head and wouldn't let me get out a word. So then I sat down and started writing it into my report. All this reptile-stuff is so far off the mark that you'd think they'd be if not embarrassed at least worried about the public's credulousness.

After that kind of afternoon, I really wasn't in the mood to go out. Schuyler (whom Leslie calls "Cat") graciously lent her limousine and driver so that the five of us could get around "comfortably." The pizza was okay. The talk, though—well, I guess it's just that I'm a little out of it. They gossiped about others in their circle (who sometimes go out with them, too), and then got into speculating on whether Lisa Mott would really get pregnant (their fascination with the notion of Lisa's getting some executive male to contract with her contrary to all the usual conditions was almost obscene), and speculation on whether Ginger would be more maternal than Lisa. I guess it *is* pretty bizarre, the idea of someone like Lisa Mott having a baby. Especially since the father wouldn't be living with her—I know from what Ginger told me that Mott wouldn't go through with it unless the father agreed to only the most minimal contact with the child—which would be a girl, Ginger said. Needless to say I didn't divulge any of this last night. But the way they talked about it… I don't know. I guess I *am* out of things.

Another thing, I was noticing that all of them wear expensive clothing—and because of Lise's trying to give me that bracelet, I began wondering which of their jewelry was *real*. After all, these are working women, they're not the types to take lovers for mercenary reasons. (At least I hope not.)

There was also a lot of gossip about executives at the Cabinet and sub-Cabinet level. Well, that's hardly surprising, considering who their lovers are. But after years of the security-minded discretion that Security impresses upon one, this kind of chat—out in public, yet—left me uneasy. Oh, and speculation about Weatherall. One of the women there last night, Susan Garcia, had a fling with Weatherall a couple of years ago. (She almost broke up with her lover Elaine Pfefferman over it, too.) They tried to pump me, especially when I admitted (after they asked me pointblank—because they know Lise has always been so close to Weatherall) that I knew Weatherall and that I'd been a part of her group in the FZ (all their lovers had been Weatherall-loyalists and a part of her network and helped support her coup, so they all knew about the Redmond compound).

The movie was awful. Don't know why we bothered. Then wine afterwards at that bar we were at the other night (their regular hangout, I gather). And then, finally, home.

Lise returns tomorrow. Depending on how busy she is, we may go somewhere, hopefully on the coast. What a week it's been. I can still hardly believe I had that incident in the subway. That I grabbed that guy like that. It already seems a long time ago…

Friday, June 29, 2096—DC

Such drama! What happened today—Lord, who knows what it all means? Lise is in a tizzy.

Every Friday afternoon there's supposed to be a meeting to review the status of the various projects. This was to be the first week they began these meetings. Lise had said I was to be present at the meetings. So were all the project managers, plus, of course, Creech herself. Lise would be at some of the meetings. Well she got back this morning and the word was out that she was going to be there. And maybe even Schuyler. (That was just a rumor—turned out to be false. I don't really see why Schuyler would come to such meetings. It's Lise's show, after all.)

So there we are at one o'clock, all of us sitting around the table (apart from the woman taking notes, I was the only service-tech present), listening to progress reports from project managers. Enright was going last because he was going to screen rough-cuts and discuss editing strategies that Creech and Lise would want to have a say in shaping. Since both Creech and Enright have become pretty hostile toward me, they weren't too happy having me sitting there. I hadn't submitted my report to Enright yet since I hadn't decided whether I wanted to go up against him. But I suspected Lise might ask me my opinion…or should I say I hoped she would? So I was a little nervous as I sat there, thinking about how awful it would be to speak my piece in front of twelve professionals and three executives.

And then, all of a sudden, Julia came in and whispered in Lise's ear. The project manager reporting just went on as though he didn't notice, but I was watching Lise's face and caught a look first of surprise, then of puzzlement, and finally of consternation. She whispered something in Julia's ear, and Julia left the room and Lise interrupted the man speaking. She announced that the aliens had destructured that damned pollution site that's been making all of us cough and weep and that they were on everybody's vid sets again, announcing it. Or rather that some subversives living in DC were announcing it and

were making a big propaganda pitch out of it. Just as Lise finished
saying this, a service-tech wheeled in a large screen on which, sure
enough, some subversive-looking type woman was holding forth on
how the aliens were on the side of the oppressed etc. and how they
had cleaned up a source of misery that the corporations had created
out of greed and carelessness.

The upshot is that the entire campaign is now jeopardized, and
Lise says we have to change the orientation and find a way to deal
with this propaganda defeat. It's clear that I don't need to worry about
objecting to Fenton's hysteria—they can see for themselves, now, that
people in DC at least wouldn't buy it. Instead, judging from everything they said this afternoon, I think they're going to try to focus on
getting people to see how the aliens did this only to dupe the public.

I don't know. I have a funny feeling about all this. I don't think the
"dupe" theory is exactly right. And I don't see the aliens as plotting
to rule the world and exploit it. It's more a matter of their believing in the anarchists' ideology and wanting to implement it without
understanding how stupid and unworkable such ideas are. I just can't
see them as evil—though I suppose I might be duped myself. But all
the times I was around aliens (mostly Sorben) I found it impossible
to believe the picture of them all our media projects are continually
constructing. I tried to talk a little about this to Lise, but she said the
details didn't matter, that basically it was a power struggle for "the
hearts and minds of the people." That the Marq'ssan did want power,
even if they weren't the evil scheming reptiles wanting to enslave all
humans that Fenton claims them to be. And that whatever the case
might be, humans must be masters of their own destiny. I couldn't
argue with that. Though I do wonder if people are as stupid as Lise insists they are—which is why she says that aspects of the power struggle must be "exaggerated" when presented to the public... I didn't
mention how glad I was to know that once the air shifts this crap away
from DC we won't have any more of it. I think Lise wishes they hadn't
done it because of the strategic loss. But she can't say that out loud.
The Executive is in a delicate position. Lise went back to work after
dinner—she's meeting Weatherall and then will be staying at the office until she finishes hammering out a statement the President can
read at a press conference tomorrow.

Chapter Eighteen

[i]

"I can't believe you acted unilaterally without even consulting us, and on such a goddam important matter!" Martha glared at Emily. "*Think* about the implications, the consequences!"

"Believe me, Martha, I have." Emily glanced at Astrea. When on their return they had found Martha's message, Astrea had suggested they spend the evening and possibly the night on their favorite ocean beach.

"It's ridiculous for you to call the action unilateral," Astrea said—very coldly, Emily noticed. "And it's presumptuous of you to be peeved at Emily for something that was largely my own accomplishment. If you have a bone to pick, it's with me." Astrea paused, then added, "I really am curious to hear what you might have to say to me about what I choose to do or not do."

Martha gaped at Astrea in a kind of shock, as though realizing for the first time that it wasn't just Emily who had gotten out of line. "Don't you see," Martha said weakly, "this will create a terrible precedent. Up until now—"

"Up until now," Emily said, "you've considered Marq'ssan powers of destructuring solely as a weapon in your war against the executives."

Martha glared again at Emily. "That's simply not true. The point is, if everyone goes off doing their own thing, we'll have nothing but chaos. We have to talk things over. The Marq'ssan—" here she gave Astrea a worried, uncertain look—"have always discussed things with us. They always discuss things before *doing* them."

"They clear every single destructuring they do on earth with you first?" Astrea asked, her voice dripping with sarcasm. "Someone should have told me I needed your permission before doing my good deed for the week."

Good deed for the week: Astrea must have picked up that little gem from Martin, Emily thought.

"I didn't mean it that way," Martha said defensively. "Of course they don't talk to me about *every*thing—but they've always consulted me about the things they do that concern the US. Because we're working together."

Emily sagged against the door frame. She was exhausted—because of the tiny, minor role she had played in the actual destructuring (apart, that is, from contacting the women activists in DC). It had been a big energy-drain for Astrea, and Astrea had suggested she could help her manage her field, merging with her and acting as a kind of steadying support, allowing Astrea to devote more of her attention to the material being destructured. Astrea had warned her afterwards that she should be sure to spend at least an hour in deep meditation, that that more than food would help her to recover from the strain. "Could I have some water?" Emily asked Martha.

"Sure. And for the goddess's sake come in and sit down. You look like you're about ready to fall down."

Emily moved into the living room, sank onto the floor, and accepted a half-liter bottle from Martha. "Look," she said as she twisted off the cap. "When I talked to Weatherall two weeks ago I told her that we were all of us different people with diverse opinions and ideas and that we respect this diversity. I told her this in the context of telling her I was speaking for myself and not for you and Hazel." Emily swallowed some water. "As we had agreed I should tell her," she said, looking into Martha's eyes.

"Yes, but this is something else. This is an *action*, Emily." Martha's hands swooped dramatically. "An important action. The whole notion of negotiation will be thrown into doubt. Don't you see—"

"But there are different ways of negotiation," Emily said. "Most of which we haven't begun to explore. Can't you see how Elizabeth's government will be plunged into confusion and disarray by our doing this? It's a visible demonstration of positive things that—"

"That may be," Martha interrupted, apparently angry again, "but why the *hell* didn't you bother to discuss this with us first? I don't understand your doing this without telling anyone in advance! You knew what you were doing when you asked me for the names of my contacts in DC!"

"You know what I think it is, Em?" Astrea still stood near the door; her voice was cool and quiet and remote, in marked contrast to Martha's hot anger. "I think Martha feels her territory has been invaded. Isn't that so, Martha?"

Martha frowned. "Territory? Of course not, that's absurd!" After an uncomfortable silence that Emily was too tired to make the effort to break, Martha added—cautiously, Emily thought—"Sorben and Magyyt have always said to me that they feel it appropriate to consult with us precisely because they aren't themselves human."

Astrea shrugged. "So I consulted with Emily and the activists in DC."

"That's not good enough," Martha said. "We went through this a long time ago, when all of us first started meeting on board *s'sbeyl*. Some of us acted without consulting the others, much to all our regret. We really cannot be doing important things without consulting the others."

"How many others?" Astrea pointedly asked. "Before either of your actions in Baton Rouge, did you consult, for instance, the women in DC? Or anywhere else for that matter?"

"But that didn't touch them," Martha said, clearly nettled, "and we can't consult the whole damned world! There are major differences between that and what you did today. What you did today could change everything!"

Emily sighed. "Do you think we could talk about this tomorrow? I'm exhausted, Martha. I'd like to go home and go to bed."

Martha stared first at Emily and then at Astrea. "I think we should have a meeting tomorrow," she said. "I'll call Sorben and see if she can make it. I think we need to do a lot of talking and thinking and rethinking."

"I agree, Martha. Only not tonight. I'm dead tired."

Martha swallowed. "Will you come too, Astrea?"

Astrea raised her eyebrows at Martha in such a way that Emily remembered with a jolt that such facial expressions were deliberate on Astrea's part. She *must* be irritated by Martha's attitude. "All right," Astrea said. "I'll come to your meeting." Emily got to her feet. "You know," Astrea said, her hand on the doorknob, "I don't know why I'm surprised—no human reaction should surprise me by now—but only a human would so begrudge an action of great beneficence to over a million people. Didn't you hear what Bonnie said about what that stuff was doing to the eyes and respiratory systems of most people living in the area?" Astrea shook her head and opened the door.

Emily nodded at Martha, who now stood in the middle of the living room with her arms hanging lankly at her sides, embarrassed, speechless, dismayed. She had expected an angry reaction from Elizabeth, not Martha. Because of Astrea's words Martha was probably at this instant realizing something new about herself, something she would rather not know. But then Astrea could shed a terribly disconcerting light on things. Emily had learned that long ago herself.

[ii]

Before the meeting Emily and Astrea walked along the waterfront; basking in the sun, they stared out at the Sound and the Olympics sharp and craggy against the hot blue sky. "Do you think Sorben will agree with Martha?" Emily asked Astrea.

"You're wondering if Sorben will think it wrong for me to have done this without consulting anyone but you and the DC activists?"

"Something like that."

"It's not likely she would put it that way," Astrea said. "We don't police one another. Sorben and the others may think it *unwise* of us to have done it the way we did, but they won't say it was *wrong*. They'll probably want to examine what we did, why we did it, and what the likely consequences are in every context they can think of."

"You mean everything's a learning experience," Emily said drily.

"Something like that, yes."

Emily sighed. "Maybe Martha will have second thoughts about her objections."

"Maybe. Her proprietary attitude is pretty blatant, don't you think?"

"Sorben will see it that way? As a proprietary attitude?"

They paused to lean against the rough stone railing and stare down at the water. "There's always been debate on the sorts of things we can do for humans and when we should do them and why. Since we have such limited resources."

"You mean the problem of not being able to do the same thing for everybody," Emily said slowly, casually looking over at the gleaming white boat tied up at the dock nearby, bobbing on the water.

"Yes. So there are generally two schools of thought. Leleynl attempts to work with individuals. The closest thing to what she does that I can think of is what Hazel does in her seminars. Except that Leleynl also teaches people about health and their bodies and those sorts of things."

Emily had heard about some of the practices they were teaching patients at the Whidbey Medical Center, practices Gina had learned from Leleynl. "And the other school must be Sorben and Magyyt's," she said. The boat, Emily saw, had a Canadian license number stenciled over its bow.

"Yes. And then there's me. Who doesn't fit with either group."

Though Astrea seldom talked about other Marq'ssan, this statement did not surprise Emily. She had had the feeling for a long time now that Astrea was something of a misfit among her own kind. Which would explain why Astrea told her and taught her things which to Emily's knowledge none of the other Marq'ssan shared with humans. "Martha's worried about losing leverage against the Executive," Emily said. "I know that's what was really bothering her. I don't think it's a genuine power thing at all. Just that the timing must seem bad to her."

"What do you mean, *genuine* power thing? Power works its way into everything, Emily."

"Yes," Emily said uncomfortably, "but I don't think there's this, well, self-serving aspect of power operating in Martha. Maybe that's what I mean..." Emily's voice trailed off uncertainly, not sure what exactly she did mean or had thought she had meant.

"Is it possible you want to reduce the question of power in this situation to a contest of the relative *goodness* of intentions?"

"I'm confused," Emily said. Whenever she tried talking to Astrea about these sorts of things she always ended up confused. Astrea refused to allow things to be simply meant. "Let me put it this way," she said. "I don't think Martha is worried about her own personal degree of control over 'actions' or over the things the Marq'ssan do or over activism in general. I don't think there's crude ego-aggrandizement behind Martha's distress."

"You mean you don't think she's *consciously* wanting to be in control," Astrea said.

"You're implying she's unconsciously wanting that?"

"But Martha herself isn't necessarily the point," Astrea said. "The thing that will be argued about—supposing we do argue at this meeting—is the extent to which it's thought proper to plan and otherwise centralize efforts, actions, strategies. What *I* scent in all this is Martha's sense of a system developing and operating. Now if you could tell me how something that is a *system* can be subversive..."

"You think there's a system being built?" Emily asked.

Astrea met her gaze. "I think that's an important question that needs to be voiced at this meeting."

"Then maybe Sorben will—" Emily frowned. It seemed *wrong* to place individual Marq'ssan on "sides," wrong to think of herself and Astrea as being on one "side" and Martha on another.

"Who knows *what* Sorben is thinking. You know why they allow me to go my own way, don't you?" Emily shook her head. "It's precisely because they know the dangers of subsuming others into one smooth system. They won't bring me into line because they know that it would be wrong for them to think that way. That the very concept of there being a line in the first place is dangerous. To put it cynically—and at the risk of distortion—I disturb them by my lack of orthodoxy, but in a sense they value that lack of orthodoxy because it means they haven't created an entirely closed system."

They turned their backs on the water and the sleek Canadian boat and began the trudge uphill. Emily wondered what sort of meetings—if any—the Executive had been holding over the last twenty-four hours. It would be interesting to see how Elizabeth reacted to a *de facto* miracle she could not claim credit for. It was to be hoped Elizabeth's people didn't get wind of the controversy this had opened among the activists. Officious as it might seem to the others, she had better warn everyone at the meeting to be discreet.

[iii]

"I think we have two things to talk about," Martha said when everyone invited had arrived and seated themselves around the table. "First, damage control. Second, lessons for the future."

"Damage control?" Emily said. "Isn't that a little strong, Martha?"

Martha's eyes moved to Emily's face. "When you see the tape we made of the President's press conference, when you read the editorial that was printed in today's *New York Times*—" Martha nodded at the copy of the editorial Emily and everyone else had been given—"I think you'll agree that that phrase isn't too strong."

"Just a minute, Martha," Hazel said. "Before you show us the tape, let me note that in general we've tried not to make our actions and behaviors into mere *re*action to the Executive's statements and deeds. What you say makes me wonder if that isn't what you're doing in this case."

"We can't ignore the way in which the things we do are subsequently manipulated by *them*," Martha said. "And although we try not to instigate reactions, we do, however, attempt to take anticipations of those reactions into account when we decide upon strategy."

Emily picked up the gauntlet. "I frankly don't see the President's statement to the press as at all relevant. Who cares what he says? He's a figurehead. If we take to listening to him, then we'll have to start analyzing soap operas as well. And all the other forms of propaganda the Executive orchestrates and manipulates."

"It's a matter of studying the consequences of certain types of actions," Martha said. Her mouth tightened. "Which I don't think you realized when you went ahead with that action."

"You're talking about propaganda responses as *consequences*? Don't you think you're placing too much emphasis on their propaganda? What about the *material* consequences?"

Martha's lips thinned. After a few seconds, she said, "We'll get to that later. Although I think they're pretty obvious, don't you?"

Emily shrugged.

"Cora?" Martha said, turning her eyes to the screen positioned at the head of the table.

At the sound of the pompous voice announcing "The President of
the United States" and at the sight of that Hollywood-produced image of The Senior Statesman, Emily cringed. "My fellow Americans,"
he intoned, sending shivers of irritation down Emily's spine. For
something to do she pulled her copy of the editorial closer and began
jotting notes down on it. *"Demonstration of superior technology,"* she
wrote, taking down a verbatim snatch of text. *"The same powers that
inflicted the Blanket on us." "Intimidation by benevolence, to show us
we are puppets in their superior hands." "Do not be deceived, my fellow
Americans." "Make no mistake." "If they were truly benevolent they
would long ago have cleaned up all our pollution instead of destroying our prisons and attacking the defensive structures of our country."
"They are not gods to be worshiped." "We will not be deceived or intimidated." "They wilfully withhold from the people of this land the
keys that would unlock the doors of environmental control and economic
prosperity." "We must be on our guard."*

After fifteen minutes Emily stopped listening. How outrageous
to be subjected to this. Why? Why waste fifteen minutes of their lives
on this crap? She looked up from her note-taking and glanced around
the table. Apparently most of the others were annoyed, too. And who
wouldn't get into a state of irritation listening to the creepy smooth
voice of the Executive's doll?

When the vid finally ended, Hazel spoke at once. "I resent your
having asked that of us, Martha. Why must we be exposed to such
meaningless, irritating drivel?"

"You could have told us in twenty-five words or less the content of
his statement," Maureen said.

Martha flushed. "I wanted you to realize how most people on this
continent are probably thinking about this action. And how they'll be
led to think about any other actions of a similar nature, should they
occur." Martha flashed a look at Emily. "If you thought the people of
DC were going to be grateful, you were sorely mistaken."

"Grateful?" Emily said. "I don't know that I was thinking in
terms of gratitude. I've never much believed that there is such a thing
as gratitude, except as something people try to pretend exists because
they don't want to see all the other stuff going on in situations where

gratitude is supposedly operating." If anybody should know, Emily thought, *I* should. Gratitude is as bogus an emotion as altruism is.

"The way I read that tape and the editorial," Cora said, "it looks to me as though they're going to push the notion that if the Marq'ssan wanted to they could be fairy godmothers to the human species but for reasons of their own choose instead to use their powers arbitrarily."

"What do *we* care what line of bullshit they push?" Hazel said. "I don't see what that has to do with *us!*"

"Their propaganda has as much or more of an effect on what people think as material facts do," Cora said. "Since apparently the point of this was to touch the lives of ordinary people instead of merely trying to get at the power structure—the usual way destructuring is used—then you *have* to take into account the way the material experience will be interpreted. There is no such thing as raw material experience!"

Hazel said, "Thank you, Cora, for sharing that brilliant insight with us."

As if, Emily thought, Cora would need to enlighten Hazel of all people about such things. "May I add one small point to this?" Emily said. "We had several motives for doing this. Among those motives was the desire to visibly demonstrate to certain people in the Executive whom I've recently been talking to the constructive sorts of things Marq'ssan power can accomplish. I wanted to show them things they may either have forgotten or never realized. I thought it might make a refreshing change from the usual approach."

Hazel said, "Which brings us to another thing. We always need to be looking for more creative as opposed to destructive ways of deploying our actions. Instead, Martha and Cora keep talking as though every single thing the Marq'ssan do on this planet should specifically fit into some grand political design. That kind of thinking is, I believe, insidious."

"No, that's *not* the point," Martha said. "Way back in the first days, when we were attempting to negotiate with the governments on board *s'sbeyl*, a situation arose in which a group of US activists made a deal with the Executive which in effect operated on the premise that the US was the world. We used the Marq'ssan's powers to our own end,

without thinking about the needs and opinions and wants of the activists from the rest of the world. I see something of that here."

"What if I were to say that this 'action' as you keep calling it was
my own idea?" Astrea said.

How odd, Emily thought. The other humans around the table
looked as though they had forgotten any Marq'ssan were present.
Martha, for instance, was now glancing at Sorben, as though recalling
Sorben's presence among them.

When no one spoke, Astrea went on, "What would you have to say
if I should choose to do such things when and where I wished on this
planet without consulting anyone at all?"

Martha flushed. "That would be your prerogative, obviously."

"Obviously?" Astrea repeated ironically. "*Obviously?* But if Emily
is involved, *then* it becomes a matter for this kind of discussion? A matter for warning, a matter for anxiety over what the Executive might
say, a matter for talking about grand political designs?"

"*I* said nothing about 'grand political designs,'" Martha pointed out.

"I for one don't see a problem here," Hazel said. "Seems to me this
kind of thing might get all of us thinking in new ways. And my god,
given Emily's description of what the air in DC was like, I can't imagine anyone in their right mind objecting to cleaning up that poison."
She glanced at Martha. "As soon object to the Marq'ssan's assistance in
Santiago after that devastating earthquake last year."

"As a matter of fact, if my memory serves me correctly," Emily
said, "the Marq'ssan's assistance, though given without any deal being
struck with the government, achieved certain positive side-effects,
such as the formation of neighborhood organizations, which are now
functioning to accomplish other things than their initial purpose."

Martha threw her hands into the air. "All right, all right, I give up.
You're all making me the heavy. When my real concern is that we not
be playing into their hands."

"But we can't know, *ever*, those kinds of things in advance!" Hazel
said. "Pretty soon you're going to start talking about cause and effect
relations!"

"Martha," Sorben said. Every head turned towards Sorben. Again,
Emily realized, they had forgotten the Marq'ssan's presence. With

Sorben that was easy enough to do, for Sorben's gray eyes, silver-gray hair, and slight body tended to blend into any background. But how could they so easily forget Astrea as well, Astrea who had chosen a human appearance as close to the edge of the plausible as could be? "You mustn't have illusions of control," Sorben said. "*We* don't. Nor aspirations toward it, either. It's both dangerous and foolish to think that way. Granted, you may not always agree with the things that others choose to do. The important thing is to live with those things. Not predict or control them. Astrea and Emily did this thing for their own reasons. It's up to them to know what their reasons are, and by the fact that they did it they've taken responsibility. That's not your problem. It *can't* be your problem. I wouldn't *dream* of demanding of Astrea that she clear such things with us in advance. She has to live with what she does, just as we do. We're not police, Martha, neither you nor I nor any of the Marq'ssan. You're able to deal with the absence of policing structures in the Free Zone, in spite of the fact that people will do violent things to one another. If you can live with that, then you can live with Astrea and Emily and whoever else might choose to do so engaging in activities not expressly decided upon by you or anyone else in this room in advance."

This was one of the longest speeches Emily had ever heard Sorben utter. She glanced sidelong at Astrea, but of course Astrea's face revealed nothing.

"I think," Hazel said when the silence had lengthened to the point of discomfort, "it will be interesting to see what sorts of things come out of it. We can think of it as, inter alia, an experiment."

Martha, her eyes restless yet subdued, nodded. "Perhaps you're right," she said. "Anybody have any idea what effect if any this may have on our broken-off negotiations with Elizabeth Weatherall?"

Astrea's elbow nudged Emily's arm. Astrea wasn't above being amused at this, Emily thought—while the very idea of Sorben being amused was inconceivable. There was no doubt about it: Astrea *was* different—from everybody, human and Marq'ssan alike.

[iv]

"Of course what really startled me was her calling me up at three in the morning and offering me a job," Emily told Hazel, concluding her carefully abridged version of her discussion with Elizabeth.

"At three in the morning? *What* job?"

Emily grinned. "She offered to make me Undersecretary of Alien Affairs. Said she'd been thinking for hours and that she had decided my being in such a position might 'save the situation.' That obviously I knew more about the Marq'ssan than any of her people, and that furthermore I was on good terms with them." Emily picked up the wine bottle. "Another glass?" Hazel nodded, and Emily refilled Hazel's glass. How had Elizabeth put it? *You aren't moved by the ordinary measures, standards, and honors. It is the Marq'ssan who intrigue you. Only they can offer you something worth your while. You wouldn't have to give that up, Emily, working with us.*

"So all of that happened two weeks ago," Hazel mused, sipping.

Emily stretched out on her back and folded her arms behind her head. "Yes. I half-thought you'd have heard from her by now." Emily turned her head so that she could look into Hazel's face. "I thought she might try offering *you* a job."

Hazel snorted. "I'm sure she knows where that would get her."

"Lisa Mott told me that she thinks Elizabeth still has a thing for you."

"Why would she tell you a thing like that?"

"Lisa is, by my guess, worried about the direction Elizabeth seems to be moving in. I think Lisa fervently wants peace with the Free Zone and the Marq'ssan." Emily stretched the muscles in her thighs, calves, and toes as far as she could. "Remember, Lisa went on one of those prison liberation actions. She *knows* how powerful the Marq'ssan are. She has sufficient imagination and intelligence to understand what Elizabeth's precipitate rush to conflict might be leading to."

"I never did know what to make of Lisa," Hazel said.

Emily shifted the conversation back on track. "When I mentioned the pollution site to Elizabeth, it was off the top of my head. But later, when I started—" her phone chirped—"to think about Elizabeth's basic psychology, it seemed to me that—" the phone chirped again— "damn, I'd better get that," Emily got to her feet.

"Emily, it's Jodie Heath. Do you have a few minutes to talk?"

Emily glanced at Hazel. "It's about Celia?" she asked.

"Yes. I saw her again today."

"Go ahead."

"She's getting worse. I finally got permission to bring her reading and writing materials, but she's so depressed she barely seemed to notice. Could only get monosyllables out of her. Frankly, I'm worried."

Emily closed her eyes and drew a deep breath. "Do you think she should have medical attention? Or do you think there's something we need to investigate?"

"I've been considering that, but I think they might use a psychiatric exam against her. Questioning her professional fitness and so on, and I know that if I could discuss this with her she would probably object on that ground in particular. A *medical* exam, though, might not be out of place—though likely her problem sleeping and so on would be cast in psychiatric terms."

"Damn it, why do we have to worry about the whole professional question?" Emily said urgently. "I can't believe Celia is still—"

Jodie interrupted. "We've been through that several times already. Let's not argue about it again. Celia and I had many conversations about it, and I think I know where she stands."

Emily stared at the originals of the cartoon series Martin had done on the restoration of elections; after the series had been widely disseminated he had framed the originals and hung them on her wall. "Do you know where she is?" Emily finally asked.

"No. They don't tell me. And Emily, I don't ask."

And probably Jodie's phone was bugged, too. "All right. Look, do you think they'll ever allow *me* a visit?" Jodie had been working on that since Celia's arrest.

"No, I don't. Since you're neither a blood relation nor legal counsel nor medical attendant, they don't have to let you see her."

Suddenly, Emily knew what to do. "Then I think you'd better get permission for Celia's mother to visit. I think it's essential. I'll take care of the travel arrangements, if you can set up a date."

"Maybe that *would* help," Jodie said. "Okay. I'll do that. It shouldn't be too difficult. These people are walking a fine line here. And the fact that Elena Salgado is a physician will do double duty for Celia herself."

Emily sighed. "I'll try to give her some idea of what to expect..."

When Emily hung up she found Hazel paging through an issue of the Miscellany's journal. "Things have deteriorated with Celia," she said to Hazel.

Hazel put the journal aside. "Maybe it's time for us to do something in conjunction with the Marq'ssan. No matter what Celia says she wants."

Emily resettled herself on the rug. "It's a moral quandary. And I think only Elena Salgado can help us come to an answer."

"Surely, if we put real pressure on them..."

"We *are* putting pressure on them," Emily said. "And as I told you before, Elizabeth has been putting pressure on them, too."

Hazel stared for awhile into her glass, then raised it to her lips. "If it weren't for Celia's situation, I'd have said we were doing all right. Compared to ten years ago, at least." She drank the rest of the wine in her glass. "I'm curious about what kinds of effects your action may have—apart from the obvious thrust of their reactive propaganda."

"It is true we have to be careful in the way we go about such things," Emily said, pressing her fingers into the rug and tracing lines of the interlocking circles patterning it. "We don't want people to start fantasizing dependence on the Marq'ssan to take care of everything for them." She lifted her gaze to Hazel's face. "There's always been that danger in the Marq'ssan doing positive things. Just as at the beginning it must have seemed a danger to do too many destructurings for the activists. The Marq'ssan have to be careful not to undercut any tendency to responsibility and independent thinking on the part of humans. I think that more than anything is the reason behind their using those powers basically for negotiations and, in certain cases, retaliation."

"Yes. I see what you mean. Let me ask you something." Hazel hesitated. "I'm not sure how to put this. But what I was wondering... when you said something at the meeting about wanting to make an impression on Elizabeth, and then when you were telling me about your discussion with her...I'm wondering if what you're trying to do with her is to sort of, well, seduce her into that fantasy you say we have to be careful to avoid."

"I'm not sure I follow," Emily said.

The rose in Hazel's cheeks deepened. "Getting her to think that if she plays the game right you'll get the Marq'ssan to fix up all sorts of critical problems that are otherwise almost insoluble." Hazel's golden gaze held Emily's. "You know how manipulative she is. Are you trying to tempt her into trying to manipulate the Marq'ssan?"

Emily laughed, but uneasily. "I'm not sure what I had in mind," she said, intensely conscious now of Hazel's sharp attention and questing mind. "I suppose I wanted her to see that she needn't think of us as absolute enemies. Things would be so much easier if the Executive had relations with us similar to those we have with Austria."

"Oh come on." Hazel scoffed. "That will never be. Austria is thousands of miles away. A different culture. Never closely associated with the piece of earth inhabited by the North American Free Zone. Can you ever imagine the Executive able to accept what we're doing?" Hazel shook her head. "Only if we agreed not to contaminate the rest of the continent. But even then that wouldn't be good enough for them. Our very *existence* threatens them. Anyway, getting the Free Zone back under Executive control was always Elizabeth's second objective—after accomplishing her first, which was pulling off her coup."

"So you think she'll be fighting us every step of the way."

"Of course she will." Hazel slanted an ironic look at Emily. "Though it's true that if she fell for the fantasy of being able to manipulate the Marq'ssan, she'd lose a lot of ground. Which is why I wondered if that was what you intended."

"I'm not sure what I intended." Emily smiled wryly. "I don't really know what I'm doing. Sort of keeping on moving, and trying this, that, and the other thing as it occurs to me. And right now most everything I do is ultimately directed toward finding a way out of Celia's detention." Emily stretched out on her back and closed her eyes.

"Martha's going back to Baton Rouge."

"Wonderful," Emily said. "Does she realize they'll bust her on sight? And whisk her away to someplace hidden?"

"Yes," Hazel said. "She knows that. But she's in such a pushy mood...I think she's itching for a confrontation."

"Great." Emily dropped into near-trance. She wanted to see Hazel's field.

"There have been discussions all week about it," Hazel said. "I think that had a lot to do with Martha's response to your action."

Emily slid into field perception. "Astrea thinks Martha is on a power-trip." Hazel's field pulsed and swirled in patterns that reminded Emily of a blackberry patch in the paradoxical density of the nearly transparent thinness of its layers of leaf-like structures. Dense yet thin nearly to the point of transparency? How different from Martha's and Celia's, Emily marveled. She had not perceived many fields, but Hazel's—like Astrea's—struck her as unique.

"Are you asleep?" Hazel asked softly.

Emily opened her eyes to show Hazel she was not—and realized she had been *seeing* Hazel's field with her eyes closed. Shocked, she stared at Hazel's face—now returned to its usual appearance—and wondered how that could be. *How* had she perceived, if not through the sensory input of her eyes?

"What is it, Em?" Hazel said anxiously. "Are you all right?"

Emily gave herself a mental shaking. "I'm fine." She sat up and smoothed her hands over her hair.

"Maybe I should go," Hazel said.

"No, no, I want to hear more about Martha's plans," Emily said. "But I'd like some tea. There's more wine if you'd like some," she added, pointing to the three-quarters empty bottle.

"Maybe I will have another glass." Hazel reached for the bottle, and Emily got up, went to the kitchen alcove, and switched on the kettle. She wished she could perceive fields while paying attention to everything else going on around her. Would she ever be able to? But wait until she told Astrea about "seeing" fields with her eyes closed. Astrea would be as fascinated as she.

All of what she did was new, brand new, never done before, Emily thought, awe-stricken. Maybe Elizabeth had after a fashion been right when she had said that the Marq'ssan "knew her price." Though "price" was a concept as alien to the Marq'ssan as chiastics was to humans—and thus the Marq'ssan could "know" no such thing as price...which Elizabeth apparently did not realize.

Chapter Nineteen

Saturday, 7/7/2096

I'm getting stronger. Life will improve vastly once the physical therapist & med-tech can be sent away. Feel purposeful, as I've never been
in my life. How interesting, having a *purpose*. Directing everything
toward one end. So as I push myself physically I am motivated as I otherwise probably would not have been. I'm even impressing the physical
therapist. This isn't what they expect from a botched suicide.

As I walked along the beach it came to me why I've given up reading
Nietzsche. Not so much my being too worn out at night to spare the
energy as my having let what he calls *ressentiment* swallow me up. For
that's what drives me now. Nietzsche would despise me. I am the sort
of person he railed against: I'm in a position of weakness, driven by
the negative, by the desire to pull down the one who won, the strong.
I am purely reactive now. Yet have I ever been anything else? All my
life reacting—to Mama, to Grandmother, & then to Rbt. As though
there were nothing else. & now I'm reacting to *her*. At any rate, I must
unconsciously have known this & thus stopped reading Nietzsche. Because to listen to his voice, to see myself through that prism, would
be intolerable. (Yet still, at moments, I obviously *do* become aware of
that prism, even if I push it away from me as soon as I notice it.)

To be filled with this driving goal, which now seems to have a life
of its own, to have taken me over...it's as though all past selves have
melted away. Every interaction with the other humans on this island
has a purpose to it, nothing is said or done idly. All observation has a
point. Every thought must be harnessed to my objective. In short, I'm
bending my entire being to defeating Elizabeth. So, Rbt. You would
approve of me, finally. Will I win? I don't know. But for me, there's
nothing left *but* this machinery of war.

Monday, 7/9/2096

Since I haven't snatched the bait, she's changed tactics and is now actively stalking me instead of merely offering herself as mine for the taking. Which sounds absurd on the face of it—after all, *mine* is the role of predator. Can she have bought another line from Elizabeth, that she's willing to risk retaliation from me? She *must* know I will eventually lash out at her. If I could find a way to disillusion her about Elizabeth…But no. If I did that, she'd be without hope.

Since my bones and muscles were aching, I took a long Jacuzzi with the water as hot as I could stand it (turning the thermostat up every time my body adjusted to the heat). It enervated me, but I was determined to stay in as long as I could in an effort to dispense with Kitty's bedtime massage as a part of my working toward full independence. So I was lying there sweating and weak with my eyes closed, my head laid back. "Are you all right?" I heard her voice ask.

I jumped—my heart thudding laboriously from the surge of adrenalin that startlement shot into my blood—& opened my eyes and scowled at her. "What are you doing in here?" & then I saw she had on only that skimpy little scrap of lace she sometimes used to wear for me.

"You look terribly hot," she said. "Don't you think you should come out now—or maybe add some cold water?" & she leaned forward toward the taps—affording me a tantalizing glimpse of her breasts. (All the worse because I could imagine so vividly the round silken feel of them—through memory, not fantasy.)

"Mind your own business." My tone was fierce. "Don't touch that faucet. Just get out."

She offered me a look of apology. (She's an actor, I reminded myself, only to forget that fact moments later.) "I'm sorry," she said, making her eyes wide. "I didn't mean to annoy you." Then she *smiled* at me—fetchingly ingenuous, hesitantly eager. "I told Kitty that since I know so well how you like things done I'd see to your massage myself."

So then I repeated everything I'd said to her before & ordered her out of the bathroom. But she ignored my words & picking up the loofah & soap knelt at the edge of the tub & bent low (her breasts slipping out of that flimsy lace thing) & attempted to soap my shoulders.

Enervated or not, my heart raced in a kind of panic, & I grabbed her wrists & yelled at her to stop playing Elizabeth's game. I informed her that there was no point in her putting herself through the pain & humiliation, that Elizabeth was lying to her if she had promised to give her a second chance.

No, no, she cried, it wasn't that, she knew she had no chance, Elizabeth had told her that she'd blown it & that she would be living on the island indefinitely. Elizabeth, she claimed, had promised her nothing.

When she kept insisting that Elizabeth hadn't instructed her to seduce me, I pointed out that she had no reason in that case to be throwing herself at me. She switched gears then & sobbed out a lot of nonsense about being frightened & needing a friend & how nice I'd been to her (oh christ, in spite of my weakness I almost struck her for saying that) once I'd found out the truth about her, how lonely she was, how she hadn't had anyone to talk to for weeks & weeks since Elizabeth hadn't let her talk to anyone & how awful she'd felt at my rebuffing her & how she thought that if I wanted her sexually then at least I'd pay some attention to her.

I wanted to get out of the tub, but not with her in the room. I was so worn out I could hardly work up the energy to maintain my anger. So go hang around Kitty, I said. No, no, Kitty didn't like her, she disapproved of her, & anyway Elizabeth had warned her not to tell anyone else why she was on the island etc. etc. Then go talk to the amazons I said. In fact, I added before she could reply, you should be living over there. I don't want you in my house. Oh, she sobbed, they *despise* me. Please don't make me leave the house, if you do I'll sleep in the gym or the garage or even outdoors, I *couldn't* live with the amazons.

By this time I knew I had to get out of that tub, even if she *was* still there. So I clambered out & ended up flat on my face, the room spinning, too weak to get up. I told her to give me the towel; she did, & I wrapped myself in it. "Now listen to me, Sally," I said when I could. "I'm very sorry for the mess you're in. & probably it is true that you've had no one to talk to & are very lonely. Knowing Elizabeth, that wouldn't surprise me at all. But there's no help for it. I won't make you leave the house—so long as you stay out of my way. Otherwise you'll have to go."

But that didn't satisfy her. Why did I hate her so, she wanted to know. Did I have any idea how she'd felt after seeing me all bleeding & broken & for weeks not even knowing if I was alive (since no one would talk to her), how she had kept going over everything, wondering what she'd done or hadn't done, thinking about how she'd let me scare her away & then I'd gone & thrown myself off the cliff...

Remember, she's an actor. It's so damned easy to forget. She actually had me *believing* her. I almost put my arms around her to comfort her! But then I remembered, & I got to my feet, slipped into my gown, & started walking. She trailed me & asked if she couldn't at least sit with me, she wouldn't talk, she'd be so still I'd forget she was even there... Before I made it out of the bathroom I staggered against the doorframe, my ears buzzing, my vision darkening. I had to accept her help downstairs. But then, when we reached the library, I threatened to turn her out of the house in the morning after I'd regained my strength. Only then would she leave.

What an idiot I am. I spent the rest of the evening remembering the feel & smell of her as she helped me back to the library. Elizabeth would be pleased. After all, because of Sally my mind strayed from its major concern to thoughts of carnal pleasure. The problem is that I know the girl must be desperate & therefore I tend to excuse her & pity her. I must be harder. I *must*.

Wednesday, 7/11/2096

Our precarious little effort at civility has collapsed. This became apparent yesterday at dinner. Since Sally's arrival here, while the three of us have happened to eat breakfast or lunch together only two or three times, we've always dined together. Earlier in the day I'd snapped at Sally for mucking about in the Long Drawing Room, which is obviously hopeless. I told her to go down to the beach & swim. The weather these days is perfect for swimming, for sunning, for enjoying. She silently straightened up from her crouch (she was of all things collecting the stuffing from the furniture) & left the room. Later in the morning when I went to the gym for PT, I saw her toiling away in one of the gardens, that glum, closed expression of suffering still on her face.

Later, when I'd finished preparing dinner & Kitty & I were filling our plates to take out to Nicole's terrace, Kitty filled a plate for Sally as well. Barely glancing at me (certainly not meeting my eyes), she said, an edge in her voice, "She says she's not eating with us. I told her I'd bring her plate to her." I shrugged & carried my plate out to the terrace. When Kitty joined me, she made her anger clear. I remembered then what Elizabeth had told all the med-techs. So now she speaks to me only when necessary. I'm surprised she doesn't join Sally.

I've caught several glimpses of her today—which could have been premeditated on the girl's part—looking pathetic, her eyes swollen from crying. Of course she has reason for crying—realizing she has nothing good to look forward to. She must be very frightened. But there is nothing I can do for her. & thus it's best if we do not speak at all.

Thursday 7/12/2096

I'm in the Music Room, listening to Bach Orchestral Suites, sipping cognac. It's a warm night with a slight breeze wafting the smell of the sea into the house—have the windows in this room open. Only the one small lamp to see by as I write in this book.

Kitty let me have it with both barrels today. Have been ruminating on it for the last half hour or so. & it came to me how Rbt would in the same situation have exploded at what he would have called "impertinence." But I don't think it's insolence or anything like that behind Kitty's decision to get away from here on the next plane out. I think she's frightened by something she is unable to understand, is feeling threatened, &—let's be honest here, entirely disgusted. I could almost feel her nausea myself. I don't blame her. She never bargained for this scene. She knew of course that she would be paid extraordinarily well & that there were conditions (I feel sure they made the job conditional on points like her agreeing to loquazene exams etc.—I know they *must* have), but none of that touches her the way my (non)relations with Sally do. I'm not quite sure what she thinks has happened between us, but it's clear that she thinks we're both horrors & she wants no part of us. Sally, she said, isn't eating & does nothing but cry. She knows from Sally that Sally & I were lovers in the past. Kitty thinks I'm being cruel to Sally. But I can see she thinks Sally is as bent as I.

So Kitty will go, & there will be no one to act as go-between for us. I don't know what to do. I can't physically kick Sally out of the house— she is, at this point, stronger than I. Also, she may well find the amazons too difficult to take. In which case I don't doubt she'd sleep outside—of course making sure that I was always aware of her doing so. & so now I must have the wreck of this girl on my conscience. One more source of pain Elizabeth inflicts on me. Even if Elizabeth hadn't spoken so vilely to me or hadn't wrecked this house, what she has done to Sally is motive enough to destroy her. Large as this house is—no, as this island is—I can't escape feeling Sally's wretched presence. But I mustn't give in. Because if I do, Elizabeth will have me precisely where she wants me. & Sally will be no happier. Remember that. Neither of us can gain by my weakness.

Friday, 7/13/2096

Friday the thirteenth. & today Kitty left. The physical therapist remains, though, still living with the amazons. The doctor visited, said I was doing "splendidly." Walking on the beach I came upon Sally huddled in weepy melancholy. Didn't speak to her.

& now that I have more privacy, tomorrow I will try to force myself to do some memory regression. I shouldn't put it off much longer.

Oh, & I've discovered one of the amazons likes baroque music. I've invited her to make free with my CD collection. This may be a promising opening.

Saturday, 7/14/2096

I've done it. I've made myself do the memory regression. It's odd how memory fades to the actual point of distortion. I'd forgotten the essence of that period of time—the sense of desperation & violence all around me. The sense of Rbt's insanity. But how could I have forgotten that? I could feel it all falling down around our ears—not only the constant repression to keep the cities "under control" (when they essentially became wastelands of violence barely kept from erupting by the city's streets etc. being bound in a strait-jacket contraption of "security," making anything beyond bare existence impossible), but the loss of support from everyone but those in Security & Military.

The unreality of Military & Security alternating between cooperation & attempting to feed one another to the sharks—as though never sure which was the more expedient strategy. Knowing that only the possession of superior physical force stood between Rbt & his fall. In the end she did have to use force against him. Imagine that. How uncivilized. & that the showdown should come at the Colorado house with people—on both sides—killed as she came after him. Somehow all that had faded from my memory. But then the psychic violence of that day probably overshadowed everything else.

So she broke through his defenses, entered, & literally occupied the house & disarmed him. I was beside myself with joy. & then there the three of us were, in that room with those walls of windows (the views that house has—as stunning as anything I can think of), but of course we weren't even aware of the view, not with the two of them flinging accusations, taunts, & insults at one another.

Her first objective was to separate him from me. So she stated her offer of my living in comfort & ease on this island. & then she stated my alternative—living with *him* at the winery house. (A godforsaken place except when taken in brief snatches, a small house in comparison with the other residences, arid atmosphere, &—I imagined—a terrible threat of claustrophobia. & with *him* for ever & ever? & in that place in particular, where my memories are of all places the most painful?) I didn't need to be persuaded, but she didn't know that & didn't give me a chance to answer. Instead she said, "No, don't give me your answer yet. Let me tell you a few things first." & then she flatly stated that since he had killed Kay he could do the same to me. I think she thought I knew that he had done that. But of course I hadn't known that. I turned to him. "*You* killed her? Is that true?"

Oh he was savage to Elizabeth, his fury on the verge of psychotic attack. (Except that she was so much stronger than he that she didn't even bother to have anyone else in the room with her when talking to us.) Last night as I was watching this scene unfold, it occurred to me that the only thing that kept him under any control at all was his desperation to keep me from leaving him. "Shooting her was the greatest sacrifice I've ever made!" he cried to me. "Listen to me, Persephone, listen to me! She begged me, she *pleaded* with me, she *ordered* me to shoot her. Because she couldn't bear what that *bitch*"—& here he jerked his head in Elizabeth's direction—"had done to her! Kay didn't believe she could ever pull herself together again, she felt destroyed by what Weatherall did to her." & then he said, suddenly cold & restrained, "It's all down on paper, too. There's a transcript. You can read it for yourself." & he looked from me to Elizabeth & gave her one of his nastiest smiles.

All the color drained from her face. "I'll find it," she said, but he shook his head at her. So she said to me, "Do you want to spend the rest of your life with a man who could kill the person he claims to have loved most?"

I had already made up my mind, so this only gave me an excuse—though I see now that I was so emotionally overloaded by all this that I hardly understood what I was hearing. "No," I said, "I don't want to live with him. I accept your offer."

& then he flung himself at me. God. I never thought to see him like that. It was horrible. I told him to let me go, that I'd hated him for years, that I was glad I could finally escape him. His "Persephone" in my ears, he said I didn't know what I was saying, that it was only the shock of the moment, that if I knew everything I wouldn't feel this way, that it was too important a decision to be made like that, that separated she'd be able to play us against one another, we needed one another, we were in one another's blood etc. etc.—repeating all the things he habitually said to me at certain times. He said, too, that he couldn't live without me, without my love. & then there came pouring out of me all the words of hate that had been locked inside me for all those years. They poured out in a flood, & he reeled under them—& understood finally that he'd lost me.

When my stream of vituperation ran out, he said (my god, the wreck his face was—I'd forgotten that, too), "It is all there for you. You can save yourself, Persephone. You will know how. It's all down in the will, everything's taken care of." & then he did it. He killed himself while we stood watching. While the hate was still heaving inside me. & then seeing him like that, a horrible panic came over me—I hadn't remembered this at all, I'd obviously blocked it out—I got down on the floor beside him, screaming, hysterical, sobbing, wanting to take back all my words, wanting to take back my denial of him. Someone stuck a needle in me. Not Elizabeth, but someone she had waiting nearby. & I dropped into unconsciousness. & then the next thing I knew I was on the plane—on Rbt's jet—& we were landing on the island. Everything was a haze because of the drugs & the shock. & then I opened the safes for Elizabeth & she talked to me & I signed papers. & then she went away & Rbt's body was buried—according to his instructions in the will.

& then I was here alone. Alone in this house as I'd never been. & everything was over. Elizabeth had told me this was to be where I would be spending the rest of my life, but I see now that I never took it in, that I didn't really believe it. That I thought that after a while Elizabeth would let me leave. (When I'd shown her what a good girl I really was?) That she would realize I was no threat to her. Foolish me. So naive.

So what was the point of reliving all that? I'm a wreck now, a wreck for having remembered. & I'm no closer to finding the transcript—except that now I know it involved what Elizabeth did to Kay. Which explains a great deal. The only clue I caught has to do with the will. I think there may still be a copy here somewhere. I suppose I'd better get it out & study it. Surely that *was* what he meant? It's clear he kept the transcript as a kind of last resort for dealing with Elizabeth. For he did threaten her with it, unequivocally. It was on his mind. That *had* to have been what he meant when he told me I could "save" myself.

I want another glass of cognac. So far I've kept myself to one glass each evening. (Except last night when I took a tranquilizer instead.)

Sunday 7/15/2096

Apart from all the financial details there's nothing in the will but instructions for burial in the same grave as Kay, under the holly tree. What strikes me as peculiar now (at the time I was too crazy to notice) is the degree of specificity in the instructions. That I be there when the grave is dug & when he is lowered into it, that the grave be dug exactly so many inches from the statue of Kay on the one hand & the trunk of the holly tree on the other... Why these numbers, these very specific details? A kind of craziness? Or is there some significance there, a hint of something I was supposed to understand? When he mentioned the will before taking the cyanide, I thought he was referring to my financial well-being. But now that I know he used the expression "save yourself," saying I would "know how," that it's all "in the will"—it seems as though there *must* be something in his burial instructions that holds the key. For everything else in the will has to do with the Estate & is essentially instructions to our financial managers...

Looking at the will, I wished Rbt hadn't named me executor—that he'd named Grandfather or someone like him—because then there'd have been a chance of someone interfering from outside. But I suppose that since Rbt had thrust most of the responsibility for overseeing his finances onto me it never occurred to him to name anyone else.

It's plain to me what I must do. I must clandestinely dig around out there. Perhaps the gravediggers were supposed to uncover something? Or no, wait...if that were the case, then there would have been the danger of Elizabeth's getting hold of it. No, maybe he gave the precise instructions so that he could be sure they *didn't* uncover it? But all this is fantasy & speculation on my part. It may have nothing to do with the transcript at all. But so far it's my best lead going. I'll have to do it in the dark. Encountering *her* bones, or *his* coffin: the thought makes my flesh creep...

Am I strong enough now to tackle such a strenuous job? I'll have to take stimulants to help me. It will have to be on a dark night. & I will *feel* my way. What a shiver just snaked down my spine. I hope this won't be for naught. Doing such a horrible thing. But if it gives me some leverage with Elizabeth... Provided she doesn't manage to take it away from me once I find it. But I must think everything out carefully—*before* I start digging.

Chapter Twenty

[i]

A sound penetrated the mists of sleep. And then repeated itself. Hazel struggled to wake up. It was the phone. She reached out and after a few seconds' groping put her hand on it and fumbled it open. "Hello?" she said as she pried her eyelids apart. Light. She closed them again. It must be morning.

"Hazel Bell, please."

Hazel cleared her throat. "This is Hazel Bell."

"Good morning, Hazel. This is Margaret Canfield. Sorry to wake you. I'm afraid I forgot how early it is out there."

Hazel's eyes flew open. "How can I help you, Margaret?"

"I have good news for you," Margaret said. "We're very close to winning Celia Espin's release. We think it will be only a matter of hours before we finish ironing out the details."

Hazel's breath caught in her throat. "Really? You mean she might be released *today*?"

"That's possible. But we have a request to make of you."

Hmm. Attaching strings this close to the release? "And what is that?"

"Elizabeth would like to meet with you."

Shit.

"She would like you to come to DC. This afternoon. She hopes to have returned with Ms. Espin from New Orleans by then."

"She's in New Orleans herself?"

"Yes. She's been engaged in some complicated, ah, horsetrading."

"I see. But why take Celia to DC?"

A beat passed, then Margaret said, "I think I'd better let Elizabeth answer that herself."

"Is my meeting her a demand?" Hazel asked, intuitively certain Margaret didn't want to be pinned down.

"The authorities in Louisiana are adamant about first releasing Ms. Espin to ODS custody. They can't otherwise save face. And they don't want her loose in Baton Rouge."

"To *ODS?*"

"Only as a formality," Margaret said. "I can assure you, ODS will not keep her." When Hazel did not immediately answer, Margaret said, "I know it sounds peculiar. But I can assure you, this was the only way we could manage it without having to take even longer before securing Ms. Espin's release."

"This is rather short notice for a meeting."

"Yes, I realize that. We can have a plane for you at SeaTac by noon, ready to leave at your convenience."

They would specially fly in a plane for *her?* What was Liz up to, anyway? "And I could bring others with me?" Hazel asked.

"Not Ms. Greenglass, Ms. Chalkins, or Ms. Kaufmann. As you know, they have been declared *persona non grata.*"

"But I could bring others?"

"We would prefer not," Margaret said. "Although we are—and Elizabeth herself will want to discuss this more fully with you—interested in pursuing further meetings with you and your, ah, colleagues. Elizabeth did say to me that if you insisted on coming accompanied you limit yourself to one person and, needless to say, one of those who have not been declared unwelcome in the US."

"Very well," Hazel said.

"Oh, excellent, I know Elizabeth will be very pleased." Margaret fairly cooed. "Someone on the plane's crew will phone you on arrival. You can then make your arrangements directly with them."

"What about hotel reservations and such?"

"We'll take care of everything."

"Very well." Hazel hung up and within a minute of doing so realized that with the unexpected prospect of Celia's release dangling before her as a carrot she had let herself be stampeded into doing exactly what she had refused to do under more deliberate conditions. She almost picked up the handset to call Margaret back and refuse the arrangement, but the thought of delaying Celia's release held her back. No, she would go through with it. Liz would have the advantage in several respects, but she should be strong enough by now to handle a brief excursion into that world again. And she could always leave as soon as Celia had been freed.

Hazel got up and peed and washed her hands and face and left her room in search of coffee. She found Martha in the kitchen. "You look as though you've just bought the Brooklyn Bridge," Martha said.

"I've just bought Celia's release." Hazel saw that it was just seven. "We'll be getting her out this afternoon, if what Canfield says is correct."

"And the price?"

Hazel shook her head. "I don't know. I'm flying out to DC this afternoon. I think I'm going to ask Emily to go along with me." It crossed her mind that Liz might have told Canfield how out-of-it Hazel always was in the morning before intaking her first infusion of caffeine.

Martha got a couple of mugs from the cupboard and poured out the coffee she'd just made. "That probably means Astrea, too, then." She shot Hazel a look.

"Emily has sound instincts where Liz is concerned," Hazel said.

"And you don't?"

Hazel reached for the mug Martha passed her and breathed in the rich fragrance. Seven o'clock in the morning, she thought. Might as well be the middle of the night as far as her brain was concerned.

[ii]

The crew asked Hazel and Emily not to use a jamming device on board lest it disturb the aircraft's electronics. Emily looked into Hazel's eyes, and Hazel nodded. And then Emily took a book from her bag—*The Political and Economic Foundations of the Arts in the Twenty-first Century*—and began reading. Hazel, admitting to herself just how keyed up she was, did not attempt to read. Most of the time she stared out the window, reviewed the two-hour talk she and Emily had had before driving to SeaTac, and thought about Liz.

Martha had argued that Hazel should call Canfield back and tell her that the meeting was off. "She caught you unprepared. You know it's a mistake. You're letting *her* set up the context and basic structures of the meeting. They probably knew you'd refuse if they'd called later in the day when you were playing with a full deck. Don't let them stampede you!"

Yes, she was allowing herself to be drawn into Liz's world—but only for a brief encounter. They might learn a great deal. And they might even accomplish something—though about this Hazel warned herself not to cherish illusions. As for handling it—if she wasn't strong enough to deal with Liz and her world for a short time, then she hadn't come very far after all.

Her gaze moved from the window to slowly sweep the cabin in which they sat entirely alone. Liz's sending this plane for them struck Hazel as a deliberate demonstration of power and wealth. There would probably be more of the same in DC. With these demonstrations Liz would be saying several things to her—*look how powerful I am now— therefore be careful with me.* She might also be saying *if you'd stayed with me you would be a part of all this.* But more subtly, Liz would be nudging her to abide by executive rules and mores, to respect the social formulas that served to keep people in line. These things worked step by step: first the ambiance, then the little attentions of courtesy that one would look boorish to refuse, the little attentions that said *we're civilized people here, we consider you civilized along with us because you know how to behave properly,* which would then set up a certain pressure of perhaps unperceived rapport and would nudge one into respecting other unwritten, unspoken pressures until finally the very thought of breaking any of these protocols would make one feel uncomfortable. Or else one could embrace the rules of the game and try to manipulate the other side by using their rules. This naturally entailed a high failure rate, especially for people like Hazel who had been service-techs all their lives. Emily, on the other hand, probably did best when playing their game, for she knew instinctively how to play it.

A voice over the intercom advised them to fasten their seatbelts and announced that they would be landing in seven minutes. Hazel finished the juice she had been sipping and peered out the window at the ground below. Probably, she thought, the war damage had been completely cleared away. Would there be relics of those last insane years before Liz had pulled off her coup, structures like those only partially dismantled in Boston? But no, they would probably see to it that DC of all places had been liberated of such structures.

Hazel touched Emily's elbow.

"Look out the window at where we're landing!" The engines' whine grew louder as they descended.

Emily looked out the window. "This is a military base," she said, sounding puzzled.

The wheels touched the runway. "Liz *hates* anything to do with Military," Hazel said. "So why in the hell are we landing *here*?" She looked at Emily. "Do you suppose——" she left her worry unstated.

"We have access to the Marq'ssan whenever we want," Emily said, her eyes as steady as her voice.

Hazel swallowed. "Yes. Of course. They wouldn't lead us into a trap, would they?"

"I don't think so. But if they do, it won't do them a damned bit of good." Emily's eyes bored into Hazel's. "Remember that."

"Of course," Hazel said, half-ashamed of her moment of panic.

The plane rolled to a stop, and the cabin door opened. A uniformed officer informed them that a car was waiting; he took their bags, which he passed to a waiting subordinate, and invited them to deplane. Trying to still her trepidation, Hazel descended the stairs to the pavement, where a gleaming gray car unlike anything she had ever seen was parked.

"I don't believe my eyes," Emily said. "A Rolls Royce, I think. Where on earth did she find it?" A woman dressed like the one who had given Hazel Liz's letter held open the back door. "Mauve interior, too. And more livery, I see." Emily grinned at Hazel. "Shall we?"

Hazel got into the car and scooted along the seat to sit near the other window. Emily piled in beside her. The uniformed woman closed Emily's door; hearing another door slam Hazel turned and looked out the back window in time to see the man who had taken their bags moving away from the car. Swiftly the car swept across the pavement, away from the plane, and accessed a deserted service road. Hazel observed that another uniformed woman sat in the front, probably an amazon.

Emily pulled out her jammer and activated it. "Why the military base?" Hazel said.

"I've no idea. Maybe it isn't tactical at all. Maybe she always comes in here. My guess is this is Andrews Air Force Base. Which isn't far from the Executive's offices."

"She used to hate anything to do with Military."

"Things have changed. Of course, it may be a further attempt to impress us."

"You mean intimidate us," Hazel said. The car approached a guardpost. The sight of uniformed men holding M-19s raised the hair on the back of her neck. The car did not stop but passed the gate, and Hazel realized they had lifted the barrier before the car had even reached the guardpost. More theatrics, she decided: a sign of things to come. Liz would be laying it on, sure to be overawing someone with a humble service-tech background who had made it big in the anarchy... If she *darling*s me I'll make her stop, Hazel resolved. I'll only let her go so far with all of this, and then I'll refuse to play.

"We're agreed that we should insist on seeing Celia before there's any talk with Elizabeth?" Emily said, referring back to their earlier discussion of tactics.

"Yes. And we insist on doing our own recording of all conversation."

"And we protest the expulsion and exclusion of Martha, Eileen, and Jill."

Those were the three points they had resolved on. They had not had time to discuss much more than that; everything else would have to be worked out in an *ad hoc* fashion. There had been discussions for weeks now on what sort of agenda they'd want if they did find themselves negotiating with Liz. But since the primary point of their negotiation seemed to be resolved—namely, first Martha's and then Celia's release—they would be starting almost fresh.

"We should try to bring in some of the DC activists," Emily said. She gave Hazel a rueful look. "I wish I'd thought to contact them before leaving Seattle."

"We must almost be there," Hazel said, noticing the familiar buildings they were passing. Which one, she wondered, did Liz have her office in? Presumably not Security Central. The car stopped several times to be given clearance past successive guardposts, then entered a roundabout in front of a relatively small yet tall white and green marble building, labeled simply as the Clarence D. Roderick Memorial Building. Hadn't Booth had his office here?

Emily switched off the jammer and slipped it back into her tunic pouch. Smiling, she took Hazel's hand and squeezed it. Hazel could not quite manage to smile back. Her apprehension seemed to be swallowing her up.

Another woman in a mauve and gray uniform appeared at Hazel's side of the car, opened the door, and conducted them past the marines standing sentry both outside and inside the building. The uniformed woman led them around the corner from the bank of elevators and using a plastic strip opened a door that concealed another elevator. No one spoke as the thickly carpeted, gray leather-walled car shot upward. The doors opened onto an airy lobby filled with a holographic sculpture of succulent fruit and flowers that in spite of the absence of human figures had a distinctly erotic flavor to it. "I'd know that sculptor's work anywhere," Emily said. "It has to be Ada Chun's. I'd be willing to bet on it."

"Emily, Hazel?" Hazel turned and faced a short round woman wearing a loose, swishy peach silk tunic. "Margaret Canfield," she said, holding out her hand to Hazel.

"Hazel Bell," Hazel said, shaking Margaret's hand.

"And you must be Emily Madden." Margaret smiled and shook her hand as well. "I hope all the arrangements have been satisfactory so far?"

"What is the news on Celia?" Hazel asked.

Margaret glanced at the service-techs behind the front desk. "Why don't we go inside," she said, gesturing at the doorway to the right.

Emily slipped her arm through Hazel's, and they followed Margaret into a large, sunny office. Before Hazel could take much of it in, she heard Liz's voice gurgling, "I'm so pleased, so pleased you've come!" Hazel glanced around and saw Liz striding to them, a glowing picture of health, impeccable grooming, and flawless beauty. *She's let her braid grow back* was Hazel's first thought. And then Liz was lightly embracing Emily, brushing cheeks with her and murmuring something about being delighted to see her again so soon. When Liz turned to her, Hazel tried to make her oddly stiff face produce a smile. Liz's eyes, she noticed, were brimming with tears as she took both of Hazel's hands between her own. "You look wonderful," Liz whispered. "I'm so glad you came."

Hazel nodded and found it hard to speak. "Hello, Liz," she said, acutely aware of Liz's grip on her hands. "Has everything worked out, with Celia?" Her eyes were fairly mesmerized by Liz's bright blue glassy gaze.

"Yes, yes, it's all worked out for the best." Liz continued to hold Hazel's hands. "She's over in Lisa Mott's office. It's all arranged that Emily is to go over there at once." Liz glanced at Emily. "For Ms. Espin's sake," she added. "I'm sure the last few weeks haven't been easy for her."

"I'd like to see her as soon as possible," Emily said.

Liz's smile flashed out. "Good. Then Dale—she's the amazon who escorted you upstairs—can take you over there now." Liz looked around. "Margaret? Will you see to it?" Liz smiled down at Hazel. "And then Hazel and I can relax and talk in my office."

Hazel emerged sufficiently from her daze to realize that Liz was neatly separating her from Emily. She turned to Emily, but Emily was already going off with Margaret—probably at this point thinking only of Celia. Hazel let Liz take her arm and draw her through Margaret's office, into her own. "What were the conditions of Celia's release?" Hazel asked, grasping at the first thing that came into her head.

"Let's sit over here, shall we." Liz steered Hazel to one of the smaller groupings of furniture. Since Liz sat in the armchair, Hazel sat on the sofa. Liz beamed at her. "I know this is silly," she said, "but I'm beside myself with joy at seeing you."

"You look well," Hazel said awkwardly, wishing Liz's warmth weren't affecting her so powerfully.

"So do you," Liz said. "You wear your PhD very well. May I offer you my belated congratulations?"

Hazel grimaced. "Thank you."

"I'm sure you'd like to know the agenda I've set up, subject—naturally—to any change you'd like to make."

Hazel mustered a smile. Of course Liz would have an "agenda" for her. "It's something of a mystery why you want this meeting now," Hazel said. "And Margaret wouldn't say."

"Who knows who might be tapping your phone?"

"Tell me what you have in mind," Hazel said.

"First, I'm leaving it up to Ms. Espin and Emily to decide whether they want to join our discussions. I'm putting a plane at their disposal, should they wish to go to either Seattle or San Diego." Liz crossed her legs. "If you want someone else to join you, I won't object, provided some of our talks are one-on-one."

Talks? It sounded as though Liz intended this to be a long drawn-out affair. "I don't understand," Hazel said. "Are you thinking of working out an agreement between the Executive and the Free Zone?"

"We already have an agreement with the Free Zone, don't we," Liz said, referring to the agreement worked out after the fall of the old Executive. "I'm hoping for something more than that."

"If it's about Martha and the others' activism," Hazel said, "then we've nothing to talk about."

Liz's long fingers smoothed her dark crimson tunic over her thigh. "No, it's not about that precisely. I would be interested, Hazel, in working out some sort of arrangement with the Marq'ssan. You see, I'd like to do business with them."

"Then Emily and Martha should be a part of our talks," Hazel said.

"Emily yes, Greenglass no." Liz's face grew a little cold. "Greenglass is completely out of the question."

So Liz still had some kind of thing against Martha. Otherwise why be so adamant? "Martha worked everything out between the Marq'ssan and the Austrians," Hazel said.

"She's *persona non grata*, Hazel. Anywhere in this country."

"You don't think that will keep her out?"

"Perhaps not," Liz said, "but it will keep her from ever managing to stay for very long."

"And if the Marq'ssan were to insist on working through her?"

"Then I suppose the whole endeavor would collapse."

Hazel sighed. "Tell me the rest." Wishing she had a NoteMaster handy, Hazel realized that she hadn't been recording this conversation.

Liz's scrutiny of Hazel intensified. "I'd like you and your people to talk with me and various others over the next few days." She hesitated. "Ultimately, I think the Marq'ssan themselves must come into it. I don't see how we can deal always through intermediaries. Not on matters of such monumental significance."

So Liz had something major in mind? "But you know how the Marq'ssan have always reasoned about this," Hazel said into the silence. "They don't actually make arrangements for themselves, but allow themselves to be used so that others may negotiate with powers that would otherwise ignore them."

"But it is the Marq'ssan we must negotiate with," Liz said. "It is frustrating and infuriating that they refuse to face us!"

"I doubt if that's going to change. Even in the early days they had no intention of ever talking to the actual heads of government themselves." Hazel restlessly shifted her legs. "I don't like this set-up, Liz. I'm unprepared. And I'm not sure I want to invite others to join me here under these conditions. I think we should be on neutral ground, which any place in DC definitely is not. And then there's the matter of living arrangements and such, which I haven't had a chance to see to myself. I think—"

"I thought," Liz said, leaning forward, "that you and Emily and whoever could stay in my house. It's enormous and very comfortable. I—"

"Oh come on, Liz." Hazel's tone was incredulous. "You don't seriously expect us to be your personal guests when we're engaged in this sort of thing?"

Liz bit her lip. "You would have all the privacy you'd like. But if that would truly make you uncomfortable, hotel accommodations can be arranged. I apologize for taking you by surprise, but when things fell into place for Espin, I experienced a burst of excitement and hope that maybe now we can work things out." She smiled. "After all, there was that goodwill gesture on your side, when the Marq'ssan rid us of that vile·pollution dump, and then *our* goodwill gesture of getting Espin freed. This morning it seemed a great basis for hope and a time to push forward."

Did Liz really expect her to believe this agenda had been created on the spur of the moment? "Have you declared Celia *persona non grata* too?" Hazel asked.

Liz's soft reddish eyebrows flew high into her forehead. "Certainly not! I never thought the Baton Rouge DA's office was correct in its detention of Espin. As a matter of fact, I'm hoping Espin will agree to go to work for the Justice Department's Human and Civil Rights Division."

Hazel's mouth dropped open. First she offered Emily a job, and now Celia. Would Celia take it? She might, Hazel thought, unless she had been disillusioned by her treatment at the hands of legal authorities. Who next? Herself? But Liz must know better than to try *her*.

"Don't look so astonished. I need people like Espin." Liz's mouth twisted. "If this Baton Rouge affair has taught me one thing, it's that I still have a lot of work to do to reform the system."

"Oh Liz," Hazel sighed.

"Yes, I know you don't agree with me." Liz uncrossed her legs and rose to her feet. "But I have this idea, Hazel, that we can work together. You and I, I mean, because there won't be the kind of distrust and ignorance getting between us that there would be if it were someone else and Greenglass." Hazel gaped at her. Could Liz possibly think she *trusted* her? Or was this some kind of rhetorical ploy? "You see," Liz said, sounding a trifle impatient, "if we *can't* talk then we're going to have escalating trouble. Because there's a very vocal, influential group within the Executive that's pushing for declaring the agreement null and void and putting out warrants for the arrest of key Free Zone leaders on treason charges."

Hazel half-laughed. "But we'd just be back to where we were before," she said. "And you know you've never been able to deal with us by force."

"*Us*," Liz hissed—and walked to the far end of the office.

Hazel turned in her chair and saw that Liz was making a phone call. She couldn't make out more than the undifferentiated murmur of her voice. Hazel closed her eyes to shut out her surroundings. *Where are my bags? I've nothing with me, not my NoteMaster, not my notes... I have to get a grip on this situation. Must insist on contacting local activists and bringing them in on this... That would be one reason for holding talks here in DC. Maybe the* only *reason...*

Liz appeared beside Hazel's chair, startling her out of her reverie. "Here, Emily would like to speak to you," she said, passing Hazel her handset.

"Yes?" Hazel said, aware of Liz's returning to her desk, offering what was probably only an illusion of privacy.

"Let's compare notes," Emily said. "I'd like to accompany Celia to San Diego, so that she doesn't have to do the trip alone surrounded by military creeps."

"Oh," Hazel said, disappointed. "Then maybe we'd better get some others out here. Liz claims she wants to do some real negotiating. Along Austrian lines."

"Really?" Emily sounded dubious.

"I thought I should get some local activists in on it, too."

"Too bad we can't call a national convention," Emily said thoughtfully. "If she's serious, I mean."

"So who do you recommend we fly out here?"

"I can return as soon as I see Celia comfortably in Elena's company," Emily said.

"Oh, that would be wonderful. And speaking of Celia, how is she?"

After a brief silence, Emily said, "I'm not sure. She's apparently close to accepting a job with the Justice Department. Though I'm going to try to talk some sense into her. I think it's too soon for her to be making important decisions."

"You think maybe you should stay with her in San Diego for a while?" Hazel asked, torn between hoping Emily would stick with the decision to return and worrying about whatever was going on with Celia.

"No, I don't think that would necessarily be the right thing. I think she needs some relaxation time. And I'm not sure that San Diego is the place for her to try to get it, considering Elena and Luis's involvements. But she doesn't want to go to Whidbey or anywhere in the Free Zone. Because she insists that there was nothing to this time spent in jail."

It sounded complicated. "Okay, if you're sure," Hazel said, relieved to know Emily would be supporting her against Liz.

"I think the way I'll work it is to return here in the morning," Emily said. "You have the names and numbers of the locals I gave you, don't you?"

"Yes," Hazel said, again wondering where her bags had been taken.

"I'll call Martha and let her know what's up, in case you're too busy at your end. And of course I'll be in touch with Astrea."

Of course? How close *were* they? Martha had given her the signal for Sorben to be used only in case of dire need.

"I'll see you in the morning then," Emily said.

Hazel returned the handset to Liz, who was sitting at her desk, talking into another handset. Liz held up her hand, signaling Hazel to wait, and then almost immediately hung up. Before Liz could speak, Hazel told her she wanted her bags, as well as to get set up so that she could begin making phone calls for lining people up for these "talks."

Liz pursued her lips. "You want to set up somewhere on your own. I understand. I'll have Margaret get you decent hotel space. For office as well as sleeping quarters, I presume?" Hazel nodded. "But you will dine with me? Lacie would be very disappointed if you didn't." Her rueful look shifted into a half-smile. "And so would I."

"Lacie's still with you?"

"We get along well, she and I."

"I remember," Hazel said drily.

"So will you dine with me?"

Hazel knew she could say no. She could even hear herself doing so. But if she did, Liz would think she did it out of trepidation. And then there would be that between them all the time they talked. She looked into Liz's eyes. "Yes, of course," she said. "I'll enjoy seeing Lacie again." She looked quickly away from Liz's slight flush. "Oh, and I'll want to rent a free-wheeler," she said, switching her attention back to the problem of how to counteract the disadvantages of the situation.

"We can supply you with one," Liz said, reaching for the phone. "I'll ask Margaret to come in and you can tell her everything you'd like to be done that you feel you can trust us with."

Hazel took one of the two chairs facing Liz's desk. Liz was making it as easy as she could, with everything gliding smoothly along, every cog in the machinery greased to prevent friction. All to make her forget that ordinarily these same structures worked against people like herself even as they worked for people like Liz.

[iii]

On Friday evening when the core group met alone, Hazel had to report that Liz had canceled the afternoon's scheduled meeting, claiming that an "unrelated matter of urgency" had arisen and was demanding her attention. So far she and Liz had had two sessions alone, which were supposed to allow "sharper, more focused" discussions of the issues. She had her doubts that this format could work, but since access to Liz was obviously important and since it wasn't clear whether there'd be negotiations otherwise, Hazel had agreed to go along with it.

"One big problem with the DC people is that they seem to have little idea of harmonious coalition politics," Pat said.

"An even more important problem," Hazel said, "is that very few activists are going to be able to participate in any of the talks because they have jobs they have to go to. We can't do everything on the weekends, and only certain people will be willing to risk getting fired for the sake of all this." *All this*—the very thought of what they were trying to do—out of the blue, for whatever reason—sometimes overwhelmed Hazel. But the problem of the activists' being tied to their jobs dogged her. She had thought, for instance, of bringing in various women she had been corresponding with since their initial contact during seminars she had given, and so she had phoned Nancy Ruiz, in Baltimore. Nancy had questioned whether what was happening here was worth her losing her job over. She would come, she said, on the weekends, if Hazel could accept her participation on such a limited basis.

"What bothers *me*," Lucille said—and Hazel realized this was to be a session in which all their misgivings and apprehensions were to be aired—"is the question of whether we should go along with this contract-writing format." Her thick dark eyebrows drew down into a vee. "I mean, neither the Free Zone nor the Marq'ssan consider the law to be an absolute. We all know it's a tool of the authority in power. And it's not *law* that will make the executives abide by anything that's agreed upon, but fear of Marq'ssan retribution. So why go through all this legalistic crap?"

"It's the League for the Return to Democracy that's behind *that*," Pat said. "But as long as we're bringing out a list of our anxieties, can

I add my misgivings about counting so heavily on an arrangement of workers being represented on the governing boards of their workplace? Unless we're careful about the selection process itself, the execs could slot in people they think can be co-opted."

"But if there were activist group input at the same time," Emily said, "surely that wouldn't be likely."

Pat delivered the *coup de grace*: "Doesn't all this come down to the fact that what we seem to be getting ourselves into is arranging some kind of reform—for which people will be obsequiously grateful to the Executive and count themselves lucky and thereby go on perpetuating the system?"

A thick silence settled over them, which Hazel eventually broke. "It isn't reform we're interested in, is it. It seems to me we're trying to set up a climate more favorable to change. As well as bring about an expansion of organization. Think of it: Sedgewick wiped out an entire spectrum of dissident organizations. How do we get such things started again?" Lucille nodded vigorously. She went on, "Apart from which, we might wonder how people can have the energy for such things if they can't even confront their employers on the most basic issues controlling their day-to-day existence. If they start by exercising some control over their workplace conditions and so on, then it would be easier for them to expand outward from that. As it is, people are grateful to hold on to their jobs, grateful to be able to buy things apart from subsistence again—what do you think this face- and body-painting craze is all about?—grateful to be able to go from one part of their city to another without having to have their identity checked or submitting to other invasions of privacy. Grateful to see violence reduced to crime and domestic abuse." Hazel reached for the barely touched deli platter and snatched up a shiny, wrinkled black olive.

"It's not that I don't see the usefulness of changing the living and working conditions for service-techs everywhere." Pat set down her beer glass. "And of course I don't want to perpetuate their misery. But I don't want to hand the Executive a plan for stabilizing their system, either. Or for guaranteeing them immunity against Marq'ssan reprisals. And it seems to me that that's what we're doing. That's certainly what's happened in Austria."

"Ah, Austria," Emily said, shaking her head. "You might be surprised about Austria, Pat. I'd say that though they are *stable* in Austria, they're nevertheless changing quite rapidly. You see, the more input people get, the more they want. It's a kind of expanding consciousness along with rising expectations. There's a certain self-educational process going on there. And the fact that it's taking place in an atmosphere of prosperity and relative tranquility is critical. I don't think it's *in spite* of prosperity and tranquility, but that peace and tranquility are almost *essential* for meaningful change. Violence just doesn't work. Violent revolution always leads to new forms of tyranny. That's because the cycle of violence is difficult to break. In my view, the better things are materially and the freer people are to express themselves and make demands and challenge authority, the more truly radical change becomes possible. Fear—and this has been exacerbated by the Sedgewick years—fear is poisonous to creativity and positive non-repressive change. If we can eliminate some of the fear by coming to certain agreements with the Executive, then we'll be much better off in the long run. People's minds grow fertile the more conditions are relaxed. While fear engenders self-censorship."

"Hear, hear," Hazel cheered, smiling. Emily almost never made speeches.

"I can see your point," Pat began, and Hazel could already hear the "but" that would begin her next sentence. Pat's next sentence, however, did not get spoken, for a knock sounded on the outside door of their suite.

"I'll get it," Hazel said, rising to her feet. Maybe Nancy had been able to get away after all. Before opening the door, she peeked out through the peep-hole. "Hey, it's Astrea," she called over her shoulder as she unlocked the door.

Astrea crossed the threshold—incongruously, Hazel thought, for it was quite certain she had not gone through the conventional procedures of most visitors to this hotel, jumping through all the security hoops the management used to assure the privacy and safety of its guests from unwanted incursions. Hazel realized that Astrea hadn't come alone. "Hazel," Astrea said, "meet Lourdes Montini."

Hazel smiled and offered her hand. "Welcome. I'm Hazel Bell."

The woman returned the greeting. "Astrea said that you were the one doing most of the talking for our side," Lourdes replied in heavily accented English.

"Oh, I forgot." Astrea held out her palm. "Take one of those and clip it to your ear, Hazel. It's a translation device."

Hazel selected one of the six earrings in Astrea's palm and fastened it to her right ear. She had worn these on five or six other occasions. The others by now had stood up and come over to them, and Astrea handed out translation ear rings to them, too.

"When we were talking Wednesday night, Emily brought up the problem of achieving a broad enough participation in these negotiations," Astrea said after she had finished making introductions. "I thought that you might like input from outside the US. When I talked with Lourdes and a few of her friends about it last night, they were extremely interested. And convinced me that now is the time to be pressing all sorts of matters." Astrea glanced at Lourdes. "Would you like to tell them, or shall I?"

A little worm of anxiety burrowed in Hazel's gut. It had become apparent that Astrea did not go about things cautiously. Astrea's appearance here and her great air of energy and enthusiasm presaged something even more unexpected than the pollution clean-up action.

Lourdes moved her glowing gaze from face to face around the circle as she spoke. "One thing that has been disturbing us for a long time is that the security forces in our country procure their weapons and equipment, drugs, and a lot of intelligence from the US. We're anxious to see that connection broken. Therefore we've—in conjunction with Astrea—come up with a plan. Which is to tell the US Executive that if the connection is not broken—if the supply of these things to the government of Brazil is not stopped—then the Marq'ssan will go after each of the companies that makes these things. We have the further idea that the first company on our list should be told that this will be so, and that they will be the first to be destructured." Lourdes' eyes turned now to Hazel. "We ask that you, Hazel, tell this person of authority you have been speaking to our demand and threat. And we, of course, will pass along the threat to the first company on our list."

Hazel looked at Astrea, but the Marq'ssan's face revealed little. Needless to say, the company at the top of that list would not find it worth losing everything just to preserve that connection. As for all the other companies involved, some would find it worth gambling that they weren't high on the list. This challenge would probably create a great deal of strife and dissension in executive circles. But wouldn't it also upset Liz and perhaps induce her to cut off negotiations?

Apparently Pat was thinking just that, for she immediately initiated an attack against the timing of the proposed challenge. And, Hazel observed, she started her first sentence with *but*.

Hazel reached for her half-empty glass of beer and tried to imagine Liz's response. Would that be the end of their "talks"? Would it send Liz off the deep end against the Marq'ssan and all opponents of the executive system? Hazel swallowed the rest of her beer in one go and nodded when Lucille offered to refill her glass.

Leave it to Astrea to create controversy.

Chapter Twenty-one

Tuesday, July 10, 2096—DC

So much work to do, between the frantic rush to make up for time lost because of all the projects' change in direction and Lise's insistence that I be a real consultant. Yesterday and today were both twelve-hour days. This weekend's barbecue seems long gone. How pleasant it was, all of us outdoors lounging on blankets with cushions and pillows, having good things to eat and drink—the atmosphere the closest thing to certain FZ gatherings that I've experienced here in DC. Everyone excited to be able to sit outside, without concern for exposure to pollution. Also a bit like the Redmond house, but without the Hazel-generated tension that characterized most of my time there. Ginger fussing, of course. Lise and Elaine Pfefferman doing the cooking. And Sherri playing her guitar and singing—such a lovely voice she has. All this in Lise's rather small yard, surrounded by its high privacy hedges, shut off from the rest of the world—for a while, anyway.

Lise told me last night that there's trouble about Mott's having a child. She's found a "suitable" executive male willing to accept her conditions. (Apparently Mott is offering him financial remuneration and favorable influence at the Executive level and all the Mott family connections to boot.) But the *Executive* is up in arms about it. The Secretary of Health is male. And he, like some of the other male Cabinet officers, objects to career-line women—and older ones at that—contracting on such terms with less-prestigious males. Usually women do not arrange their own contracts. (Lise sarcastically remarked to me that maybe Rogers might not have objected if Mott had had her uncle arrange the contract *for* her.) These men insist that women must do one or the other, but not both. And that if they make an exception for someone as visible as Mott, other career-line women will want to do the same, which would throw the executive system and executive society into chaos.

Too sleepy to continue writing. These twelve-hour days are murder. Don't even have time to read any more.

Wednesday, July 11, 2096—DC

What are Hazel and the others up to now? Lise just told me Hazel arrived in town yesterday. For "talks" with Weatherall. As a result, Lise appears to be up in the air about what's going to happen with all our media projects—we're now, apparently, on hold until further notice from Weatherall.

It was confusing enough when the Marq'ssan eliminated that horrible pollution site. I mean, no one quite knew how to feel about it. (Except that everyone was secretly dancing and singing for joy.) Mom and Dad, for instance, were deeply confused. What they saw on vid made them wonder what was going on. They couldn't understand why the President was coming out against the aliens for doing something beneficial. I mentioned this to Lise, and I think she took my point seriously, since the day after that, they started coming out with the new line of making lists of similar things the Marq'ssan could do very easily if they felt like it.

"We're fighting for the hearts and minds of the American people," Lise is always telling me. "That's the war that counts. Winning that war is the only way the aliens can get what they want." I think she sometimes senses my uneasiness at this constant deliberate management of people's thinking and perceptions. Oh, I can see how it's necessary. But then I think of how many years I was ignorant, how many years I was deliberately managed in that way (all through the war, for instance, when I was living with Lise—who was *in control* of all the media then!—and working for Security, and *still* didn't suspect). Lise likes to talk about how I'm one of the "insiders" and how intelligent I am. But what did that matter before they let me in on their secrets? Mom and Dad aren't stupid. Yet all they have to go on are these "filters" and "angles" and "slants" and "saturations" and so on. I think of how they sometimes sit there and seriously try to analyze all the bits of information that get through—knowing they have only partial truth, but still trying their damnedest to understand. But Lise has this image of service-techs—except for a few of us, the ones she knows personally... I should feel good, I guess, at being one of the insiders, though as far as I can tell it's pure accident that I am. I'm no one special. And the accident is my being Lise's lover.

I mentioned Venn's counterargument once to Lise, to see what she would say. Venn had argued that the executives' contention that the FZ wanted to make the rest of the country like the FZ wasn't a bad thing, that I could see for myself that the FZ is a very livable place. My thought was that that was because it was on such a small scale and could afford to stay out of international politics. (I had other thoughts, too, but I kept them to myself—Venn might have begun wondering about me if I'd said them out loud.) Lise replied that the FZ wasn't bad—yet—because they hoped to persuade the rest of the planet to go their way. And because of the way the Marq'ssan are, this would be a "war" being fought for generations to come, until they finally managed to reduce the entire planet to defenselessness. But that once everyone dismantled their governments and their defense systems and law and order etc., then the aliens would take outright control of the planet and use it for whatever purpose they were so far concealing from us. That this was what is at stake in our "propaganda war." Not the danger of the anarchists taking over. Anarchists like Martha Greenglass and Hazel would simply be swept aside because there would be no need for them then. We would be easy prey to the aliens.

This may be correct—I don't know, how can I know such things? But Fenton's comic-book picture of the aliens as reptilian monsters isn't. It would have to be a much more subtle thing. Lise agrees. She said she was thinking at the time she approved that "slant" that it would be a simple enough image to be "readily accessible" to ordinary people. But I think it would be too ludicrous for people to believe in. ("Oh, you'd be surprised, Annie, at what people will believe if it's presented in the right manner.") So now the question is how to construct an image both "accessible" and "plausible"—and I want there to be truth in it. This is what I'm always wanting to argue to Lise, that we be sure we don't actually lie, even if we do omit certain things, or package them. She agreed, saying that lies out of whole cloth eventually entailed all sorts of problems.

Time to put this away and see if Lise is ready for bed. I know *I* am.

Friday, July 13, 2096—DC

The shit is about to hit the fan. Lise gave me the details last night. At an Executive meeting yesterday morning Mott requested final approval for having a child since she'd gotten the contract drawn up and signed. But Rogers, when pressed by Mott, said that as long as she was working and in a position of responsibility, her having a child was "out of the question."

Lise—she said she could see that Mott was close to losing it, so that she, Lise, had better try to argue *for* her— said, "But while he was Chief of Security Services, Sedgewick had *two* children."

Lise said the men exchanged a certain kind of glance around the table. Then Steinmetz said, "But when a male has children he isn't subject to the hormonal fluctuations afflicting a woman before pregnancy while menstruating, during pregnancy, and then afterwards while nursing. Thus women's control, while tenuous to start with, is necessarily grossly attenuated during all stages of child-bearing." Lise said he chuckled then and added, "I should know. I've been through it twice myself, and last year my daughter had a child and I saw it again."

Mott said: "I wouldn't be nursing the child myself."

After more negative comments from the men, Weatherall finally said something. She, I gather, has been trying to act "neutral" around the men. As has Cat Schuyler, who I know to be on Mott's side, at least from what she says when we're all socializing together. As for the other women at the meeting, those at the sub-Cabinet level of course said nothing, since they hardly ever enter any discussion unless asked (Lise, though she's considered sub-Cabinet level, is in every way an exception), and probably their bosses had told them to keep their mouths shut on the subject. Lise isn't sure what Danforth thinks. But Steadman and Seely, she says, are pissed at Mott for "rocking the boat," for threatening all of them with the loss of their power by reminding the men of their "female physiology." Lise scoffs at this and says that the men never let them forget it and therefore don't need reminders. That Seely and Steadman are simply "gutless." So anyway, Weatherall said, "Would you gentlemen be satisfied if Mott went on leave during the course of her pregnancy? Or if she had another woman carry the pregnancy for her?"

According to Lise, gasps were heard around the table—and one of those gasping was Mott herself. Rogers, Lise said, couldn't think of any objections to these alternatives, though he said he still didn't see how he could give Mott permission to procreate. One of the other males, I forget who, said it wasn't seemly. That every executive child, even girls, should have the exclusive attention of its mother, and that furthermore it was essential that child-raising be overseen by the executive male father. (It's true that mainly professionals use the services of surrogates.) I gather that Weatherall again deployed Sedgewick as an example and pointed out that he had hardly seen his children until they were adults. And that most executive children were first cared for by service-techs and then sent away to school and almost never got the kind of maternal attention they were mythologizing. But after saying this, Weatherall changed the subject. Lise says that Weatherall will pursue it individually with the males. I wonder. Weatherall can dump any one of them if she so chose—could dump Rogers and therefore, presumably, could twist his arm hard enough to make him sign the consent.

My guess—and it's an uninformed one, since I don't know that much about what's going on—is that Weatherall herself is worried about losing power if she's seen as unable to carry the point for Mott. Security, as everyone now realizes, is a powerful, dangerous force that must be controlled and leashed. Mott has done that for Weatherall. And considering what a hard act to follow Sedgewick was, that's pretty damned impressive. And to think those stupid fools claim to worry about Mott's hormones! What was it Sedgewick had wrong with him? It must have been a hell of a lot worse than pregnancy could ever be! It's so obvious, why don't they see it? Maybe they do. Maybe it's just an excuse. Lise, though, I don't think, is so sure herself. Sometimes executive women puzzle me. They have superstitions about sex that completely blow me away whenever I come up against them. But then what do I know.

Sunday, July 15, 2096—DC

Had a lazy Sunday morning—met Leslie at one of those outdoor cafe places. I was a little nervous about their letting me in, since it's mainly executives that go there. But they looked me over and decided I was all right. Fortunately Leslie was already there, waiting. Both of us were free, since Cat like Lise had to go to the special session of the Executive this morning. (For all I know they could still be at it, though probably the reason Lise isn't home yet is because she's working out some new statement or speech for Sellwyn.) Anyway, we had cafe-au-lait and croissants and fruit (for an extravagant sum, but it went on Cat's account). And then we read the Sunday papers. Though to tell the truth I find it hard now to read them seriously. That's what knowing too much can do for you.

So what does Weatherall think now of her cherished darling? Lise has been irritated about Weatherall being so "excited" and "pleased" at Hazel's being in DC and meeting with her. I hadn't realized that Lise doesn't like Hazel and never did. She never let on until now. And then of course when Hazel threw another of her little bombshells at them, Lise said she wasn't at all surprised. Lise seems worried about what this could do to the Executive—that Weatherall could lose her grip. Not only is it a matter of so many defense contractors turning the pressure up, but the fact that the Marq'ssan and the FZ are now openly meddling in a foreign policy matter makes them seem more of a threat than ever. Lise thinks this will end Weatherall's willingness to negotiate.

But back to Leslie. She wanted to have what Ginger calls "girltalk" (a thoroughly disgusting concept and term). Told me how she and Cat had met. Their "history." All very romantic. Then she wanted me to reciprocate in kind. Ugh. I was as sketchy as I could be. I told her how I met Lise, thinking she'd turn up her nose, but it didn't faze her the way it would someone like straight-as-an-arrow Hazel. (Should have guessed by the way Leslie dresses and the paint on her legs, knees, face, and arms that she's probably been in that scene, too—who knows how old she is; she's probably had longevity treatments.) Didn't mention the drugs, though. If she's been in the scene she'd assume it. If not what does it matter. Just said Lise and I were slow getting off.

(Didn't say either how we didn't really click until some time after the rape.) But Leslie hardly noticed how abbreviated my story was—too busy going after whatever I was willing to give her about Weatherall in those days. God people are hot for her. Any little tidbit turns the wheels in their heads. So I described the scene at that party where Lise and I were standing watching Weatherall and that hungry red-headed vulture gobble one another up for dinner. And so now that story will make the rounds, I'm sure. No one will know if it's apocryphal, but they'll tell it with relish and say *It's just like the bitch, you know?* And if it gets back to either Lise or Weatherall they'll know I told it, but it won't matter. It's a fairly harmless piece of gossip. And considering how Leslie had her hooks into me, I'm pleased at the way I managed to avoid making any major indiscretions.

Guess I'd better get in that little car and zip on down to Mom and Dad's for their outdoor do. They're in a state of bliss at being able to spend summer weekends and evenings out-of-doors in that little square of grass they share with all the other people in their building. *The good times are coming back, honey,* Mom said on the phone yesterday. I hope so. People deserve a break after so many bad times.

Tuesday, July 17, 2096—DC

I remember hearing about surrogate pregnancies for professionals (not about anyone I actually knew personally, just that they do happen). And no one has ever breathed a suggestion that Mott herself couldn't physically carry a pregnancy to term, which would be the only reason an executive woman would have for hiring a surrogate. But the real reason has to do with all the crap those men were spouting in that Executive meeting. (No one ever suggests that service-tech women can't keep working during *their* pregnancies.) I have the sneaking suspicion that Weatherall worked this out as a compromise so that Mott could go on being Chief of Security. On the other hand, by going the surrogate route she can pay lip service to the hormonal crap. Weatherall must have really sat on the men to get them to go along with it.

Lise said Mott said Ginger is "thrilled" and "beside herself with excitement" at "their decision." Hunh. Can Ginger really be interested in

being in that awful condition for nine months and then going through
the agony of labor at the end? (The descriptions I've read in old novels make me sure I'd never voluntarily go through such a thing.) And
then, after all that, breastfeeding? Lise says Mott and Ginger think this
will make Ginger feel more a "full partner in the experience." That
though the baby will have Mott's and that executive male's genes, it
will be a physical part of Ginger and thus bonded to her.

I suppose this may be what Ginger's always wanted but couldn't
have because she's not hetero and thus not of the right "profile" for
the Dept. of Health. Who knows. In fact, it's one of those things you
simply *don't* talk about to anyone. Not even to your lover.

Wait until the news gets out. The uproar will really be something.
And then Ginger will be at the center of it all, right along with Mott.
Consider how embarrassed she gets when anyone notices much less
fusses over her the way she herself does with everyone she likes. I can
still remember how she used to blush at the things Hazel would say
and do at that Redmond house.

It's getting late. I have to bathe and depilate my legs and do my
hair. No time any more for reading. Well, I'll have plenty of time in
Pennsylvania for reading. Even more time than when I was living in
the FZ, since there I had to spend so much time writing reports and
meeting my agents.

Thursday, July 19, 2096—DC

There's been no time to write. All last night after I got home the
phone kept ringing. Elaine and Susan and the others calling, pumping
me for details. Lise said, when I briefly saw her at the office this afternoon, that word has started getting around, and Weatherall is already
taking flak. That it looked as though they were going to have to mount
a mini-propaganda campaign just for executives. (Well of course, who
but executives would care that Mott was doing this?) Don't know how
it will work since they won't be using the usual media for getting it
across. How *do* executives communicate in that way? Or *do* they? I
never much thought about this before, but while I was eating dinner
alone I kept thinking about what Lise had said and things she'd said at
other times and realized that she always talks as if there is some kind

of executive "community" out there and "executive opinion," which is like public opinion (only more powerful) that Weatherall and the rest of the Executive have to play to. I'm sure if I came straight out and asked her about it she wouldn't tell me and would be irritated to boot. (At my putting it into words. Lise likes to keep certain things unstated.) So I'll have to see what I can piece together for myself. (The way Mom and Dad try to piece things together from the media "news" they're exposed to? I hope not. That would be pretty damned pathetic.)

Funny how everything is so open and so secret all at the same time. Like the open secret about the President. Though it's not *that* far off, since the Cabinet is most of the Executive (except for Weatherall and Lise) and mostly the Senate is for show, but of course the Senate is mostly executives who are concerned to "work with" the Executive. The only thing that isn't real is the President. And whatever Greenglass and those people may say, elections and public opinion do act as a kind of pressure on the Executive. Why otherwise would they spend so much time and money worrying about public opinion? What could an election by such ignorant, non-caring people mean, anyway? It didn't do much for the country in the last century when they still went by that system. People like Lise were still controlling things, only with less finesse. And obviously the problems with that system were what made everything come close to breaking down. Too much greed. Too much chaos. And this playing to instant public opinion (fear of not being re-elected) led to all kinds of stupidity just to get re-elected. No, I understand that part of it. It's just that Lise hasn't explained it all to me.

But then who ever explains everything? Some things you just have to figure out for yourself. One good thing about being back in DC like this is that I have a better chance of learning about these things than I ever had before. Especially since Lise talks to me so much now, which she never used to do.

Chapter Twenty-two

Monday, 7/16/2096

The house is so quiet it's like a tomb. Haven't seen Sally since that time on the beach Friday. Nor signs *of* her. Now that Kitty is gone, I'm doing all the clean-up work in the kitchen. Sally seems not to be helping herself to the food I prepare. (Or indeed any foodstuffs at all that I can perceive.) Where is she? Upstairs in her room? Or wandering around the island or house? Surely the amazons would have noticed if… No, I must not think that way. She is *not* my responsibility. It's Elizabeth's fault for doing this to her. I will not let myself care deeply enough to be used. I will not. I must steel myself to accept this girl's tragedy (if that is, indeed, what it is).

Dreamed last night of Rbt & Kay, a dream that is pervading the whole of this very hot, sweaty day. I dreamed that I was out by the graves, digging around near the holly tree, & unearthed the top of Rbt's coffin. That was truly horrible, yet when the coffin opened & he climbed up out of the grave, I was not horrified—or even frightened—but *pleased*. As though that had been my intention in digging around out there all along. "I will show you where to look," were his first words. & then he went to the statue, which was further out from the holly tree, just on the other side of his grave, & lifted Kay—the statue had become a living, breathing woman—down off the pedestal & opened it, revealing a heavy steel safety-box. Rbt then took my thumb & pressed it against the recog-plate, & the thing buzzed, & the top of the box lifted. & there was the transcript. When I turned around, Rbt & Kay were gone, & I was left in the dark with the wind blowing in a gale all around me & the transcript beckoning.

A symbolic dream, or one with a real clue? Is it possible Rbt once told me something that was a clue that I didn't recognize as such since I didn't know anything about the transcript at the time? Is it possible my unconscious could have worked out the connection for me? I'm afraid it must be a wish-fulfillment dream. (As for Rbt taking Kay off her pedestal: did he *have* her on a pedestal, ever?) Should I attempt to remove the statue from its pedestal? Just to see? Would it be possible for me to do it? I hesitate to vandalize it, just on the whim of a dream. On the other hand, it would be a much cleaner place to start than digging up the soil near Rbt's grave. Well, I will think about it. I don't have a sense of urgency. My instincts tell me that I must take care not to go too fast, not to be rash—because this will probably be my only chance & I don't want to throw it away by tipping my hand to Elizabeth & letting her take the transcript from me without a fight.

Oh, one bit of progress that is encouraging: Jasmine (she's invited me to call her "Jazzy"—her nickname among her friends & colleagues) accepted a glass of cognac last night. She's been here to listen to music three nights in a row. I discovered she plays the piano, so I invited her to use the Bechstein whenever she pleases. (She's dreadful, of course, but then she's never been able to have first-rate teachers or regular access to a piano.) She may be writing reports on me, but I will behave with her as though she is not. I can't afford to be as principled as I've tried to be in the past.

I have so much on my mind. Which is, I suppose, why I'm writing in this book at one in the afternoon instead of slaving away at all the damned labor that this house & its grounds cry out for.

Later

It's two-thirty in the morning & I'm exhausted, but I must write a little about what's happened, to get it down, to attempt to make sense of it. I don't want to believe I've done myself in. No. I suppose I don't know how to think about what follows. Or to understand much of what already is & has been. My mind racing in spite of the exhaustion. I could knock myself out, but I want to write these details while they're still fresh in my mind, want to get down verbatim speeches so that I can examine them later & keep my memory from straying into its usual distortions & imprecisions.

My worry about her not eating & the fact that I hadn't laid eyes on her made me decide to stake out the kitchen—sitting quietly in Nicole's room with the door cracked. I did this from three to six; then I prepared a meal, which I ate in Nicole's room; after which I cleaned up the kitchen & returned to Nicole's room with the cognac bottle. I stayed there until about eleven—sitting in the dark once the daylight had gone. & still that girl did not come into the kitchen. I realized she probably wasn't going to. Either she had a supply of food somewhere else, or she wasn't eating. Or… I couldn't bear not knowing. So I climbed the stairs to the top floor & started checking every room along the main hall. I finally found her in one of the smallest, most cramped of the staff rooms. Sitting in the dark, by the open window, staring out at the ocean. (The only thing one can say for those rooms on the top floor is that they have wonderful views.) The room was stifling hot, & no air in it was stirring. There were dozens of empty water bottles in a garbage sack beside her chair. When I opened the door & came in, she turned her head, saw it was me, then turned again to stare out the window. "It's like an oven in here," I said, irritated at her for having closeted herself in this dinky little place when she could have had one of the corner rooms or moved to a room on another floor—& certainly could have spent time down on the beach, where it would be very cool at that hour. I knew damned well she hadn't been out of that room except to use the bathroom connecting this room with another. It was obvious.

She said nothing. "When did you last eat?" I said next. (This whole scene rather left me at a loss—I hardly knew *what* to say to her. This sort of self-immolation is like an assault on anyone who has the misfortune to observe it.) "I don't know." She spoke in a mumble. So I took her through a sort of catalog. "This noon?" No. "This morning?" No, again. & on & on until it became clear that she probably hadn't eaten since Kitty's departure—if even then, for she admitted she wasn't even sure what day it was or when Kitty had left. (As though it were so long ago—but given the state she was in, it's not surprising that she'd lose all sense of time.) So then I yelled at her. "Why the fuck not? I've been cooking & leaving it out for you with notes about finding dishes in the warming oven or the refrigerator, & you don't even bother to eat?" My anger got through to her. She turned from the window & looked at me, & though I had only the light from the hall by which to see her, the slackness of her face, the dullness of her eyes shocked me. "Your house, your food," she said. "You don't want me here." & then, as she turned back to the window, she added, "& besides, I'm on a crash diet. I'm too fat."

Without thinking, I went over to her & grabbed her by the shoulders & wrenched her around. The look of alarm on her face & the way she raised her hands to shield her face drove the knife in even further. [May someone do the same to you someday, Elizabeth. May you feel that pain in your heart & then that guilt making your stomach heave, making your hands tremble.] I went & sat on the bed. I didn't know what to do. Probably I should have left, but I couldn't. After a while I said, "I shouldn't have said you weren't welcome in my house. Obviously you have as much a right to be living here as I have. Because like me, you have no choice. I didn't realize at the time that you couldn't stay with the amazons. I suppose Elizabeth specifically told you you couldn't. Since you'd be no good to her plans if you lived over there. I'm sorry for all this. I know it's as much a nightmare for you as it is for me. Please, you mustn't stay up here like this. & you're not fat, for godsake." I don't know why I added that—it's so obvious her body is gorgeous. But I do know that some girls lose all sense of perspective about their bodies, especially when their livelihood depends on their physical attractiveness.

"It must be that I'm fat," she said, her voice quivering & breathy. "She said when she told me I had to live here that you—" she swallowed, & I waited for her to finish.

"What did she tell you?" I urged her to continue.

She swallowed again. "She said I had to come here to live for good. & that all the time you were in the clinic convalescing you were thinking about *me*. About...sex with me. So I thought... But you don't want me any more. It must be because of all the rich food I've been eating here. I knew I shouldn't go off my diet like that. But it's hard, here, to—" she stopped again.

"Did she tell you why she wants you to have sex with me?" I asked her.

She shook her head. "She didn't *say* she wanted me to have sex with you. She didn't tell me anything except that I would have to come here & stay here, & that you would be wanting to have sex with me. That's all she said."

"Tell me the rest, Sally," I pressed her. "Please. You know that it's hopeless, she'll never free you even if she gets what she wants from me. Because you know too much. Your only hope is with me."

Her eyes filled with tears. "But she didn't *tell* me anything else. I did ask her for another chance, but she said it was too late. She said the reason she was telling me that about you was that I would have to get along here the best I could. But that it shouldn't be bad because you liked me so much & because you would need me because of your poor health & the lack of staff here." By this point Sally was crying.

I was too wrought up & couldn't properly see her face. Yet for some reason I felt that she was telling me the truth. Worse, I couldn't stand not trying to comfort her. So I got up from the bed & went to her & put my arms around her. She clutched at me & sobbed horribly, those sounds that wrench out of one, that one never wants another soul to hear. Yes, I know she's an actor, but I don't believe she had a script for this scene. Or for any of the other scenes since my rejection of her last advance. When she finally quieted down, I drew her over to the bed, & we sat down together. "Look," I said, "let me explain to you what I think is happening."

She sniffed & reached into her pocket & pulled out an enormous wad of Kleenex (further evidence that she has been crying without an audience) & let go of my hand in order to blow her nose. "I think Elizabeth is hoping I'll become extremely attached to you," I said. "& that she believes that once I'm completely besotted she'll be able to use that against me. By either threatening you with harm or by separating us. Or something else along those lines." There might be other ways, involving Sally's cooperation, but I saw no point in bringing any doubts I have about her into the conversation. That is all for me to work out for myself, privately.

"Harm me?" Sally's voice quavered. "You mean *physically*?"

"The idea shocks you?"

"I don't think she's that kind of person," she said in a faltering voice. As though she were thinking it over for the first time. "I mean, she's very, well, hard. But she never—"

She broke off, & I guessed she was comparing Elizabeth's treatment of her to mine. That was hardly a happy thought. "She's very determined. Not to say desperate," I said.

"Oh no," Sally whispered. "We're trapped here. There's no way off this island without *their* stopping us."

"Yes. That's right," I said. "& that's always been true. & I hope you understand," I added ruthlessly, "that even if you are playing her game, it's doubtful she'll keep any bargain she might have struck with you. She doesn't take that kind of risk. You know too much about things she has to keep quiet."

"There's no bargain," Sally said quickly. "I swear to you, all that's past. She was furious with me for lying to her & conspiring with you against her before. She said that's why she was sending me here to stay."

Dealing with Sally without outright excising her must be a problem for Elizabeth. She can't put her in a detention facility, because trials & such are now necessary (except of course for Security & Military employees, who are tried secretly by their respective internal security institutions). What else could Elizabeth do with her? A mental institution would present certain problems unless it was some small place run by the Company, & even then it might be dicey for her, given the number of enemies Elizabeth has. Anything else would be equally risky & expensive... No, this would be an ideal situation. Except that it was more than that. Even without Sally's active cooperation, Elizabeth could expect to reap an advantage from sending Sally here.

"I want you to understand what the situation is," I told her. "In the first place, if you value your own well-being, you'll do your best not to appear to have succeeded with me. Because the amazons would pass that on to Elizabeth. & you'd do best if you're still working for her to tell Elizabeth I won't have anything to do with you. Because then she's less likely to harm you in order to coerce me."

"I'll do everything you say," Sally said eagerly. "But I'm *not* reporting to her anymore." By the hall light I could see her face, lifted to me, growing radiant. "You can see that I'm not. I haven't talked at all with the amazons." I got up from the bed, as did she. I opened my mouth to say something to coax her down to the kitchen to eat, but she threw her arms around me & pressed herself against me. "We're friends now, aren't we?" she asked, pleading.

I gently detached her from me. "Yes," I said, "we're friends. Let's go downstairs & find you something to eat. Aren't you famished?"

"Oh yes," she admitted. "Half the time I've been up here I've been thinking about food." Hesitantly, she touched my shoulder. "But you really don't think I'm too fat?"

"Don't be silly," I said. "I'm not a vid audience."

"Then you *are* still…attracted to me?"

It was hard keeping the impatience—or was it irritation?—out of my voice. "Look, Sally, you don't have to go through that now. It's completely unnecessary. It will be like it was the other time after you told me the truth." I put my arm around her & drew her out into the relatively bright hall. "But we've talked enough. Let's go down to the kitchen."

When we got to the head of the stairs she darted a kiss on my cheek & gave me a shy smile & thanked me. Which made me feel more of a shit than ever.

So now we have this new situation. Undoubtedly Elizabeth will get wind of it & move in on us. Or maybe by some fluke she won't. But if she reels Sally in before I've made my move, she'll get everything out of the girl by loquazene & will know she has some leverage against me. Unlike Sally, I don't put anything past Elizabeth, no matter what she says to the contrary. She's a desperate & driven woman. Rbt knew that whatever is in the transcript would spell ruin for her. & since whatever it was she did to Kay was bad enough to lead to Kay's death (if, that is, Rbt was telling the truth—& it's never possible to know: but why would Elizabeth be after the transcript if he *hadn't* been telling the truth?), that's prima facie evidence that Elizabeth can't be trusted not to harm Sally.

If not tomorrow night, then the next.

Thursday, 7/19/2096

She's like a new person. It worries me, her sudden euphoria & easiness with me. As though every stage we've been through—especially the first one, when she was so cool, distant, poised, & sure of herself—has been a role she's been specially trained for. Her eager trust takes me aback, makes me want to do something to frighten her, to remind her of everything that's gone down between us. She laughs, her eyes sparkle at me, she smiles, she takes my arm & urges me out to walk the beach with her. It occurred to me when I caught a glimpse of my-self in the mirror this afternoon that maybe it's the radical change in my appearance. So this evening I reminded her that though they'd re-made my face & I wore my hair differently, I was still the same person & she should try not to forget it. She nodded, but I think she shrugged it off the way one does when coming up against something one des-perately wishes not to be true. The confusion of feeling & sensation that comes over me at times, especially when she touches me, makes me want to strike out at her, to put her at a distance. Yet there's this other part of me that wants to comfort her for everything's she been through (& undoubtedly will in the future be going through). I must find some way to explain to her why she must pull herself back for both our sakes. It's like being on a hair-trigger. Have to be all control around her. To keep her warmth from sending us both to the devil.

Fortunately she finds Jazzy so intimidating that I've no trouble get-ting her to leave when Jazzy comes up for her evening visit to the Music Room. Why, I wonder, is she so spooked by the amazons? I'm sure there's a story there, that it isn't simply antipathy. Considering the way she's been spilling stories of her childhood (how her parents essentially sold her to the vid industry when she hit age twelve) & adolescence, I'm sure she'll tell me eventually. It's as though a dam has burst. She talks & talks & talks, her eyes anxiously on my face, watching for every slightest reaction.

So tired. & I don't want to keep this book out longer than I need to. Though I've made it clear she's not to barge in on me after I've gone to bed, there's no telling what she might do, now that I've caved.

Saturday, 7/21/2096

Well. I've really done it now. I'm a fool, is what I am. I can just hear Rbt scathing at me for my weakness. I know better than to be starry-eyed. (Would such a state ever again be possible for me? Not unless I found myself totally amnesiac.) Still, the intensity of it... I suppose there were warning signs that I should have caught. Yet my preoccupation with making my explorations as well as with the problem of keeping Sally in ignorance of them claimed all my attention. I was sitting there in my chair in the Music Room half-listening to a Mozart piano concerto & had a moment before decided that I would put a sedative in Sally's wine just before her bedtime when Sally came into the room & knelt on the floor at my feet. I barely registered her presence. I suppose it was that initial inattention that lost me control of the situation.

I came fully awake to Sally's presence only when I felt her pressing against me—her arms around my waist & her face against my thighs. Christ. She's *never* had the nerve to come on to me like that. Half-hysterical (I fully admit I was completely without control) I grabbed her hair & shot out of the chair like a madwoman. I shouted at her, something like, "Are you crazy?" & "What the fuck do you think you're doing?"

Sprawled on her back (which is how she landed when I shoved her off in the process of getting out of that chair), her glittering green eyes stared up at me. "Don't be angry with me, please don't be angry with me," she said, very hoarse, her mouth quivering. So I launched into the same old song—hadn't I made it clear that it wasn't necessary—& added something about how if she didn't stop this she'd spoil everything between us. Then I ordered her to get off the floor (for she hadn't moved) & said we both needed a drink. So I reached a hand down to her, to help her up. Another mistake. She stood there, her eyes that beautiful rain-washed green, looking up into my face; & then she asked me if I'd lied about her being too fat. This constantly recurring thing, happening yet again, was beginning to fray my nerves. I didn't feel I could stand much more of it, considering how difficult I was finding it to keep control of myself (much less her). So I said, very harshly, that I didn't understand her motives, that I didn't do such things with someone neither willing nor paid to do it, & that if she kept this kind of thing up she'd end up out of the house, regardless of her desire to stay away from the amazons.

"Don't you understand?" She flung the words at me. "I'm in *love* with you! I *want* you to make love to me!"

That hit me hard; I could hardly breathe for the blow. My first impulse was to physically hurt her. But I didn't. Some part of me coiled up, taut and gnarled, & held me back. & then I was able to think a little & said, "What about your lover in prison?" trying to bring her back to reality.

"I've been wanting to explain to you about that," she said, looking suddenly apprehensive. I looked at her for a long moment before suggesting we open a bottle of wine. I could see she liked the idea, so I went to the cabinet where I kept a supply & pulled out a Cabernet Sauvignon & a couple of glasses. When we were finally sitting down—she on the sofa, me back in my chair—sipping, I told her (feeling somewhat resigned to this further entanglement) to start explaining.

The basic story was that she & her lover had been cooling toward one another for some time when her lover had been busted. That it was mainly guilt & a sense of obligation that had made her go through with playing Weatherall's game. So you lied to me, I said. No, no, she said, I never said I was still in love with her, only that I was doing it for my lover, & it was true, she was still my lover when she was busted. & then she started in on how she had fallen in love with me even though she knew it was crazy, that she thought it must have been my being so nice to her after she had told me the truth, & that she had been wishing all that time that we could be lovers then, because, she said, she knew it would be different than it had been during those months I'd been so angry at her when I thought of her as a paid spy.

I told her that she shouldn't imagine sex between us could be any different than it had been before, that I was bent, that I had never had a "normal" sexual relationship in my life.

"But I *know* it would be different. Because look at how different it is between us now. Just the way you talk to me—"

I told her that I was incapable of more than superficial relationships, that I had never even had a *friendship*, which fact alone said a great deal about what kind of person I am. She flew off the sofa & threw herself at me, babbling nonsense. Everything would be different, I'd see. She had been *glad* when Weatherall had told her she would be coming back here. Nothing else would matter. It would just be us, apart from a world we didn't need.

And when she touched my lips with her own, I couldn't help myself.

What an excuse. I *know* better. I shouldn't be so weak as to not refuse what she so freely offers. I've nothing to offer anyone. She should know this. But infatuation is often blind. & when she crashes down to earth, when her eyes open, it will be bleak, possibly grim. Because here we are on this island. Just her, me, & the amazons—our inescapable reality.

But now I must finish my preparations to go out to the holly bush & see what I can see. She is out cold—not from a sedative, but from too much alcohol, which I poured down her in great quantities, while hardly drinking anything myself. Which discrepancy between us made me feel devious & managing in the slimiest of ways.

If I find it, then what? But no, better just to see if I *can* find it. & worry about everything else later.

Chapter Twenty-three

[i]

Mama's voice calls her out of the dark. From outside the dream, this voice and hand touching her forehead pull her away from the tightly locked, choking closet of horror, and the world expands to include Mama, who is untouched—miraculously—by the stench burning Celia's face and the inside of her nostrils. "Are you awake now, baby?" Mama asks, her voice soothingly real, stronger than the horror.

Celia's throat tastes of vomit. Like her throat and stomach, the inside of her mouth burns (though not, she realizes, her face or nostrils). "Water!" She's gasping. "I need water." To wash away the taste and the traces of filth. She needs a shower, too. She will get up and shower once she is able to brave that blind, enclosed, vulnerable-making space. Mama takes her hand away, and Celia feels her weight lifting from the bed. She opens her eyes to watch her mother going out into the hall where the ceiling light dimly glows. She recalls that first time they had screwed a low wattage bulb into the light socket. They had decided they needed something not too bright that could bridge the dark in the middle of the night when Celia needed a little but not too much light.

Mama returns with a glass of water. "Every night since you've been back," she says.

Celia swallows and swallows, drinking down most of the water. When she takes the glass away from her mouth she says, "I'm sorry. And you have to work in the morning, too."

"I'll go back to sleep very easily. But I'm worried about you, Cee."

She started having the dreams again in jail. "I thought I was going to be okay." Mama waits; her head inclines slightly, urging Celia to continue. "I was proud of myself, Mama. For being able to handle going into that jail to see Martha. Strip-searched each time. And when

they busted me, I thought it would be all right. I was tense, but I refused to show my fear." Celia's throat tightens. "But it was like being
suspended in limbo forever. No touch with the outside world. When
you came to visit me that time..." Celia shrugs. "I hardly remember
it now. Your visit, I mean. And yet the physical details of all those different cells are etched in my mind, so vividly, more real than anything
else, giving me this feeling of nothingness. Even while we're sitting
here. As though some part of me is still sitting in one of those cells,
just as some part of my unconscious mind is still back in that nightmare, emerging from its dark corner only at night, in my dreams."
Celia swallows the rest of the water.

Mama puts the glass on the night table and wraps her arms around
Celia, holding her close against her warm, solid body. Without speaking, Mama tells her that this immediate warmth and comfort is real,
is solid, is also a part of her.

[ii]

Celia sits on a bench in the enclosed garden behind the clinic, staring
at the crimson bougainvilleas sharp against the dazzling white-washed
wall. *They* are waiting: Danforth's PA called again that morning, and
then shortly afterwards, the lawyer heading the Division of Human
and Civil Rights called. Is she ill? Danforth's PA wanted to know. They
would like me to be ill, Celia thinks, it would be the easiest way to discredit me. But: No, no, I just feel I need some time to think it over, Ms.
Hampton, and I'm sure you understand that life in backcountry jails is
less than salutary. Oh her hurried rejoinder, this executive so anxious
not to be made to listen to details about cockroaches and boredom
and stinking, clammy heat. And the head of the Division, anxious to
"confirm" that nothing about her confinement had been "abusive."
Sometimes now it seems that some of those Free Zone people and the
Marq'ssan are correct about jails. But no, Celia's rational mind eventually reasserts, it's a matter of reform needed, not abolition.

Unfortunate, being taken first to Mott's office. Mott so ostentatiously affable and concerned, *oh do do do please help us we are working for the same ends you know Celia we need people like you people
with integrity and ability and determination...* All the while Celia
from some quirk of memory every time she sees or even thinks of

Mott recalls the feel of the railing pressing against her thighs as she is forced to stand handcuffed on that bridge listening to her talking about going renegade, reliving that moment of near-screaming vulnerability, the railing not even waist high and she with her hands behind her back unable even to clutch the railing if something should happen... Is it possible to work with people like Mott and Weatherall? But is it possible to work with people like Martha Greenglass? If she chooses to work with neither, she will be without support. Will the system bury her, silence her, muzzle her if she goes to work within it? To go on working with the anarchists would be to work to break from the system, to associate herself with the anarchists' lack of respect for the order of law, to put herself outside her profession.

Celia shifts on her seat and looks away from the bougainvillea that seems, now, too gaudy for her taste. If she had a daisy perhaps she would pull the petals off to find the answer to this seeming binary question. But no daisies grow in this garden. Daisies require too much water to survive here.

[iii]

As the meeting for San Diego's committee contributing to the National Registry breaks up, Celia signals Evelyn. When the room is empty of all but the two of them, Celia asks, "Do you have time for a drink?"

Evelyn scans Celia's face. Slowly she nods. "Sure. Anything to do with the meeting?"

Celia shakes her head. "Only indirectly." Celia's obligation to the Search and Alert Program is only one of many concerns she feels must be considered in her decision.

They drive downtown to a place near the County Court House, a little bar patronized by professionals (the majority of whom are attorneys). Once they are served their drinks—gin for Celia, white wine for Evelyn—Celia says, "I'm trying to decide whether or not to accept a job with the Justice Department. In the Division of Human and Civil Rights."

Evelyn's eyes widen; she sips her wine. Then, setting her glass down on the exact center of the little square of white and yellow cardboard, she remarks, "Sounds to me as though someone's decided they'd better co-opt you for their own good."

Celia, the stem between her fingers, twists and turns the liqueur glass around and around and around while staring down at the crystal clear gin inside it. "That's a possibility," she says. "What I'm wondering is whether or not it would be feasible for me to work from inside the system."

"Would they insist you give up making statements, insist you stop sitting on all your human rights committees?"

"They've been cagey on the subject." Celia looks up from her glass and sees that the skepticism on Evelyn's face has deepened. "They say that I would have to get things cleared through the head of the Division as all US Government employees do."

Evelyn's eyes narrow. "You want advice, Celia?"

Celia bites her lip. "I think they're going to go after me if I turn them down. In which case I'll be more or less useless at the things I've been trying to do." She lifts the glass to her lips, inhales its fragrance of juniper berries, and takes a small, burning swallow. "I could imagine the Search and Alert Project tying in with the Division's efforts at current enforcement. I could be tipped off when one of the located creeps steps out of line and then instigate action. Don't you think?" Celia realizes she is nearly pleading with Evelyn to assure her she can continue to be of use working for the Government.

"But the crimes we find them committing will probably all be municipal or state violations," Evelyn says. "In which case your being in the Justice Department wouldn't help us all that much."

"But I might be able to build better liaisons—" Celia halts when she sees the look on Evelyn's face.

"You asked my opinion," Evelyn says. "I think they want to stop you. You're dangerous because you've built up a massive network that enables you to accomplish things. It's not just the Dowsanto case, you know. That would be kidstuff to them if it weren't for everything else you're into, not to mention your connections with the Free Zone."

Celia tries to smile. "Thanks for your honesty, Evelyn. I appreciate it. I guess I wanted to believe it could work."

"What precisely do you think their response will be?" Evelyn asks after a while.

Celia shrugs. "Probably a campaign to discredit me as a crazy or a radical. Maybe try to get me disbarred. All those sorts of things. I'm sure they'll be on my tail, watching."

"The way we watch the torturers in the National Registry," Evelyn says wryly. "But Celia, think of it this way: some of us will fight alongside you to the death. I think there's more of us than we know. People are starting to come out of the woodwork now that the worst seems to be past. You won't be alone."

Celia realizes they are talking as if she has made her decision.

[iv]

Luis closes the door and returns to his chair behind the desk. *If you're tired, Celia, then for godsake just go live in the Free Zone. Because you'd probably accomplish more there than you would working for those Washington bastards. What they extracted from us in return for the clinics should have been telling enough.* Celia hasn't tried to talk to Luis about the job offer since he gave his opinion that second night she was home.

"I called Danforth's office today," Celia says. Luis's face goes blank. "I declined to accept the job."

His eyes warm; he nods. "I'm not surprised. And you've prepared yourself for consequences?"

Celia swallows. "Yes. Evelyn Wakoski thinks I will get plenty of support."

"Provided their tactics are obvious," Luis says. "You've told Elena?"

"Yes. I actually decided a few days ago." She licks her lips. "But I had to nerve myself to take the plunge."

"That's natural." A smile lights up his face. "I'm proud of you, Cee. Just remember, it won't be anything like the other fight. Things are different." He strokes his moustache. "Not that it will be easy."

Dirty tricks, character assassination, psychological warfare. Not as horrible as torture and murder, but effective nonetheless.

Chapter Twenty-four

Sunday, 7/22/2096

Have to keep calm. My first impulse was to lug it up to that room on the top floor & sit in there & read until I'd figured out what makes the damned thing so important to Elizabeth. But prudence prevailed.

The dream was slightly off. Though the pedestal was the key, I almost failed to search it thoroughly when I couldn't find a way to get under the base of the statue. But feeling around the sides, I found the seam, which made me experiment. & then just as in the dream, the box opened at my touch.

The box is a heavy-gauge steel, hard-wired safe. I suspected the thing would be thick, because of its housing, but not *that* enormous. What could it possibly be a transcript *of?* I imagined it to be a transcript of Kay talking to Rbt, revealing what Elizabeth had done to her. But it's bigger than any book I've ever laid eyes on. I didn't stay & glance through it because the amazon assigned to the immediate grounds of the house was due to pass soon on her rounds. So at the right moment tonight I'll go back out & snatch a handful of pages so that I can start reading—skimming, probably, since it would take me days to read & I don't need to know the details, just what it was that Elizabeth did to Kay that was too terrible for Elizabeth to let out.

Fortunate that I still have to sleep in that damned brace-contraption— gives me a good reason to sleep apart from Sally. The way things are going between us... No. This is just a little spot of intensity that will pass of itself. She carries both of us on the wave of her enthusiasm... So hard, keeping her from making love to me. But all this will pass. The electricity will dwindle to a trickle & finally cease—as long, that is, as I keep things (viz., myself) controlled.

Tuesday, 7/24/2096

Can hardly wait the half-hour before I can go out there & snatch the next installment. Stayed up half the night reading—not skimming— the nearly three-hundred page handful I took from the safe last night. I can't understand my fascination with it. I suppose it's because of everything I've heard about Kay. & because it involves Elizabeth. I still haven't come across anything that must be kept absolutely secret. Probably I should take a handful of pages from the bottom of the safe, because that's likely where the answer lies. But I'm too anxious to read on from where I left off.

Staying up so late I ended up sleeping part of the afternoon, Sally curled up beside me, pleased because I didn't send her away during my nap.

Seems to me I'm going to have to read the whole thing, figure out what's what, then make at least one copy of the entire transcript, maybe more copies of selective bits, & divide the copies into smaller packages that can be secreted all over the island, in the woods, maybe, buried in the ground, secreted within tree hollows and in the rocks above the tide line. I'll make up one of those whimsical mnemonic systems that a tutor taught me when I was about seven or eight years old. If I make enough parcels & let Elizabeth know there are literally dozens of them lying around waiting to be discovered, she'll never feel safe & will know she can never be sure she can recover them all herself.

Friday, 7/27/2096

It's like leading a double life. Reading half the night, then dragging myself out of bed in the morning (physical therapy, household labor all to be done as usual), then the afternoon nap (which Sally would now hate for me to give up), & then the wait for the next install-ment...all the while there's this dialogue (is that the right word?) go-ing on in my head day & night. I even dream about them! I'm starting to see what it is about the transcript that Elizabeth dare not lose con-trol of. As for Kay...it's clear to me now that the things he said about her were no exaggeration. For all Kay's careful talk (how well I know the stress of careful talk myself!) I can't help but identify with her;

I know it's going to kill me, whatever it is that happens to her by the end of the transcript.

Jazzy was upstairs with me in the Music Room a while ago. Got mellow drinking my cognac. Started reminiscing about her childhood. She's five years younger than I. She was only an infant at the time of the Blanket, so she has no memories of anything before it. Before the World War, actually. She's new at all this. Was, like other of the amazons, recruited out of secondary school by someone who sounds as though she has only a tenuous relation to Security. (Probably a strong enough relation, only one not publicly acknowledged. I remember how such things work.) She has been indiscreet in letting me know about her recruitment, which makes her a little vulnerable to me. I gather she's lonely out here. Not particularly close to any of the others. Is celibate & fancies neither men nor women. (Is that possible?) But she had a strong friendship with another girl in secondary school. Which suggests to me that she will be susceptible to forming a strong bond with me.

& now I will go into the Small Study, ease open the French windows, & thieve the last—no, probably the penultimate—installment. I feel like an addict preparing to cook up my fix.

Sunday, 7/29/2096

(or should I say Monday morning?)

It's five a.m. & I've finished it, I've read the entire thing. I should go to bed now & think about it tomorrow. After all, it will soon be time to be waking up, & Sally will be wondering at my lazing in bed—again. Got almost no sleep last night, either.

I am stunned. As far as I can make out, not only would the masses be aghast at what this transcript reveals, but most executives as well—for entirely different reasons. Most people wouldn't be able to stand hearing such a tale, & so they would turn on her for it. For disgracing the executive system. For making fools of the Executive.

But Allison Bennett's involvement? Rbt never breathed even the faintest condemnation of *her*—all that time he kept talking about finding her so that he could use her sorely needed propaganda expertise. & to think even *Mama* knew about it. Doesn't that worry Elizabeth? Of course Mama didn't know the *details*, but she knew Kay was alive when the rest of the world thought her dead! Mama is a living witness.

I'm so excited by the possibility of having a *future* that my hands are shaking. But *basta*. Must get some sleep.

Monday, 7/30/2096

Have been thinking a great deal about Sally's place in all this. It's clear Elizabeth is capable of…incredible things. Her grasp of psychology combined with her ambition & no-holds-barred attitude makes her nearly invincible. Therefore I can all too easily imagine her using Sally against me. & there's no way to hide what's happening between Sally & me—her face gives us away.

Today I let her talk me into walking with her on the beach, she hanging on my arm. & after a while I said to hell with it & sank down onto the sand with her; & we kissed. & we shared a moment that touched me powerfully. Sally was sitting close beside me with her head on my shoulder. Softly she half-breathed my name: the first time she's ever used it to me. Sort of a tentative experiment, to see how it felt. I hugged her tightly, but we did not speak of it. We watched the waves for a while & then came back to the house for my nap. Which I will continue to take. I need to be able to go on working at night. I've copied the electronic files from the data disk Rbt left in the pedestal to my personal terminal and have made a start on making three additional flimsy copies. I already have a few packets that I've labeled with a statement providing the appropriate context that would make clear the significance of each particular segment. During tomorrow's walk with Sally, I will begin looking for hiding places outside. In the meantime, I will start caching packets inside the house & in the gym & perhaps even in the gardens.

Tuesday, 7/31/2096

Two important discoveries tonight: first, Jazzy's visits to me & my Music Room are clandestine. & second, it is she who makes most of the occasional necessary trips in the boat to the mainland. (Only three of them are trained to run the boat.) Probably someone accompanies her for security reasons, though I saw no way of confirming that guess without arousing her suspicions at the nature of my interest. But this means that that boat's system will respond to her prints. This could be important.

As for her coming here secretly—I suppose she could be deceiving me, working out one of Elizabeth's plots. But I doubt it. Must find a way to dig her in deep enough that she'll feel she'd have something to lose by turning on me. She apparently likes me, in spite of everything. Just as I mustn't underestimate how little such liking matters when it gets down to critical situations, I mustn't underestimate how much such things can count for. It all depends. The girl must be terribly lonely. Otherwise how could she have overcome all the affective obstacles to forming this bond with me?

This afternoon, after our nap, I asked Sally whether she had a decent Internet connection—thinking I'd broach the subject of trying to find a way to contact grandfather. Turns out that Elizabeth had Sally's implant fried right after recruiting her.

I've finally finished hiding all the packets of the copies of the transcript. Should I now return the original to the pedestal, or hide it, too? & what about its storage on my hard-disk?

Hard to make these decisions when they could be so damned critical.

Soon, soon I will decide how to make my move on Elizabeth. But I want to let things go further with Jazzy & see if I can get Jazzy to send Grandfather a note... But in any case, I must prepare for Elizabeth's next move.

Thursday, 8/2/2096

My confidence in Sally was shaken this afternoon. Niggling doubts still pursue me, though most of my mind rejects them.

We lay down as usual for our nap. I dozed off. When I woke, I found her asleep—she sometimes does sleep a bit during our naps, but not often. Usually when I wake I make love to her & then we bathe, after which we start preparing our evening meal. I leaned on my elbow to watch her sleeping face. So remarkably smooth & lovely with its dusting of freckles & those thick dark lashes curling against her cheekbone. When she is awake I usually notice only her eyes & sometimes her mouth, but asleep like this I looked instead at her cheekbones, her jawline, her neck, her ears... Until I noticed the earring. Something about it pricked my suspicions & prompted me to detach it from her ear. She woke, of course, at my touch. I gestured her to be silent & snapped off the outer shell of the pendant—revealing what could only be a transmitter.

She gasped, & I motioned her to remove the other earring. That one was empty. Before she could speak, I got up &—Sally trailing me—carried the earrings into the Small Study. Then I led her back to the library. Weeping, she swore up & down that she hadn't known, that it had never occurred to her that her personal possessions could have been tampered with. We went up to her room & I went through her jewel boxes & clothing inch by inch, button by button. I found three other bugs.

I have no way to be sure of anything. Must simply trust the girl. It's not worth holding her responsible for the bug—we'd be back where we were, only in perhaps worse shape. Just one more inconclusive piece of evidence. Like everything else to do with Sally...& lord she has been all loveliness, permeating so much of the last week with an almost painful sweetness. To tell the truth, I don't want to give that up, not just yet.

I know, Rbt, I'm being a fool. I can hear your remonstrations loud & clear.

Chapter Twenty-five

[i]

"So, what do you think about the way things are going?" Hazel asked Nancy after the waiter had taken their order.

Nancy's dark brown eyes followed the progress of two executive men trailing the restaurant's manager (a professional) across the dining room to a bay window that overlooked the courtyard. She said, "My view is rather limited, don't you think?" Her gaze settled on Hazel's face. "I'm only here on the weekends, and most of the talking goes on during the week." Her bare brown arm reached across the white place setting; she lifted her water glass to her lips and sipped from it. "And besides, everything's so complicated, there are so many different things involved that I can't see the whole picture." She set her glass down and returned her hand to her lap.

"There's a lot of pressure," Hazel said slowly, "to keep tacking on new demands. Because so many things are wanted. I can understand that. But I'm not sure that's what we need to do. What we're after is more than the fulfillment of the demands we're putting forward. We want to nudge change in a favorable direction. And since the effects of the things one does are seldom predictable..." No one could say they were organized, no one could say they were at all prepared with a well-thought out plan. It had never occurred to them that the Executive would be willing even to consider their demands, much less fulfill them. The result: chaos, chance, confusion. The principle danger of their disorganization lay in Liz's taking advantage of their lack of structure by imposing her own—whether through the simple tool of drawing up "agendas" for talks, or through more complex and less perceptible means.

The waiter returned with coffee for Hazel and juice for Nancy. Hazel's throat caught as she watched Nancy eye the juice with what looked like awe before sipping a tiny amount from the glass. Nancy caught Hazel's eye and flushed. "It's so full of flavor," she said—apologizing.

"I know. For you it's juice. For me it was Chinese cuisine. A new world opening before one—the only question being how one chooses to create and structure that world." One could long for the Good Life and do anything to get it. One could ignore that new world and deny any importance to sensory experience. Or one could begin a sort of quest or voyage... Hazel touched the rim of her coffee cup to her lips and inhaled the fragrance of the rich dark liquid rising wetly into her face.

"You felt that, too?"

Hazel smiled. "There's so much to enjoy. And I'm still finding new tastes, new perceptions. It gets to be habit-forming, you know."

"I had the feeling that these things were temptations that I was supposed to resist." Nancy spoke so low that Hazel had to lean forward to hear.

"No, no, not temptations! Why would you think that?"

Nancy made a face. "Well, for a couple of reasons. First, some of the activists I've met here despise such things. They always order that old dishwater beer we've been drinking all our lives. You heard what they said when there was that discussion about what to order last night? That it was not only a waste of money to order something better-tasting, but also petty even to think about what you drink. That anything would do. That nothing matters but the Revolution."

Hazel sighed. *The Revolution.* "Well I have two responses to that," she said. "First, it's petty if you devote your entire existence to obtaining such things or worrying about, say, which beer is the best. But I don't accept the argument that if you enjoy something you should give it up strictly because it's a materialistic pleasure. Second, those particular people mean by "revolution" something different than *I* mean. Actually, I'm not sure *what* they mean. But whenever people have had revolutions in the past, it usually meant that only a few things changed while the structures of authority and hierarchy were perpetuated—in a slightly re-packaged form. I really don't know if there's any connection between this idea of having to drink lousy beer and holding onto the structures of authority and hierarchy. But since

the people who you heard talking that way last night aren't interested
in dismantling hierarchy, I don't think you need to accept their dogmatic assertions as gospel." Hazel took another sip of coffee. "Talk it
over with others, think about it, and then decide for yourself." Hazel
smiled. "But then on this subject maybe I'm being self-serving: you
see, I happen to think pleasure is important." Hazel observed their
waiter enter the dining room with a large tray on his shoulder. Their
breakfast? she wondered. She looked back at Nancy. "Talk to Emily
Madden about this sometime. One of her chief interests in life is aesthetic expression and pleasure."

The waiter lowered the tray onto a stand and placed a platter of
fruit and cheese, a bowl of thick creamy yogurt, a basket of breads
and rolls, and a dish of butter on the table between them. Hazel lifted
the napkin from the bread basket, and the warm yeasty smell made
her mouth water. When the waiter had gone, Nancy gingerly spooned
pieces of the cut fruit onto her plate. Aware of Nancy's likely self-
consciousness at engaging in unfamiliar behaviors and physical movements in surroundings that were probably socially intimidating, Hazel
asked her what she thought of the plan for establishing a Marq'ssan-
tech network for activists throughout the country.

"As long as *they* couldn't just tap in whenever they wanted to,"
Nancy said, glancing up from the croissant that was falling apart as
she struggled to butter it, "then I think it's a good idea."

Hazel nodded. "The only things that worry me have to do with
so much Marq'ssan tech being so widely distributed. Though Sorben
keeps saying there's no way the Executive's scientists could ever figure
out how any of it works, I still have nightmares of their getting hold
of these things and spending years reverse-engineering them until
finally they *do* make a breakthrough that would be devastating." The
other thing that worried her had to do with the Executive's changing
its mind—again—about how it chose to deal with dissent. If they did,
people found to be using such technology would be marked.

"What an appalling thought! It would mean—"

"But Sorben doesn't believe they could ever figure any of it out
without first achieving a conceptual leap she thinks their philosophy
and politics makes impossible," Hazel said quickly. "And since I know
nothing about Marq'ssan technology and Sorben knows everything

about it and a great deal about the state of science and philosophy and politics on this planet, I think we can take her word for it, don't you?"

"Do you think a separate network will help the activists to work better together? I mean, to get past some of the most serious differences of opinion?"

Hazel spooned yogurt over the fruit she'd heaped on her plate. "I don't know. Probably not. But it would sure as hell make it easier for us to deal with the Executive in centralized situations like the one we're in now." Centralization, Hazel thought, was the key to the problem. They didn't *want* to be centralized, any more than the Steering Committee wanted Seattle to make decisions for the rest of the Free Zone. But the way they were going about it now certainly did make them centralized.

"I need to get away from here for a few days," Hazel said. "I need to get back to the Free Zone. To re-ground myself. In case things about this situation and place are getting to me."

Nancy's face took on that intense look that usually meant she was thinking strenuously. "Does that have something to do with what you once said about how differently you feel when you leave the Free Zone and have to deal with ordinary aspects of life here that are so different?" she asked.

"Partly," Hazel said. "And partly that Liz has gone out of her way to set me up." Nancy's eyebrows flew up, her eyes widened, her mouth opened—inducing Hazel to elaborate, "Not set-up in any malevolent sense, rather that she's making everything as easy and comfortable for me as she knows how. She's hardly played on our previous relationship at all. And she has so focused on me that I'm forced to play a central role in the negotiating—to boost my ego, I suspect, and to put me off-guard. And then there are all the little things. I've no doubt that her people have emphasized certain things to the management of this hotel and restaurant." Nancy's gaze moved around the room, as though to check out her surroundings with fresh eyes. "If someone hadn't spoken to the management, all of us would be getting rather different treatment and demeanor from the staff." Nancy nodded vigorously: in the ordinary course of events in a hotel like this she, Nancy—in her tight-fitting jeans and nylon tanktop—and she, Hazel—in her Free

Zone garb—would have been made to feel like insects mounting a disgusting invasion on this dining room.

Nancy spoke in a half-whisper. "So you think you might be not noticing things you'd ordinarily be feeling and seeing? That it might be lulling you?"

"That sounds a little strong, doesn't it. But I guess that's exactly why I want to go back. Apart from wanting more than phone conversations with people who have more experience with these kinds of negotiations than I."

"Oh, but nobody could really have *this* kind of experience," Nancy said. "There's never been anything this far-reaching, has there?"

Hazel's uneasiness about the negotiations coming to nothing returned full force. "We don't know if this is far-reaching or not," Hazel said. "They could be using it as a fishing expedition to find out what we want and what we're willing to give."

Nancy chased an elusive melon ball with her spoon as it slipped and slid around her plate. When she'd captured it, she popped it into her mouth and glanced at Hazel and offered her a sheepish smile.

Knowing Liz and her plans for the Free Zone, Hazel had to wonder if Liz had something nasty up her sleeve. It would be characteristic, certainly, if she did. But paranoia came easily in DC. Definitely, she needed some time away.

[ii]

"Please get out of your vehicle," the amazon said after studying Hazel's ID.

"Why?"

The amazon looked impatient. "We don't permit guests to drive their own vehicles past the gate. We'll run you up to the house and then back here when you've finished."

Was this the way they usually treated "guests"? They hadn't put her through this the evening she had come here to dine with Liz. Had she been exempted then because Liz had specially ordered it? Or was it because she had been Liz's—and not Lacie's—guest? Swallowing her irritation, Hazel stepped out of the car; the two uniformed women watched her as though on the alert for a threatening move. Did Liz have anti-aircraft weapons emplaced on the roof of this house, too?

Had the measures taken at the Redmond house been temporary, as Liz had always claimed?

The amazon drove her around to the side of the house, then stopped under a portico. As Hazel got out of the car Lacie appeared in the doorway, smiling. "Hello, hello," she cried and wrapped Hazel in a surprisingly tight hug. "I'm so glad you could come to see me, Hazel!"

Arms linked, they walked into the house and down a long hallway. Lacie stopped and opened the door to a narrow steep stairwell. "I was hoping for a chance to see you," Hazel said as they separated to mount the stairs. Should she comment on the weight Lacie had lost? Or would Lacie prefer that she not call attention to it? "Although I'm surprised to be here in DC for this long. I thought it would be only for a couple of days." Hazel's sandals clattered on the bare wood steps as she followed Lacie, whose soft slippered feet made no sound that could be heard over the swish of the silky gown she wore.

Lacie glanced back over her shoulder. "Liz says you and she are holding important talks."

"Well," Hazel said, "they could be. If anything comes of them."

Lacie stopped at the second landing they came to and opened the door. They emerged into a deeply carpeted hall. Paintings of aristocrats in towering white-powdered wigs dancing and playing the harpsichord hung at close intervals along the flowery-papered walls. They passed three closed doors, then turned the corner into a shorter hallway. Lacie opened the first door they came to and gestured Hazel in. "My bedroom is right across the hall," she said. "But this room, too, is mine. Well almost all mine. I share it with one other person." Lacie's eyebrows lifted. "I think you might know her? She was with Liz before you went renegade. Maxine?"

"Oh," Hazel said. "Yes, I remember Maxine. I think I met her a few times." Hazel recalled a woman who had sometimes arrived in the mornings at Liz's apartment before Hazel had gone, but she could not conjure up the woman's face.

A table set for lunch stood near the windows that covered most of one wall, overlooking an extensive formal garden and an immaculate, tree-shaded green lawn. "We can walk in the garden after lunch," Lacie said as they seated themselves. "There's a really beautiful trout pond and fountains, and even a Henry Moore statue."

"Sounds nice," Hazel said politely, reflecting that back in Redmond Lacie wouldn't have known a Henry Moore from a Giacometti (no more than she herself would have). But then life in a house like this might well be educational.

As they worked their way through the elaborate meal it occurred to Hazel that in her role of hostess Lacie seemed to be imitating Liz as the latter had been when Hazel had dined with her the first evening of her stay in DC. "How do you like living in DC?" Hazel asked, buttering a slice of French bread.

"Well," Lacie said, "I love living in this house and working for Liz. But to tell the truth, I'm not that crazy about the city." She wrinkled her nose. "Until the Marq'ssan got rid of that pollution mess a few weeks back, I couldn't even walk in the garden. Can you believe it? Not that I go out much. I guess I'm not much of a city girl, growing up in the country like I did." Lacie took a long drink of water. "And then, everything seems to be pretty violent around here. Which isn't what I'm used to." She shrugged. "But why go out? Sometimes it almost seems like living in the Redmond house, except that we had to be so worried about security all the time those thugs were after Liz."

And they weren't worried now? Hazel speared a crisp green bean and a slice of potato with her fork. "Somehow I thought you'd want to stay in the Free Zone. It never occurred to me you'd end up moving out here when Liz did."

"I like her a lot, Hazel." Lacie's plump, pink lips curved in a soft smile. "She's always been so nice to me. So appreciative. I've never known anyone like her. It never occurred to me *not* to move out here with her."

"All that executive-service-tech stuff doesn't bother you?"

Pink slightly darker than the pattern marking Lacie's face crept into the pale powdered spaces naked of paint. "Oh, I think you made too big a deal of that, you know? I can see that maybe Liz didn't treat Ginger the way she should have, and that some of those executives living at the house were real bitches, but the advantages outweighed the disadvantages, at least for me. Not everybody is the same, you know. Once we started eating separately, things weren't as tense. And actually it allowed us to be freer and gave us more time to ourselves. It's a good thing to be able to spend your free time separate from your employer." She smiled and waved her hand at the delicately furnished room. "I'd much rather be up here watching vid or reading or chatting with Maxine than hanging around downstairs with Liz—who's hardly ever around, anyway." Lacie grinned. "My special thing in this house is service for Liz, but since she's almost never around, I don't have much of it to do."

Lacie clearly enjoyed her position of privileged dependence. It would take a great deal, Hazel saw, to disenchant her. Lacie might have done most of her growing up in the Free Zone, but she had spent all of her adult life with Liz.

"She thinks very highly of you."

Startled, Hazel looked up from her plate to catch the expression of wistfulness suffusing Lacie's face. Could Lacie be *in love* with Liz? Could she be Liz's *lover*? "You must know a lot about Liz by now," Hazel said. Those serving executives like Liz probably picked up a great deal about what their employers were up to, even when their employers took care to fall silent every time a service-tech came into the room.

"Not as much as you do." Lacie slid Hazel a questing look. "Are you sorry you left her?"

Hazel grinned. "Not for a second. I like determining my own life. For me that's the key to everything."

"Nobody can completely determine their own life."

"Of course not. But certain circumstances are more conducive to self-determination than others."

"Different people have different wants and needs." Lacie stared down at the garden.

Hazel wiped her mouth on her napkin. "I would be silly to dispute that." She laid her napkin beside her plate and drank the last swallow of water in her glass.

Lacie looked at her and smiled. "Would you like to see the garden now?"

Hazel summoned up a smile to match Lacie's. "Sure. I've only seen two Henry Moores in my life. And I always did like dahlias."

Assured, slim, poised, Lacie rose and led Hazel back down the stairs. Ten years, Hazel thought. Ten years of adulthood with Liz, and Hazel could barely make out that young woman so eager to talk about the growing seasons of spinach and broccoli and Walla Walla sweets. But then Lacie had—or thought she had—made her choice. And that was that.

[iii]

"I suppose," Liz said, "you have to report back to Greenglass." The silver and amethyst bracelets covering most of her right forearm flashed and glinted in the sunlight as her fingers crept back to the long dangling loops of silver and amethyst chain wound several times around her neck.

Hazel remembered that jewelry. Liz had been wearing it the first night they had gone out together. "Trying to bait me, Liz?" Did she know that Martha had been with them in their hotel suite nearly every weekend of the negotiations?

"Why else would you go off just when we're so close to agreeing on at least a few things?"

Hazel shifted into a cross-legged position. Liz's informality during their talks sometimes made Hazel feel as at home here as she would be talking to friends in the Free Zone. Usually they sat on the floor, moving about as they wished, taking breaks to use the telephone or the bathroom, drinking juice and water and only loosely following any sort of agenda. "Maybe I just want a few days to myself in more natural surroundings," Hazel said.

"You'd be so selfish at a time like this?"

"It needn't be selfish," Hazel said.

Liz's gaze grew uncomfortably intense. After a long silence, she said, "Is it a lover, Hazel?"

"No. Not that that's any of your business."

"Sorry. I've so pointedly refrained from asking..." A wry smile flitted over Liz's face, then vanished. "I could find out such things about you, Hazel. But I never have, you know. I've always respected your privacy."

Hazel swallowed. "I'm glad for that. Where those sorts of things are concerned, I've never doubted your integrity, Liz."

Liz's eyes brightened. "I'm glad you still know that much about me," she said.

"To get back to the Lake Erie project," Hazel said. "If we think of it as a sort of experimental prototype for future cooperative efforts and perhaps publicize it as such, then we might want to design later projects to have a built-in flexibility responsive to what we learn as the project unfolds."

"Last night I was thinking about the few projects we undertook in cooperation with the aliens just after the Blanket," Liz said. "And I got to thinking how differently everything might have turned out if we had been able to sit down and talk the way you and I are doing now." She twisted a strand of the silver and amethyst chain so tightly around her fingers that the nails and tips of her fingers went livid. "If that bastard could see us now!"

"Who?" Hazel asked, confused at Liz's non sequitur.

"Sedgewick." Liz's eyes gleamed. "He must be rolling over in his grave. Not just the fact that we're trying to do business with aliens and anarchists, but the way you and I are sitting here on the floor discussing things so informally, so chattily, so *easily*. Like women!"

Liz thought of herself as—in her own way—revolutionary? As a trail-blazer?

Liz leaned forward. "I think you must have realized by now what a restraining effect I exercised over that bastard for all those years. If it hadn't been for me, he would have been like that all the time. It was only after I left him that he went to such extremes."

Hazel said nothing. Surely Liz did not expect a pat on the back?

"But I wish it were true that we really were doing business with the aliens," Liz said, changing the subject. "Surely there must be something of ours they would want to trade in? Think, Hazel, how this world would change if we could engage in actual *trade* with the inhabitants of another planet!"

Opening a vast, new market? Hazel said, "The Marq'ssan don't trade." She had told Liz this once before. The issue of "trade" appeared to be an *idée fixe* with her.

"But they obviously trade with the Free Zone. What is it you give them for all the technology they put at your disposal?"

"They don't trade, Liz. They offer gifts to us. Gifts without strings attached. All they ever require of us is thoughtful and honest dealings."

Liz's eyes narrowed. "Nothing is ever free, Hazel. Strangers don't bestow such lavish generosity and expect nothing in return. Don't you people worry about the enormity of the bill when the aliens finally tender it?"

"No," Hazel said, "we don't. They just don't think in such ways, Liz. They aren't human! And they aren't strangers, either. Not any more."

Liz drained her juice glass and gathered up the papers strewn around her. "I'm afraid I have to stop early today. I didn't realize you'd be leaving town tonight. We can take it, then, that your people here and in Buffalo and Cleveland will be in touch with Enright's people?"

"While in return, you will push through that legislation and get corporate support for it."

"We'll work it out the way cats avoiding a fight do. One step at a time, each side watching the other." In one rippling movement she rose gracefully to her feet. "Could I by any chance talk you into coming with me? I'm going down to see how my house is coming along and have a brief meeting with the builder. It's lovely down there. All green rolling hills and meadows." Liz smiled down at Hazel. "Far from the furor of DC, though only a few minutes by jet from Andrews."

Hazel scrambled to her feet. "I have to talk to the others a bit before I go. It's just as well we're stopping early today."

Her face blank, Liz nodded. "I understand."

What was it Lacie had said when Hazel had asked her if she thought Liz had changed over the last ten years? Something about her becoming more tightly controlled, tauter, but often manic, sometimes to the point of frenzy. Just now, for the first time, Hazel sensed this in Liz. Had Hazel only now noticed it because of Lacie's mentioning it to her? With her hands in her tunic pockets, her head easy on her shoulders, her mouth and eyes both smiling, Liz offered an ostentatiously casual posture as proof of her easy relaxed control. Posed or unaffected? Hazel debated as she left Liz's office. Did her grasp of such vast power come so easily to her, did the constant uncertainty of her continuing hold on power leave her so untouched? No, Hazel thought, nodding at Margaret Canfield as she passed through the latter's office. No being could hold that much power and remain the same self.

Chapter Twenty-six

Thursday, August 2, 2096—DC

Heart's still pounding, hands shaking. How the hell was I to know *she* was in there? No one warned me. And I never knock on the door of that room. Not only would I feel funny knocking, but Lise would be upset if I did. So it never occurred to me… And I guess I assumed that if Weatherall were to drop by to discuss something important, they would go into Lise's study—a room Lise hardly ever uses. (She has to have a study, it's *de rigeur*. My guess is that she goes in there only to take care of her personal finances and the household accounts.)

The look that woman gave me when she saw me standing there. What could I do? I didn't think I should try to creep out unheard, once I'd made the blunder of going in. That's all I'd need, to look as if I'd been in there eavesdropping on them and was on my sneaky way out. Thank god Lise stuck up for me. The way she snapped at Weatherall! Oh those blazing blue eyes, enough to make me drop dead in my tracks. I don't know, somehow it's hard to imagine her now in everyday settings and moods—eating, bathing, playing tennis, skiing, etc. as in the Redmond days. She was a super-hedonist back then. But now?

I should probably try to forget what I heard. Yet I'm also curious. Will Lise tell me more, when Weatherall has gone? (Which reminds me: must be ready to close this file the instant the door opens.) Lise was saying something about how no one would believe Guatemala had produced or was even interested in supplying Brazil. Weatherall interrupted at that point, and then Lise saw me. They could have seen me before then if they weren't so intent on whatever it was they were discussing. Supplying Brazil with what? The only thing I can think of where Brazil is concerned is the Marq'ssan threat against defense industries if the US goes on sending arms to Brazil. Could it be that they're talking about a way to get around that ultimatum? But surely such a thin subterfuge would inevitably be exposed. Everyone knows what a puppet Guatemala is.

Lord. I feel like warning Lise that such a ploy would only backfire in the end. That they'll look like liars and fools if they try such a thing. Why does it matter that they supply Brazil with these things, anyway? It seems so petty a thing to stick at. Especially considering what horrible creeps are currently governing Brazil. But I suppose

Saturday, August 4, 2096—DC

Had to stop because Lise came in. (And of course she doesn't knock on my door any more than I knock on hers.) Lise rueful about my walking in on her conversation with Weatherall. Not blaming me, but wishing it hadn't happened. She's given orders to Elly that in the future should Weatherall or some other member of the Executive come to talk to her I be warned... When I asked Lise if Weatherall was really pissed at me, she said it didn't matter, that Weatherall would forget about it in a day or two. Bull. Knowing Weatherall, I'm sure it will be added to the lengthy mental dossier on me she carries around in her head. In the past she's shown she has a very long memory for trivial detail where I'm concerned.

Yesterday Lise called me into her office to talk to me about some extremely sensitive, extremely secret projects. She will be doing almost all the actual writing in these projects herself—that's how secret they are. There's to be only one professional involved (to make a video). I'm to help her with writing, as well as to handle the production of various circulars and pamphlets and things. Because, she says, she knows she can trust me with such "utterly sensitive" material. I'm not sure what it is yet, except that it has to do with propagandizing executives. (Which is why, she said, only the one absolutely essential professional will be let in on the project.) Julia will be doing some of the work. But most of it will be done by Lise and me. One of the projects has to do with Mott's pregnancy. The other thing, Lise was a bit cagier about—said she'd tell me more later, as I needed to know. But my overall impression was that most of the projects have to do with convincing "the executive community" that Weatherall's policy vis-à-vis the anarchists and the aliens is the correct one. Lise thinks she might be ready to have me do some typesetting for her by the middle of next week. Of all my projects, these may prove the most interesting of all.

I wonder what it would be like to know what's going on the way people like Lise, Weatherall, and Hazel always seem to do? (But *of course* they know what's going on: they're the ones doing the things that "go on.")

Will settle down with a novel now, until it's time to get ready for the party. My first chance to read fiction in weeks.

Sunday, August 5, 2096—DC

Mott asked that Lise and I come early, about forty-five minutes before the party was to start. So we did. When I saw Mott and Ginger together, the expression "radiant as a bride" came into my mind. (Which is strange, considering how talk about brides and marriage and all that crap has always turned me off.) Their happiness and pride—well, it was bursting out all over. We drank a toast in champagne—with even Mott having some of the champagne for the occasion. She delicately gave us to understand that Ginger's had the first medical treatment. Which I think means she'll soon begin menstruating. We didn't talk explicitly about it—too weird a subject: the thought of a woman's deliberately returning her body to a primitive state... Why can't they do all that in the lab? As I was standing there sipping champagne, my stomach went queasy from my thinking not only of that but also about how Ginger would be having a fertilized egg implanted inside her body, to grow. And that struck me as even more gross than the menstruation routine. Still, they seem amazingly happy.

And last night their happiness was contagious. I don't think I've seen Lise look so happy and relaxed for years. She kept giving me brimming looks, squeezing my hand and surreptitiously caressing my arm as though she too were going to burst. And later, when we were walking the two blocks home, she bubbled over telling me how happy I was making her. Some of that was the champagne, I suppose, though I *do* think she's happier lately. It feels as though all the troubles between us are past. All that time we were walking home with our arms twined I kept thinking of how she had defended me to Weatherall the other day.

Most of the other couples sparkled, too. We did a lot of dancing—Mott had hired a trio of amusing musicians who wore paint on their faces and bodies, and dresses. Hard to explain, but they wore those things in a kind of satirical way. Which probably made a few of my peers feel a little uncomfortable even as they were laughing at some of the songs and repartee the trio offered us. And so a good time was had by all, with only one little incident marring it. I think it was Susan who started making cracks about the males on the Executive. Well, it's clear to see that everybody discusses this thing within couples. But there's a kind of taboo against more public discussion. So Elaine got annoyed with Susan and snapped at her. No one looked at anyone else, and then one of the executives told some anecdote or other about the anarchists who are, as gossip has it, overrunning DC. (They like such exaggerations. I haven't laid eyes on a single one of them myself.)

After we got home we made love, and after that Lise confided to me that Mott's having a baby with Ginger signified a triumph for all executive women. That it meant that not only could women hold the most powerful positions but that they could also control maternity and other private matters as they had never before been allowed to. That finally women were truly free of male control, that they need never be the pawns of men again. Is this true, I wonder? Lise never seemed dissatisfied before, not even during our early years together. If Lise hadn't said this, and if the whole issue of Mott's pregnancy hadn't raised such a ruckus, it would never have occurred to me that executive women were dissatisfied with their lot. Not even in that house at Redmond did they talk in such a way. They all hated Sedgewick and Booth for failing to appreciate the Women's Network, but I didn't know they felt like *pawns*. Well, maybe it's just Lise. Maybe the others don't see Mott's pregnancy in such a light... But now I want to finish my novel. Poor Lise will probably be working until after midnight tonight. So I'll have the whole evening to read. Which I'd better take advantage of, since I may be too busy to read another novel for weeks to come.

Wednesday, August 8, 2096—DC

Finally, that first forty-five-minute documentary over which there's been so much trouble is completed. Screened the finished version today for all the project managers, Lise, and Schuyler. Must say even *I* am impressed. Hard to believe this came out of the same trashy hysterical stuff they started with. What they ended up doing was taking what they call the "balanced approach": they posed the question of whether or not allying ourselves with the Marq'ssan is genuinely beneficial or will be ultimately destructive to our values and culture and freedom. Presented the pros and cons. They let the scientists and old photos and film-clips show how formidable, extensive, and unfathomable Marq'ssan technology is. *Naturally* what happened in the course of the documentary is that a "middle ground" was "found" between declaring total war on the Marq'ssan and anarchists and making ourselves wholehearted allies with them. And of course along the way, they presented Lise's (and, I gather, others'—probably Weatherall's) theory that the Marq'ssan hope to lull us into lowering our guard and that their most immediate intention is to let anarchy and chaos loose on the world so that humans will be totally at their mercy. The argument was made—mostly by way of shots of "interviews" with Enderby and Rossellini—that we can take advantage of the Marq'ssan's willingness to share beneficent technology while holding the line politically. That clearly the aliens would long ago have destroyed the planet if they'd wanted to, that what matters is preserving our culture and values and freedom and not allowing our society to break down as the Marq'ssan are thinking it will. To tell the truth, they did it so convincingly (all those film-clips of Martha Greenglass certainly helped) that while I was watching it I was almost persuaded by it, even though I tend not to believe most theories people devise about the aliens. The technique of presenting a "middle ground" is an effective one. They're going to show the documentary tomorrow night during prime-time and distribute it as an extra on circulating soap DVDs. And I gather various organizations will show it to groups of people and encourage discussion of it. Which must mean Lise thinks this documentary could have a powerful effect on the public.

That image of the spaceship out in the desert, though...it remains after everything else fades. Isn't that curious? And of course it conjures such memories of those days...

Friday, August 10, 2096—DC

Have been expecting Lise to ask me to do that typesetting for her. But she's said nothing about it. Wonder if this has anything to do with what she was so upset about last night? Yesterday at work everyone I talked to was in a euphoric mood about the documentary. There was a kind of pleasurable anticipation, waiting for the compliments and raves to flow in on Friday. But last night when Lise finally got home she was in a terrible mood. I think there was an Executive meeting, but I'm not sure because she didn't specifically mention it or talk about it. But she came to me in my room (when she stays out late I usually just sleep in my own bed) and asked me to hold her. She was all trembly and weepy.

So we lay quietly for a while, softly cuddling in the dark, not speaking. But after a while she started mumbling to me. About how frightened she sometimes gets. That most of the time she just tries to forget and just does things without thinking about them. I had no idea what she was talking about. But then she started talking about the old days—the Civil War, and the World War, and then about fighting Sedgewick and Booth, about how those days were so much harder and more dangerous, about how much more was at stake then, and why should it get to her like this, that she had borne a lot of responsibility for a long time now. So I began to guess what she was talking about. "I'm having moments of thinking I might not even mind if the men dumped us now," she said. "Maybe it would be just as well, because the fight just goes on and on, you know."

What finally emerged is that she thinks the Executive is coming to some kind of crisis. That Weatherall may have to force the resignations of Rogers and Steinmetz. But that it would be a test of her power whether she could do so now or not. And that Weatherall herself wasn't sure that the crisis wouldn't break her power, but thought that if she didn't force the resignations, certain policy directions would be shifted, maybe even reversed, and that if that happened some of them might not feel like staying around much longer. Mott, I gathered, in particular. I'm confused about what the issue is, except that some of it has to do with Mott's pregnancy and some of it centers on Weatherall's talks with the anarchists.

After a while I fetched Lise some wine. After that I made love to her. And then she fell asleep. I stayed awake for a while, though, to piece together what she'd said to me. I think I have it right, though I can't be sure. I wish I understood why the males are so upset about Mott. I understand how hardliners can be pissed at Weatherall's talking to the anarchists. But this whole Mott problem, that's something else. And somehow I have the impression from Lise that where the males are concerned, it's even more threatening than negotiating with the anarchists.

Sunday, August 12, 2096—DC

Stayed up most of the night typesetting the "white paper" that's labeled as coming from Weatherall's office. Then slept all morning. Tonight I'll have to go back to the office to correct the proofs. Lise is out of town until tomorrow, for which I'm grateful. I don't know what I'd say to her if I were to see her today. Maybe I'm too tired to be thinking straight. But what she wrote for this "white paper" bothers me. I can't get it out of my head. At a certain point when I realized what Lise's major argument was, I started to feel sick. Basically she argues that executives shouldn't be short-sighted in their greed. That they should think about where their "true interests" lie, as the executives who brought about the Executive Transformation did. (What in god's name is the Executive Transformation? I think the reason I couldn't go right to sleep once I got home was because I kept trying to guess what it could be.) And then a parallel was drawn, which Lise kept stressing throughout the entire paper, between the current situation with anarchist-inspired demands being made on the corporations by workers in chemical plants and the people living in their surrounding communities, and how the Guatemalan ruling class in the late '30s and early '40s had to be shown how by "giving up a little one could gain a great deal."

The entire "white paper" consists of those sorts of arguments and analogies. I didn't understand half of it, but it's clear Lise has a cynical view of the executive system. I guess it's her cynicism that bothers me more than anything. I mean all that bullshit she's talked to me about responsibility and taking care of public interests and all that. But when it comes down to it, the only recourse is to appeal to other executives' greed and desire for power. The few lines about responsibility were just a thin cover she wasted almost no time on at all. The overall tone stinks of corruption of the worst sort.

So tired. But can't sleep, not in the middle of the day. Maybe I should go to the office now and finish the job. And then try to get to bed early.

Tuesday, August 14, 2096—DC

Had a long talk with Lise last night about the white paper—or, to be more specific, about her cynicism about the executive system. She pled guilty to cynicism when dealing with "certain types of executives" as she calls them. Says a lot of them are interested only in wealth and power. Not all, but a lot. But that that doesn't affect the basic truth that the executive system is managing to preserve freedom and a good standard of living and peace and tranquility etc. for the entire population. That the alternatives would lead to disaster. And that for that reason one had to put up with a certain amount of corruption, though Weatherall was trying to change that. She said that the Civil War, the World War, and then Sedgewick's Reign of Terror had demoralized executives, had made many of them cynical—and that cynicism makes people ripe for corruption. Weatherall was hoping that she could change that, could reform the executive system to the fine instrument it had been before the Blanket.

I suppose I see her point. But I find it disquieting to be forced to accept corruption as a matter of convenience, to be forced into cynicism. Isn't it bad enough, I said, that the public is basically hoodwinked every day of the year? But to have to con, bribe, or flatter executives into going along with reforms that might cut into their massive profits... (Lise doesn't argue that their profits are massive. How can she, considering how much she has been making lately because of insider tips that—as she often tells me—keep doubling her holdings every year?)

What a world, what a world. And I think of Mom and Dad and know they'd never in a thousand years comprehend any of it. Because first you have to start more or less over, knocking down the house of cards you've taken for "reality," and slowly build up a new house— never knowing, of course, if any of the walls will stand, since there's never any way to be sure you've finally got hold of the truth.

Truth? Does even Lise know what it is? She must. But that she's so easily lied to me on so many levels all these years... And every time I've had a new revelation I've thought *now I finally understand, now I finally have the truth.* Hah. Bah-humbug.

Time for a bath. Lise will probably be home soon. She claimed her meeting with Weatherall would be short. I think I'll take a glass of something into my bath so that I won't be jumping down Lise's throat when she gets home. She seems to be under a lot of pressure, and I don't want to add to it. She needs me as she never has before. Well, I won't let her down. And she knows it, too. That's how we are these days. And for that at least I'm glad.

Chapter Twenty-seven

Sunday, 8/5/2096

I'm moving as if in a dream, a lovely dream I wish never to waken from. Tonight I discovered how beautifully Sally reads. But I should have guessed—it should have been obvious that as an actor she knows how to read lines aloud. She read poetry to me, from one of the books of women poets Elizabeth sent me so long ago. Sally, it turns out, would have liked to have done serious theater. But there never was any question of that. She started with the soaps at age twelve. & they never wanted her for anything else. I think I'm to understand from what she's said that those who act in the soaps have little choice about their roles. They are assigned. Their lives are mapped out. Even her "private life" was a scripted show largely for public consumption. That is, she had little of a genuine private life, since most of her "leisure" (during the time she became a favorite) had to be spent acting out a "private life" the "fans" would be fascinated with, usually following a loose script, though sometimes acting explicitly scripted scenes for fan magazines to pick up on & generate gossip out of.

This was worse than my situation with Rbt. To hear Sally talk, my life has been a luxury of privacy.

Oh the little things we do together. This morning weeding the garden together; planting spinach for a fall crop (will we even be here then?); & of course our favorite thing, walking on the beach after lunch before our "nap." I don't think I've ever been so relaxed in my adult life. How can this be, considering that I'm teetering on the edge of either catastrophe or release? Yet I have a sense of being swept up within a flowing current she & I both share & generate.

It's as frightening as it is wonderful, though. This afternoon she grew more persistent in her caresses, pressing her lips against my (clothed)

breast & belly. I protested to her to make her rein herself in. Why? she wanted to know, why can't she make love to me? How explain the fear I have, the fear that surges up at the very thought of letting myself go in that way? Irrational, yes. But if I were to let her make love to me, she would see no reason to restrain herself in any way (& why should she?) as I, too, yielded control—& then where would we be?

I keep putting off my decision. I'm loath to relinquish this state of bliss, can't get my mind & body out of the present tense to reach into the future. It's dangerous, living for the moment. I don't *have* all the time in the world. Elizabeth may at any moment snatch Sally away. It would take only one phone call from her to the amazons. & then Sally would be gone.

Wednesday, 8/8/2096

If anyone had ever told me I could fall into greater madness than that I shared with Rbt...no, I wouldn't have believed it. With Rbt it was dangerous because of what discovery would have meant. But this is a different kind of danger. Not to mention that I am allowing myself to be diverted from what should be most important to me: saving our future—yes, *our* future, Sally's & mine. Though she knows nothing of my efforts, nothing of what otherwise faces us (naively she imagines we'll be living here undisturbed for ever & ever amen), it is both our futures that I must manage, hers as well as mine. I can't bear thinking of a future without her. I won't always feel so strongly, surely I won't. It's madness, of a sort Rbt would never have understood. I don't believe he ever felt this kind of joy (that simple but swelling pleasure triggered by a shared glance or by the sensation of our fingers touching). He knew well, of course, the intensity of passion (though an intensity he understood to be bounded in a way the one I share with Sally seems not to be), the craving for which drove his sexual excesses. I love the intensity even as I fear it. Oh these terrors of mine, lurking, threatening to swallow me whole. Sally's fears seem trivial compared to my own. She finds nothing frightening in our lack of control, our lack of emotional restraint. But we've worked out our "bargain": she will brave her fears if I will brave mine.

Why why why, she would not stop asking, why would I not let her make love to me. Her touches & embraces drove me wild—she wouldn't heed me & I wouldn't/couldn't be rough with her to make her desist. Such a sweeping combination of sweetness & fear—the piercing sweetness of her fingers & breath soft on my face, her words of love (she's so gentle, I've never known anyone so gentle in my life, except perhaps Marie when she'd tuck me in bed, hold me in her lap & read to me, take me to concerts). Such sweetness is a gift unearned, undeserved, a gift impossible to repay. One can only accept it as the wondrous thing it is. It undid me, though, & I wept. Her lovely eyes waiting, her hands tender & steady—compelling me to try to explain something I barely understood myself. I sought for speech, & there came out of me halting, shaky words of fear. But of what? she wanted to know. I don't understand it myself, I admitted to her. It's all the fears Rbt taught me. I see that now. Fear of uncontrol, fear of rejection, fear of betrayal...all those things that add up to a fear to trust anyone (but Rbt) with this flood of emotion & sexuality. & even with Rbt I didn't trust him as completely as he thought I did. In some ways I never let go entirely because I knew he would condemn despise scorn me if I did. I always had to be Persephone with him, & it was he who invented Persephone.

Sally gently derided my fear. Lured me on. In a panic I reminded her of her own sexual fears. & told her that it would give me great pleasure to use the dildo with her but that I knew she had too great a fear of it even to suggest it. She looked shocked at my saying this— shocked, I suppose, that I could have such a thought about her when I'm feeling about her as I do. So then we talked about our respective fears. & lord I don't know whose idea it was, but we ended by agreeing to this bargain: if I would let her make love to me then she would allow the dildo. & all this discussed & arranged with the most incredible intensity, our eyes locked, our fingers twined.

& so I let her make love to me today. I was so tense that I thought I wouldn't be able to come (though I often come simply from caressing her). & then it happened...& it hardly seemed frightening afterwards, though I'm frightened again now at how far we are going, she & I. This is nothing like anything I've known. With Sally I'm neither Rbt nor Persephone. I keep wondering how this can be. Who am I? What am I? Somebody both old & new. & something of a stranger at that.

Saturday, 8/11/2096

How can I get enough of a grip on myself to *think*? My brain is like gauze. I *must* decide whether to write to Elizabeth or try to subvert Jazzy. Instead I walk on the beach with Sally, dig in the garden, listen to her reading to me. & we make love half our waking hours. Sally slipped into my bed this morning & woke me by making love to me (& I still in my brace, too). Oh. Of all my pleasures, ever, the experience of waking like that... No. I mustn't dwell on it, not now. I need a series of cold showers, perhaps. For surely all this can wait until I've dealt with Elizabeth.

But can it? Will we ever be like this again?

& then doubt nags me, that things may turn out badly with Elizabeth, that I may end up dead. & though it won't matter to me if I'm dead, still the thought clutches at my throat & makes me anxious to live for this wonderful moment as I can.

Rbt would say I deserve to lose to Elizabeth. Because I don't even care about her now—about revenge, that is. I want a future for us. I don't want this to be all we have, to be cut off by Elizabeth when she chooses. I know she'll take Sally from me eventually. In a matter of weeks...or even days.

I must move to protect this precious thing, this vast ocean deep we share together. I must prevent Elizabeth's poisoning polluting invading our sea.

Monday, 8/13/2096

Jazzy has a ten-day furlough that begins on Friday. She is allowed a choice of Boston, New York, or DC (Elizabeth generously pays for food & lodging for these furloughs—perks to sweeten the dullness of isolation), & she says she's already signed up for Boston, along with the other amazon on furlough that week. I'm a little nervous about this because it's possible that even if they go directly to Boston they might still be loquazene-tested, though I don't really see why they

would be—Elizabeth has no reason to distrust them, & they are being paid to write reports on me. & no one knows of the hours Jazzy's
snatched here.

At any rate, I've gotten Jazzy to agree to mail two letters for me—
one to Grandfather & one to Mama. We happened on the subject
when Jazzy started talking about how she misses her mother, whom
she hasn't seen for two years. Jazzy is originally from the South. She
generally doesn't have the time or money to travel to see her. (She's
hoping things will change because this job pays so well.) So I told
her how terrible it was for me not to see any of my relatives, I even
showed her the letter Elizabeth wrote me telling me about her forged
response to Mama's letter. This shocked her—she can't imagine why
Elizabeth won't allow me contact with my own mother. ("Even people
in prison!" she exclaimed indignantly.) I must say, I wasn't expecting
that degree of naiveté. So tonight I will begin drafting my letters.
(Oh Grandfather, I can hardly wait to see Elizabeth's face when you or
your attorney confront her! Not even Elizabeth can brush aside Varley
Raines.) & then when I've done that I'll think about a letter to Elizabeth. Do I send it simultaneously? Or do I wait to see what happens
with Grandfather & Mama? & a more important question: do I try to
defuse in advance Elizabeth's tale-bearing? & do I mention my possession of something Elizabeth badly wants & mention this as the reason
for Elizabeth's holding me here incommunicado?

Oh it's so tricky. But now that I have someone to mail letters for me,
anything is possible.

Tuesday, 8/14/2096

How difficult sending her upstairs to sleep. She doesn't understand
why I won't let her spend nights with me. But the less she knows of
what I'm doing, the safer she will be.

Today...oh, today we went even farther...one part of me is almost
delirious with happiness, while another part of me, fiercely jealous
of these precious experiences, insists that when this time has passed,
such happiness will never again be within my grasp. Grasp? What a
strange way to talk about it. But that fierce, poignant voice already la-
menting what some part of me knows must pass, that voice speaks of

experiences as something that one takes, seizes, tries to hold onto. Yet I don't think the rest of me feels that way at all. More like accepting a gift that has fallen into my lap through no doing or merit of my own. I'm tempted almost to call it a passively experienced thing, yet I cannot conceive of this leaping of my heart, this eagerness & excitement, as *passive*. No, I see now—the active/passive dualism is inappropriate here, must inevitably distort whatever is happening between us & within me. Allowing oneself to participate without restraint cannot be described in such terms.

What happened today... (I know I'm attempting to write about all this because that part of me already poignant & jealous & regretful predicts to me that I will later long for traces of this time with which to seek—futilely—to relive these emotions & pleasures.) What happened is that I held Sally to her part of our bargain. & it was nothing like any other time I've used the dildo. With Rbt, I think, it was as much a desire to exercise a permitted aggression against him as a desire to touch him as deeply and sensually as he touched me. & then later, when I used it those few times on Sally, it was to humiliate her; she was a symbol to me then for many things. But I was gentle with her, & timely. How curious, that what she most minded was the look of the thing—on me. ("You are so beautiful," she said, "but that thing is so ugly!") Kneeling over her—her luminous green eyes sometimes closed, sometimes fixed on my face—a flood of love words gushed out of me (the taste of her vulva yet on my tongue & lips), words that I've never said to a soul (never dared to say), & I could feel us—both of us—carried away on the swelling flow of them, & all Sally's little gasps & cries (she already coming before I entered her) & all this moving me so powerfully that I too came as I was pushing into her, my hands sliding over her smooth slick thighs, my tongue in her ear & her palms pressing into my back, her breathless cries in my ears... What was it in her eyes—love, yes (her eyes swim with love), but more—a sort of wide-eyed trust that elates me almost past bearing, fills me to bursting. Afterwards we lay quietly in the late afternoon heat, the sun streaming in through the tall library windows drenching us, our legs tangled, my fingers in her hair, her fingers lightly touching my arm,

her lips trailing tiny kisses over my shoulder & collarbone... Those
moments of ineffable fullness I will never forget, ever.

Wednesday, 8/15/2096

Because Jazzy came tonight & we talked a bit more, & because Sally
went up to bed as soon as Jazzy arrived & (I found when I went up to her
after Jazzy had gone) fell fast asleep, I am stalked by chilling thoughts
about Elizabeth. In the end what it comes down to is what I know of
her through that transcript. It has been haunting my dreams, despite
my absorption with Sally. What drove me to read the entire transcript
(rather than merely hunting for the incriminating parts) was my need
to figure out just what it was Elizabeth was doing to Kay & what it
was she intended for her. Kay's distress at the end when she found out
how trivially Elizabeth chose to use her—this cuts too closely to my
own situation with Sally & my fear that Elizabeth hopes to use Sally
against me. Yet what she did to Kay, or tried to do...there lurks in me
a deeper fear than that Elizabeth hopes to use Sally to control me. The
deeper fear is that Elizabeth is fucking with my mind—because she
so obviously fucked with Kay's mind in the eeriest, spookiest way. One
can achieve certain crude forms of brainwashing, that's been known
for more than a century. The religious sects of the last century used
those techniques better than anyone. But much more was involved in
what she attempted with Kay. As I read the transcript I kept thinking she was going to make Kay identify strongly with her, make her
excessively dependent on her. Yet she didn't take that approach, which
would seem to have been the obvious one. (& god knows it would
have been easier on Kay.) No, she kept a certain distance. Or do I have
this wrong: was it possible Elizabeth was trying for that, but that Kay
resisted her too strongly? No. That's not it. Elizabeth could have used
Kay's vulnerability during those post-closet episodes to greater advantage. Instead, she seemed each time to be extremely careful to keep
a certain distance so that Kay, putting herself in some fashion back
together again, would again find that distance for herself, would again
cling to her perception of Elizabeth as her enemy.

My body is covered with gooseflesh. Here I sit in the middle of the
night with only one dim light burning. & what is in that transcript

seems at this moment far more real than anything that happens in the daytime between Sally & me. At this moment anything seems possible. For instance, that Elizabeth is playing some deep game that I can't begin to fathom. Actually, that seems *certain*, rather than merely possible. I have thus far fallen into her trap—with Jazzy, with Sally, with the transcript…

No. I mustn't think that way. I have a winning hand if only I can keep my face from giving it away. I will press my bet & keep pushing the ante higher & higher. She will lose, I will win. Unless she manages to cheat & I (or Grandfather) can't keep her from getting away with it.

I'll sleep now & hope dreams of Elizabeth don't wake me.

Sedgewick's Island, Maine
August 16, 2096

Dear Grandfather,

I'm writing to you for the first time since my father's death because at last I am able to do so, now that one of my guards has agreed to mail a letter for me. (Two letters, actually—one to Mama as well as one to you.) Since Elizabeth Weatherall brought me here I've been allowed to correspond only at her discretion. Until recently she allowed me to send a few letters—carefully censored—to Mama. But a few weeks ago she wrote to tell me that she had written to Mama in my name in such a way that Mama would be permanently alienated from me. I don't know if she's done the same with you.

I have no idea what information you have on my situation, or what Weatherall has told you (if anything) about me. In my confused and vulnerable state of mind following Papa's death I agreed to assign her a comprehensive power of attorney (as well as to sign a will making over the entire estate to her in the event of my death). I have no way of revoking it though I would like very much to do so, for I cannot leave the island except at her orders. I must admit to you, Grandfather, that at first I believed I deserved this punishment. I've done things to be ashamed of, and she knows about them. They aren't things for which I could be prosecuted in a court of law, however. It is a matter of personal, not criminal, shame. I think I must have believed all this time that those shameful things were the reason she kept me isolated here. I had some idea that she thought I wasn't fit to be out in the world. As time passed I even hoped that she might come to change her mind, to forgive me. It was only after the first year (I was very upset that first year, filled with guilt, remorse, and grief) that I began to realize what a lifetime spent alone would mean—and I having lived only twenty-one years when all this started (and of those twenty-one, six were spent in a strange painful existence living the life my father required of me).

Recently, however, I've discovered (from her own admission) that her true reason for sequestering me here is fear that documents Papa had hidden on this island would get out. She *literally* tore this once beautiful mansion apart looking for them. But she did not find them. After a long search of my own, I located the documents. They are indeed damning, far more so than any of my wrongdoings. Hers could not only land her in a court of law, but bring down her entire administration. Of that I've no doubt at all.

Grandfather, all I ask for is a chance to tell you my case in person. I don't believe I deserve to be deprived of my liberty and the love of my family. I acknowledge that you may wish to wash your hands of me once you learn everything there is to know about me. But those wrongdoings aren't the true reason I am deprived of my liberty. On the contrary, Weatherall's crimes are the reason for my imprisonment.

It may be that if Weatherall did what she wrote me she would do Mama will not read my letter. I ask one more favor of you: that you please explain to Mama that I did not write whatever obnoxious thing she received in my name and that I would have written to her many times since her visit if I'd been able. As for why I didn't tell her anything of my situation when she visited me, it was because Weatherall threatened to tell her my shame (as well as other things she would have invented at that time to compound my guilt). Since I didn't fully comprehend the perilousness of my situation, my shame and fear of Mama's learning of it restrained me.

I would like so much to see you again, Grandfather—if you would allow me to. Please find some way to make that possible. Or I really will begin to believe that no one on earth even remembers my existence, that I am indeed the non-person Weatherall has chosen to make me.
With love and hope,
Alexandra

Sedgewick's Island, Maine
August 16, 2096

Dear Mama,

Elizabeth has not let me write to you since I put the Paris apartment in your name. (This letter is being smuggled out and mailed by one of my guards.) A few weeks ago she wrote and told me you were becoming a "nuisance" and that she would therefore write you a letter in my name that she hoped would alienate you to the point of never trying to communicate with me again. Whatever it was that she wrote you (using my name), I beg you to disregard it. I've written nothing to you—because she would not let me. The truth is she's very frightened of you and me joining forces together against her. I've found a set of documents my father left in my possession (though I didn't realize it all these years), documents Elizabeth is desperate to get her hands on. At the same time, it is apparent that you are one of the few living witnesses who could corroborate the veracity of these documents. Be careful of her, Mama. I don't think you realize just how much you know that could pose a threat to Elizabeth's power. Sometimes people know things without being aware of their significance.

I need an attorney, Mama—to revoke the comprehensive power of attorney I assigned to Elizabeth. As you know, I think Papa's settling the entire estate on me alone was unfair (although not as unfair as Elizabeth's unchallenged possession of it).

Oh, Mama, I would so like to be able to begin *living*. Remember all our dreams about what it would be like when I had finally grown up? You can't know how hard it's been for me, having all that snatched from me, first by Papa and then by Elizabeth.

Help me, Mama, please. Together we can fight Elizabeth. She isn't omnipotent. Serve her with a writ of Habeas Corpus for me. And then let me revoke the power of attorney. My escape from her control would be that simple, it would take just those two steps. And then we would have a wonderful future, you and I, living the life we used to dream of.

I'm so lonely for you, Mama.

Your loving

Alexandra

Friday, 8/17/68

Jazzy's off, & hopefully my letters with her. It's possible she will hand them over to Elizabeth, but I don't think so. She was almost casual about doing this for me. I loaded her down with CDs for her trip & a bottle of cognac. I considered giving her something expensive but concluded that doing so would have raised her suspicions & made her feel she was betraying her trust as an amazon. I had gotten out old clippings from the *E.T.* of Mama—ostensibly to show her cherished photos, but more essentially to allay any doubts she might have about someone named Raines being my mother. (Service-techs don't always understand executive social mores.) Showed her pictures of Mama & me from my childhood. All this done subtly, to answer any questions that might be lurking around the edges of her consciousness. Also showed her pictures of Grandfather.

No, the most difficult thing was deciding whether or not to sign my letter to Grandfather with "Rosebud." Decided against it. It might irk him if Elizabeth has gotten to him. Better this way, to keep a slight distance & let him decide for himself. I'm feeling fairly confident that whatever he thinks of the incest he will stand by me to the extent of dealing with Elizabeth even if he washes his hands of me afterwards. It will annoy him that Elizabeth has done this to *his* granddaughter. & it will probably also vex him that Elizabeth has had the free use of the Sedgewick estate though Rbt didn't intend it. He didn't like Rbt, but the males stick together on things like wills. His attitude will be that Rbt had the right to do with his estate as he pleased & that Elizabeth had no business overturning his will through sleight-of-hand (especially against the confused twenty-one-year old that I was at the time I signed that damned power of attorney).

As for writing to Elizabeth…I'll wait a while before I take that step. Perhaps two weeks? Surely if Grandfather & Mama are going to help me they'll have freed me by then… Oh lord, how my stomach lurched just now, how my heart accelerated, writing those words…my hands are trembling from the excitement of that thought. Two weeks! Is it *possible*? How will I get through them? Thank god for Sally—these days have been slipping through my fingers like grains of sand. Oh, it's too much, my cup is overflowing! If I can have both—freedom & Sally, too…I wouldn't even care about ruining Elizabeth.

Chapter Twenty-eight

[i]

"Oh I *wish*," Andrea said passionately, taking hold of Astrea's sleeve, "we could see what silm is like! I *wish* we could go to Marqeuei and *see* it!"

"Yeah," Sandy breathed, his brown eyes widening into saucers at the thought. "There'd be nothing like it. Because it's *completely* different, right Astrea?"

Astrea nodded solemnly. "*Completely* different. So different that I don't have the words in human languages to describe it."

"Oh," Sandy sighed. "Oh." He watched Astrea's face as though hoping to catch a glimpse of that *completely* different world that he wished so badly to know or imagine.

"You two must be getting tired," Beatrice said. "It's after nine."

"Couldn't you tell us another story, Astrea?" Andrea begged. "You tell better stories than anyone."

Ariadne grinned at Emily. "After all, *we* can only tell stories about turning the world upside down. Pretty dull stuff."

"But Ari," Sandy said, "all your stories are *earth* stuff!"

"I'm glad you like my stories," Astrea said, "but I'm finished telling them for the night. I'm interested now in having a discussion about the negotiations."

Andrea made a face. "Yuck."

Sandy groaned. "Boring adult stuff. I'd rather go to bed than listen to *that* kind of stuff."

"I have to agree that Astrea's stories are really special." Martha's voice and eyes were wistful.

Emily had some idea of how Martha must be feeling. The first time Astrea had told her about childhood incidents on Marqeuei she had been taken aback and then charmed at the thought of Marq'ssan as playful, mischievous children. But what had grown to be even more interesting were the inadvertent insights into aspects of child-raising and moral and cultural transmission from adults to the young.

As Sandy and Andrea left the room Emily heard Andrea loudly whispering, "Imagine learning how to get your own food like that so that you'd never have to eat again..."

Sandy said, "But what about really yummy food? I wouldn't want to give up strawberries." The outer door of the barn closed, cutting off their conversation.

"Once the individual projects get going it won't seem quite so centralized," Hazel said. "It will become clearer then that the most important work is going on at the local level."

Emily leaned back against the pile of pillows behind her. "I think Elizabeth will be surprised when it finally dawns on her that once certain processes are set into motion they can't be easily controlled from the top."

"The reason I came tonight," Fred, one of the three Whidbey scientists who had dropped in about half an hour ago, said, "was to ask what it is you expect of us." He spoke directly to Hazel, though his eyes occasionally slewed sideways, as though to check on Astrea. "We don't see ourselves as political types. And so we're concerned to make it clear that our participation in the Lake Erie clean-up is less for ideological reasons than for the scientific and technical interest the project holds for us."

Hazel looked at Martha. "You want to address that, Martha?"

Martha set down the bottle of beer she had just opened. "We're not asking you to be our political or ideological *representatives*," Martha said. "It's more a matter of our preferring to work with Free Zone scientists who have become accustomed to working without the usual sorts of management constraints non-Free Zone scientists are used to. As well as our knowing you can be counted on to speak out against the invidious when necessary. I know at least two of you have worked on civil projects around the Free Zone, which means you're used to working cooperatively with citizen groups." Martha retrieved her beer, started to lift it to her lips, then paused. "In other words, we feel you'll exert a certain ideological kick by your very presence because you won't find it useful or easy to put up with executive-style shit."

The three of them exchanged glances. "You think there will be conflicts, then?" Sarah queried.

"For you, I imagine there will be minor conflicts, more in the nature of irritations. The real conflicts are going to have to do with the corporations in the area that will go right on polluting in spite of the deal the Executive is making with us. Those conflicts won't concern you except to the extent that we'll be relying on you to help us detect such violations."

Fred asked, "Will all the engineering and constructions crews be local?"

"More or less," Hazel said. "And there will be other scientists on the team—some of whom we can assume will be there specifically to spy on the Marq'ssan." She grinned. "They even have a name for such spies now—xenologists."

Fred looked worried. "What do we do about *them*?"

"Nothing. It doesn't much matter, you know." Hazel looked at Astrea. "Does it, Astrea?"

Astrea shook her head. "How could it? All they'll see if they watch us destructuring anything is a person with her eyes closed."

"Maybe they'll have instruments that can measure things that can't be seen with the naked eye," Sarah said.

"Fine," Astrea said. "I've got no problem with that."

Beatrice, who had begun to wind a skein of bright blue yarn onto a warping board she had propped against the wall, said over her shoulder, "Maybe it would be a good thing if they were to have more exposure to the Marq'ssan. It might open their eyes a little."

Martha choked on her beer. When she got her windpipe clear, she said, "They see only what it's convenient for them to see."

Beatrice said, "But there sometimes comes a time when certain things can't be ignored. Which is where I find the most value in these projects."

"That and trying to generate local political infrastructures and to develop in local people the methods and skills needed to challenge the system," Laura said.

This talk is all a matter of reassurance, Emily thought. Hazel needed to talk to the Steering Committee crowd and to come here to Sweetwater only to acquire reassurance about her arrangements with

Elizabeth. Also, since no one quite knew what they were doing, they probably needed to keep repeating the obvious. Except, of course, for the scientists who didn't want to believe they were politically involved at all. And if she, Emily, were to air some of her opinions? But no, it would only confuse them. Enough to have discussed it privately with Hazel and Astrea.

Emily finished the water in her glass, set it down on the rug, and closed her eyes. It would be interesting to see if she could "see" both Hazel and Astrea's fields. Always they looked different when either of them was engaged with other persons. But she had never seen their fields in the same room together.

This time when she dropped into field perception, Emily's awareness of her own field came to her without intention or warning, astonishing and physically dizzying her. It had never even occurred to her that she might be able to perceive her own field. Yet lying back against the cushions, she took in her own self as if she were standing above her body, staring down—though not at a body, but at a watery rippling texture of melding yet stable patterns of colors of a certain depth in spite of the lack of opacity... She realized she could make out the fields of the *pillows*, of the glass beside her, of the rug, the floor beneath the rug, the barn's foundation, the earth beneath... And then, perhaps because of her wild excitement, she lost it.

"Emily, are you all right?" a quiet voice said into her ear.

Emily opened her eyes to find Beatrice kneeling beside her. "Oh, Beatrice...yes, of course, I'm fine," Emily said, wondering if she had been acting strangely.

"The way you sighed, after conking out like that...you had the strangest expression on your face."

Emily offered her a sheepish smile. "I guess I was nodding off. And then I must have suddenly jerked awake."

Satisfied, Beatrice returned to her warping board.

Emily rose to her feet, collected her glass, and left the room under the pretense of fetching herself a refill. What she wanted was to learn what else she could "see" in that room. Could it be possible she had really made out the fields of those physical objects? Or had she imagined it? Had she perhaps gone to sleep and dreamed it? Only Astrea could tell her if she had truly "seen" those things. But if she *had*... Emily

pushed open the outside door and stepped out into the dark, starry
night. She would take a walk to give herself time to compose herself,
time to tame her excitement. Too bad she and Astrea had to return
Hazel to DC in the morning. But duty first. And *then* they would see.

See? With her eyes closed? She needed a new word for this perception unknown to humans. But for now, *see* would have to do.

[ii]

Hazel got into the two-seater waiting at the landing site. "What
next?" Astrea asked Emily.

Emily watched the two-seater drive off. "I wanted to talk with you
about something that happened to me last night." She pulled her eyes
from the viewscreen to look at Astrea. "Unless you have something
else planned?"

"Nothing firm," Astrea said. "I had some notion of dropping in
on Lourdes and her crowd to see how things were going down there.
But since I made no arrangements with them, I can always do that
another time." She gestured at the viewscreen. "Where to?"

"How about my old beach place?"

Astrea grinned. "Oh, are you planning on visiting family and
friends?"

Emily grinned back. "Not family, but maybe friends, if we feel
like it."

The amber light flashed, and before Emily drew her next breath
she felt the pressure of the pod lifting off. "I've been thinking about
some of the things you told Andrea and Sandy last night," she said.

"About Marq'ssan childhood?"

"Yes. Especially about the importance placed on teaching the
young to become physically self-sufficient."

"We do believe—just about all Marq'ssan, I think—that the existence and inescapable reality of our hierarchical structures stemmed
directly from the assignment of roles in the provision of food, especially since it was a structure that was learned during infancy and
constantly reproduced in a multiplicity of forms throughout each
Marq'ssan's life."

"But I wonder that it was thought best to simply eliminate the need for food provision altogether in order to eliminate that structure," Emily said. "That's such an extreme solution."

"It does seem extreme, yes. But the *affective* context surrounding food—first with regard to the infant-food provider bond and then later the more conscious division of such responsibilities and burdens by ambients—made it an almost insurmountable problem otherwise." Astrea made an odd little gesture with her hands (Brazilian? Emily wondered). "Of course I know this only intellectually, since they'd arrived at this solution before my own birth. So I know nothing of what it might be like to be dependent on others for food, say, to the extent that Sorben or Magyyt do. Or what it might be like to be assigned to the role of food producer. I do know that young children are eager to outgrow the digestive stage of their development in order to achieve new stages of independence—as well as to feel more and more an accepted member of Marq'ssan society though of course another part of the child wants at the same time to cling to that dependence. But Marq'ssan society provides new, more satisfying structures for the child that replace that particular structure."

"I wonder if humans' problems might come down to this same structural problem to do with food and dependence, only with respect to gender rather than ambient role assignment."

"I wouldn't jump to conclusions like that," Astrea said cautiously. "I know that on the face of it the relation between ambient on the one hand and gender and class and perhaps race on the other *seem* analogical, but humans and Marq'ssan have entirely different biological structures, conceptual configurations, and histories."

"Yet it might be instructive to study and think about such structures and their implications."

"Yes, oh yes, I'd have to agree with that."

"Just on the crude level, examining who does the actual growing and preparation of food would bring out the obvious fact that farm workers and workers in the tube-food industry get paid less than almost anyone else. Even maintenance workers of every sort rate higher wages than farm workers." Emily recalled the figures in reports she had read while working for her father. Farm workers made very little in credit—they were largely paid "in kind"—i.e., they lived "for

free" in substandard housing and ate "free" tubefood distributed each
Saturday morning at the storehouse that was a standard feature of
each workers' housing compound.

"Oh, I'm sure it's worth examining such things. My only caveat is
that you be careful not to reduce your problems to that one relation in
particular," Astrea said.

The amber light flashed again. It seemed as though they had just
taken off, Emily thought, watching the viewscreen as the pod deceler-
ated and landed on the beach. How *did* these pods work? They had no
visible instruments, no visible computer system, no visible fuel source:
how could she not *see* at least traces of the necessary mechanics needed to run the pod?

As they walked along the beach Emily stared up at the house that
used to be hers. She conjectured that her father would not sell it in
case she decided to "make her peace" with him (as he liked to call
it). *Never is a long time, Emily. When you've had enough independence
you'll realize how important the oldest and surest ties really are.* The
sort of ties she formed were not even imaginable to him. He had never
understood her, and once she had learned to manipulate him, he had
given up any attempt to do so. He had known she had her "own opinions" on things, but because she played the roles he wanted of her he
ignored everything else about her. As long as she had kept her "difference of opinions" to herself, as long as her "own affairs" did not
inconvenience or embarrass him, it hadn't mattered to him how she
spent her "free time." He had acknowledged she led a "double life"
but said that his son would have, too, *as sons always do*, and that she
had a right to enjoy herself as she could.

"When you said you wanted to talk, I assume you weren't referring to Marq'ssan child-raising practices," Astrea said, breaking into
Emily's ruminations.

Emily realized she had been standing in one spot staring up at the
house for a long time. She turned her back on the house and looked
at Astrea, whose reddish-gold skin glowed in the glittering light of
brilliant sun and reflective sea. "I'm not sure what it is that happened
last night," Emily said. "I think I saw the fields of my own body, the
pillows I was lying on, the rug, floor, foundation, and earth beneath
me, and the glass beside me. But I'm not sure. Before I went to bed

last night I tried to see the field of my own body and the floor and so on, but I wasn't able to." Emily bit her lip. "It's possible I dreamed it, but I don't think so. I didn't *feel* as though I'd dropped off to sleep, though that's what I told Beatrice when she asked me if something was wrong."

Astrea stood without moving, her face immobile, her eyes un-blinking. The strangeness of this immobility made Emily uncomfort-able until she realized that Astrea must be thinking too intently to be giving even minimal attention to her facial responses. After perhaps a minute Astrea's face returned to life, and she touched Emily's fore-arm. "Let's sit for a while." They moved above the water line and sat on completely dry sand hot from the morning sun. "I think it's pos-sible," Astrea said. Her greenish-gold eyes moved over Emily's face. "What you've been doing is tightly focusing on individuals. But what you've described here is something different. You agree?"

Emily tried to compare last night's experience with her other ex-periences of field perception. "Yes," she said slowly as a myriad cha-otic thoughts and fragments of memory tumbled through her mind, "I think I see what you're saying. Last night I wasn't *focused* at all. My attention was somehow *diffuse*. I didn't begin as I usually do—which is to be already concentrating on the individual whose field I intend to see, and then while still concentrating on that individual slipping into field perception. Instead I slipped into it without being concentrated, and the first thing I became aware of was my own field."

"Do you think you could do it again, right now?"

"I couldn't last night. But of course I can try."

"Try to be as loose and diffuse and non-focused as you were last night. Don't concentrate on your own field, for instance, or on the beach. Or on my field. Just try slipping into the state you recognize by feel as the state conducive to field perception."

"Oh," Emily said, beginning to see what Astrea might be driving at. "Maybe I was trying too hard when I tried to do it a second time last night?"

"Perhaps."

Emily stretched out on the sand, closed her eyes, and tensed her muscles from toes to neck, then released the tension from her body, segment by segment. Soon her awareness shrank to the feel of the sand beneath her, the sun on her body, the bright reddish light filtering through her eyelids, the smell of the sea in her nostrils and the taste of it on her tongue, the roar of the surf in her ears. She proceeded through the now-familiar stages that led her to slip into field perception and, without noticing the moment of transition, found herself "seeing" her own and other fields. Only Astrea's seemed different now, perhaps of less depth than Emily usually "saw" when perceiving it. And as Emily's perception swept wider, it dawned on her that that vivid complex multi-textured field(s?) must be *the ocean*, and her excitement grew and grew until it almost exploded, as would a bubble reaching its maximum circumference.

"Astrea," she said softly, wondering if diverting a part of her attention would break her perception, "I can *see* the ocean. I can see fields within fields!"

"And you perceive my field and your own?"

"Yes," Emily said, "all at the same time. It's so peculiar, I keep thinking I must be going to lose it for lack of concentration!"

"That is how we Marq'ssan 'see' all the time, Emily."

Emily gasped. "Like *this*! But what of what humans think of vision and the other senses?"

"That too—only differently. Leleynl says it must be differently. For we never lose our perception of fields. A specialist on human physiology on Marqeuei showed me how to simulate the perceptual experience humans call vision. It's very flat, isn't it, compared to how you are 'seeing' now."

Emily sighed. "Everything's so much more beautiful this way."

"So much more complex," Astrea corrected.

"But I wouldn't be able to function if I always 'saw' this way," Emily said sadly.

"How do you know?"

"It would be impossible."

"But it's too new for you to know that."

"How, for instance, do you read my body movements and the expressions on my face?" Emily asked.

"There are different modes of perception. You've experienced two of them so far. And when we are with humans we use approximations of human sensory organs to help us mediate between your world and

Marq'ssan bodies. It's a part of what I was telling you about the human forms we adopt and the way they function to mediate between a physically hostile environment and the need for cosmetic disguise on the one hand and our Marq'ssan bodies on the other. But when I use a more intense mode of perception of human faces and body movements, I don't 'see' as a human would, though I probably perceive more. We can perceive as microscopically as we wish—that is, right down to the sub-atomic level. Which is, of course, how we are able to construct and destructure as we wish."

"You mean," Emily said, groping for a metaphor by which she might understand something so wholly alien to her patterns of thought and perception, "that it's a little like focusing a lens to different powers for different purposes?"

After a few seconds, Astrea said, "Maybe it's something like that, yes. It might work to think of it that way. What I suggest you do is attempt—still holding your diffuse perception—very very slowly to focus more closely on my field, as though gradually narrowing the spatial area you are taking in while trying to achieve more depth in your perception. At some point, if this method works, you would be perceiving my field as you usually do; but it would be interesting to see if you could go on shifting the mode of perception to greater and greater depth or intensity or whatever it is we're talking about."

Emily caught her breath. "All right," she said. "I'll try." Emily shifted so that Astrea's field rather than the ocean constituted the center and the ocean slid to the periphery of the scope of her perception. Then, conceptualizing her modulation of perception as the twisting of a camera lens for focus, Emily "watched" Astrea's field almost imperceptibly change. "What is it I'm seeing?" she said, perplexed and curious at the shadowy chiaroscuro that eliminated nearly all color from her perception. "I wish I understood, Astrea. It's gotten dark, with shadows, and I can hardly distinguish your field from everything around you."

"Yes," Astrea said, "that's all right." After a few seconds, she added, "I've just now shifted into that mode of perception myself, to see if I can follow you and see what it is you're doing."

"Should I keep shifting the focus?" Emily asked. She already felt comfortable using that speech metaphor and method of visualizing the modulations she was making in her modes of perception.

"Yes," Astrea said. "Go on. We'll talk later about what these different modes are."

Cautiously Emily effected another turn of the lens. "Oh!" she cried. "I'm seeing your field now the way I usually see it!"

"Now see if you can get deeper or closer or whatever it is."

Emily feared she wouldn't be able to switch out of this mode, since it had been the one she had "seen" in without change up until last night. Still, she tried another turn of the lens—and gasped. "Astrea! You've turned into a lot of phosphorescent-like rivers of color rushing along at dizzying speed!"

"All right," Astrea said. "Now see if you can focus in more tightly—getting closer. That might not be the same as you've been doing to get this far. See if you can find a way to move that you haven't tried before."

"I don't know how to 'move' without a visualization metaphor," Emily said. "What other sorts of things beside focusing a lens would be appropriate do you think?"

"I suppose you should stick to visual metaphors," Astrea said. "Though they might not be the most appropriate in the long run, they seem to be the ones you engage with most often when it comes to field perception. How about sticking with the camera metaphor, but thinking of zooming in for a close-up the way vid cameras do?"

"It's hard," Emily said after spending a few seconds considering this suggestion. She had never before had to think about what faculty did the perceiving, and Astrea's suggestion seemed to entail the conceptualization of such a faculty. Emily drew a deep breath and tried to visualize that faculty as slightly apart from her "self" (whatever she meant by that)—physically, mentally, emotionally, as an instrument that provided views by means of a complex set of lenses that could be changed and adjusted and manipulated quite apart from her own mind and body. She imagined being able to choose from a set of lenses that could be easily exchanged for one another and chose a lens that would zoom her close in. Then she visualized exchanging this lens for the one she was currently using. To her astonishment, as she did this, her perception went dark, darker than any shut-up room she had ever been in, a dark that threatened to suffocate her. But she concentrated on fitting the new lens to her viewing apparatus, and the brilliantly phosphorescent rivers of motion reappeared—at the very moment her new lens clicked into place. *The metaphor is working! Or else that wouldn't have happened, would it?*

She contemplated her next step: "zooming in on" one of those rivers. Should she elongate the lens manually, or program it to work automatically? Emily decided to try doing it manually first, even though she had already used that visualization with her other, simpler lens metaphor. In her mind's eye, she put her fingers to the lens's plastic rim and slowly began twisting. As the lens elongated the rivers enlarged, and soon she could see that the rivers were made up of tiny particles of light. Emily moved closer and closer. The particles of light forming the rivers, it soon became apparent, had within them little constellations of particles whirling rapidly, erratically, frenetically. "Astrea, I'm deep inside the rivers of light," Emily said. "I see particles whirling within the larger particles that form the rivers of light."

"All right," Astrea said, her voice sounding strange. "Try now to go back to a more abstract level of perception, to the point where you can distinguish my field. And then, once you've done that, shift your attention onto one of the large rocks behind us and see if you can reach the rivers of light flowing in the rock you choose to focus on."

Emily did as Astrea instructed and without trouble found the "rivers of light" in the rock. "I can't believe it's so easy!"

"Are you getting tired?"

"I'm feeling a little washed out."

"Then we'd better not do much more. I don't know what kind of drain all this might be making on your reserves of energy."

"I think I'm all right," Emily said, anxious to continue.

"Tell me when you've had enough. I'm trying to keep an eye on you, but I don't know that much about human energy systems. What I want you to do now is see if you can find a replicated pattern in the way those rivers of light move in the rock."

"Should I go inside one of the rivers, or look at the rivers in relation to one another?"

"Look at the rivers in relation to one another."

After "staring" for a long time at the ever-moving rivers, Emily thought she perceived two separate patterns. "One of them is a kind of spiraling of the rivers," Emily said, "but then, behind that pattern—behind? Can that be right? Underneath it, or maybe it's on another plane? Anyway, I think I see another pattern like big blobs that are constantly moving—much more slowly than the things making up the rivers of light—and changing shape and size."

"Okay," Astrea said, "that sounds like it might be what I'm wanting you to 'see'—it's hard for me to know, you realize, because I don't *see*, and consequently what I perceive cannot be described in visual terms, making it necessary for me to extrapolate the structures you describe and find a corollary in what *I* perceive."

"Oh," Emily said, a little nonplused by this revelation (which, she realized, she should have expected).

"I want you to 'watch' carefully now. I intend to extend my field until it's almost merging with the rock's field."

Almost at once Emily 'saw' the presence of a new set of patterns. The colors making up the rivers of light she assumed must be Astrea's field varied little from the phosphorescent colors of the rocks' rivers of light, but the patterns of the spirals and the blobs looked distinctly different, though she, Emily, might not have noticed such differences before she had discovered the patterns in the rock's field. "I see what must be your field quite clearly," Emily said.

"I'm going to encircle the rock's field with my own now," Astrea said, and as she spoke her field appeared right up against all the edges of the rock's field, as though it had always been that way. "And now I'm going to merge my field with the rock's." Suddenly the patterns became so complex Emily could not make them out.

"What happened? I can't see either your patterns or the rock's!"

"That's because they're all overlapping now. But see how I can withdraw," Astrea said, and the patterns returned to the previous configuration, that of Astrea's field encircling the rock's. "Someone tired or inexperienced risks losing the definition of their own field through merging should, say, they not hold the exact memory of their own configurations—not just the patterns, but every unfolding of those patterns at that particular place in time—or the sense of the relation between their own field and the rock's. It doesn't happen often, except with children. But since only Marq'ssan with the very strongest field management ever undertake to teach children chiastics, that almost never happens, and when it does, the teacher is usually able to reconstruct the child's patterns."

Emily shivered with the first wave of fear sweeping over her since the outset of this journey of exploration. "How horrible."

"Don't worry, Emily," Astrea said. "You've done nothing to risk your own field. You've only been scanning."

"That's what you call this, 'scanning'?"

"Yes. There are many different kinds of scan, but this one is the most common. Would you like to see what happens during destructuring?"

"Yes, yes, I would!" Emily grew *very* excited. "I've always wanted to know about that!"

"Pay attention," Astrea said. "It happens quickly, so quickly you may not see it."

Emily strained to "watch"—and gasped as in quick succession—perhaps in a split-second—the blobs in the rock's field blurred together and the spirals spun outwards and the rivers of light blinked out. "Oh," Emily panted, "Astrea, I'm feeling sick…I can't breathe…" Light exploded in Emily's head; she heard a wave crashing against the rocks near her—the first she had heard for what seemed like hours—and she felt drops of sweat running down her body. She fought for breath, she fought to open her eyes, but exhausted, she fell back, down, down, down into a spinning, plunging, lightless chasm.

Chapter Twenty-nine

Monday, 8/20/2096

For the last twenty hours I've done nothing but brood about how I might as well slit my throat. (Couldn't face the thought of the cliff again.) So finally, not half an hour ago, I went into Rbt's room & combed through the rubble to find that antique gold-handled razor he always had himself shaved with. But just as I was lifting it to my throat, that oil portrait of the two of us that used to hang above the mantel in his bedroom (but had been tossed into the fireplace) caught my eye. It was as though I could hear Rbt saying to me *are you going to let that bitch get away with it when you're so damned close to nailing her? It's* her *doing, using the girl against you. Forget the girl & deal with that bitch as she deserves—for me, for Kay, & above all for yourself goddam it!*

I find it hard to care. Is it really worth it, revenge? I hate her, & I know what has happened is her doing. She set out to destroy me, months & months ago. (*Why? Can it really be the damned transcript? How could such machinations possibly get her closer to finding the transcript, unless she thought they would break me into pieces?*) It's so Machiavellian; but what she did to Kay proves she's capable of the most convoluted, indecipherable stratagems… No, Rbt is right, I should forget the girl & destroy Elizabeth. & then, when I've done that, kill myself. There's nothing more beyond destroying Elizabeth that I can imagine living for. She's taken everything from me.

But go slowly, Alexandra. First write it down. Write down the things that endlessly repeat themselves in your head. Maybe if they are written down it will become unnecessary to go over & over & over them. Can't believe it's been less than twenty-four hours. Feels like weeks.

Lying there with the girl on my mattress in the library. Just awakened from my nap. I was caressing her, had that Mozart concerto she likes so well playing on the stereo (no, she probably didn't like it, probably only said so to please me), so I didn't hear Elizabeth's jet land. When I heard the door open I thought it must be an amazon, or the physical therapist. I looked up, an expostulation on my lips ("damned intruder," I think I began to snarl), & saw it was Elizabeth. The sight of her shocked me mute. My first thought was that Jazzy had betrayed me. Elizabeth came over to the mattress, stared down at us, & smiled—pure insolence, with malice aforethought. Probably she knew where we'd be at that time of day. Undoubtedly she knew everything there was to know about how I spent my days with the girl. "What a charming sight," she drawled, or something like that.

I whipped the sheet up to cover the girl's nakedness. "Go into the Small Study and I'll immediately join you there," I said.

Elizabeth took a few steps away from the mattress. "There's no reason we can't talk in here," she said. Then she crooked her finger. "Quickly, Sally. Go upstairs & pack your things."

The girl clutched my arm. "No," she quavered, "I don't want to leave her. I won't. I'm staying with her, that's what I really want."

I thought the girl was afraid of Elizabeth's using force on her, god help me. The grip she had on my arm... "Leave Sally out of this," I said. "I can assure you you'll regret it if you don't." My mind was racing, calculating how best to spring my threat on Elizabeth.

Elizabeth laughed with what can only be described as contempt. "Tell her, Sally. Tell her about our bargain." She didn't look at the girl when she said this, but spoke directly to me, as though taunting me.

"I don't care about that," Sally cried. "I'm in love with her, & she loves me, & we're staying together no matter what. I won't go!"

Elizabeth laughed again. "If you don't tell her, I will," she said.

"I don't care what your bargain was," I told Elizabeth. "All that's past. What I have to say to you—"

Elizabeth interrupted me: "I hope you didn't believe any of Sally's tales about lovers in prison? Or any of her other stories? All of them were my inventions. To be used one at a time, as needed."

Was that the moment fear first got me by the throat?

"Please, Alexandra," Sally said, pressing herself close, twining her arms & legs around my limbs. "Please don't be angry with me. I don't care about any of that now, please don't let her turn you against me."

"Sally's principle passion in life is something she has in common with your so charming brother Daniel," Elizabeth said. "Sally's final reward, once she's finished the job, is to have unlimited access to plugging in. Her own apparatus & someone to take care of her. A lifetime of reward & pleasure. But then I *had* to come up with something extravagant to reward such, ah, unattractive work."

"Is that true?" I asked the girl. But I already knew by the way she was sobbing & clutching at me.

"I don't want that now, I only want to be with you!" she shrieked as I began extricating myself from her grip.

Elizabeth smirked—no, sneered, really—in gleeful gratification.

I struggled to my feet, fighting against the girl's grip on my knees as she shrieked her phony protestations of love. God it was horrible, that word issuing out of her like sticky tentacles snaking around me, all but strangling me. "You're like an onion," I said to her. "You're like an onion with layer after layer after layer that one peels, to find nothing inside. Layers & tissues of lies."

"She's an actor," Elizabeth said.

I suppose I'd thought that even actors feel things, that even actors have a substance under the layers & layers & layers of lies.

I can't remember exactly what happened next, except that Elizabeth made the girl go upstairs & pack, telling her that she'd have an amazon "assist" her if she didn't. That made the girl slink out from under her sheet, grab her clothing, & flee. I turned and stood with my back to the room staring out the long window at the knee-high grass & weeds that had overtaken the lawn.

"Would you like to keep her?" Elizabeth asked me—with such utter & casual cool as to take my breath away.

"I don't want her. Besides, you so obviously owe her."

"Yes, but it's for me to decide when she's done enough for her reward."

I was so far gone that I had actually forgotten about the transcript. Until, that is, she said, "I'm going to search this room, Alexandra. You might as well go into another room & wait there so that I won't be aggravated by your presence."

I waited in the hall.

When she finished, she went upstairs, presumably to talk to the girl. I went back into the library & started re-shelving the books that lay in piles all over the room. After a while Elizabeth returned & perched on a corner of the desk. First she said a few things designed to rub salt in the wound. & then she suggested we "do business." When Elizabeth finally decided that even in my debilitated state (I'm sure she knew damned well how distraught I was) she wasn't going to get anywhere with me, she left. Taking the girl with her. & now I'm alone, entirely alone in this house.

& to think that I thought I'd need to protect the girl from Elizabeth, gullible fool that I am.

Sedgewick's Island, Maine
August 21, 2096

Dear Elizabeth:

It's time, I think, that we begin laying our cards on the table. Yes, I do have possession of copies of the transcript. I know all about you. I know why my father hated you, I know all that you did to Kay Zeldin, I know how you manipulated the Executive and deceived the world. You see, I've read the entire transcript, front to back. Doing so was quite an education.

It won't do you a bit of good to put me under loquazene. If you do, I'll self-destruct the instant my brain begins to respond to the drug. You know how powerful my use of self-hypnotic suggestion has become since I needed to use it to resist the constant, intense pain caused by my injuries. Second, you should remember my ability to keep myself asleep against all attempts to use chemical stimulants to rouse me. There's no doubt in my mind that any attempt by you to learn about the location of the copies—and there are more than one, you know—of the transcript will trigger my death. I've made sure of that, Elizabeth. And if I die, the chances of your exposure will markedly increase. It's *possible* something could go wrong and your exposure not take place, but it's not *likely*. Before tampering with me, I urge you to consider your chances most carefully.

I, of course, have little to lose. I'm not feeling particularly attached to my life just now, which is why I choose this moment to confront you. You do understand I wouldn't now be satisfied merely to be allowed circumscribed jaunts off the island. I would want, for instance, control of the Sedgewick Estate placed into my own hands. You may choose to murder me. But is your possession of the Estate important enough to risk the revelations and exposure my death would entail?

Of course you may decide to stall...but I warn you that would be unwise. You really haven't fathomed *all* the longterm safeguards my father planted. After all, it's only been five years. Perhaps you've gotten a little sloppy? My father was not brilliant; but his mind in certain areas of human thought certainly had (thank god!) few equals. You know what those areas are as well as anybody could. So think about that, too.

You might in fact now realize, Elizabeth, what a pity it is that you didn't take advantage of my naiveté that day I chose you over my father. We both would have been spared a great deal if you had. But that moment is long gone. Just remember when you're laying your schemes that I've learned everything I know from you and my father. Who ever had such teachers as I? Remember, too, that I've little reason to cling to life. That makes a difference. Perhaps you forgot that in your calculations?

I'll be hearing from you shortly, Elizabeth. Your clock has begun to run.

With the utmost sincerity,

Alexandra

Wednesday, 8/22/2096

This morning I'm thinking about yesterday's letter to Elizabeth. She may have gotten it already. In fact, she might have gotten it yesterday, since they probably faxed it to her. Or else, if they're under orders not to open my letters themselves, they will hand-deliver it, in which case it could take longer, even though yesterday was one of their supply drop days.

This house is of a quiet I've never in my life experienced. The only sounds are of birds & the surf. & occasionally wind against the windows & boards creaking. An inhuman silence in every sense of the word.

I've spent the last two days thinking not about the transcript situation, nor about whether Mama & Grandfather have received my letters, but about why Elizabeth used that girl in such a way against me. It makes no sense on the face of it. As I pointed out in the letter, I'm so depressed & demoralized, I have so little attachment to anyone or anything, that it's harder for her to get at me now than if she'd allowed me my illusions about the girl, or if she'd never sent me the girl in the first place.

Because of what I know about Elizabeth from having read the transcript, I know she's capable of playing a very deep game—& that she's unlikely to indulge in the pettier forms of revenge for personal gratification when she can, instead, reap a greater profit & a grander scale of revenge through more devious & long-range methods.

It seems so pointless. She's proven me a gullible fool, yes. She's shown me I have no one & nothing to care for & no one who cares (or could care) for me. I can see very clearly that that was her object with the girl & everything else, too. But to what end? For her *real* object must be to retrieve all copies of the transcript. How does my near-destruction help accomplish *that*?

Yet some treacherous stupid voice in my head keeps wondering about the girl's fate, a thing that I should be far from even thinking about. She will be given loquazene (for surely Elizabeth doesn't trust her) & then? But what does it matter? The girl is nothing to me. Nothing at all.

It's only eleven a.m. & already I'm thinking of sleep. All that's left now is to wait for Mama, for Grandfather, for Elizabeth to react. Soon, everything will be over. & it's for that that I'm *really* waiting.

Friday, 8/23/2096

Elizabeth is insane. Or else she's trying to drive *me* insane. All the time I was reading that transcript I never let myself fully identify with Kay. Sometimes it seems as though I've spent half my life avoiding that identification. But I can escape it no longer. Unlike Kay, however, I have the most potent of weapons to use against Elizabeth, a weapon I will *not* allow her to disarm me of. Now that I'm able to think again— after almost forty-eight hours of craziness (that's the only word I have for it, craziness, madness, near-delirium).

I must go through it step by step. (I may need notes later.) Start with her arrival here Wednesday afternoon...

God. I'm shivering. I'm sitting in the sunshine & I'm shivering at the very thought of her arrival & what followed. Will I fall back into madness when I try to describe it?

It was maybe two-thirty or three. I heard the jet & went upstairs to get a view of the plane. It was Rbt's jet. & lo & behold she stepped out & descended the stairs & stood chatting with an amazon for a few minutes before striding through the weeds & grass (that came only to her knees, so long are her legs). She was wearing a shade of green that reminded me of Key Lime Pie, sort of a creamy muted lime. & she was carrying a suitcase (I knew from the fact that she was carrying it herself that she had told them to stay away from the house—otherwise one of them would have carried it for her). I had quite a time of it speculating about the contents of that suitcase. When she got to the house she rang the bell that I can't remember ever having been rung (since there's never been any need for visitors to announce their presence here). Then I heard her call out my name. I considered making her find me, but decided that might put me at a disadvantage, might be interpretable as reluctance to see her. So I went to her. I paused at the head of the stairs & saw her waiting there in the hall below with her hands on her hips, her head thrown back. "Here I am, Ms.

Sedgewick," Elizabeth called up to me. "Must I come up or will you come down?"

For some reason I can't quite put my finger on, I didn't want her up-stairs. So I went down the stairs & tried to get a grip, tried to remind myself that I, not she, held the advantage. When I reached the foot of the stairs I suggested we go into the Small Study.

"Just like dear old Sedgewick," Elizabeth drawled. "But then sum-moning me here to lavish personal attention on him was also one of his tricks, too. If his binges wouldn't draw me, he'd stooped to threats. History *does* repeat itself." I was close enough to Elizabeth to see that her brilliant smile didn't hide the tightness around her eyes, the rigid-ity of her mouth & jaw. "These poor pathetic Sedgewicks." She put her arm around my shoulders as we processed to the Small Study.

I was thoroughly confused. I didn't see the angle she was taking. I think I mostly assumed she was shaken up & consequently babbling non-sequiturs as they came into her head. More fool I.

In the Small Study she half-pushed me to the sofa and plumped down beside me, & though she released my shoulders, her arm rested along the back of the sofa, her hand inches from my neck. I had a strange prickling awareness of that hand & arm. "Do you remember that time when you came to DC & you defied him & he put you under house arrest?" she said. Of course I remembered. What did that have to do with anything? "You were *so* pathetic," Elizabeth said.

Her fingers brushed my neck, then withdrew. At that point I began seriously considering how to get off that sofa without losing points to her. If I got up & moved away, she would at the very least say some-thing nasty; but I also worried that she might hold me there by force. Those were the kind of vibes she was giving off. Super aggressive. I see now that these vibes triggered certain physical & psychological responses I had been through so many times with Rbt—that's how I knew we were skating close to violence. She had that same vibrating tautness about her, that same dangerous glitter in her eye just daring me to push her. And for a few seconds I wondered if I should have waited to see what Mama & Grandfather would do before showing her my cards.

"I couldn't do much for you that time because I was having troubles with him myself," Elizabeth said. "That day you arrived, he came on with some very impressive threats." The corners of her mouth twitched a little. "He'd begun realizing he was probably going to lose me. But also, of course, he wanted attention I hadn't been giving him. & so we had a round of hardball. & you, poor thing, were caught in the crossfire." At this point Elizabeth swiveled a little, so that she was sitting sideways on the sofa with her body turned toward me; with her other hand she took hold of my face. (How could she have known how Rbt used to do that to me?) "Do you remember my whisking you out of the house & taking you to the Diana & telling you that you'd learn to manage him & would someday be glad to be his daughter? You couldn't believe you'd ever care for such things." Elizabeth smiled nastily. "But you did, as I knew you would. You quickly learned to do with him as I had done for years & years. Only *I* never played disgusting sex games with him."

I shook my head in spite of the pressure of her hand gripping my face. "All I wanted was to survive. I didn't want his power. I thought it horrible. All the killing. All the ugliness. All I wanted was to lead my own life, but that was the one thing he wouldn't let me do."

Elizabeth leaned even closer. "Poor little Persephone," she hissed.

I went wild. I tried to jerk myself free, to struggle to my feet, to escape her. But she was ready for that & held me down. I think the thought went through my head that she was insane, that she couldn't be reasoned with. It wasn't an irrational conclusion to leap to. But the use of that name had been calculated. She had just been waiting for the intensity to build sufficiently before springing it on me. Now that I think about it, I realize she had understood a great deal from reading what I wrote in this book last winter & spring. That in some areas—the most vulnerable ones—she might understand me as well as I understood myself. But at the time I could only feel I was caught up in a mad nightmare.

I managed to clout her kneecap effectively enough to make her cry out. My aim was to make it difficult for her to pursue me—for I knew that even if I got off the sofa she'd catch me in no time at all if I hadn't first disabled her. And I knew that in my relatively weak physical condition (even if I'd been in great shape that woman could have killed me with her bare hands if she had set out to do so) I'd have to be strategic in my maneuvers. But my slam into her knee seemed to enrage her—or so I thought at the time—into a berserker state, which scared the shit out of me, given her strength & size & level of skill.

In short, I got pinned under her on the floor, & she pummeled me, mostly my face. There was a lot of blood—from my mouth & nose, mainly. & she didn't stop until I pleaded with her, until I promised not to fight her or try to run. She was savage. Nothing at all like Rbt, really. Terror yawned in this horrible empty abyss that hollowed my stomach. Even in his worst rages against me... No, the difference is that he didn't hate me, & she does. I could feel how she'd like to go on & on & on beating me until there was nothing left. It was like something Rbt once made me watch. When she did stop, she panted something about how "good" it felt to be beating me, that she'd owed Rbt that for years for something she'd once had to take from him. & I had this eerie feeling that for a few seconds it had been Rbt not me she thought she had pinned under her. But she clicked back to me, confusing me. I think now that she was always in control, that she knew exactly what she was doing with me, that she wanted me to think she was confused & insane & out of control in order to further terrorize me.

"You talk about what I should have done five years ago, you like to babble on about your so-called naiveté." Her face loomed frighteningly close over mine, thrusting & enraged; a spray of spit showered my face as she talked. "But we both know perfectly well that your naiveté ended when you climbed into that bastard's bed. No, *this* is what I should have done with you five years ago. But frankly, I didn't want anything to do with you. The very thought of you made my flesh creep." She made a sound of disgust in her throat. "What you did with your own father was bad enough. But then, later, when I discovered you were a female version of him—christ. Monster doesn't begin to name what you are." Her mouth stretched into a grimace meant to be a smile. "You said in your letter that you know all about me. Well consider this, Persephone: I know *everything* about you."

I think it must have been then that I started crying. I don't know for certain. I was hardly aware of anything but terrible fear. I don't know what it was about her saying that to me that made me so much more afraid than I've ever been. Her violence frightened me, but not like that. & of course there was her using that name again. Letting me know she was going to cram that down my throat, that I was helpless to stop her.

Helpless—yes, I felt helpless. Somehow I forgot how powerful my weapon is. It was as though I were facing some more horrible—because untouchable—version of Rbt at his most terrible.

"& of course now your true sentiments are emerging," she went on. "All that crap about not wanting the Estate, about not caring for power or wealth. All a part of your little games."

"I *don't* care about it," I choked out. "All I care about is being free. & it's obvious I can't be free unless I have control of the Estate. Believe me, if you wanted a share I wouldn't hesitate a second," I blurted out, remembering the transcript & hoping to somehow negotiate with her—even with her body on top of me crushing me making it hard for me to breathe.

"Still playing the demure little girl, Persephone? It won't work with me. I know all those games, don't forget that I was brought up that way, too." She rolled off me. "You're making a mess of the floor," she said. "Good thing I took all the best carpets from the house." I stared at her, shocked to see her undressing! "I'm going for a swim," she said. "& so are you. As long as I have to spend the day out here with you, I might as well get something out of it. Come on, get out of your clothes. They're in tatters & quite disgustingly bloody now anyway."

I sat up & looked down at my tunic & saw she'd torn it without my noticing. There was blood everywhere. & my eyes persisted in leaking, the tears mixing with the blood still trickling from my nose. "I'm not going swimming," I said, trying to pull my tunic back over my chemise (which was also torn).

"Oh yes you are." She gave me one of those long speculative looks—a look suggesting that she'd love to lay into me again.

"I'm having a bath & some aspirin."

"You're having those when I say so," Elizabeth stated. "But right now you're going swimming with me."

So I took my clothes off & to my shame followed her (I think she glories in brazen nudity) naked outside through the woods & down to the beach. When we got to the cliff she asked me if that was the place, & I said it was, & she made a remark that flicked me on the raw, I don't remember now what it was. When we got down onto the beach she grabbed my arm & forced me out into the water with her. I wasn't at all surprised when she got sadistic, dunking me & holding my head under. I swallowed a lot of saltwater, & some of the stuff went up my nose, burning my wounds. I thought she might be going to drown me, but then her hatred of me was foremost in my mind. The panic overtaking me almost burst my heart as the adrenalin exploded in my body. Her sadistic water games were somehow the last straw, & by the time she stopped, I was sobbing & clutching at her. Passive, I let her hold me...& touch me. Now I wonder how if the thought of me makes her flesh creep she could do that. I got so cold out there in the water (I'd forgotten, how the ocean up here never gets very warm), I had gooseflesh, my teeth were chattering, my pulse racing, & there I was clutching at her, my face pressed against her breast, & I let her handle me. That's what she did, handle me. & then carried me (I can't believe how strong she is) out of the water, onto the beach, set me down on the sand & stretched out beside me. What followed—I can't go into. Only to put down one particular thing she said that strikes me as especially peculiar—something about how I should have known about the girl, how I should never have trusted her, how those girls are never trustworthy, that the only women worth giving one's love to are executive women, that she knew that firsthand & that if I were more experienced I would know it too.

She stayed overnight & most of the next morning. We never talked about the transcript. Instead, there was more craziness. No, I can't write any more of it. I should make myself do it, but I can't. Her beating me again...all to terrorize me. Everything she did was to confuse me, terrorize me, humiliate me. Where does she think it will get her? She surely doesn't believe she can sustain this kind of thing, does she? I can see through it all, now that I've had a little space for thinking.

Does she think she can make me give up the transcript this way? I won't. I may have lost that round, but next time I'll be prepared for her. Next time...oh god, the thought of seeing her again makes my stomach heave. But I must. I must deal with her, & it can't be through the mail, either. I must think of an aggressive strategy so that she can't continue hers. & must find a way to protect myself against her easy use of violence.

I know what Rbt would do in this situation. He'd kill her. He'd devise a method & then the next time she came he'd do it. There's nothing to lose, after all. But I won't do that. I don't have the will to murder in me, not even to murder her.

Oh I'm so tired, I'm so confused, I'm so...ravaged. Let's be honest, Alexandra: your main hope is Grandfather. Grandfather & Mama. I need them. Otherwise... Otherwise she might win.

Maybe I should forget revenge & just kill myself now. I don't think I can bear much more. I'm just not that strong. Rbt was certainly right about that.

Chapter Thirty

Sunday, August 19, 2096—DC

A big party at Cat Schuyler's last night—had a hangover this morning, and so did Lise. It's been years since I've been to a party of that size and type. It's almost impossible not to drink too much at such affairs—you're driven to it by the intrinsically brittle, depressing, on-the-make atmosphere. Though it was a mainly couples party, there was plenty of sexual action, with short-term pairings creeping off into private parts of the house and into the dark of the yard. Cat had had the old swimming pool cleaned and filled, and some people were skinny-dipping, almost all of them service-techs, of course—hardly any executives deigned to indulge in such spontaneous frivolous behavior, except, of course, for Weatherall—whom I was flabbergasted to see there: she's never at the mainly couples parties that I've been attending here—but I suspect there was a lot of politicking involved that I being a mere service-tech didn't pick up on.

But before I get caught up in the party, I should describe the exhibit Lise and I went to yesterday afternoon. It was so strange, so weird that I found it creepy. I'm not sure what Lise thought, except that she too seemed a little uneasy. It was in a small house near the river. The entire house, actually, was a part of the exhibit. Or almost all of the house. It's called "psychokinetic" or "living" art. Apparently Weatherall is funding it. Though there's a high admission charge and films are being made from it and books are being written about it, it's still very expensive to produce—three years of preparation went into it, and the exhibit itself (or whatever you're supposed to call it) takes years to run. Her name (as "patron") was on the sign in front of the house and will be on all the films and books that result from the exhibit.

As far as I can make out, it's a cross between a psych experiment and a twenty-four-hour-a-day soap opera that never ends. These trained actors have "deep-studied" their roles for a minimum of a year before they enter the "psychokinetic stage" (which is most of the house). Besides the actors there's a staff consisting of service-techs that take care of technical matters and supplies (food, clothing, etc.), a team of writers and psychologists who determine the "course and flow" of the "dramaturgy," and several "interpretive analysts" who spend a lot of time watching the players either through the one-way glass the outer walls of the house are constructed of or on vid monitors (the inside of the house being honeycombed with vid cameras and microphones). These "interpretive analysts" write articles and books, talk to the team of writers about what is "really" happening in the house, and conduct the tours for the gallery goers (mainly professionals and executives) who come to view this "art." And then there are film crews and other writers and all sorts of projects spinning off from this exhibit. What I saw of it was pretty depressing—and, as I said before, creepy. According to the interpretive analyst we talked to, some people are really fascinated by this and keep coming back once or twice (or more) a week.

I guess it was a fitting prelude to the party. Which was at first okay. Everyone made a big deal about Mott and Ginger. (Will Ginger ever stop blushing?) Lise looked like she might be going to relax, but then Cat led her away—to chat, I think, with Danforth and Mott. My guess is they were talking about the Executive's crisis—specifically about the need to get rid of Rogers and Steinmetz. According to Lise, the easiest way is for the Executive to vote a two-thirds majority for their resignations—with at least two of the votes coming from Defense, Security, and State (i.e., O'Leary, Mott, and Seely). Neither Lise nor Weatherall get a vote, of course, since they're only "ex-officio members." The "hard way" is to marshal enough pressure from outside the Executive to force them out. I gather Weatherall will have to throw some weight around to get the Executive to vote as she wants them to. Well, she's used to doing that, and every single one of them was appointed by her. Still…eight of the voting members are men, while only five are women. And Seely might not side with the other women. There's a third possibility: pressuring them to resign. Lise hinted darkly about this. I've been wondering if that means Weatherall has dirt on them. I wouldn't put it past her.

But to get back to the party.

Ugh. I don't *really* want to think about it. (Was that why I drank so much?) I shouldn't get so mad, it's of no significance whatsoever, nothing to make a big deal about. After all, I'm a woman of a reasonably mature age...it's not like I'm an impressionable young girl. And Weatherall has always been outrageous...

I was chatting with Leslie and Julia. Actually, Leslie was flirting with Julia (who hadn't been invited into the little meeting going on with Cat, Lise, Mott, and Danforth). We were hovering near the buffet. I was listening to the band and watching the few people who were dancing and considering looking for Ginger or Susan. (I'm always the same at these kinds of parties—just trying to find somebody I know to hang out with rather than mingling—too old, I guess, to be as adventurous as I used to be in the early Colorado days.) Anyway, I spotted Weatherall when she came into the room and saw that executive who took me shopping at her elbow. (I can never remember that woman's name—she works for Cat and had obviously been assigned to handle the door.) My guess is that this executive was trying to steer Weatherall off to the meeting—but Weatherall always does what she damned well pleases, which in this case was making an entrance into the room and spreading her glitter-glamour around. She looked her most stunning—smoothly tanned, her braided hair worn in a coronet, and her clothes absolutely fabulous—the fabric a strong off-white that up close showed an incredibly thin, purplish crimson stripe running through it. (The *feel* of the fabric was wonderful, too, I have reason to know.) Oh, and lots of gold around her forearms and throat.

Weatherall worked her way across the room toward us—or toward the buffet, probably. (The amazons in the Redmond house didn't call her Big Liz for nothing.) I could tell Leslie was tracking Weatherall with an eagle eye, and as she got closer, Leslie went into some obvious routines. I tried not to cringe at this and had just about decided to go in search of Ginger when suddenly Weatherall was right there in front of us—and showering her so fervently sought-after attention on *me*. Our little set-to a couple of weeks back was still fresh in my mind, so her attention was even more unwelcome than usual. But she acted

as though that scene in Lise's study hadn't happened—she kissed me
on the cheek and gushed about how lovely it was seeing me after so
many years, that I was as "charming" as ever. Her arm went around
my waist and immediately started a downward slide; soon, to my total
mortification, her hand started investigating the lines of my hips and
buttocks. I imagine I turned that shade that Lise calls "aubergine."
All the while Weatherall cooed a line at me and stared down my cleavage (since I'd worn one of those skimpy summer dresses Lise is always
after me to wear).

If just anyone talked in that silky slick come-on voice, they'd sound
ridiculous. But with Weatherall...maybe it's that everything is so exaggerated about her—but done with such confidence—that she can
pull off tones and manners that no one else could? And then, too, she
radiates the attitude that all the teasing and flirtation is a game she's
playing with you against everybody else, just a silly frippery game not
to be taken seriously—but with this ambiguous undertow of seriousness lurking beneath the surface. She kept calling me "Annie," too—
which no one but Lise does. I suppose she picked that up at the Redmond house and remembered it... At any rate, I sensed Julia's grave
stare and Leslie's wild excitement, so I tried to bring them into the
conversation by introducing them to Weatherall. Of Julia she said—
nodding coolly to her—that they'd "of course already met," and she
barely registered Leslie's existence, which surprised me a little, since I
was sure she'd be delighted to sweep Leslie away for an exciting little
quickie back in the bushes or wherever it was people were doing it.
But her only response to the introductions was to chide me for calling
her Ms. Weatherall and to go through all that "call me Liz" stuff.

Oh hell, I've just reread what I've written so far and seen that I'm
not being entirely honest in the way I'm describing it. (I can see me
years later looking back and getting all indignant and self-righteous.)
I was embarrassed and blushing, true. But at the same time, I was
playing her game. Because in that situation I somehow found it necessary to play—for fear of looking ridiculous, I guess. I know I should
have gotten cold and dignified, but I had this nagging suspicion that
if I did that I'd just look silly and priggish. (Weatherall has a way of
doing that to people.) But on the other hand I kept remembering that
incident years ago when I almost did go to bed with her—and some of

the remarks Weatherall was dropping made me wonder if she didn't still remember it too, unlikely though it would be. I'd promised Lise after that incident that I'd never under any circumstances have sex with Weatherall. She insisted that the only reason Weatherall would dally with me would be in aid of breaking us up—not that Lise meant to cast aspersions on my attractiveness (and anyway we both know Weatherall isn't all that fastidious), but that this was one of her aims, and my getting in any way entangled with Weatherall would work against us... After that incident Weatherall never did lay a finger on me. And she was reasonably polite to me in the Redmond house. (Actually, during those few months before Hazel started getting so difficult, Weatherall was at her most mellow.)

So Weatherall edged me toward the buffet and asked me to help her decide what to "nibble on"—since I, she said, knew her "tastes and appetites." I couldn't see any way to get out of it, so I played her game. And then as she "nibbled" she switched to talking about what good reports she'd been getting from Lise about how "helpful" I'd been and how wonderful it was that they had someone like me they could trust to do such important and confidential work... So for a while I got plenty of that kind of pep-talk (which I loathe and detest and consider a sort of put-down, as though I need such stroking to be induced to perform what I'm perfectly willing to do as requested)...and then noticed that Weatherall was edging me out of the room with her.

How extricate yourself—gracefully—from that kind of situation? I kept thinking about how if it hadn't been for my promise to Lise I might just go through with it—it would have been the path of least resistance, and the woman is, to be honest, incredibly sexy. I never felt so gauche in my life. Somehow we were suddenly in a little alcove off the room (which suggests that Weatherall had a certain familiarity with it) and Weatherall was kissing me and had her hand down the front of my dress... At the first opportunity I made my breathless, gauche announcement that I had promised Lise not to dally (a lie, since I'd only promised her about Weatherall). Weatherall first countered that Lise wouldn't mind, then said Lise would never know. Right. When everyone in the room had probably noticed our "slipping away" together. So then she wanted to know whether I found her attractive. (She obviously knew that at that moment, anyway, I did. But

she wanted to make me say it.) She let me go, of course—but only after making me feel like a silly little ingénue faced with her first seduc-
tion attempt. She said that it didn't matter, it was nothing, she'd only
thought it would be fun and for her part she'd always been attracted to
me, as I surely must remember... Which was all a lot of bullshit.

I'm blushing at the very memory of it. Haven't told Lise anything.
Should I? In case someone gossips to her? Or in case Weatherall herself hints at something to her? If I do tell Lise she'll get pissed (at both
me and Weatherall, I suspect).

I feel like an idiot. Should have stopped her from leading me into
that alcove.

Think I'll read a murder mystery. Was supposed to go visit Mom
and Dad today, but I'm just not up to it.

Monday, August 20, 2096—DC

I'd better start from the beginning. It's confusing enough as it is—
but I suspect that's because I'm getting so little information—only the
bare minimum, as is proper with such high-security affairs. I do understand that. And I do understand that the less I know the better. At
first when Lise called me into her office and sternly said she'd agreed
to let Weatherall "borrow" me, I thought she was talking about our
personal affairs, that Weatherall had been making trouble between
Lise and me. But then I realized, when Lise started talking about my
taking leave from the Office of Information and returning to my Security status on contingency special assignment, that it was probably
the other way around—that Weatherall had probably come on to me
because she had picked me for this special assignment. (Hazel once
claimed that Weatherall makes a point of using sex for reinforcing
loyalty.) It struck me that Lise knew very little about the assignment
and had no intention of going over to Weatherall's office with me.
Something about her unsmiling stiffness made me think she wasn't
happy about my taking this assignment but that she felt it necessary.
When after meeting with Weatherall I finally returned to Lise's office
and told her I'd be leaving town in the morning, she grimaced and
said only that in that case she'd make it home for dinner since there
was no telling how long I'd be gone. We're eating late—she said she'd

be home around eight-thirty, which gives me roughly forty-five minutes before I have to start packing. Knowing Lise, she'll want to spend
the rest of the evening and night together and will insist on watching
me pack if I'm not packed by the time she gets home.

So I went over to Weatherall's office, and her PA took me straight
in to the inner sanctum. Who should be in there with Weatherall but
Hazel? They were just finishing their session, Weatherall said. Hazel
made some smalltalk with me, then left.

Weatherall gave me a quick glance and picked up a handset and
murmured something I couldn't hear into it. Then we sat down on
the floor where she and Hazel had been, and after I declined an offer
of water or juice, she made heavy eye contact and started telling me
slowly and carefully about how she had an extremely important, high-
est-secret job that she wanted to entrust to me. (That was the word she
used, "entrust.") That she understood that I was to have been assigned
to run actors on vid projects because of the talent I'd shown running
agents in the Free Zone. A very delicate and highly confidential situation had arisen that she had chosen me to handle, if I was agreeable.
She mentioned the inevitability of loquazene examinations. Of course
as a Security employee I had waived all objections to *them* more than
twenty years ago. I would be reporting directly to her and must promise never to reveal even the slightest detail of the assignment to anyone but her and those she might designate, not even to Lise. I would
be working with one other person—one of her amazons—who would
know something of what was going on, but I was to keep my discussions with this amazon to a minimum. Then she said that it was
customary for the payscale to be considerably elevated for this sort of
assignment; the figure she named was double my salary at the Office
of Information. On the other hand, there would be no regular hours.
She didn't know how stressful a job it would be, but that if it proved
to be a hardship I would be compensated.

When I agreed to all her conditions, Weatherall picked up her
handset and a few seconds later one of her liveried amazons came
in, whom she introduced to me as "DG." This was the person I'd be
working with. There would be service-techs and other amazons, but
basically the two of us would be in control (and apparently I was to

be one step up from DG, for it would be me reporting, not DG). Then Weatherall explained the "assignment."

This was where it got weird. Obviously this DG already knew a lot about it. In fact, DG already knew the person—an actor—we would be handling. This actor had been on a special assignment and had gotten far more involved and had learned far more than had originally been intended, which might not have been a problem except that her affections had been "turned"—that was the word Weatherall used. I asked her if she was a potential renegade or whether she had been doubling, but Weatherall wouldn't give me a straight answer. This actor was apparently depressed. And Weatherall said it was her "speculation" that the actor might out of spite try to reveal the information she shouldn't have acquired. Our job was to hold her in the secluded safehouse we would be taking her to and keep her quiet. We weren't to allow her to talk even to us about whatever it is she knows (going so far as to use a sedative injection when necessary), but we were most especially to make sure she didn't talk about it to the others on the scene.

Up until this point I had no problem with the assignment. But when she explained the part about encouraging the actor to plug in... Christ, I wanted right out. Weatherall pointed out rather defensively at my unspoken reaction that actors are always plugging in anyway. And that this actor had done it quite often before her assignment, and that she, Weatherall, had promised her as a part of her compensation for the assignment unlimited access to it. There followed a discussion of the perimeters of the area that was not to be discussed—since we might not otherwise realize when she was getting close to talking about the forbidden. Basically she's not supposed to talk about anything that's happened in the last nine months. Nor about islands. (???) Nor about Weatherall. Nor about someone named Alexandra. I have a feeling DG knows what this is all about. I'm glad I don't.

But now I must pack. DG and I will be picking up this actor, Sally McGuire is her name, at seven-thirty tomorrow morning. And then it's off to the wilds of Idaho.

Wednesday August 22, 2096—Idaho

What an exhausting day and night! It's not all that easy conveying a heavily doped woman across the country—first by plane then helicopter then van…into the back of beyond. It's quite beautiful here—or at least that's my impression. I haven't had time yet to get outside and see for myself. It's green and cool—we're in the middle of what seems to be forest, and there's a river nearby. I don't know what I expected Idaho to look like. I am, after all, a city girl.

I took Weatherall's suggestion of lightening Sally's tranq dosages on arrival: and what resulted yesterday evening was an outburst of crying and shrieking as the tranq began wearing off. So then I had to give her a sedative. I can't help but feel sorry for her, even if she's probably done something awful (though Weatherall wouldn't specifically *say* Sally had been doubling, that's certainly the impression I'm getting). When Weatherall saw us off it became clear how intensely Sally hates her—even in her heavily doped state she gave off strong vibes of hatred and vengefulness. In spite of this, Weatherall seemed not to bear her a grudge. In fact, in my final briefing Weatherall even suggested to me that I try being as much a "friend" to Sally as the restrictions on what Sally can say allow, that Sally's rehabilitation might be helped by kindness.

Our prisoner certainly is beautiful. Though she looks terrible at the moment, I can see how stunning she must be when she's in top form. Creamy ivory skin, almond-shaped green eyes, silky hair that's almost red, sharp yet delicate bone structure; and her every movement wonderfully graceful—even when drugged. Her hands are the most beautiful I've ever seen. But her eyes are always dull from the tranqs, except of course last night, when they first got very wild and then puffed and swollen and red with crying before we put her to sleep.

This morning when I showed her the apparatus she roused from her lethargy to curse Weatherall and insist that she wouldn't have that thing in her room, that she'd destroy it if it were left there. Considering the amount of emotional pain she's suffering, I find it puzzling that she's able to pass up such a soothing escape, given what Weatherall said about Sally's past use of the apparatus.

But I'm exhausted. Being around someone in a zombie state is tiring. I'm going to ask to have some books sent. Maybe before I drop off to sleep I'll make up a reading list. It's going to be excruciatingly boring out here if I don't have books to read. That much is clear. (DG certainly is no conversationalist.)

Friday, August 24, 2096—Idaho

Yesterday a difficult day. I had a long talk with Sally about the tranqs—how she'd be more comfortable on a lower dosage and that we were all agreeable to a lower dosage if only she would keep herself from getting hysterical. So we tried again...and I ended up listening to her talk non-stop for a couple of hours about acceptable subjects—mostly about being a teen on longevity drugs (this horrifies me; it never occurred to me they'd give such drugs to teens—she says they did it to prolong late adolescence, even though there's a great risk of screwing up hormonal processes etc.) while playing two teen roles consecutively on the soaps. And then I realized who Sally was—I mean, I realized that she'd been Maeve in that soap about an ad agency I used to watch faithfully during the later Colorado days. Which surprised me, because it means she's a lot older than she looks. (Not that age can ever be guessed from a person's appearance.)

This morning I faxed straight into Weatherall's personal terminal my first weekly report (which is always to be made on Fridays, except in cases of crisis or emergency). At the end of my report I appended a question I should have asked on Monday but which only occurred to me last night in the middle of an insomniac night—namely how long this assignment will last. At around three a.m. I realized that this kind of thing could go on for years. Apparently, my question caused Weatherall concern, for she phoned me this afternoon. First, she said (her voice was a little strained, I thought, though maybe I imagined this), she was considering "bringing Sally back into the situation" (whatever that means), because in spite of everything, Sally might still be useful. Then she said that she felt that with sufficient time Sally would grow less bitter and put everything behind her, which was all that would be necessary for other arrangements to be made. That it was Sally's hysteria and wildness that necessitated her isolation. That Sally wasn't, at heart, an enemy, but that the intensity of her emotions had put her beyond reason or loyalty. I gathered from all this that Weatherall doesn't intend retribution for whatever it is Sally has done. I wouldn't have expected this of her. Perhaps she isn't as bad as I've always thought. Weatherall specially commended me for my approach in dealing with Sally yesterday re the tranq dosage. I'm even to be allowed to take her out for walks at my discretion (with, of course, a fully outfitted escort of amazons accompanying us).

I never imagined it would be so easy working for Weatherall. The little contact I had with her when she was still at the Redmond house and I was running agents in Seattle suggested she could be a first class bitch to anyone unlucky enough to work directly under her. (We all knew that Hazel fared so well because Hazel was nearly her match— not to mention the object of her adoration.)

One aspect of the conversation was not so pleasant—Weatherall says she wants all mail to and from me subject to her eye. Even to and from Lise. "As a matter of precaution," is how she put it. This, I can't help feeling, is designed to drive a wedge between Lise and me. But I didn't dare say so.

Later

Can't sleep. About fifteen minutes after I turned off the light it occurred to me that Weatherall wants me to plug Sally in against her will. The very thought of it gives me the shivers. I can't recall Weatherall's exact words (I've been trying, but they elude me). But I'm sure that she hinted at my doing this in her call.

No, that's crazy. She wouldn't. One might as soon kill a person as plug them in.

But her telling me the general whereabouts on Sally's skull for where the plug was likely to be and suggesting I get Sally to show it to me... It's so small. I guess I expected a regular-sized socket. But it was so tiny I would never have found it myself. Sally, showing me, began reminiscing about the day she had had it done—she was only thirteen at the time. (Even though the legal age for it is fifteen.) She'd thought—and had, in fact, continued to think until only very recently—that plugging in was something all the rich and famous did, that it was "chic to the max" (her expression, so typical of the way she talks), that doing so was a sign of privilege. She and all her friends became addicted to it. Of course I've always known it was highly addictive—though because it's a psychological addiction I suppose I tended to discount its strength. It fills you with such euphoria that it makes real life seem at best dull, at worst flat, jagged, ugly, unreal, even tawdry by comparison, and one's sense of anxiety increases when one returns to ordinary consciousness. She said that for her as an actor the net effect of plugging in had been to get her more heavily into her roles—not only because doing well would earn her more time plugging in, but also because the roles themselves—i.e., "living the soap"—began to seem an escape from ordinary uncontrollable reality, which—after plugging in—made her feel helpless in a way living her roles did not.

Then she told me that she's done a lot of thinking about all this over the last few months. At which I warned her to say no more, gave her her evening sedative, wished her goodnight, and came in here to read. I checked on her a few minutes ago and she's of course sound asleep. Unlike me.

Surely I'm reading too much into Weatherall's words. Surely I can take at face value her regret for Sally's anguish and her wish that it be alleviated?

No, what am I saying? Weatherall is no fount of sympathy! My interpretation *must* be right.

I won't do it. Not even if she explicitly orders me to. And I won't encourage Sally to ask for it, either.

All things considered, it would have been even more of a disaster than I suspected at the time if I'd let Weatherall seduce me. At least I don't have *that* on my back now, too.

Chapter Thirty-one

[i]

Emily managed to arrange to dine with Lisa Mott that evening, despite the short notice. And Hazel, though puzzled at the request, agreed to come to the Diana to talk with Emily after Lisa had left, however late that might be.

When Emily finished with the phone, she started the Jacuzzi filling and opened her attaché case and pulled out the last five issues of *The Executive Times*. These issues had brought her to DC. When she and Astrea had "returned to civilization" that morning, Emily had dutifully made herself purchase not only the current issue but also those she had missed over the last week. The one standing task—apart from trying to keep Celia out of detention—she had long ago assigned herself was a daily reading of the *E.T.* as a kind of monitoring of the Executive and the executive system. No matter how tedious and aggravating such reading got to be, Emily always forced herself to do it, first because she had easy access to the paper, and second because she knew how to read it.

The need to read behind the words and between the lines of the *E.T.*, Emily mused as she sank into the churning hot water, had made all attempts to expose the Executive through publicization of fragments of the *E.T.* fail—that and the deliberately cultivated reputation of the *E.T.* as a right-wing fanatical newspaper whose articles and editorials were for the most part lunatic-fringe fantasy. A couple of years past when the Rainbow Press had published a book written back in the seventies that had analyzed the *E.T.* in detail, Venn had described to her how the author of the book had not only been unable to get it published but had also been denied tenure and lost all chances of holding a job in any reputable university because his colleagues had ridiculed the book as a paranoiac fantasy for "taking seriously"

the "rantings and ravings" of the whacko right-wing press. By flying in the face of what seemed to be obvious (an illusion Emily knew the Executive worked diligently to create and maintain), the man had discredited himself.

Every time activists attempted to expose the executive system via publicization of the *E.T.*, they ran up against a stone wall of deafness and incomprehension. One could read out loud an *E.T.* editorial from which Emily could plainly learn a great deal about Executive policy debates and find most people unable to get beyond the bombast and the otherwise seemingly innocuous words. "These are extremists—what have they to do with our political system?" most people would say. And of course the major media organizations regularly ridiculed the *E.T.* as lunatic-fringe. If the *New York Times* did not take the *E.T.* seriously, why, then, should the ordinary person? Too, executives meeting with criticism among their own ranks for withholding the truth from non-executives always pointed out that "the truth" was there for all to see if they "really wanted to"—the assumption being that only executives wanted to accept that level of "responsibility," just as self-hypnosis, self-defense, and other survival skills virtually universal among executives were "available" to those not too "lazy" to make use of them.

What a shocking transition, Emily thought. After four days and nights spent alone with Astrea, first healing from the depletion her over-exertion had brought on and then continuing their explorations, returning to DC's executive world and the need to corner Lisa Mott created a strain that jerked at her perceptions and her consciousness. How did Astrea exist in this world with humans—who must be so much more alien to her than the executive world seemed just now to Emily—without breaking down? Emily conceived a new respect and admiration for the Marq'ssan who had been living for decades on this planet. To remain here plunged in the ugliness and corruption of human relations when they could return whenever they wished to a world lacking such stress and pain seemed not only extraordinary but incomprehensible. The more she learned of them, the more unfathomable they became—even (or especially) Astrea.

[ii]

They worked through the usual round of smalltalk—the weather, mutual acquaintances, members of their families, tidbits of gossip— circling around the chief piece of personal news between them, viz., Lisa's (or should it be called Ginger's?) pregnancy. But Emily eventually had to ask after Ginger, and when she did, Lisa's cheeks grew rosy. "I suppose you've heard all about our pregnancy," she said. Emily nodded. Lisa forced a smile. "She's thrilled about it, though she doesn't like the amount of publicity and controversy it's generating."

Emily sipped her spiced tomato juice before replying. "Did this controversy have anything to do with the reason for Steinmetz's trip to the Rose Garden?"

Lisa flashed a sharp look at her. "How did you arrive at *that* conclusion?"

Emily smiled. "I know how to read the *E.T.* as well as you do, Lisa. Or *nearly* as well. The only other halfway plausible reason for his resignation would be opposition to the negotiations."

Lisa stared into her glass and swirled the ice cubes until she had raised a mild pink vortex along the sides. "Perhaps he really does want to return to the happy pursuit of making money after having rendered five long years of public service in the Cabinet," she said, not looking up.

"Yes, and perhaps the temperature will drop sixty degrees in the next hour and it will snow by midnight."

Lisa looked up. "You surely don't think I'm going to tell you Executive business, do you?"

"I thought we were talking about your pregnancy," Emily said.

"How many years have I known you?" Lisa archly queried. Their service-tech arrived and served the first course. When she had gone, Lisa said, "It's obvious you're using everything I've told you to the fullest advantage. That hotel over there is swollen now with dissidents eager to get in on the negotiation gravy train." She smiled sourly. "And all at the Executive's expense, too. I've been damned generous with you, Emily. Lay off your fishing expedition."

"You think the negotiations are going too far?" Emily speared a fat juicy shrimp.

"I don't know. Elizabeth isn't all that forthcoming about what deals she's making with Hazel." She frowned. "Elizabeth is *too* secretive, if you ask me. I've always thought her one of the coldest and most calculating decision-makers I've known, but I'm beginning to wonder if she isn't getting carried away by Hazel."

Emily finished chewing and swallowing her mouthful of shrimp, then said, "I can assure you, Elizabeth's not giving anything away. Which is why it's taking so long to work out even the preliminary things. She likes to leave things vague, she likes loopholes because she doesn't want to be pinned down by the letter of her agreements." Emily smiled. "But Martha is experienced enough to spot such problem areas. As for the swelling number of activists in the hotel—it's a matter of growing enthusiasm as even skeptics begin to wonder if there isn't something going on that's worth their while."

Lisa neatly sliced another bite off her serving of fried mozzarella. "It's hard work, keeping track of that many activists swarming the Capitol." She slid the bite into her mouth.

"Speaking of keeping track of activists..."

Lisa—her mouth still full—raised her eyebrows.

"I want to talk to you about Celia Espin."

Lisa, swallowing, shook her head. "Can't we leave her out of the conversation just once, Emily? Do you know how sick I am of your insisting on talking about her?"

Emily watched her sip her juice. "The last time I saw you I'd just arrived in DC to fetch Celia from your office. She had just been through a terrible ordeal."

Lisa's mouth bunched up as though she had bit into something putrid. "Not so terrible an ordeal. A few boring weeks sitting in detention. Nothing extreme, nothing horrible. As she herself confirmed. The only thing she had to complain about were cockroaches for Christ's sake!" Lisa glared at Emily. "Which is something I don't appreciate discussing over dinner!"

"For you or me maybe it wouldn't be an ordeal," Emily said, keeping her voice low and level despite her vexation. "I wouldn't know about that, since I've never had the experience myself." Emily's eyes bored into Lisa's. "But for Celia, who has been through what you cannot even begin to imagine, forcing herself to visit clients in detention centers is a feat more heroic than you or I can ever know." Emily smiled tightly. "Of course, what you are doing with the pregnancy takes a lot of courage, for you're flying in the face of tradition, against your socialization. Yet somehow I wonder how that matches up against the courage of someone like Celia, whom you so consistently choose to despise."

Lisa fingered her glass. "I had nothing to do with what happened to her. I did everything I could to help her, and you know it. Yet you persist in blaming me for—"

"Cut the bullshit, Lisa. I've *never* blamed you for what happened to Celia. You're letting your own guilt for who knows what sins fabricate such an interpretation and translate it into hostility toward Celia herself."

Lisa's lips trembled. "What is it you want to know?" she said in a hoarse, low voice.

Emily took a swallow of water and tried to get better control of her anger. Lisa's weakness, she reminded herself as she had so many times in the past, was something she had to accept. Only Lisa could change herself, and that was most unlikely. "I'm concerned about Celia's situation," Emily said. "As you know, she is opposed to anarchy. Which as far as I can tell is the sole reason she's still willing to live in the executive system. You also know she turned down Danforth's job offer. What concerns me is the likelihood of future harassment because she has chosen to remain independent."

"Don't worry," Lisa said bitterly. "No one's going to touch her. Believe me. We'd have to be pretty stupid to harass her now."

Emily shook her head. "You *know* what I'm talking about, Lisa. I want you to make it clear to Elizabeth that any attempt to discredit Celia will call forth swift and costly retaliation. I personally guarantee it."

Lisa shoved her barely touched plate of fried mozzarella to one side. "You've completely ruined my appetite," she said. "Believe me, after what happened in Baton Rouge we've no desire to provoke new situations with her. As long, that is, as she obeys the laws you claim she's so fond of." Lisa poured more water into her water goblet. "Was there anything else? We might as well get through everything you intend to dump on me all at once."

"One more warning," Emily said, watching Lisa's face. "Tell Elizabeth that if the Executive decides to circumvent the prohibition against arms sales to Brazil by using Guatemala or any other government as a go-between—" Emily noticed Lisa's eyes first widening and then reflexively narrowing—"we'll hit the first defense contractor on our list without even discussing it."

"Why tell *me* this? Why not have Hazel tell Elizabeth directly?"

"Because I haven't discussed with Hazel or any of the others the indications in the *E.T.* suggesting that the Executive is planning to do just that." Emily smiled sardonically. "I don't want to spoil the negotiations. And if I tell Hazel my suspicions I think she'll have a difficult time continuing her talks with Elizabeth. This is all my idea—I've discussed it with Astrea, and she's agreed we'll simply take care of it ourselves. Our Brazilian contacts will know if the arms keep flowing, and if they do, we—Astrea and I—will determine how you've managed it. I also want to warn you that we have contacts in Guatemala and many of the other places you might try." Emily took a long swallow of water and looked Lisa in the eye. "I'm very serious about this, Lisa."

Lisa ran her tongue over her lips. "Why don't you talk to Elizabeth yourself?"

Emily shook her head. "I've several reasons for not wanting to talk to Elizabeth, but perhaps the strongest reason is that I can't stomach the thought. Our last meeting left a foul taste in my mouth."

Lisa attempted a weak smile. "I know what you mean. I've been *there*, too. We all have. Given what Elizabeth is like." She pressed her lips together for a few seconds, then continued, "But you're way off base, you know. The Executive wouldn't—"

Emily interrupted. "I know how the Executive thinks and what arms contractors are like. The latter, especially, I know well—I grew up around them, Lisa. And I know that even if it's so small in the larger scheme of things, this particular concession is bound to be sticking in the Executive's throat."

Lisa sighed. "All right, I'll pass your messages on. But I tell you, I resent your using me as your personal messenger girl. It's—"

"Come off it," Emily said, again interrupting. "You know as well as I do this is a matter of great importance. If you'd like, though,"

Emily sarcastically added, "next time I'll talk instead to the reception-ist in Elizabeth's office."

Lisa fiddled with her butter knife. "The point is taken," she said after a couple of beats. "But I want you to know I still don't appreci-ate having to deliver your threats to Elizabeth. She has this habit of snarling when——"

A syrupy voice behind Emily cut across Lisa's words. "Well, well, well. It's Lisa Mott, isn't it?"

Lisa's head snapped up; her gaze, hardening, fixed above Emily's head. "I beg your pardon?" she said in the iciest tone of voice Emily had ever heard her use.

"You should be begging pardon from *all* of us, dear."

Emily turned in her seat to look and immediately noticed how in-tensely the green eyes of the woman standing two feet in back of her chair—obviously maternal line—glittered with anger. The second thing Emily noticed was that the woman had the dubious distinction of being the only executive in the room wearing face jewelry.

"My dear Felice," Lisa said, fairly hissing. "Your kind's envy is entirely pointless. Times are changing, in case you hadn't noticed."

The woman's mouth stretched into a complacent smile. "Oh, I've noticed. I certainly have noticed. If anyone had told me ten years ago that a bunch of renegades would be sitting in the Executive and that Sedgewick's successor would be a renegade embracing maternity, I would have told her she was nuts. And if anyone had told me this ren-egade trying at middle-aged maternity would be Lisa Mott, I would have laughed my head off." The woman glanced down at Emily. "I do beg your pardon, dear, for interrupting like this. Since Lisa seems un-interested in observing the courtesies, allow me to introduce myself. Felice Raines." She extended her hand to Emily.

Emily extended her own, but the woman squeezed her fingers rather than shook her hand. "Emily Madden. How do you do."

Felice wrinkled her nose. "Hmmm...the name's familiar..." Emily waited for her father's name to click. But rather than asking if Emily was related to Barclay Madden, Felice instead said, "Are you the one who started the Collage Miscellany?"

Startled, Emily nodded. "Or let's say I initially helped finance and fundraise the foundation. The artists actually started it themselves."

Felice smiled. "Every time I'm in a town with a Collage Miscellany I make a point of stopping in to see its current exhibit. I've even bought a few pieces."

"If you'll excuse us, Felice," Lisa said. The sharpness of her voice cut through the chitchat like a knife. "I'm sure Emily would be delighted to discuss the finer points of art patronage when we've finished."

Felice's smile grew venomous. "Sorry, dear, I only stopped by to ask you to give Elizabeth a message from me." She glanced down at Emily and added in a stage whisper, "I know some of Lisa's relations quite well—she's a terrible embarrassment to them. It's a pity really, everyone thought she had done *so* well in her career before she went renegade—"

The table violently jolted and rocked; Emily turned just in time to rescue her water goblet from its near crash into her half-consumed plate of shrimp. Lisa, now on her feet, stood poised for flight. "I'm sure you'll both excuse me if—" she began, but Felice interrupted her.

"Of course I'll excuse you, dear. But you needn't run away on my account—I'll go as soon as I've given you the message."

"Another one?" Lisa's sneer was bitter. "Just call me Mercury, messenger to the gods."

Felice chuckled. "Tell Elizabeth I give her less than two weeks more in power." She chortled with glee. "As for the rest of her crew, I'm sure you'll all be gone within a month. I'd be willing to lay odds on *that*." Unable to resist snatching a glimpse of Felice's face as she said this, Emily again twisted around in her seat.

"Christ, you can't be spinning *that* out of the *E.T.*," Lisa said. "I can't imagine what privileged information you think you have. If you think the Executive will fall because of my maternity—"

"No, dear, though it might eventually do you all in, that's not what I'm going on. It is, as you say, privileged information. I imagine Elizabeth will know what I'm referring to as soon as you tell her." Her eyes glistened with malice; she again laughed. "I'd love to see the look on her face when you tell her. But alas and alack I've other fish to fry." Felice leaned forward. "Oh, and you might tell her one other thing. Tell her that I've got a splendid memory and that I retain a vivid impression of a certain New Year's Eve." Felice turned to go, then glanced back over her shoulder. "She'll know *exactly* what I mean."

Emily watched the extravagantly dressed woman mince across the room to the lounge Debra had said she was working this evening.

"I'm sorry, Emily," Lisa said. "But I've had more than I can take. I don't want to offend you, but I'm going now."

"Indeed."

"I'm surprised someone hasn't taken a contract out on that bitch," Lisa said bitterly. "She's had it coming to her for years."

Felice Raines, Emily thought, trying to place the so-familiar name. "Perhaps we can get together another time when things are less, ah, chaotic," Emily said. She smiled. "And I *would* like to tender to both you and Ginger my best wishes for the pregnancy."

Lisa pushed her hair back from her face and smiled slightly. "Thanks, Emily. I'll pass it on to Ginger. God knows there are few enough good wishes for our endeavor."

When Lisa had gone Emily summoned their service-tech and gave her the news that they would not be eating the rest of the meal. The server nodded discreetly and, pointing out that she would still be charged for the full service of dinner, said she would have Emily's account billed.

Upstairs in her room Emily phoned Hazel. Since she would be meeting with the latter earlier than she had expected, she would have a little time before Debra got off work to do the exercises Astrea had devised for her. Thinking about how Lisa must be feeling, she almost regretted her attack against her. Almost. For Lisa would, of course, rationalize away any qualms she might be feeling. Lisa Mott wouldn't be a successful Chief of Security if she didn't routinely dispose of qualms with the greatest of ease. And as a longtime SIC officer, she had years of practice behind her.

Chapter Thirty-two

Saturday, 8/25/2096

At this rate I'm going to crack up. Every slightest noise makes me about jump out of my skin, even when I know there's no way for Elizabeth to be here since my ear is constantly listening for the drone of her jet. My programming myself to wake up through the night every time there's the slightest sound has proven to be a double-edged sword. Every time the amazons make their rounds I wake, ready to bound out of the house. Sleeping on the mattress I dragged into the front hall is, I suppose, stupid, but still I feel I can hear more there than from any other place in the house. I've cached food, water, a flashlight, a large sharp kitchen knife, & a thermo-blanket out in the woods. Which is absurd, of course: a simple heat-sensor would locate me in no time. & always I sleep with a knife beside me. But what I imagine doing with it is not plunging it into Elizabeth but holding it to my throat & using it should she make the slightest move toward me. I'm close to being out of control, so stretched, so wired from my mental state of alert. & then the horrible dreams & nightmares—half the night I don't know whether I'm Kay, Rbt, Sally—or me. Or all of them/us. Keep thinking how lucky Kay was to escape from Elizabeth to Rbt—if only she had known it! Elizabeth makes Rbt look like a saint. With him one could at least count on limits. With Elizabeth there is no limit. If she can, she will destroy me. The only thing restraining her is her desire to lay hands on my copies of the transcript.

Jazzy is due to return on Sunday. The earliest she'll come here will be Monday evening. & then presumably she will be decent enough to tell me whether she mailed the letters. Surely Elizabeth would have taunted me with having foiled my attempt to reach Grandfather &

Mama if Jazzy had betrayed me. There's hope in me yet, though it gets slimmer with every day that passes.

But suppose I did get my chance—will anyone believe a word I say? I have this terrible feeling that Grandfather & Mama will think I'm insane & lock me away in an institution. I don't know if I can even speak coherent sentences—I haven't spoken to anyone since Elizabeth left. The physical therapist hasn't come around. & then last night I caught sight of myself in a mirror & saw that my face had turned into a swollen mass of bruises. I think my nose must be broken. Because I blocked the pain that first bit of time Elizabeth let me sleep, I hadn't been aware of the extent of the damage. But worst of all, my face is no longer Alexandra Sedgewick's face.

I still have the transcript. It is my ace in the hole, no matter what Elizabeth tries. None of them can deny the truth of it. & Mama was a witness. Surely Mama won't let Elizabeth win?

But I have no faith in Mama's taking my part. As for Grandfather, it's just as likely he'll wash his hands of me as help me.

Had to stop writing for a while, my hands were trembling too much to hold the pen. I must assume I'm all alone in this battle against Elizabeth. Maybe I *am* crazy. Maybe I've imagined there's a transcript. Maybe I've imagined this entire nightmare I'm trapped in.

Tuesday, 8/28/2096

Where do I start? So much has happened…& most amazing is the fact that I managed to hold onto this book in spite of everything. I was able to take only what I could carry in a waterproof pack on my back, a pack already filled with emergency equipment & rations. So I took only one set of clothing & this book, my notes on the amazons, the data disk holding a copy of the transcript, & the letter Elizabeth wrote to me telling me she had forged a letter in my name to Mama.

Start first with my waking before dawn & my terror at hearing them in the house—they'd entered through the back (I later discovered they'd gotten in through a top floor window the girl had left open unbeknownst to me—I'd locked & otherwise secured every other window & door in the house)—& of course I thought they were amazons accompanying Elizabeth. Knife clutched in fist, I crept off my mattress & slipped into the closet under the stairs, leaving the door cracked. They—three *males*—walked right by. They paused to stare at my mattress. If they spoke, though, I heard nothing. Then two of them went up the stairs, & the third began a stealthy search of the first floor.

After about thirty minutes they met at the foot of the stairs. "Where the hell is she?" the one who had searched the downstairs demanded. "Could she be out wandering the island at this hour? The guards are still around, which has to mean they haven't moved her."

"We'll have to mount an outdoors search—the old man'll give us hell if we go back without her & can't say we've thoroughly searched."

"What he doesn't know—" one of them began.

"What if he doesn't believe us & drips some loquazene into our veins?" the original speaker said, his voice rising. "I've been working for him for twenty years. You can't bullshit Varley Raines & hope to get away with it. Believe me, I've seen a few damned fools try."

"All right, man," the second said. "So we'll search. Better get out our topo maps."

At the mention of Grandfather's name I knew he must have sent them to rescue me. So it was all a matter of revealing my presence without their shooting me. (I knew damned well they'd be armed to the teeth—gorillas out on this kind of job would likely be carrying everything from throwing knives to blowtorches to handguns to M-19s.) I decided to call out my presence before opening the closet door. So I cracked the door open, took a deep breath, & said (my damned voice shook so badly that as I spoke I worried they wouldn't be able to understand a word I was saying), "I'm Alexandra Sedgewick. Are you looking for me?"

Sure enough they jumped, whirled, & reached for their guns, then dropped into a crouch with their backs making a triangle as they faced out in three directions.

"Don't shoot," I said. "I'm in the closet under the stairs. If you lower your weapons I'll come out, slowly."

"Okay, but don't try anything cute," one of them warned.

I slowly opened the door & crept out into the hall. One of them shone a beam from a flashlight on my face. "This isn't Alexandra Sedgewick!" the downstairs searcher exclaimed.

"I *am* Alexandra Sedgewick," I said as steadily as I could. "They've surgically reconstructed my face. But my fingerprints are the same. & my voice. & my memories. If you take me to my grandfather I'll prove who I am."

A long discussion ensued. Which is why we ended up having to wait through the whole day before fleeing the island. When dawn began streaking the sky, we continued our discussion in the cellar. They wouldn't let me out of their sight—to protect me, they said, but I understood it to be a precaution in case I happened to be one of Elizabeth's operatives. But I talked by phone to Grandfather—who was on a yacht anchored only two miles off the island. They explained the situation to him, & so I answered a series of silly questions that presumably only I would know the answer to. It was bizarre—talking to him but saying nothing of significance. & it was such a long, long day: I was terrified the whole time Elizabeth would come & find me with Grandfather's gorillas in the cellar.

The day seemed interminable. We left the house at ten. I decided not to take the transcript—Elizabeth hadn't found it yet, so there was no reason to believe she would find it in whatever length of time elapsed before I managed to take legal control of the island. The sea was frighteningly choppy, & rowing in the dark intensified my fear. But we signaled the yacht, & when we saw a light signaling in return, I knew we'd make it. The relief & excitement hyped me up, made me more of a wreck than I'd yet been. I found it so hard to believe that the nightmare was over that I began imagining all sorts of terrible things that might yet happen. Besides capsizing & drowning, I imagined Grandfather refusing to believe me to be Alexandra Sedgewick. I imagined his testing my fingerprints only to find that they no longer matched my old prints—that Elizabeth had somehow managed to remake my fingerprints as well as my face. By the time we reached the yacht I was trembling so badly, my limbs had grown so enervated, that I could hardly climb aboard. Right there on the deck Grandfather stared at me for a long time. Frightened by his motionless silence, yet overwhelmed by my relief, I began to weep. Finally I made a move toward him. To my utter relief he held open his arms & embraced me. "Your mother," he said, "is standing by, waiting to hear from you. She's in my apartment in New York. After I've given the order to head for the mainland where I've got a jet waiting, we'll go inside & call to let her know you're safe."

He took charge of everything. I collapsed into a chair on the deck & he put a snifter of cognac in my hand. His doing that said more than any words could have.

Some time in the middle of the night we arrived at his New York apartment. Mama shrieked when she saw me—at the mess of my face, &, of course, at the fact that I no longer looked like myself. But she soon found a bright spot: about the fourth thing she said to me (the second thing had been about the need to get a plastic surgeon to attend to my nose) was, "Well at least you no longer resemble Sedgewick." & then, having had her say, she bustled me into a Jacuzzi & found a gown for me. I drank another cognac with Grandfather. He told me how he had gotten Peter Grace, who had always handled Rbt's affairs, to tell him the location of the island. Mercifully grandfather refrained from demanding explanations. As soon as I finished the cognac I went to bed. I slept for ten hours straight.

I felt certain he would demand to know *everything* when I woke. But when I saw him he asked nothing & said only that his attorney would be arriving shortly. When the attorney arrived I signed a statement that he had prepared revoking Elizabeth's power of attorney. I could hardly believe how simple it was: with one stroke of the pen I gained my autonomy & freedom. The ease of it dazed me. I still haven't taken it in.

It was then that I knew I must say something to him. I started out by telling him that I felt it would be better for him to hear the worst from me than to hear it from Elizabeth. But he stopped me, said he didn't want to know. & that he would see to it that she'd have no access to him. His eyes told me that as long as he didn't know it wouldn't matter to him. My first thought was that Elizabeth might then go public— until I realized that my possession of the transcript would be enough to keep her silent. I saw my next move must be to contact Elizabeth & inform her that the power of attorney she held was no longer valid.

When I called her office (Grandfather having supplied me with her PA's number), my announcement of who I was brought first disbelief, then consternation. Elizabeth came onto the line at once. The things I said to her made my identity clear—for only I could know all the things she had done to me. My pleasure as I ordered her to clear my property of her people, as I ordered her to vacate my houses, as I told her to begin preparing an accounting of her executorship of the Estate, is indescribable. Though she made a few threats about revealing the incest, I mentioned the transcript—& left her speechless. At one point in our conversation I reminded her that holding a person against their will is a felony. She scoffed at the implied threat, but it gave me pleasure voicing it.

When I finished talking to Elizabeth, I let Mama drag me off to the plastic surgeon she had chosen for me.

But it's late & I'm too tired to describe more of the day's events.

The very idea of having a life to live...*stupefies* me. That I can do anything I want leaves me breathless. I haven't had a chance to *want* for a very long time. Since before Rbt. Almost I've forgotten how.

It isn't too late... Surely it isn't? I've won my freedom. Surely that must mean something?

Chapter Thirty-three

Monday, September 3, 2096—Idaho

Tomorrow it will be two weeks since I began this assignment. Already it feels like months. So this is what Weatherall was saying I should be using my "potential" for? If I'd wanted this kind of job I would have become a mental health worker. The very thought of Sally lying on that bed staring up at the ceiling (as I know she is doing when she isn't sleeping) oppresses me.

On Saturday I couldn't stand it any longer: I forced Sally to dress and go outdoors with me. We'd only taken a few steps when she began complaining about being too weak to go on. Well of course she was weak and shaky, she'd done nothing but lie on that damned bed for days!

It occurred to me last night as I tossed and turned that she must be very close to the edge. I'm not sure "being kind" is what she needs. (But then neither is plugging in.) As for the other things plaguing me... At the top of the list, I suppose, is Weatherall's statement that she was thinking of sending Sally back in. I keep wondering why she would even consider such a thing, given this loyalty problem she apparently has—and of what possible use someone in Sally's condition could be in any operation. After long consideration, it seems that rather than Weatherall deluding herself about Sally's stability, it's more likely that she might be intending to make some really horrid use of her. In my last report, I asked Weatherall if she would prefer me to steer Sally to plugging in (which I *will* not do) or brace her up for this possible return to the field, but got no response.

Yesterday I had the idea of getting Sally to watch the last soap she had been in. Actually, as Sally explained to me during one of our conversations last week, the soap she played in had a "twin" soap running concurrently with hers (the two are usually shown consecutively, since the viewers of the one always watch the other), with some of the characters moving back and forth between the "twins." The basic set-up is historical—the French and English royal courts in the second half of the sixteenth century. (Sally's soap focuses mainly on the court of Elizabeth I, while the twin's focuses on the French court—Catherine de Medici and the scheming Jesuits and dissident protestants etc.) Sally had what she called a strong role—but it came to an end when her character was beheaded (she played Mary Queen of Scots). Originally she had been considered for the role of the famous mistress of one of the French rulers.

So I went into her room at the right hour and turned on the vid set (which as far as I can tell she hasn't watched even once since our arrival here). At first she was interested in the English court soap—because she knew most of the actors in it. But after a while I could tell she wasn't paying attention. So I gave up and turned it off. I made some kind of comment about how interesting it was to learn that soap stars found soaps boring.

"I was remembering what it was like," she said. "I can tell you that the people we just saw in that soap…well, they spend their time shuttling from the make-believe reality of the soap scenario to the make-believe lives of soap stars that we're persuaded to play, to plugging in. Those are the three atmospheres soap players live in. You can't imagine what it's like. I did that from the age of twelve. That's more than half my life. It's about all I knew of life until last December." I cautioned her not to talk about last December. She shrugged. "I didn't know there was anything else but these roles. How could I? Often in these soaps the actors start taking on the identities of the characters they're playing. I suppose it's the plugging in that does it." She glanced at my eyes, then away. An eerie, haunted look came into her face. "That can make it awfully tough. Like when your character gets killed off the way mine was last fall."

She wasn't joking. Still, I had this terrible urge to laugh. A nervous urge, I suppose. In a way I think I can see some of what she was talking about—there's something in it that reminds me of the double life I was leading in Seattle.

She's a sad case. I'm getting too involved emotionally; I can feel her tugging at me, and it worries me. Weatherall's advice about being friendly (when Sally is really a prisoner, and the reason she's a prisoner is because she was turned—though I'm finding it almost impossible to feel animosity toward her, or even distrust) was, I'm beginning to think, a mistake. I know the point is to make Sally feel she's in a safe environment with people she can trust—to make it easier for her to surrender control to that damned apparatus. But the toll it's taking on *me*—I don't feel at all objective.

Tuesday, September 4, 2096—Idaho

Today I asked Sally why, if plugging in does such damage to one's brain, actors—who presumably have to remember their lines and so on—are allowed to do it at all. Her answer: they are allowed only snatches of it—tantalizing snatches. That that's how most casual users get by. But that it is difficult to control oneself. Which is why none of them are allowed to own their own apparatus.

We had this conversation while taking a short (and I mean *short*) walk in the woods around the house. After she had explained this to me she said, "You can see now why I'm afraid to use the apparatus you had in my room. Maybe the first and even second time I used it I'd be able to exercise some self-control—though just supposing I could, I'd probably get even more depressed than I already am—but it wouldn't be long before I'd be plugged in for keeps." She gave me a long stare, and I felt that she was for the first time really looking at me. "Why do you want that to happen to me? I've been thinking about this, and I just don't understand it. You've been really nice to me. Not like them." She jerked her head in the direction of the amazons tagging along with us at what they considered to be a "discreet" distance.

What could I say? That I had my orders? Or preach at her about loyalty (which, now that I think about it, doesn't really have that much to do with the issue of plugging someone in for life)? So I came out with the thing that's become a formula now: "We can't discuss that." She said nothing, only looked at me—and something in her eyes, and the way the corners of her mouth pulled up in a certain way, made me feel like an ass. I never expected an actor to be so intelligent. She understands too much for my own comfort. But then I suppose my impression of actors as stupid comes from all that stereotyping hype and gossip about actors' lives that according to Sally is manufactured for public consumption.

It was at this point that she insisted on going back to the house. It's interesting to note that she waited until we got back before acting out. Now that I've written all this I see that it must have been the conversation we had (or didn't have) on our walk that triggered the tantrum. At any rate, not long after I took her to her room she started stamping around the room, slamming doors and drawers, even throwing the vid set onto the floor (though not breaking it, since its plastic is too durable to be easily damaged). "Do you have any idea," she shrieked at me, "what it's like to know that the person you love and who loves you believes you don't because some damned bitch told her so?"

I'd already activated the call signal I always carry in my pocket. But she was taking another breath, so I grabbed her and put my hand over her mouth—terrified that she would say more—really, terrified. My heart was going like crazy. *I don't want to know* whatever it is that Weatherall is trying to keep quiet. Hell, who knows, if *I* find out I might end up in Sally's situation, too. At the same time, I felt furious with her for pulling this on me—for we've gradually worked down to almost no tranqs at all. I'd trusted her—otherwise why would I have been taking her for walks? By her indifference to my safety she was endangering me. A voice in my head kept repeating that she didn't give a damn how I fared. I felt like shaking her, even punching her—it was strange, having such a violent feeling toward her, when we'd been so friendly only a few minutes before. She struggled to get my hand off her mouth and babbled something I fortunately couldn't make out (I was convinced she was going to bite my hand, but she didn't). It seemed to take hours before DG and one of her crew flew into the room and plunged the hypodermic into Sally's vein. It couldn't have been more than a minute. Still… This whole thing just gets worse and worse. Why am I so angry at her? It's stupid of me to expect her to play by these imaginary rules I've made up for this situation. Because after all this is not just a situation to her, it's possibly a struggle for her life or at any rate is of the heaviest significance to her future existence. In other words, it means a lot more to her than it does to me.

I'm too involved, and that's the truth. Maybe I should suggest this to Weatherall in my next report? Would she replace me if I said this?

After all, they pulled me out of Seattle because they thought I was too emotionally involved with Venn.

Who knows. You can never tell what executives are going to decide about such things. The only reason I ever know what's going on with Lise is my years of experience with her. Guess I'll read in the bathtub now for a while. Maybe that will get my mind off Sally. Writing about her certainly hasn't.

Wednesday, September 5, 2096—Idaho

Well the shit's hitting the fan now. Phone call tonight from Weatherall. I'm to return to DC tomorrow—for "an extensive and thorough evaluation of the operation." As far as I could make out on the phone, Weatherall is getting impatient with the lack of "progress." When I asked her what she meant by "progress," she irritably said I should know exactly what she meant, that she shouldn't have to spell it out for me. Which is to say she either didn't want to talk about plugging in over the phone or she doesn't want to explicitly order me to do it. (Leaving her clear of any implied guilt, I suppose?) Well I'm not going to do her dirtywork for her. The longer this assignment goes on, the firmer I am on that. She picked the wrong person for this job, if that's what she's expecting. But without going into this aspect of it, I'm going to suggest she get someone else for the job—on the grounds that I'm getting too close to Sally. Of course the danger of that is that she might decide on a loquazene interrogation. God, I hope not, I hate that stuff. You never know what you've said (and there's no way of finding out), unconscious like that you're completely at the mercy of whatever the examiner feels like asking you. Maybe I won't push her to replace me after all. Weatherall's response might be worse than remaining in the situation.

Friday, September 7, 2096—Idaho

Returned so late last night that I slept in. When I finally saw Sally this morning, she would hardly speak to me. According to DG, Sally had to be heavily tranqed yesterday, for when she discovered I'd gone she regressed into the old hysteria. She hasn't been hysterical today—but then she's pretty doped up. When I checked on her a little while ago she showed some thaw and said she'd thought I'd gone for good. Then promised not to act out on me. So I'll lighten her next dosage. (It's all so bizarre—seems even more bizarre after yesterday's flying visit to DC.)

Actually, that's not the truth at all. I made up all this nonsense about her promise not to "act out" etc. for DG, so that I could justify taking Sally off tranqs altogether, hopefully in the near future. I need to come to a decision, and I don't feel I can do it without talking seriously to Sally. And time is running out.

Christ, what a mess. I can't believe it's come to this, that I could even be considering this. But after what Weatherall said to me yesterday, I feel like I'm caught in a trap.

Maybe the truth is that I've had it. Or maybe the fact that I've gone renegade before... But no. It's more that there have been too many things I've been finding it hard to live with—and now *this*. If I don't get Sally plugged in, Weatherall will come and do it herself. That's the bottom line. "Do it any way you like," she said. "Either get her to try little samples to remind her of the enormous pleasure she's been denying herself—and I tell you frankly, this *was* what she wanted from me, it was to be her reward for her role in the operation—or, if you can't manage that, simply plug her in by force. Though if you do that, leave everyone but DG out of it and be discreet."

Be discreet! My god, it's a *felony*, besides being appallingly immoral! When I expressed dismay, Weatherall made a big thing about how this was pleasure, not pain, that we're talking about. I wanted to say but what about consciousness! But I didn't, because by that point I could see that that would only raise her suspicions. She has me backed into a corner. Sort of. Oh, she can't *make* me do it. But if I don't...well, it will happen anyway. And then I'll have a lot of difficulties to face. I keep thinking the difficulties couldn't be too bad, because Lise would stand by me. But I have this feeling that if Weatherall went all out to alienate Lise from me, she could do it. And if Lise were alienated from me, Weatherall could make my life a misery. After all, I still work for Security. She could have Mott dump me in some godawful job in some horrible backwater.

I keep remembering what Venn said to me that last time I saw her.

If I'm likely to end up going back to Seattle anyway, then I might as well make a decision of conscience about Sally and go renegade. Which means I have to get her side of the story and find out just what the hell is going on. If she's done something truly horrendous, but my god it's hard to believe that—not only because of what I know of Sally, but because of Weatherall's attitude—it's simply not the attitude she would be likely to take toward someone who has committed large scale treachery. And even so, I'm just not sure I'd agree with permanently plugging her in. So I've got to get her off the tranqs so I can talk to her. I've only got a couple of days' leeway before Weatherall will personally take control of the situation. She was so hard, so cold, so *wired* that for a minute there I thought she was going to jump on her jet that very night.

So this is how it happens. This is how "traitors" are made... Or at least *some* traitors. I don't suppose all renegades are persons of conscience. No, of course they're not. Though everybody in Security will say I was corrupted or bought or something like that. I'm sure Weatherall will see to *that*. Damn her for getting me into this. I feel bad about Lise. I know she'll never understand, even if I call her from Seattle and try to explain it. By that point Weatherall will already have gotten to her and poisoned her against me.

It's so ironic. Because of Weatherall I learned how to conceal my true feelings, how to deceive, how to plot details for various scenarios, how to strategize clandestine operations. And now I will use those skills to betray her.

Saturday, September 9, 2096—Idaho

Before I heard even a word of Sally's story I began conspiring with her. First thing in the morning I went into her room, wakened her, and whispered to her that I wanted her to act a role, that I couldn't explain why now, but that I'd explain later. At first she was confused, but then to my surprise quite perked up. Perhaps it was a feeling that I must be on her side and that my lying to the others could mean only good for her?

At any rate, we went out for a walk right after breakfast, and by god she made a damned good show. She even *laughed* and linked arms with me. (What an actor, to be able to transcend her misery just like that.) Later, when we were inside, she played a game of scrabble with me—out in the main lounge—and was the image of good humor. She even provided an explanatory circumstance for DG and the others—namely that she was happy and relieved to find that I was back "for good." I caught a strange look in DG's eye, but I could see she bought it.

Then after lunch Sally went to her room, supposedly for a nap. I joined her there after about half an hour. From then on we spoke in near-whispers nonstop for the next hour and a half. What a horrifying story she told. At one point I began to wonder if she'd made the whole thing up. But when I compared it with Weatherall's demarcation of the boundaries of the "forbidden" areas of speech, I realized they jibed perfectly. I'd never be able to live with myself if I didn't try to get her out of this situation—even if she does prove to be a traitor. By the story *she* tells, there's not the slightest hint of treachery or the slightest shade of national security endangerment. All I can see is some bizarre plot by Weatherall for unknown purposes. But if this woman involved really is Sedgewick's daughter (and I can't imagine who else would have his name and be so important to Weatherall and so wealthy into the bargain), it *must* be pretty strange.

The story Sally tells is this: Weatherall recruited Sally to pose as one of those expensive courtesans certain executive women keep. The promised reward was as much plugging in as she wanted. She was to spy on this woman—Alexandra, Sally calls her—and make reports to Weatherall. When she first arrived on this island (somewhere in the north Atlantic, Sally doesn't know exactly where), she found herself in a large household full of not only service-techs but a crew of professors brought there to amuse this Alexandra, and an enormous contingent of armed guards. Alexandra immediately suspected Sally of being Weatherall's spy and was cruel to her. (Sally didn't go into specifics and said it wasn't important, that what could a sneak expect.) But things changed when Alexandra exposed the first layer of her cover—at which point another layer came into play. Weatherall apparently gave Sally several layers of cover for just such eventualities, for Weatherall, it seems, expected Alexandra to see through some of the various layers. (Sally talks as if this woman is brilliant, even a genius.) But after this top layer was peeled off, Alexandra grew friendly with Sally and made a sort of pact with her, to the end of fooling Weatherall. But of course Sally still reported to Weatherall—except that after a while Sally reported exactly what Alexandra told her to report, because, Sally said, she started to "really like" Alexandra (now that she was being nice to her).

Things took a dramatic turn when Alexandra threw herself off a cliff and an emergency crew arrived and carried her away to a secure medical facility. Weatherall pulled Sally back in, slammed her with several loquazene interrogations, and generally got into a rage with her. Sally spent weeks more or less locked away in a single room. Sounds damned close to solitary confinement if you ask me. She hints that she was roughed up a little, too, by some amazons. Says all she did while locked away was think about what had happened to Alexandra and wonder why she had wanted to kill herself. Finally Weatherall announced that she would give Sally another chance and sent her back to the island, where Alexandra, now patched up and with a new face, had been returned. But everything was different. There was no one on the island but guards and medical attendants. The house had been wrecked. And Alexandra would have nothing to do with Sally. Worse, Sally recognized one of the guards (they were Weatherall's amazons) and felt in a very difficult situation. Sally thought Weatherall had just abandoned her there to punish her for her treachery, thinking Alexandra would be nasty to her... There followed more or less a love story...brought to an end by Weatherall's arriving and telling Alexandra the "truth"—namely that she'd been recruited with the prospect of a lifetime of plugging in as her motivation. Alexandra then refused to talk to Sally. (What an idiot! I must say I can't have too much sympathy for her if she'd let Weatherall come between them like that. Unless of course *she* never loved Sally herself.) Sally was crushed. Is crushed. According to Sally, the only thing Alexandra said to her was that she was "like an onion," all layers of skin with nothing inside. When she told me this, tears began rolling down her cheeks. "Maybe she's right," Sally whispered to me. "Maybe I was caught by the role, the way the soaps sometimes catch us. Maybe I'm not *really* in love, maybe there's nothing to me but *roles*!" This so disturbed me that I had to point out that falling in love with Alexandra had never been a part of "the role" Weatherall had assigned her. This seemed to comfort her a little. How horrible that she is tormented by such doubts about her own feelings and experience of reality. Even in the worst moments of living my double life I never doubted that I had a real, feeling, authentic self.

So Weatherall dragged her away and crammed her full of drugs to get her to shut up. Which is, of course, where I came into the story.

So why does Sally deserve to have her mind wiped? I can't see a shred of reason to justify such an extreme measure. I keep remembering how Weatherall talked about Sally's being "turned." So she fell in love with the mark, which is a no-no. But Sally's not a regular operative.

In the meantime Sedgewick's daughter (if that's who she is) is now living alone except for guards on this deserted island. Why? Why is Weatherall keeping her there? Sally says she doesn't know.

Too many whys. I'm sure I'll never know all the answers. God knows Weatherall isn't about to tell me.

I'm exhausted—too much intensity, too much talking and thinking. Maybe after sleep I'll have a fresh handle on everything. But tomorrow night, if all goes well, we'll head for the Free Zone, which isn't that far from here. Lucky, isn't it, that Weatherall chose this of all places to send us.

And then I'll be seeing Venn and Marlene and—but no, I don't dare think about of any of that until it's all over. It can only distract me. And if ever I needed my wits about me, it's now.

Chapter Thirty-four

Monday, 9/3/2096

Finally, things are moving. Grandfather thinks my impatience absurd, given how long I've already waited. It took time to assemble the necessary complement of gorillas before returning to the island. Elizabeth's amazons had gone, however. My relief at finding the house intact was immense—I had had this nagging feeling that she might decide to set fire to the entire island, to burn the house to the ground or even bomb it. I kept telling myself that it wouldn't matter if she did that, that I hated the place. But already I'm starting to feel differently about it. I wouldn't want to live there again. But I see now that if I'm free to come & go I might want to stay there for short breaks.

The ocean is in my blood.

While I waited on the jet, the gorillas combed through the house room by room, closet by closet until they could assure me the house was totally uninhabited. Before opening the pedestal on the statue, I wandered through the house, seeing it with new eyes. Then I packed two suitcases—dressing gowns & jewelry, mostly, since I won't be wearing any of my other clothes (out-of-date & ill-fitting now). & then, as though without a will of my own, I climbed to the top floor & went into Sally's room. To lay her ghost, perhaps (since I can't seem to stop dreaming about her). I've no idea whether Elizabeth keeps her bargains with her pawns. I suppose that's why I keep wondering about the girl.

I found the letter stuck into a sock she'd left under the bed. I saw the sock from the doorway when I came in. It looked as though she'd forgotten it in her hurry to pack & leave. I don't know why, but I bent down & picked it up & immediately felt the paper inside.

What to make of the letter? Another of Elizabeth's stratagems? Or the girl's attempt to assuage her guilty conscience?

After I retrieved the transcript I flew out here to the Colorado house & made arrangements for sending work crews up to the island to restore the house. I will stay here until I finish my thinking—for I have to decide what to do next. My thirst for revenge has been considerably slaked, but I still have the score of that last outrageous visit of hers to settle. The things she did & said to me... I need to tell her what I think of her & how angry I am at her savage violation of me. I'd love to pummel her—but I won't. More effective, I think, to use words against her.

Alexandra,

I can't blame you for hating me. I tried once to tell you what the original "deal" was, but I just couldn't do it, I was so afraid you'd despise me for it. As long as you thought I was doing it to help a friend, you didn't think the worst of me. But for a selfish reason like plugging in? I was in a kind of daze when Weatherall proposed the deal to me. The character I'd been living had died, I was at loose ends. The idea of getting to plug in whenever I wanted, well, back then I was *living* for those times I got to plug in. Plugging in was what I cared about the most. None of the love affairs I had were what I could now call real love.

Everything changed for me when I fell in love with you. It seemed like a miracle when I came back to your island the second time and we loved each other. I never imagined you could love someone like me (even after Weatherall, by saying you lusted after me, gave me a little hope). Then when it all happened—

I guess it was too good to be true. You would have realized all my faults and everything eventually, even if she hadn't come and told you about me.

I wish I could stay here with you, even if it meant staying out of your way, like before. You don't know how

But there's no more time, I have to get down there before she sends somebody up here after me. Maybe you'll read this, maybe you won't.

But at least in my head I've said goodbye to you, even though we couldn't downstairs.

I'll always love you, no matter what.

Sally

Tuesday, 9/4/2096

It's too quiet in this house, too lonely, though the mountain views are breathtaking. This may be the most beautiful of all Rbt's houses. Yet as I float through its rooms, memories of the last time we were here—all three of us, Rbt, Elizabeth, & me—seem to lurk like phantoms. Once I whirled, thinking I saw a shadow moving in a mirror, half-expecting to find Rbt (or his shade) standing behind me, just out of range of the mirror. Or, like a vampire, there without reflection. But his body is buried on the island—how strange to have such thoughts *here* when such fancies never crossed my mind all the time I was within yards of his grave.

I suppose I'm still jumpy about Elizabeth, even though I know I'm safe from her. She knows that if she harms me she'll be exposed. (While Mama, on the contrary, needs special protection: Mama is a witness & apparently was foolish enough to remind Elizabeth of it.)

But Sally's letter, not Elizabeth or Rbt, dominates my thoughts. Stupidly I keep rereading it, because, I suppose, I want to believe what it says. It's so painful thinking about her at all—it would be better if I could simply forget her, wipe her from my memory. For it is her betrayal that has been the most devastating thing of all. Needless to say, I haven't told Grandfather or Mama anything about Sally (or, now that I think of it, many other of the details, either). I keep wondering what has happened to her. Has she claimed her reward & sunk herself into a near-comatose existence? Or has Elizabeth reneged on the deal &—& what? I don't know. My mind goes numb when I think of what Elizabeth is capable & then think of Sally. If Sally's letter had even a grain of truth in it, then Elizabeth will not reward her. I wish I'd paid more attention to their interactions when we were all in the same room together. But I couldn't bear even to glance at her, I didn't want to see the look of revealed complicity & collusion, the triumph & scorn & amusement at Sally's success in duping me, &, possibly, a look of intimacy between them. It seems almost certain they were lovers. Isn't that how Elizabeth works? Rbt recounted enough examples of this for me to be certain of her modus operandi with Sally. In which case Sally would be in love with Elizabeth, &... Why the act at the end, of declaring she wouldn't go? To further distress me? To drive the knife in another millimeter?

No more of this. I'll have a cognac & listen to some music...here by myself.

Why am I alone now? Oh yes, because I wanted to think.

No. That's a lie. The truth is, it's because I have no one. I could still be at Grandfather's apartment. But...what was it he said to me about Mama? "There's one thing you should understand about Felice. She has always wanted more. She will never have enough, no matter what you give her. Like me, you'll have to find your own way to come to terms with this. That doesn't mean she doesn't love one, so you must try not to take it personally. She's always been this way & she always will."

It's as though I know no one else in the world but these blood relatives of mine. How does one start a life at the age of twenty-six as though born naked into the world (albeit wealthy)?

When Elizabeth vacates the house in Georgetown, should I move to DC?

No. That's a bad place to live. I will visit, but never live there for good.

I could simply move from one residence to another—there are enough of them (unless Elizabeth has sold some of them) to keep me endlessly circulating...

Too restless to read. Nietzsche no good for me right now. Too far from my immediate grasp, too much a reproach to my manifest weakness.

Cognac. I'll sit on the terrace & sip cognac while I stare out at the mountains & savor my freedom.

If I've won, why do I feel so hollow inside?

But when I decide what to do about Elizabeth & act on it, I'll feel better. & then I'll create a life for myself.

Wednesday, 9/5/2096

Grandfather phoned today, to say Elizabeth has been calling, desperate to get hold of me. He wouldn't tell her where I am or give her a means of reaching me, for which I'm grateful. She must be hoping to work a deal with me. Maybe trade me all the incriminating stuff she has for the transcript? But I won't give it up. That much I do know. I would be a fool to give it up. I wonder if she's weighing the likelihood of my taking revenge? As opposed to being interested in having her serve special interests I may have? It's possible she might think this, since she can't imagine that I really don't want that kind of power.

Of course, there's a third possibility. That she's thinking of trying to use Sally against me. Again. But if she trots Sally out, throws her at me...

In any event, whether I'm ready to face her now or not, I'm returning to New York. I'm not ready yet to be alone. I will talk with Grandfather—to try to get a feel for the current political situation, for Elizabeth's position these days, for the general climate of things. Perhaps I will let Mama drag me to some of her parties & events.

& then begin seeing to the Estate. Including assessments of how it has fared under Elizabeth. & taking possession of the Georgetown house. & I want to know what she did with all the art & antiques she took from the island house. Rbt told me of her passion for art, far stronger than in most people. Even when she couldn't afford it.

Still I'm writing about her. For how much longer?

Thursday, 9/6/2096

Today for the first time in my life I coped with public air travel. Grandfather wanted to send his jet back to pick me up, but I refused—it'd be an absurd waste, & I had no trouble getting a flight out. Actually, it was an awful experience, even flying first class. (I'm so glad I had Mama's face jewelry behind which to hide the bruises.) Guards with M-19s all over the airport & various checkpoints to pass through. I suppose if I'd insisted on having airline personnel seeing to everything for me (as Grandfather suggested) it wouldn't have been so dreadful. How fortunate that Grandfather's PA was waiting for me at the gate as I disembarked, for the very thought of going through all that hassle again had worked me into the jitters. Interesting, though, seeing how in the first class section they seat men on the right side of the aisle & women on the left. Mostly men, of course, were in first class, & all but one of the few women were career-line. The males appeared not to see me; I got a few glances from the women, but not one of them spoke to me. It was almost like being invisible. Except, of course, to the service-techs. I doubt I'll put up with public air travel again in the future.

Tomorrow I'm to "take possession" of Rbt's apartment—I suppose I'll stay there, since I won't have any excuse to hang around here after that. Grace has the keys & reported over the phone today that he's begun an audit & has started compiling a report for my inspection. & that it will be less than a month before every residence has been cleared of Weatherall's possessions & the locks changed (which I naturally insisted upon). As a precaution I will, for a while anyway, have new security personnel attending to all property. As I recall I don't much like Rbt's apartment here—the total hyper-modern experience, I used to call it. My theory is he liked hyper-modern as much as he did because that was the rage at the time he was advancing so meteorically, & so it held a nostalgic set of associations for him. Maybe I should just gut the apartment & redo it? Or I could sell it, get rid of it altogether. I can always stay with Grandfather (though Mama doesn't—she usually stays at the Dolly Madison Club). But I think, in spite of everything, that Grandfather still likes me. He's been a little reserved, but that may be his natural style.

I know I should be thinking about how to use the transcript against Elizabeth, but it seems whenever I try to think about Elizabeth I end up brooding about Sally. I keep reviewing that last scene with her— it's the letter she left, I suppose, wrenching at me, filling me with doubts (or should I be rash & say *hopes*?). Even though I know how skilled an actor she is, flashes of sheer conviction that she was genuinely afraid of Elizabeth come over me, & I begin worrying about her safety. (Such a familiar train of thought for me, it must be that I still can't take in that she was in every way cooperating with Elizabeth.) Her trembling—well, apart from superb acting, that could have been the excitement of the moment, I suppose. Yet...Elizabeth's suggestion about the amazon taking her upstairs & Sally's assiduous avoidance of them… It seems that it could be the case that she had reason to fear the amazons. Or to fear that even if she had this bargain with Elizabeth, once Elizabeth had used her she wouldn't keep her side of it. It is this, I think, that worries me most. Though I'm a fool for caring what happens to her, I do. I can't lose my deep sense of her. Surely she couldn't have fabricated *everything* about herself, her life? She would have to be a genius to do so, she'd have to have a most remarkable memory & a tough control that would surpass that of even the Company's best clandestine officers.

Of course, that might be what she is.

If I demand an interview with Sally, to make sure she's safe, I risk making even more of a fool of myself. I can imagine them laughing at me, together. Or Elizabeth's trying some new tactic for controlling me through Sally.

Best just to wipe Sally from my memory. As though she never existed. & deal with Elizabeth accordingly.

Friday, 9/7/2096

Moved into the apartment today—ugly, ugly, ugly. I almost decided to go check in at the Dolly Madison. (Mama had me made a member last week.) But I'm not ready for dealing with people like that yet. & besides, I'm too afraid to shed my gorillas, which I'd have to do at any women's club. Elizabeth with her amazons can go anywhere, do anything. I'd put nothing past her. (I hope Mama is being careful. I worry that her desire to thumb her nose at Elizabeth will make her careless.)

Had a long talk with Grandfather today. About the Executive, politics, the economy, the aliens, the executive system, & of course, about Elizabeth. He cautioned me against letting my desire to pull Elizabeth down wreck havoc on the world at large. He said he has no idea what damage I could do with the transcript, but that he thinks it must be considerable for Elizabeth to have gone to such lengths to isolate me.

Basically, his message is that I must be careful not to do anything to bring down the Executive. That Elizabeth is the best thing that's happened to the country since the Transformation. That not only is she finding a way of dealing with the aliens to our advantage (as opposed to the Chinese who, Grandfather gloated, just last week lost several satellites & a nearly-completed space station to alien "destructuring"), but that the economy is in the midst of a strong recovery, & that given the way things are going now they might soon return to the kind of normalcy the executive system had achieved in the '60s & '70s.

Most executives, he said, have come out sharply against Rbt & Rbt's policies & see a need to keep both Military & Security under tight control. Though Mott isn't charismatic & is obviously not a great leader, she has enough rapport within Security & enough of an organizational sense that she's managed to put Security's house in order in a very impressive way, & executives trust her to keep such a tiger reined in. There's widespread fear about the potential for using Security the way Rbt did. & as a proof of how people feel about this, Grandfather says that though there's general anger & disapproval at career-line Mott's having a baby (such weird, shocking news) with a service-tech partner carrying the pregnancy & with the male playing an insignificant role, still people are going to put up with it because of their confidence in Mott's control of Security. At one point he also said, giving me a very grave look, that I shouldn't even *think* about forcing Elizabeth to give me a high-level post, that my name & association with Rbt will make people extremely hostile to & distrustful of me, even people who were supposedly his friends & allies. When I told him I had no interest in such things, he snorted as though he didn't believe me.

It was like a paean to Elizabeth. She's a "necessary evil," he says. I must curb her to protect myself but avoid destroying her. No one but she would be able to pull off what she's doing with the aliens. He apparently places great store by this, which astonishes me: I never imagined he'd come around to thinking it a good thing to deal with the aliens & anarchists!

He suggested he arrange a maternity contract for me. I goggled at him. Then, after a while, I told him that it was inconceivable to me. "What are you going to do with your life?" he asked me. "I can't see you living the way Felice does. Working in Security or any other Department of the Executive is out of the question. & I don't see you working for a private corporation, either." I said I needed some time to think about what to do, that I didn't want to rush into a commitment before scraping my life into a semblance of order. I mentioned that I wanted to get a grip on the business of the Estate, too. & that that would keep me busy for some time. He just raised his eyebrows & said something like "Oh, so you're thinking of playing at *that* game of power." It's true that if I wanted to get involved in high finance & business I wouldn't have to go to work for some damned male executive—I already knew that. But what a deadly boring thought. I didn't try to explain to him that I just want to find out what I should know about the Estate.

So what will I do? Apart from acquiring some electronic musical instruments and learning to play them & trying to compose on them (a fantasy neither Grandmother nor Rbt would indulge me in), I don't have the faintest idea. Whereas while I was on the island I thought that life stretched endlessly before me without my having a chance to live it, now I have this hollow feeling that it stretches endlessly before me but that I'm not creative enough to find a worthwhile way to live it. Still, it's too soon for me to feel bored & useless. This is only my twelfth day of freedom.

Saturday, 9/8/2096

I've talked with her on the phone & made the arrangement. She's to come here tomorrow morning at ten. To this apartment. Alone, without guards. No recording devices. Just the two of us to talk, privately. She wants this meeting more than I do—otherwise she wouldn't be so willing to come here to this apartment rather than my going to DC to her office. (Grace assures me she has begun the process of vacating the Georgetown House; I cautioned him about all the art in that house, as well as the things she ripped out of the island house. He says there's an inventory & tells me she & her people will be out by midnight Monday.) Perhaps, though, she wants to keep me away from her office? But it stands to reason she must be worried about the transcript. She must be as afraid of me as I am of her. Yet I wouldn't put it past her to try something new… & I keep dreaming about Sally. Awful dreams. About Sally & *her*. I haven't decided yet whether or not to bring the subject of Sally into our dealings. There's so much to lose if I do... I'm going out tonight to the theater, by myself. I'm excited, but frightened, too. Have this terror of being recognized, even though my face is new. Of people giving me looks or saying things to me, especially after what Grandfather said about how most people feel about Rbt. As though I carry a mark on my forehead identifying me as Sedgewick's daughter.

Monday, 9/10/2096

Where to begin? It's so complicated a story that I hardly know how to organize the details. Well, start with Elizabeth's arrival here on Sunday morning: I had coffee & fruit & croissants for her (having settled on stunning her with my civility in pointed contrast with her mad savagery, the slowly fading traces of which still mark my face).

When the gorilla showed her into the living room I suffered an emotional rush so powerful it almost knocked me off my feet. The sheer size of that woman (magnified by the mirrored floors & ceiling of that damned hyper-modern room) made my knees shake. I'm reasonably large myself, but *she*...! My first thoughts were horrible flashbacks of memory—of her holding my head under the water so ruthlessly I'd felt certain she meant to drown me, of her using her fist to rape me first on the beach & then later after she pushed me on the stairs & I lost balance & fell sprawling, of the filth she flung at me & oh god I was remembering all this, & my heart pounding with fear, my face burning with shame—until the wave of anger hit me, overwhelming the fear & shame, almost swallowing me up. I actually slipped my hand into my pocket & took hold of the little low caliber palm pistol I had armed myself with. I think she saw all this happening with me—but she pretended to ignore it & nonchalantly began checking the room for on-site recorders. We both used jammers, neither of us taking any chances. I wondered about her wearing a recorder, but decided all the jamming equipment I had running—& my gorilla's electronic inspection of her before they let her into this room with me—must be assurance enough.

She started by asking me—as though making social chitchat—if I'd enjoyed the play I'd gone to see the night before. The point of this was to make me aware of her surveillance of me. I countered by asking her if the book she had made Kay write in still existed. Obviously that vexed her, for, waving a thickly buttered fragment of croissant to gesture to the floor & ceiling, she remarked on how "tacky" this apartment is & said that for her part she never understood why Rbt had had it anyway, when DC was so close, & that the one time she'd come here it had occurred to her that this room must have been designed to enhance his "sexual games" with me & the thought had been so revolting she'd decided never to come here again.

Of course this made my blood boil. & not having a retort ready made it worse. "Is that what you've been requesting an appointment to say?" I asked.

She bent over, took hold of her attaché case & pulled it into her lap. I fingered the pistol as she opened it (even knowing the gorillas must have searched it for weapons). She pulled out a sheaf of papers that she tossed in my direction with one flick of the wrist. I did not retrieve them from their scattered fall over the floor. "They're copies of your diary & transcripts of Sally's loquazene interrogations," she said. Her lips curved in a sneer. "It's a matter of establishing what sort of credibility you'd have if you attempt something stupid."

"The copies of the diary," I said, "wouldn't be credible since you don't have the original. No expert would ever agree to verify them as being mine since it's well known anything can be done cutting & pasting & so on with an optical scanner. As for the loquazene interrogations, showing them to anyone would be illegal."

"None of that matters," she said. "It won't matter to executive society at large. & to tell you the truth, Alexandra, no one would ever want to take your part. I never saw a bunch of people so eager to dissociate themselves from their former connections as your father's supporters were after I reformed the Executive. You think they want you coming around reminding them of things they'd rather forget?"

"But the transcript shows what a fool you made of everyone," I said. "I could take that transcript to George Booth, for instance. He'd know how to use it."

She laughed. "That old git? He's washed up, he's lost everything. Who'd even give him the time of day, much less *listen* to anything he tried to say?" & she leaned forward to butter another croissant. I should have known she'd hang so tough—that she wouldn't give an inch without a fight. She ate a couple of bites of the croissant & said, "Actually, apart from assuring you that I'll more than match anything you throw at me, I've come to offer you a job. In Security. Overseas, a nice comfortable embassy job. You've got skills, though of course we don't do things your father's way these days."

"You think I'd take a job from you?" I laughed. "& here's my Grandfather wanting to arrange a maternity contract for me. Christ, you neither of you seem to——"

"A maternity contract?" she interrupted. "Surely you're joking! Even a silly cunt like you can't think I'd permit the Secretary of Health to allow you—depraved as you are & carrying such obviously defective genes—to reproduce?"

I'd long ago known I would never trust myself to have a child—but to have *her* insult me this way, & to call me that name, was more than I could take. Recklessly I flung down the gauntlet: "Before we go any further, I want you to know what I've arranged for the Kay Zeldin transcript." Her face went very still. "In the event of my death or of my not making a regularly appointed contact, the transcript will be given to Martha Greenglass or Hazel Bell or one of the other Free Zone leaders." This was a lie: I'd arranged nothing—so far. It was because of my catch-up reading of the *E.T.* that these names came so readily to my lips.

The most astonishing thing happened as I delivered this threat: all the color drained from her face—even from her lips—& her skin went a sick, greasy white; the croissant dropped out of her hand onto the floor, sweat broke out on her white-gray face, & she began gasping for breath. I watched, astonished, as she tore at the neck of her tunic until she'd loosened it. She said, gasping out the words, "How did you find out? You don't have the contacts, you couldn't possibly know——" But she caught herself here, & the color began coming back into her face.

"Would you like some water, Elizabeth?" I asked. My brain raced & sped trying to make connections. The first & obvious question was how her negotiations with the anarchists could matter so much to her. The second question was whether there was some special significance to my threat that I knew nothing about. It seemed obvious there was, given what she had started to say while her thoughts were still scrambled.

"Yes, please," she said. Wanting time to recover, I guessed. I went to the cabinet where half-liter bottles of water are stored and fetched two; I handed one to Elizabeth with a glass & helped myself to the other. "& of course Mama is a witness to how you were keeping Kay Zeldin," I said as I twisted the cap off the bottle. "Like a prisoner in a twentieth-century concentration camp, is how Mama put it." I poured water into a glass. "Whatever you might say about *me*, there's nothing wrong with Mama's credibility."

She gulped most of the water before answering. "Let's trade dirt, Alexandra." Her voice was still perceptibly unsteady. "You give me all your copies of the transcript, I'll give you all the loquazene interrogation transcripts & my copies of your diary."

I shook my head. "You think I'd trust you? After the way you've treated me? & besides, it wouldn't be an equal trade. What would anyone care about my relationship with Rbt? Especially if I live the rest of my life in obscurity?" I managed to smile at her. "No, I'm not the one with a reputation & power to lose."

She licked her lips. "Then what in the hell do you want from me?"

I shrugged. "Have I made any demands on you?"

"You just threatened me, Alexandra, not five minutes ago."

"I only told you what would happen if I were to die or disappear," I said. Then it came to me what I needed to say next, to force her to face the possible consequences for everything she had done to me. "But of course," I added, "this would be true in the event of my suicide, too."

She looked horrified. "What the fuck can I say to that?"

"You're the one who's made such a mess of my life, who's made me feel the way I do," I said. This wasn't the entire truth. I've hated myself a long time now. But after everything she's done to me, it was true that at that moment, even now that I was free, I could feel the hopelessness creeping back over me.

She swallowed the rest of the water & set the glass down on the table with a snap so violent I thought the glass would shatter. "Let me tell you about Sally," she offered.

Was this what I'd been—unconsciously—hoping for when I brought up suicide (apart from wanting to frighten her & make her feel guilty, supposing such a thing is possible for someone as savage as she is)? But I wasn't sure I wanted to know about Sally. "You think you can manipulate me through her the way you hoped to manipulate my father through Kay?"

She shook her head. "No. The situation isn't the same. That is, I've no control over the girl at all. She's such an emotional mess that I've had to sedate her."

"What, you aren't keeping your side of the bargain with her?" I asked, trying to make my voice & face rigid, cold, emotionless.

"She doesn't want it," Elizabeth said.

"What did you do to her to make her so distraught, & why?" I asked. "Surely she played her part to perfection. What more could you have asked of her?"

"For godsake, you fool, the girl is in love with you!" she shouted at me. "If you didn't spend your entire goddam existence feeling sorry for yourself you wouldn't have pushed her away without the slightest doubt of her complicity. Don't you see—"

"She's a damned good actor," I shouted back.

She kept silent for a while, then shrugged. "So it isn't Sally you want. Then what? Must I find you another lover? What is it I have to do to keep you from wrecking my life?"

Wrecking her life? I wish I understood what it is about my threatening to give the transcript to the Free Zone leaders that had her so freaked.

Thoughts of Sally's letter kept crossing my mind; worse, the need to know she was all right pressed all the more strongly on me now that I knew I could probably force Elizabeth to let me see the girl's situation for myself. But the thought of facing the girl, of possibly being subjected to another piece of playacting & manipulation, made me sick to my stomach. How would I know the truth? It occurred to me I'd have a better chance of gauging for myself if I made Elizabeth take me to Sally without giving the latter advance notice. "All right," I said, "I'll see her. On one condition."

She looked relieved—thus reviving my suspicions. "What's your condition?"

"That we go to her at once, without warning."

She looked a little panicked at this. "But that's not possible," she said. "I'm keeping Sally in a safehouse about seventy-five miles outside Coeur d'Alene, Idaho."

"Idaho! Why in the hell—"

She interrupted, flashing me an angry look. "I just told you I can't control her. It was either get her away from everybody or jail her, & I wasn't ready to go that far with her when I know—" She broke off, & though I pressed her to finish, she refused.

"Well I don't see why we can't simply go," I finally said.

"But security & transportation arrangements would have to be made—"

"We'll make them as we go," I said, determined to make sure she had no chance of delivering a warning.

It would have been easier if I'd finished getting a pilot & insurance & a maintenance contract for Rbt's jet lined up, but a call to Grandfather got me instant access to his jet, & a second call a reservation for a charter chopper out of Coeur d'Alene (since the safehouse was in the middle of nowhere). & so we made our slow way to Sally. Five minutes before our arrival I allowed Elizabeth to radio her security crew at the safehouse to notify them of our arrival. I certainly didn't want to risk their firing on us by mistake.

When we piled out of the chopper, a well-dressed service-tech & a number of amazons carrying M-19s greeted us. Calling the service-tech "Anne," Elizabeth announced we'd come to visit Sally. Anne's eyes darted back & forth between my face & Elizabeth's; her dark face was ashy, her hands fairly writhing. We entered the house, & Anne led the way to Sally's room. My heart thudded painfully when Anne opened Sally's door; oddly enough it was a worse moment than facing Elizabeth that morning had been. Once the door was open, everything happened in a blur: I heard a cry from Sally, then was almost knocked over as she flung herself at me. Apparently Elizabeth drew Anne away, for I found myself alone with Sally with the door closed. Before I could say anything she started asking me about my nose & the other bruises. Everything was so out of control, so crazy that all I did was attempt to respond to each new thing—I didn't have the toughness to be cold to her, to assess her veracity, to hold myself apart from her. She had no idea that I'd gotten free of Elizabeth & concluded that Elizabeth had brought me to the safehouse by force. So I told her that I'd escaped & had gotten the upper hand with Elizabeth. Once she knew that I was no longer Elizabeth's prisoner, she said she could "explain" everything if only I'd listen to her, & please couldn't I forgive her.

The upshot was that the four of us—Elizabeth, Sally, Anne, & myself—flew back to New York together. Elizabeth said nothing to—or about—Sally. I assume she regards my taking Sally from her as yet one more headache. Obviously if I ever decided to press charges (abduction, etc.) against Elizabeth, Sally would be a prime witness in the case. All of which strengthens my sense that the threat of my death & the transcript's being passed on to the Free Zone leaders (which would somehow "wreck" her life) is more terrible than the threat of her possible prosecution on felony charges.

When we got back to the apartment (having left Elizabeth & Anne at the airport, where they boarded Elizabeth's jet), Sally poured out a tale about Elizabeth's attempt to get her plugged in—&, according to what *Anne* had told Sally, *permanently* plugged in, as a way of negating the threat that Sally posed. Further, Anne had not only told Sally about Elizabeth's plan (Elizabeth had apparently given Anne an ultimatum about accomplishing this objective) but had hatched a plot for the two of them to escape to the Free Zone that very night—Anne, apparently, having decided to go renegade. I have to say that Sally has a talent for endearing herself to others. She & Anne had been convinced, when the amazon had told them about Elizabeth's impending arrival, that Elizabeth, losing patience, had come to plug Sally in herself.

We'll be going to DC tomorrow to take possession of the house. One of the first orders of business will be to set up a meeting with Anne. Sally's anxious to properly thank her, & I want to talk to Anne myself, since Sally believes she has contacts in the Free Zone. In particular, I want to ask her about Elizabeth's relations with Free Zone leaders. I probably won't get anywhere, but it's a start. I need to find out what matters so critically to Elizabeth. After what she did to Sally, there's no doubt in my mind that she must be punished—by me.

Chapter Thirty-five

Hazel input the address Anne had given her into the vehicle's system. According to the map that appeared onscreen, the address was not far from Liz's house. It would be easy driving there, since that neighborhood lacked any mass-auto facilities. It must, she thought as she pulled into traffic, be Allison Bennett's house. How else would Anne be living in such a neighborhood?

Per Anne's request, she had destroyed the note as soon as she had read it. The mystery of a private messenger and the level of confidentiality Anne begged of her lent an air of urgency to the otherwise uncommunicative message: *Please come to see me in the morning at the address below. It's a matter of great importance to me. If anyone asks, say you tried contacting me at the Office of Information, found I was out, and decided to drop in on me at home.*

Since Anne's move to DC Hazel had seen her only that one time in Liz's office; Anne's friendliness then had been perfunctory rather than effusive. The mystery of Anne's wanting to see her privately had combined with the emotional backwash from the scene with Liz to sabotage a good part of the night's sleep. How could she have guessed that any of that had been going on in Liz's head for all these weeks? Or that her refusal to go see Liz's new house ("the first of its kind, architecturally, anywhere in the world") would trigger such an outburst?

*Every afternoon that I sit here with you I have this fantasy, Hazel, a fantasy I half-expect to happen. I imagine you calling me "Rapunzel" and unbraiding me. I imagine you—*But Hazel had made her stop, had threatened to leave if she didn't. *I know you still have an attraction to me, I can* feel *it. What is it, faithfulness to someone else, is that why you keep me at arm's length?* The image of Liz wringing her hands, visibly restraining herself from touching her, had become etched in

Hazel's memory, giving the lie to their mostly business-like dealings their three late afternoons a week.

Hazel glanced at the number on the gate and confirmed that this large old house was indeed the address Anne had given her. She encountered an amazon at the door but otherwise failed to perceive special security precautions of the sort with which Liz surrounded her house. Summoned by the amazon, Anne greeted her as though she had just decided to drop in and visit. "Come upstairs with me, I've a sitting room up there," she said, taking Hazel's arm.

As they climbed the stairs Hazel babbled about how she had called the Office of Information and learned that Anne had taken the day off and had decided to chance her being home and receiving visitors. Anne responded in kind, and somehow they reached the sitting room by the time they had exhausted the spurious subject.

"Thank you so much for coming, Hazel." Anne leaned against the closed door. "I was afraid you wouldn't. Because of, well, the coolness between us the last few years." Her dark eyes glittered with a sudden welling of tears. She swallowed. "I never should have left the Free Zone. I know that now. I guess I've been pretty stupid about certain things."

"What is it?" Hazel asked, vaguely alarmed: Anne looked so *shaken*.

Anne put the back of her hand to her forehead. "I need your help. Something's happened that's made me see that I can't simply leave— maybe I never could? I guess I always thought that if I didn't like it here I could just go back whenever I wanted to." She blinked rapidly, and Hazel saw that she was on the edge of tears. "The difference here—it makes me feel awful, about myself and about so many things. Everything's so, well...corrupt." She took a deep breath. "What I'm saying is, I want to go back to the Free Zone. But I need help. Because Weatherall—" She put her hands to her cheeks.

"What you're saying is that you can't be comfortable, you can't be *yourself* in their construction of reality," Hazel said softly.

Anne mumbled something inarticulate.

Hazel went to her and cupped her palms over Anne's shoulders. "I'll help you, of course I will, Anne," she said softly. "Just tell me what you need from me and I'll do my best."

Anne dropped her hands from her face. "You're probably thinking *I told you so*, aren't you."

Hazel shook her head. "I'm too busy wondering what Liz has to do with all this."

Anne laughed shortly and stepped back. "A lot. Almost everything. Although... Who knows how much longer I would have been able to stay? Even though I didn't know it until everything happened, it had been getting harder and harder."

"Do you feel like telling me about it?"

Anne suggested they sit down, & they settled themselves on the floor. Anne stared at the rug & drew a deep breath. "I've been having doubts about my work and about living here almost from the first week I moved here. But a few weeks ago Weatherall 'borrowed' me from the Office of Information for a special assignment." As Anne talked her long, bony fingers pleated and unpleated the fabric belt girding the waist of the gown she wore. Occasionally she raised her eyes to meet Hazel's. "The assignment involved handling a prisoner. This prisoner was to be kept in a safehouse somewhere in Idaho in the vicinity of Coeur d'Alene. Weatherall told me the prisoner was very upset and would probably have to be kept tranquilized, and that part of the payment for her services for the job she had done for Weatherall was access at will to an apparatus for plugging in."

Hazel gasped.

"It seems that actors are ordinarily given limited access to plugging in. So they develop a taste for it." Anne swallowed and cleared her throat before going on. "At a certain point Weatherall told me that she expected the prisoner to plug herself in permanently. Thereby solving a certain problem for Weatherall—the problem being that she had not only been 'turned' in the course of her work for Weatherall, but had also learned too much about something Weatherall wanted kept quiet. And since the prisoner was upset and angry at Weatherall, Weatherall was afraid she would blab this information if not forcibly prevented from doing so."

"My god," Hazel said. "You're saying that Liz hoped this woman would fry her brains and thus negate herself as a threat to Liz's security?"

"Yes. But it turned out this woman—her name is Sally—didn't want to plug in at all. I wasn't supposed to let her talk to me or anyone else about certain dangerous topics. But as time went on I began to get hints of what was going on. I *liked* her, Hazel. She's had a terrible life. *That* we were allowed to talk about. But I was beginning to realize that she had become terribly unhappy because she had fallen in love with someone the job had brought her into contact with. And that *that* was what Weatherall meant by 'turned.' Still, there wasn't anything I could do for her but try to pull her out of her depression. Which is what I did, until Weatherall started upping the pressure on me. But last week she called me back to DC and told me to plug Sally in whether she wanted it or not. It was then I decided to go renegade and escape with Sally."

Hazel whispered. "She told you to do *that?*"

Anne's eyes looked bleakly into Hazel's. "I pretended to be willing to go along with it. If I'd objected, Weatherall would have done it herself and made sure I paid for my rebellion." She swallowed convulsively. "Who knows what she would have done to me then, given all the things I knew because of that assignment. So when I returned to Idaho, I got Sally to tell me everything she knew. It turned out she had been hired to pretend she was a courtesan to make it easier for Weatherall to manage Sedgewick's daughter Alexandra, whom she had been keeping on an island off the coast of Maine since Sedgewick's death." Hazel gaped at her. "I know, it sounds totally off the wall. I think I might not have believed it if Sally had told me that straight off. But at this point I'd believe almost any weird thing someone might tell me about Weatherall. Anyway. This Alexandra tried to suicide by throwing herself off a cliff...it's a long and ugly story, I won't go into the details Sally gave me. But basically the woman was put back together again, and Sally, who had been locked away the whole time this woman was in medical treatment, was returned to the island. And she found everything changed. New guards. No staff. The entire house wrecked—by Weatherall. Alexandra wanting nothing to do with Sally, who was by this time in love with her. But it turns out Alexandra was in love with Sally, too, and eventually they worked things out... at which point Weatherall appeared on the scene and dragged Sally away. She also told Alexandra about the original deal—of Sally's job of spying on and pretending to fall in love with Alexandra. Alexandra believed Weatherall. Hence Sally's distraught state.

"After Sally told me her story, I told her about my plan for our escape to the Free Zone. We were going to do it Sunday night." Anne fell silent.

"But you didn't escape, did you," Hazel said, afraid Anne said no more because Liz had come and plugged Sally in herself.

Anne managed to smile. "We didn't have to. On Sunday afternoon Weatherall arrived—with Alexandra. At first I thought she'd come to plug Sally in herself. But it turns out that somehow Alexandra not only escaped her confinement, but also has enough of a hold over Weatherall that she was able to force her to release Sally as well. So the four of us flew back east, Sally and Alexandra staying in New York, and Weatherall and me coming back to DC."

"But that's wonderful!" Hazel said. "It sounds as though everything worked out fine."

Anne nodded. "On the plane back Weatherall was very complimentary to me. And said she'd like me to transfer to her office. That she needed loyal, bright, trustworthy people like me she could count on." Anne said this in a voice devoid of all expression.

"Oh shit," Hazel said.

"There's no way I'll go to work for her."

"I can see why you don't feel you can leave openly. How do you want to do it? I can contact a Marq'ssan immediately, you know. Are you in that big a hurry?"

"I—" Anne began, but stopped as a phone chirped. "Excuse me," she said, pulling a handset out of her pocket. "This is Anne Hawthorne," she said softly into the phone. "Oh! But of course, yes, that would be fine... Yes, that's fine. See you then." She returned the handset to her pocket. "Believe it or not, that was Alexandra Sedgewick. She's on her way over here with Sally."

Hazel said, "Would you like me to leave?"

"No, not unless you wouldn't be comfortable meeting them. I was thinking that, well, maybe you should know all this about Weatherall. Because of the negotiations."

Anne *had* changed. Hazel said, "She won't be expecting it."

"Who won't be expecting what?"

"Liz won't be expecting you to go renegade. It's my guess she'd trust you with almost anything."

"But why? I don't understand. Everyone's made such a big thing about my having gone renegade with Allison."

"It's because of something you said to me that first time I took you into Seattle from the Redmond house. You said that if we were caught by Sedgewick's people we'd deserve everything we'd get, because we were traitors. You remember that?"

Anne frowned. "*I* said that?"

Hazel smiled. "And when I told Liz you'd said that—for she was pretty suspicious of you up to that point—all doubts she had about you vanished."

"So she thought I'd do more or less anything—" Anne began, then stopped as a chime tinkled somewhere in the room. "They've arrived," she said. "That's the signal that I've got a guest downstairs."

The strange thing, Hazel thought as she waited for Anne's return, was that though she found the story bizarre, nothing in her protested that Liz couldn't have done such a thing. The intent to forcibly plug someone in...that wrenched in the worst way, it made her so sick she didn't know how she could bear to face Liz again. *When I am in power,* Liz used to say in the Redmond days. *When I am in power there will be no more human rights abuse.* If she confronted Liz, would Liz deny that she had intended Anne to do that? Probably. And act hurt that Hazel could believe such a thing of her.

Anne ushered in two women, one an executive, very tall (though not as tall as Liz), with striking eyes in a pale, bruised face, the other a petite service-tech, very pretty, reddish-haired. Hazel got up from the floor, and Anne closed the door. "I'd like you to meet a friend of mine from the Free Zone, Hazel Bell," she said to the women. "Hazel, meet Alexandra Sedgewick and Sally McGuire." Hazel shook hands with them.

"I know your name from the newspapers," Alexandra Sedgewick said to Hazel. "You're one of the women negotiating with the Executive, aren't you?"

"Yes, I'm that Hazel Bell."

"Why don't we sit down," Anne said.

So they settled on the floor, Anne and Hazel in their previous places and Alexandra and Sally with their backs against the sofa. After a
few moments in which no one said anything, Anne got up and went
over to a cupboard, muttering something about getting everyone some
water to drink, and returned with glasses and bottles for everyone.
After each of them opened a bottle and emptied it into the glass provided, the silence returned.

They don't know, Hazel thought, that I know about what happened out in Idaho. Should she say something if Anne didn't? "Are
you any relation to the Sedgewick who used to be Chief of Security?"
Hazel was surprised to hear herself ask.

Alexandra's gaze swung sharply onto Hazel's face. "Yes," she said
dryly. "His daughter."

Hazel hurriedly swallowed another sip of water. How stupid of
her to have asked such a bald question. "You don't look anything like
him," she said for lack of anything else to say that could possibly follow such a question and answer.

Alexandra flushed scarlet. "You met him?"

Hazel nodded.

Alexandra swallowed. "I'm so sorry." She glanced at Anne. "I had
no idea. Maybe I should—"

Hazel realized that Alexandra assumed that she, Hazel—perhaps
because Anne had identified her as a Free Zone activist?—must have
met Sedgewick under the worst of circumstances. "A few weeks before she and I went renegade I was Elizabeth Weatherall's secretary,"
Hazel said quickly.

Alexandra's breath rushed out. "Oh, I see." Then, after two or
three seconds, she stared hard at Hazel and frowned. "You know, I
thought there was something familiar about your name…and now I
think I know what it is. Though I'm not sure… There were reports
about Elizabeth that my father sometimes told me about. I suppose
they were after you, too?" Hazel nodded. "Well there was one report
that especially caught my attention." Her smile was self-deprecating.
"I had rather adolescent romantic preoccupations at the time."

Out of the corner of her eye, Hazel caught Sally's look of surprised interest.

"There was a report about Elizabeth that he found incredible. But when he had a chance to question the witness himself, he had to accept it as true. The report was that Elizabeth caught a naval intelligence officer breaking into her house. That she began to beat him, to get information out of him. But that the woman with her—the lover and secretary who had gone renegade with her—made her stop." Alexandra's smile grew bitter. "I was positively starry-eyed at the thought of love having that kind of power."

"I was that person," Hazel said. "How strange to think of such a thing going into a report."

"But now you are a Free Zone leader?"

"Not a leader," Hazel said. "We don't have leaders, exactly. Just an activist."

"All right. An activist. But you first went to the Free Zone with Elizabeth?"

"Yes. After about a year, we had a parting of the ways, Liz and I. And now, as you're obviously thinking, here I am negotiating with her."

"Am I being too intrusive?"

Hazel laughed. "The only person who might mind is Liz herself. Though I doubt that."

"It's common knowledge," Anne said, "that Elizabeth Weatherall still has a thing for Hazel."

Alexandra looked startled.

"Come on, Anne, surely we have better things to talk about than that," Hazel said, trying to nerve herself to take the gauche plunge. "Why don't you tell them—for I presume you said nothing on your way up here—"that I know about what went down this weekend out in Idaho."

Anne flashed her an amused look. "I guess I *don't* need to tell them, since you just did."

"We wanted to see you, Anne, to thank you for everything," Sally said. "And—" she glanced at Alexandra. "Would it be indiscreet, do you think, for me to...?"

"Go ahead," Alexandra said softly. Hazel noticed that their hands, resting on the floor between them, were just lightly touching, little finger to little finger.

"We wanted to offer help," Sally said. "Alexandra can help you if you feel you need to get away. In case Weatherall, well, if it's bad for you to have been involved in all that. I mean—"

"I know what you mean," Anne said, smiling. "Thank you. Actually, that's the reason Hazel is here. She's going to help me get to the Free Zone."

"I have a plane," Alexandra said. "It's at your service. All I need is an hour's notice."

Hazel looked at Anne. "That might be better," Hazel said. "You could go this afternoon. Unless you'd rather call in the Marq'ssan?"

Anne looked at Alexandra. "Thanks very much. I think I will take you up on your offer." She bit her lip. "Lise is out of town, and I said goodbye to my parents last night. The sooner I leave, the better."

"I can have the plane ready to go whenever you like."

"I've already packed everything I'm going to be able to take with me," Anne said. "How about...one o'clock?"

Alexandra nodded. "One o'clock it is." And she dug into her tunic pocket and pulled out a handset.

It was settled, so quickly, so simply. What must Anne be feeling, turning her back on everything she had always thought she loved? Leaving Allison, for whom she had—with anguish—gone renegade once before?

Anne shifted closer to Hazel and under cover of Alexandra's phone call whispered, "I can't believe it's happening so fast."

Hazel took Anne's hand. "But at least this time," she whispered back, "you know what you're going to and that that's where you want to be."

"Yes. This time it's my decision," she said, as though realizing it for the first time. "I don't really believe I'm in danger now. It's just that I don't want to stay here, I don't want to work for people who..." Anne folded Hazel into a hug. "I feel like I'm going home," she whispered.

Hazel, inhaling Anne's flowery scent, pressed her close. "You are, Anne," she whispered back. "You are going home."

[ii]

As they waited for the plane to take off ("just to make sure," Alexandra said, "that there's no unexpected hitch") they sipped water and chatted. Why, Hazel wondered, had she agreed to come out here in Alexandra's car to see Anne off? Why had she let herself be talked into leaving her own car at the hotel and riding in Alexandra's? And why had Alexandra pressed her to do so?

"There's something I've been wondering," Alexandra said, "but I didn't want to ask Anne herself. And that is why she's living in Allison Bennett's house."

Hazel looked at Alexandra. "She was Allison's lover. For years and years. Long before I knew her and Liz. It must be close to twenty years they've been together."

"And she's leaving like that, without even saying goodbye?" Sally asked.

The small, sleek plane inched out from the apron, positioned itself at the head of the runway, and halted. And then it raced down the runway and lifted into the air.

Alexandra's driver started the engine. "What is Allison Bennett like?" Alexandra asked.

"She's an executive woman. She's been close to Liz for years. Has known her all her life. I imagine, though I'm not that up-to-date on Liz's personal relations, that they're still very close." Hazel's gaze met Alexandra's. "Why do you ask?" The car pulled out.

"It shouldn't be difficult to understand why I might be inquisitive about Elizabeth."

The car entered the access road, and they sped away from the small private airport Hazel hadn't known existed. "I have the strangest feeling," Hazel said, "that there's something you want from me."

Alexandra's gaze flickered. "Information," she said. "One of the reasons I wanted to see Anne today was to ask her for an introduction to someone in your group—which I assumed she could arrange because of what Sally had told me about Anne's certainty of getting help from people in the Free Zone."

"What sort of information?"

Alexandra toyed with one of her rings. "This is difficult. Very difficult," she said. "And I'm terribly awkward because I'm so unused to talking to people."

Hazel waited. What could Sedgewick's daughter want to ask a Free Zone activist?

"You're closely involved in the negotiations, aren't you."

"I talk with Liz three times a week."

"Which is why your name is in the paper so often." Alexandra gnawed at her lip. "Everything I've heard and read makes it clear that the negotiations are important, that they may be the best thing to have happened to this country in years. Consequently, I have some scruples about pursuing a matter that could be construed as being merely a personal affair." Her lips wavered in a hesitant smile that vanished as quickly as it had appeared. "You see, I hate Elizabeth. For what she did to Sally, for what she did to me. You can have no idea how——" Frowning, she stopped herself, then drew a deep breath. "What I'm trying to say is, to find out what I want to know might require telling you things that would impact on you personally in a way that might affect the negotiations."

Hazel smoothed her fingers over the leather upholstery. "I don't see what you could possibly say to inspire more negative feelings in me about Liz than I already have." During the two hours she had spent alone at the hotel that morning after her meeting with Anne, she had thought of how she would have to face Liz with everything she had learned from Anne and had wondered if she could bring herself to go on with the afternoon meetings. But the expression on Alexandra's face...

Hazel's heart thudded heavily as a sense of dread possessed her. She became convinced that Alexandra's revelation would shatter something that still lived deep inside her, vulnerable yet protected despite everything that had happened between them ten years ago, despite even the sickness she felt from Anne's revelation. She did not want to know what Alexandra was talking about. But she would not stop Alexandra from telling her, either.

"I was wondering," Alexandra said, "if there were any other reason besides protection of the negotiations that Elizabeth would have for not wanting something, ah, negative, to get out to you, Martha Greenglass, or others of the Free Zone activists."

Hazel noticed that Alexandra had switched to saying "activists" instead of "leaders." She had known very few executives to be that quick to learn. "Yes," Hazel said. "I think I know why. Because of

what Anne mentioned earlier. That she still has a 'thing' for me."
Hazel looked into Alexandra's eyes. "It's true. Crazy as it may seem."

Alexandra's breath soughed out in a great rush. "Yes, yes, I see.
That fits everything I know." Hazel glanced out the window and saw
that they were on the freeway. "To be honest, there's another reason besides not wanting to spoil the negotiations that concerns me,"
Alexandra said after a long silence. "The reason I was able to force her
to take me to Sally was her fear that I would kill myself if she didn't."
Hazel looked at Alexandra. "You see, I told her I'd arranged for a certain box of documents to be given to you or Martha Greenglass if I
were to die." Hazel gasped. "It was a shot in the dark and affected her
more than I'd anticipated. My idea had been to threaten to give you
and Greenglass ammunition, to threaten to screw up her negotiations.
I'd had no idea there was this other thing, too." Alexandra smiled
faintly. "You can see why I might hesitate to go ahead and inform you
about the documents now. In a way, *not* telling you is a guarantee she
won't have me excised."

Hazel put her hand to her mouth as hot bile surged into her throat.

"Are you all right?"

Hazel swallowed several times to clear the acrid, horrid stuff out
of her mouth. "Just feeling a little sick at all this."

"Oh fuck, you were her lover. Is it possible you still—I hadn't
thought—"

"No, I'm not still in love with her," Hazel said. "It's not that. It's
just that...I did love her once, intensely, and..."

"I know about that," Alexandra said quickly. "I understand too
well. I—" But she broke off before finishing her sentence and shook
her head.

"This has to do with the reason she kept you there?"

Alexandra made a sound in her throat. "Christ this is hard to talk
about. I know it sounds awful, but I could use a drink. This is so...
May I ask you, Hazel, if you would mind coming over to my house and
talking with me before going back to the hotel? I can't see how..."
Her hands twisted in her lap.

"All right," Hazel said, wishing they could erase everything that
had been said and go on as though nothing had been started.

Alexandra spoke to the driver over the intercom. Then she said, very low, "And besides, Sally should be spared all this." She put her hand on Sally's. "I don't want her to know something Elizabeth would feel it worth harming her for. She wouldn't hurt you, Hazel, because of how she feels about you. But anyone else…"

They did not speak again until the car turned into the drive that Hazel had thought belonged to Liz. Jerked out of her sick dread, Hazel said, "Here? We're stopping at Liz's? What the hell is—"

"No," Alexandra said, "this is *my* house. She used it as her own, but it belongs to me."

"Oh," Hazel said weakly, noticing now that the guards were male and did not wear the mauve and gray livery all Liz's guards and service-techs wore. A feeling of nightmare stole over her as the car stopped at the front door and a service-tech stepped out of the house and opened the car door.

Numbly Hazel followed Alexandra and Sally into the house, watched them wrangle briefly about whether or not Sally should be present, then walked with Alexandra through the house until they came to a room full of books and heavy dark furniture, a room she had never seen on her previous visits to this house. Hazel collapsed in one of a pair of enormous leather-upholstered chairs and watched as Alexandra got out a bottle of cognac, drew its cork, and poured at least two ounces each into a couple of snifters.

Alexandra took the mate to Hazel's chair, and for a minute or two they sipped the smooth, fiery liquid in silence. "You look as terrible as I feel," Alexandra said. "I'm in such a state I'm literally shaking. I keep wondering if I'm making a terrible mistake."

"You'd better tell me," Hazel said. "Or else I'll ask her myself."

Alexandra choked, and her teeth clinked against her glass as she jerked it away from her mouth. "You'd do that?"

"I have to know now, though I dread knowing," Hazel said. "You were right to hesitate to ask me what you wanted to know. Once you asked me it was already too late." She again lifted the glass to her lips, inhaled deeply, and sipped.

"You're from the Free Zone. So probably you've at least heard of Kay Zeldin," Alexandra said.

Hazel's head jerked up. "Yes. She's known as our 'founding mother.' I've read her book. And heard stories told of her."

"She was once very close to my father," Alexandra said.

Startled, Hazel labored to recall all that Kay had written about Sedgewick. It had been a long time since she'd read that book. "This thing has to do with Kay Zeldin?"

"It has everything to do with her."

"Oh, wait," Hazel said as relief suddenly flooded her. "I know what it is. Liz has already told me."

"What?" Alexandra cried. "She's *told* you? But why then would she go to such lengths to keep you from finding out?"

Hazel frowned. "Oh, I see. Could she have forgotten she told me?" Dread crept back into her heart. "You *are* talking about her having personally captured Kay, aren't you?"

"Christ, no," Alexandra said.

"Oh." Hazel took another swallow of cognac. "All right, go on."

"Everyone thinks Kay was executed shortly after she was captured," Alexandra said, her voice tremoring. "But she wasn't. Elizabeth kept her alive."

Hazel almost dropped her glass. "I don't understand. Why would—" Hazel stopped, and her mind shut down: she waited in a suspended state of dread for something she would not try to imagine. She crossed her legs to make her knees stop shaking, but even pressed tightly together they still trembled violently.

"She thought she saw a use for her. You see, my father had a breakdown after Kay brought down the Executive and dumped him on the island. He couldn't take it, her betraying him. He was...well, severely depressed. Anyway, once they resumed contact with the outside world, Elizabeth ran things for a while in his name because he wouldn't." Alexandra paused.

"Yes, she told me that," Hazel said after a while.

Alexandra got up from her chair. "This is much harder to talk about than I ever imagined." She fetched the bottle. "I've never talked with anyone about this." She tilted the bottle against the lip of Hazel's snifter, and Hazel watched the golden liquor stream down the curve of the glass. "Only a little sparring with Elizabeth." Alexandra moved the bottle from Hazel's glass to her own. "I read it in the dead of night. It's different, talking about it like this with an unwarped human being with the ordinary emotional responses common to most human beings."

Shivering, Hazel downed another mouthful of cognac. "There are documents, you're saying?"

"Yes. An enormous transcript of several thousand pages. Mostly of conversations between Elizabeth and Kay. And a few with Allison Bennett."

"Allison! *Allison* was in on this?"

"Yes," Alexandra said. "Elizabeth couldn't have done it alone. I suppose she knows whom she can trust."

It had been Allison who had helped Liz drag her down to the under-basement of the Redmond house; it had been Allison who had helped keep her from sleeping; it had been Allison who had helped conduct her loquazene interrogation. Yes, Hazel could believe Allison might have been involved.

"I don't know how to describe what Elizabeth did to Kay," Alexandra said. "I really don't. She kept her in solitary confinement, but that wasn't all. She used all sorts of psychological machinations against her. Kay was strong and resisted her for a long time. But Elizabeth put more and more pressure on her. And knew her most vulnerable spot. And Kay began falling apart." Alexandra gulped more cognac. "I guess that's how you could describe it. She just couldn't take any more."

"What are you saying?" Hazel whispered, closing her eyes to stop the rush of hot tears leaking from her eyes.

"It's hard for me to describe," Alexandra's voice went on. "She had these rules she forced Kay to follow. And would then punish her when she didn't follow them. No one could have held out forever. And then after a while it became clear Kay wasn't eating. She lost a lot of weight. Elizabeth had her force-fed. It's hard to tell from the transcript what Kay was feeling because she had to be so careful about what she said to Elizabeth, because of Elizabeth punishing her. But I think——"

"Stop!" Hazel couldn't bear the images flooding into her mind.

"I'm sorry," Alexandra whispered.

Hazel pressed her glass against her chattering teeth and swallowed and swallowed until the cognac scalded the back of her throat. She coughed, and her eyes streamed. "How long," she said when she got her voice back, "how long did this go on? You're not saying Kay is still—"

"No, no," Alexandra said hurriedly. "She's not alive. No. What happened, you see... Well, all I know for certain is that the capture was in October. And Kay died on January 12. At least that's the date my father and Elizabeth have given me."

"January 12," Hazel numbly repeated. "Did Elizabeth—"

"No. Let me finish. What Elizabeth wanted with Kay was to use her to control my father. Because of his obsession with her. And his terrible depression. She wanted to give him Kay back—made 'safe.' I think that's how she put it to Kay. Kay was to go to the island with him and be whatever my father wanted of her. So that he would recover and take back control of the Executive. Elizabeth told Kay that since it was her fault he had broken down, it was fitting that she be the instrument of his recovery. Kay couldn't take any more. So she said she would do as Elizabeth wanted. My father came then and took her away." Alexandra swallowed. "I don't know for sure what happened after that. Only that just before he died—" Alexandra's voice broke. Hazel wrenched her gaze onto Alexandra's face and saw that she, too, was weeping. "Christ it was ugly, when Elizabeth finally had my father cornered in that house in Colorado, and the three of us were in that room together. She wanted to split us apart—I know now it was because she was worried about the transcript, she wanted to use me against him to make him surrender his copy of it." Alexandra wiped her eyes and nose before continuing. "So she said to me did I really want to go with him who claimed to love me so much, didn't I know that he had killed Kay himself, even though he avowed the greatest love for her." Alexandra grabbed the bottle, poured more into her glass and quickly drank from it.

"*He* killed her?"

"He said she begged him to, that she was so miserable with what Elizabeth had done to her that she couldn't bear to live. That he didn't want to do it and that he never regretted anything so much, but that he hadn't been able to withstand her pleas. So he killed her. Sometimes he lied, but I don't think he was lying about this." Alexandra looked into Hazel's eyes. "He killed himself only seconds after he told me this. I believe him. Especially after reading the transcript. Kay was starving herself. I can't imagine him having her force-fed. So she probably would have died anyway."

Hazel put her hands to her face and covered her eyes. "So she was already like that, long before I met her," she whispered. "There was always that inside her, between us. And I didn't even know." She dropped her hands and looked at Alexandra, who sat scrunched up in her chair with her arms wrapped around her body. "It's not beyond what I've gradually become able to believe about her. It's just... my god. How can she bear to be the person she is? How can she *live* with herself?"

Alexandra made a barking sound in her throat. "Believe me, people can. I know of people worse than she. It's just that it's *her* I hate."

"What am I going to do?"

Alexandra whispered. "I've fucked everything up, haven't I. I really have. And now there's no going back."

Hazel reached for the bottle and poured more cognac into her own glass. "I should read the transcript myself," she said, though her mind screamed back at her that she couldn't do it.

"Are you sure you want to?"

Hazel sipped, then said, "I should. Before seeing her. Because of Kay. To try to understand, to know what happened, if I can. Before I confront her." Hazel saw it then, that she would confront Liz. There could be no other way.

"The negotiations," Alexandra said, her voice regretful.

"There are others involved," Hazel said. "There's a good chance the negotiations have gone too far for easily breaking off now—some of the projects agreed upon have already begun to be implemented, you know. Probably they can survive without my contacts with her."

They drank in silence for a long time. Hazel felt the skin on her face stretching as the traces of her tears dried. She felt both drunk and depressed.

"Perhaps you can use the transcript to help your negotiations."

Hazel looked at Alexandra. "Blackmail her, you mean?"

"She would be ruined among executives if any of it ever got out."

Hazel said, "I couldn't do that kind of thing." She sipped. "That doesn't bother you, the thought of the Free Zone benefiting like that? Revenge means that much to you?"

"I don't know what I think about political affairs. I've never had much of a chance to think about such things. First there was my father and his methods and politics. Which I hated. To have to watch him do what he did to this country." Alexandra bit her lip. Hazel waited, and after a few seconds she continued. "All that time I thought Elizabeth was perfect. When I heard she had formed a renegade band and was trying to pull a coup, I rejoiced, I rooted for her." Alexandra's laugh rang harshly in the silence. "But later, her prisoner, I watched from my island—via the newspapers—and decided she wasn't as wonderful as I'd thought. Of course from a distance it's easy to pick out other people's mistakes. And I'm an outsider. I've never participated in that world in such a way as to make me feel a part of it. So I don't know. I suppose it's a matter of what one thinks is important. And I don't know about that. I've never had to think about that except in the most egocentric terms. I'm the worst egocentric I've ever known, bar my father. I've spent my life wrapped up in my own problems, first with my father, then with my exile on that island, and finally with Sally and Elizabeth. In short, I'm a confused, immature, stunted creature who's never been made to grow up."

A strange woman, Hazel thought. To sit there and say such things about herself, as though she were talking about someone other than herself. "You've suffered," Hazel said, "I can tell you've suffered."

Alexandra shrugged, and her mouth slid into an eerie half-smile. "So? Suffering isn't a passport to maturity. *Au contraire*, I'd say." She got to her feet and held out her hand. "I suggest we go find Sally and see if we can't find a piece of normalcy, at least for long enough to give our bodies the chance to recover from this session. Unless you want to go on talking?"

Hazel rose shakily to her feet. "I think I'd like to go home now," she said. And lie in her dark bedroom in the hotel suite and try to find enough peace of mind to make thinking possible. But at the thought of thinking, Hazel's mind shied: *too soon, it's too soon. I can't bear it just now*... Would she be ready for the next scheduled meeting with Liz? Could she actually walk into Liz's office and look into her eyes and...

"I'll have the driver bring the car around," Alexandra said. "I don't have a copy of the transcript here in this house, but I can——"

"No," Hazel said. "I couldn't look at it tonight, I need some time, it's all still such a shock——"

"Of course." Alexandra took a handset from a pocket in her tunic. "I understand. I didn't feel that way about her, but when I read it, there was this horror——" She interrupted herself to request that the driver bring the car around to the front door.

Hazel stared at Alexandra. Her head felt muzzy, her tongue thick and clumsy. "You think of this," she said haltingly, "you think of this—of my finding out—as her punishment?"

"I'm sorry for your pain." Alexandra touched her hand to Hazel's shoulder. "I didn't realize what it would mean to you."

"That's not important. But—what happens when I tell her I know? What then? Will it matter to her? Won't it matter more to her to keep others from knowing?" Maybe, Hazel speculated, it would be so great a blow to Liz's illusions about their relationship that it would, instead, kill all the illusions and any remnant of affection she might still feel—if indeed she did feel such a thing—for her?

"I don't know," Alexandra said. "Maybe all she'll care about is revenging herself on me." Her strange, intense gaze bore down into Hazel's. "She will probably bend everything she has to my destruction." Her mouth twisted. "I've certainly thrown away my leverage over her in one precipitate shot." Her eyes seemed to grow larger and darker. "Or perhaps you're right and she'll simply try to control the damage as best she can."

"Yes," Hazel said. "Yes. I think that's exactly what she'll do. You see, the reason I left her for good... Well. When it came down to it, she chose what you call damage control over me."

"But then she never believed she'd entirely lost you, did she," Alexandra said softly. "This time..." Alexandra's eyes glittered. "This time everything is different."

Suddenly revolted by Alexandra in her role of avenging angel, Hazel turned from the strange dark eyes, slipped away from the light hand on her shoulder, and opened the door. These executives, she thought, these executives... But she could find no words with which to complete the thought.

Chapter Thirty-six

[i]

Emily listened to the wind rustling through the leaves of the eucalyptus and the scrub, to the plaintive hooting of an owl. Twisting around inside her sleeping bag, she shifted onto her side, setting the hammock into motion. She should look at her watch to see how late it was getting, for the morning felt advanced, the way it sometimes did when one woke for the second time of the morning in a tent. But lazy, Emily lay with her eyes closed, aware of the cloudless blue sky above, certain Celia or Elena would come to wake her if it got too late since Celia was due at the airport by eleven—and Celia, no matter what the appointment, never failed to be punctual (if she could help it).

Emily heard the back door open as though on cue. She rolled over to face the house and set up a fresh wave of oscillations in the hammock. "Yes, yes, I'm getting up," she said as she opened her eyes.

Garbed in her bright terrycloth robe, her hair wrapped in a towel she'd shaped into a turban, Celia bore a mug in each hand. As she approached, Emily caught a whiff of the coffee and reached eagerly for the mug Celia extended to her. "People who sleep outdoors shouldn't expect room service," Celia said. "But in special cases, exceptions *are* made in this house."

Emily grinned: Celia *hated* her sleeping out here in the hammock, though she generally made her objections in a sort of teasing half-humorous grumble that left Emily free to disregard them. When four years ago Celia, Elena, and Luis had moved into this house and Emily had taken to staying with them from time to time, Celia had at first assumed that Emily couldn't face sleeping on the sofa-bed in the living room and so had offered her own bed, which Emily had refused. Emily had then told Celia of how when she had lived in her beach house she had often slept in a hammock on the terrace; vaguely remembering seeing the hammock on the terrace of Emily's beach house, Celia had reluctantly believed her and come to accept it as simply one more strangeness between them, though she still insisted that sleeping out of doors wasn't safe, that who knew what might happen if one weren't securely barricaded behind closed doors.

"It's early yet," Celia said. "Only seven-thirty. I couldn't sleep for excitement, believe it or not. I was up at six-thirty, writing more notes. Then I showered and made coffee. I thought I'd let Mama and Luis sleep for another half hour before I make breakfast."

Emily sipped her coffee. "So you thought you wouldn't bother sparing me."

"People who sleep outdoors in hammocks should expect to be awakened at dawn, when all the birds start making a racket and the sky gets bright." Celia's eyes fairly danced.

"Actually, I did wake then, but I fell back to sleep. Don't you know, Cee, that people who lie around in hammocks are notoriously lazy? It's almost like lying in a bathtub. The rocking movement and the hammock taking the shape of your body the way water does is very soothing."

Celia stretched out on the vinyl chaise lounge. "Perhaps," she said, "but sleeping outdoors in the city isn't all that safe a thing to do." She raised her mug to her lips and drank.

Naturally Celia would be concerned about safety—an understandable *idée fixe* for one with her experiences—though in fact Celia had been "safely" locked in her house when she had been abducted.

"I suppose I won't know until I get there and talk to others in the party what the real story about Hazel's withdrawal from the negotiations is all about," Celia said.

"My conjecture," Emily said, "and I do mean conjecture, for I don't have any inside information on this, is that one of two things— or maybe both—is involved. Hazel may have decided that at this rate the negotiations could go on forever and that if that's the case she has other things to do with her life. Or that she didn't feel comfortable taking such a prominent role—this being a collective project. And so she found withdrawal from the negotiations the best way of making certain of a broader level of participation. Or, maybe it was Elizabeth's doing. Elizabeth may have realized what an enormous project this was turning into—which, I imagine, she never had any idea of at the out-set, but which now she apparently finds not uncongenial to her own policies—and decided that she couldn't afford the time and energy this level of personal involvement was demanding of her, and that moreover others in the Executive were more competent and better suited for dealing with specific issues." Emily drank a long swallow of coffee. "But the important thing is that the Executive is interested in keeping the negotiations going—for now, at least. From some of the stuff I've seen in executive publications, it appears that Elizabeth and her people have made a strong case that the negotiations are in the broader interests of the executive system."

"So they're finally getting some sense into their heads," Celia said with what Emily interpreted as smug satisfaction.

"I wouldn't be so sanguine. This *could* be only temporary. And be-sides, given the kind of reasoning they're using to justify the negotia-tions, I can't see the 'sense' you think they're getting into their heads."

"The important thing is that there's dialogue and change," Celia said. "As long as people are talking to one another instead of killing and torturing anyone who opens their mouth in dissent, things are at least civilized and people are open to reason."

"Let's wait to see what happens."

"Yes. Let's wait and see before judging."

"Hey, Cee. Here's an idea. Why don't you demand they open Balboa Park and the beaches to the general public?"

Celia's eyebrows lifted. "Are you serious?"

"Of course. It's always bothered me that the most refreshing plac-es in San Diego are the private preserve of executives and their privi-leged guests."

Celia frowned. "There are more important demands to be made," she said. "And since we know they'll concede a finite amount, what's the point in even trying? It'll simply detract from our other demands."

"I'm serious, Cee. Public access to parks and beaches and the like is an important resource in helping people living in cities to cope."

Celia stared meditatively into her coffee cup. After a while she looked up. "They'd never agree. They'd hold out on that even more than they would on issues of workplace conditions."

"Doesn't that say something about how important such a demand must be, then?"

"Not important enough to throw everything else away for!"

"Don't be silly. They're not going to stop the negotiations because you demand public access to parks."

"Apart from which," Celia said stiffly, "a lot of my time in DC is going to be spent meeting with both Bar Association and Human Rights people."

"It was just a thought," Emily said. Her bladder was beginning to make itself felt. Nevertheless, she took another sip of coffee. "You know, Cee, there are certain things about you I don't think I'll ever understand."

Celia looked Emily in the eye. "What do you mean? Because I think other things more important than getting non-executives into Balboa Park?"

"Not exactly. I can understand your reasoning on that, even if I don't agree with it. But other things..." Maybe she was being rash, raising an issue she hadn't discussed with Celia since her release. "I find it difficult to comprehend," Emily said, choosing her words with care, "though I accept it, your choosing to go through an experience you knew could break you, all for the sake of a principle no one in this entire damned world respects. Except maybe a few idealists here and there—and whether they'd remain idealists after what you've been through, I seriously doubt."

Celia's forehead wrinkled. "You're talking about my detention on Martha's account?"

"Yes. I don't understand why you wouldn't let the Marq'ssan spring you."

"You talk about my *choosing*," Celia said. "I didn't think of it as being a matter of choice at all. If I'd agreed to the Marq'ssan's offer, I would have been in collusion with outright defiance of the law. I *don't* support anarchy, Emily. You know that. So why do you talk about my *choosing* detention?"

"That's what I don't understand—your not thinking of yourself as having a choice. For godsake, Cee, think about the state you were in by the end of that detention! If you don't have the choice for self-preservation, I don't see—"

"You've *never* understood my values!" Celia's fist smacked her thigh. "Apart from my refusal to see anarchy as a choice, think of it this way: if I'd done as Martha had done I'd be forever barred to my home, my work, living with my family. All that's of paramount value to me would have been lost. Not to mention my self-respect, for yielding out of cowardice!"

"Cowardice?" Emily repeated. "I suppose that's what you would have accused yourself of if you'd broken under torture, too?"

Celia's face blanched, looked sickly against the bright orange of the towel binding her hair. "I have my principles, Emily. Which you *must* respect."

"Accept," Emily said. "I *accept* them. I don't agree that slavish adherence to such principles demands *respect*. Your ethics leaves out an evaluation of the other side of the equation. It doesn't all fall to one side, Cee. The way you talk, people aren't allowed to feel, aren't allowed the flexibility the so-called law is granted. 'The law' as you call it gets twisted every-which-way that's convenient for whoever has the authority to manipulate it. It's their *tool*, and that's all it is. Not some standard binding both sides. I *accept* that you have this religion, Celia, but I don't understand it, and I see now that I'll never understand it. I can understand your doing what you can to keep your home and family, yes, I can understand that. *That* I see as self-preservation. But as for your religion..." The pressure on her bladder made it increasingly difficult for Emily to stay here talking to Celia. But she couldn't run into the house now, or Celia would misunderstand.

Celia set her empty coffee mug on the table beside her chair and removed the towel from her head and began combing her hair with a pick she pulled from her pocket. "I know you don't understand, Emily. Few people do. If everyone felt and acted as I did the world would be a model place to live in." Celia produced a wry grin. "I don't expect that ever to happen—since that would be utopia." Emily shivered: Celia's words conjured up no utopia *she'd* ever care to live in. "But I'm a realist for all that." At Emily's skeptical look, Celia said, "Oh yes I am, Em. Realist enough to know how to spend my limited time and energy. But if I'd given up and gone along with the Greenglass Method, I wouldn't be on my way to DC today. I'd be living in exile, unable to do the things I do best, far away from Mama and Luis. I'd be unhappy, Em, whereas now, this morning—" a smile (so rare, lately) lit up Celia's face—"I'm off to the wars again. I'm alive and kicking, Em, doing what I choose to do. I *do* know what's best for myself, even if my well-meaning friends think otherwise."

"If I don't run into the bathroom within the next half minute I'm going to have an embarrassing accident," Emily said, cautiously slipping out of the hammock.

Celia burst into laughter. "*I'm* not stopping you," she said.

Emily, not daring to laugh, pressed her lips together and fled into the house.

[ii]

The bus dropped Emily about a mile and a half from the beach house. As she walked along the road's sandy shoulder she thought about the excitement that Celia had through the course of the morning allowed to sweep over her. How, Emily wondered, could Celia get so excited and feel such obvious *hope* after everything she had experienced? Celia seemed to recognize no risk in pursuing her dogged course—though on this score Emily felt no fear for Celia herself, not after the chat she'd had with Lisa—unless, of course, negotiations soured. If that should happen, the outcome for Celia would be unpredictable. Even knowing some of the Executive's key players involved—Elizabeth and Lisa and a few others like Allison Bennett—Emily could not feel confident that the Executive would not revert to its old methods. It wasn't so much personalities and personal values that seemed to matter in determining the shape of policies and events as the structures themselves. Celia didn't believe this, of course. Her mistrust of Lisa and Elizabeth sprang from other sources than lack of faith in their ability to withstand the pressures of their situation. How far could Celia, Hazel, Martha, and the others (possibly thousands of them) push? Could they push far enough for the structures, reaching the ultimate point of the little stretch and flexibility they had, to break? Or would the structures, resisting, merely break Elizabeth and Lisa and the others for demanding greater flexibility than the system could bear?

But Celia could not conceptualize the problem in this way: she started with the structures in their most idealistic visualization (namely, an abstract notion of The Law) and hoped to conform the people to the structures, hoped to purify the system until it came into line with the delineations of the abstract structures she believed in so fervently. And so she went after individuals, always after individuals and their perceived (or not perceived, depending on who called it) infractions against the Law. She and those sharing her religion would like to purge from among the administrators of the structures those individuals who did not conform to some idealized version (on which they probably would never be able to agree among themselves), would like to try to force all others to obey... It was an uphill, never-ending, contentious battle, for people never agreed upon what those structures are, what they permit, or how flexible they can be without breaking... And thus the endless wrangles throughout written history...stretching on into infinity... And for this uphill, never-to-be-won struggle Celia still maintained zest and zeal? The thought of this astonished Emily. Besides stubbornness, Celia possessed a resilience and energy that any other human being could envy. But as it astonished it also confounded Emily and saddened her. It seemed a sheer waste of talent, energy, even joy.

Emily approached the beach house and wondered if her thumbprint would still grant her access. She had not tried coming in through the gate of the house, had not tried entering the walled enclosure of the property since she had fled it a decade earlier. If she could not get in, she would have a long two hours' wait for Astrea. Emily glanced up and down the road and along the wall running beside the road. Finding no eyes visibly watching her, she lifted her thumb and pressed it against the plate. She sighed as the little green light blinked on then off. So he *had* kept everything as it had been. Unless, of course, military security police had ransacked the place? But she would not go inside the house and so would never see whether they had or not... Emily located the hidden latch on the gate, sprang it, and pulled it open. Might he have had some kind of signal attached to the lock in case she *should* come back? She wouldn't put it past him; it was the kind of thing he'd do, though posting a twenty-four-hour guard was even more likely, and she knew from her previous visits to the beach that he had done no such thing.

She walked through the scrub-grown yard, under the stand of eucalyptus, and around the dazzling white south side of the house. The ocean called her, its heady fresh salty smell, its rhythmic pounding against the beach, its glittering blue blaze of light stretching as far as the horizon. Emily broke into a run and began undressing when she reached the beach. She would swim, but this time she would scan as she submerged, doing something it had never before occurred to her to try, combining two pleasures, two sensations into one unique experience. She would do a thing no one—human or Marq'ssan—had ever before done.

[iii]

In-structuring, con-structuring, re-structuring, yes, when Astrea explained it she could see their vast differences. But when she *showed* examples of them—creating, for instance, a small stone out of the residue of de-structuring, or "con-structing" it out of the matter of sand (much easier to believe in) or "re-structuring" it by wholly rearranging the structure of another thing, say, seaweed or saltwater, she could see their similarities as well as their differences. Re-structuring incurred the least risk one took to the integrity of one's own field, was least draining to one's own energy, while in-structuring was the most taxing and the riskiest. All three required both knowledge and experience—for how could one impose a new structure without knowing in advance what that structure was to be? These three were infinitely more difficult than destructuring, which involved little knowledge of the structures involved.

When the time for what they called "practice" came, Emily accomplished what Astrea called "simple re-structuring." She nearly panicked at the thought that she might "lose" her field, even though Astrea had assured her that if necessary she could help her to "regain" it. All these structurings demanded a great deal more than destructurings: one had to put one's very field on the line when manipulating these structures, one had to merge her own field with that of the structure one was tampering with. When at last Emily scanned the small stone she had made in every mode she had so far discovered, she dropped field perception in order to *see* it with her own eyes, in order to *feel* its reality. What had been seaweed now looked and felt like a stone. Elated, she looked from the stone to Astrea and skittered into giggles she found herself hard-pressed to control. "I can't believe I did that!" She crowed with triumph. "Astrea, are you sure you didn't do it *for* me?" Another wave of giggles overcame her; helpless to keep herself sober, she stared at Astrea's puzzled face and struggled to straighten her own.

"You aren't serious?" Astrea said when the giggles had been quelled.

"It's so hard to believe. That a *human* could do such things. That *I* could. Scanning is one thing…but transforming *matter*! It's mind-boggling. And frightening, too. Why, if I could do this, then other people could too. And the thought of that ever happening scares the shit out of me."

"No, it couldn't happen. Not unless they understood how to change their brains. None of that could possibly occur to them because it's so far outside the models in which they think." A smile came to her face, a smile that reached her eyes. (*Is she* consciously *smiling for me?*) "Our secret is safe, Emily. And you will never abuse it." Her smile faded. "In fact you are less likely to abuse it than I. Which is a strange thing for a Marq'ssan to be saying to a human."

Emily experienced a powerful upsurge of affection for Astrea, and pride and fear—fear of what she did not yet know of herself. "It's a terrible power." Emily stared out at the never-ceasing progression of waves. "It's even more responsibility than that my privilege had already thrust upon me. And I've never met that responsibility in a way I could feel satisfied with." She picked up a handful of sand and let it sift through her fingers. "I'm a dilettante, Astrea," she said, looking at the Marq'ssan. "I live for my own pleasure and comfort."

"So am I, Emily. What do you think I'm doing away from Marqeuei, anyway? It's all an adventure to me. As for your own pleasure and comfort, you at least understand how these things are tied up with larger things. Which is more than I can say for most humans."

Emily sat close beside Astrea. Slipping back into field perception, she merged fields with the Marq'ssan. In a while she would tell Astrea about how she had scanned while treading water a hundred yards from shore. And then maybe later when the moon rose they would swim out from shore and both scan and merge and enjoy this new form of earthly pleasure, Marq'ssan and human together.

Marq'ssan and human had come a long way together in twenty years. But Emily understood, now, that they had only begun. Who knew what new forms and structures they would discover (or invent) in the coming years?

Seattle
March 1986 – July 1986
revised May 1998

Afterword

Yesterday I read that Philip Agee had died. Although the Marq'ssan Cycle's SIC is an invention of my own imagination, Agee's *Inside the Company: CIA Diary*, which he wrote after serving twelve years as an officer in the US Central Intelligence Agency, helped shape my image of what such an institution could become following a nearly invisible, oligarchic coup like that of my fictional Executive Transformation. The January 9, 2008, *Agence-Presse* article by Anthony Boadle notes that Agee's eyes were opened to the CIA's Cold War agenda—that of keeping traditional elites in power through political repression and torture—while working as a case officer in South America. Boadle quotes Agee:

> It was a time in the 70s when the worst imaginable horrors were going on in Latin America—Argentina, Brazil, Chile, Uruguay, Paraguay, Guatemala, El Salvador—they were military dictatorships with death squads, all with the backing of the CIA and the U.S. government. That was what motivated me to name all the names and work with journalists who were interested in knowing just who the CIA were in their countries.

I've been asked many times over the past year how I could have been so prescient about the US Government's open embrace of torture and its dismissal of many of the provisions of civil liberties set forth in the Bill of Rights. (Today, after all, is the sixth anniversary of the US's notorious gulag in Guantanamo Bay.) When I wrote the Marq'ssan Cycle I did not see myself as predicting a possible future, however, but rather as coming to an understanding of the world in which I was living in the mid-1980s and creating a vision of hope by imagining a profound change in the way human beings interact to make a world in which everyone can thrive.

The fundamental premise on which all my hope rests refuses the widely accepted generalization that human nature is immutable (as well, of course, as the cynical assumption of many political scientists and religious fundamentalists that human beings are basically evil). If we are not to self-destruct as a species, we must change, must learn to live with ourselves and in the world, and I believe that we can do that. I reject the eschatological sense of looming apocalypse that did not vanish with the passing of the Millennium year; and I reject the view that what we have now in the US is inevitable.

Could I have created a realistic hope without taking into account the ordinary level of political, social, economic, and gender violence that pervades our world? For myself, the answer is No. A gentler, easier version of reality would have rendered my vision of change less plausible.

Reading these books isn't easy. I have seen their effect on people close to me. And I know that the violence they depict (which nominally, at least, is considerably less than that found in many bestselling thrillers) necessarily reduces the size of their audience. After I finished the first draft of *Blood in the Fruit* (the last third of which I subsequently deleted and rewrote), I fell into a fit of self-hating recrimination, during which I questioned my own sanity, fearing that both my obsession with my characters and the violence of the narrative might be symptoms of psychosis. Recently, looking back over my intense correspondence with Kath Wilham during the years I was writing the Marq'ssan Cycle, I found the following passage in a letter dated January 3, 1986, about five days after I'd hit the bottom of my post-novel depression:

> Last night after we hung up I thought about the need to sift through [...] so much debris [and it occurred to me] that I should perhaps attempt to archeologize (I know that's not a word: but I needed something better than excavate, because that's not exactly what I'm after, & "logize" should be in the word somewhere). [...] The little bit of distance I have now doesn't shrink the proportions of the peril I felt myself to have been in [while writing *Blood in the Fruit*]. I just see it differently now. & see a great need to try to

understand as best I can. In some ways I feel my survival depends upon it. My survival as that of a creature moving into/through/ around/toward (it's so vague & non-linear that I hesitate to use any of the prepositions I can think of) certain areas. [...]

I think you understand what I mean when I talk about the survival of this process I feel myself to have become (is that right? Can I think of my self as a process? Shit there aren't any words to hand that strike me as appropriate: we need more vocabulary, desperately we need new words & forms if we are to continue on like this). For shorthand I'm always referring to this process as "my writing," but that's just a rough convenience. You pinpoint my clumsiness with the socio-cultural structures as what I'm up against. & in a way it is as though the two of us have been at war against these structures for as long as we've been thinking alongside one another & together. [...]

There's a longstanding convention [characterizing] women writers [...] that many feminist literary historians have uncovered, & that's the fear of being swallowed by madness. Some of [the literary historians] have made sense of [this fear] by talking about the difference between male & female ego-formation in western society. Men [they say] have such strong ego-boundaries that they have little to fear venturing very deeply into the monsters of their [...] imaginations. [& the convention has it that] women typically have such weak boundaries [...] that there's a terror of completely losing their (sane) selves. [...]

Well I can see in my own case how this works. Some of it is guilt [...] concerning the indulgence of my own imagination. The guilt for having lain awake half the night enjoying the fantasy of invention. Or of writing any of it down & hiding it as a shameful guilty pleasure. (I don't know where I got the idea that it was shameful. Maybe being reproved for not going to sleep?) It was either [writing down my imaginative inventions] or reading fiction [late into the night, for most of my childhood and adolescence]. Then, later, [I indulged in] the guilty pleasure of composing music, which after a while I began to keep secret (because at first I got in trouble for improvising instead of practicing my lesson—though much later, in high school, people wanted me to improvise, and it became a positive value, though I still had the sense of doing something I shouldn't be doing). Even when I came out into the open with my composing (having to do with taking theory class, & my theory teacher— one of the women who helped me become the self I am today— encouraged my composing), I still had guilty feelings about it, which when I got to Illinois & met up with the composition faculty helped do-in my composing. Then when I was in History, a bit more of the same, only with a certain positive ambivalence, since I found myself rewarded for my imaginative work. [...]

It starts out as a feeling that because I'm going against the grain of the most common way of seeing things that I'm perverse. But then after a while that feeling grows, perhaps because my mind begins to dwell in a counter-reality, one that hardly anyone else can even glimpse, & I feel taken over into a different world which feels half-crazy; & it's obsessiveness that enables me to do that. (How else would I have the energy to construct this other universe that refuses the commonly accepted?) One way to feel less crazy is to find ways of sharing this other reality with other people. & that's what has happened with these books, mostly. In this case, though, this other way of looking is more & more embedded in this other universe (I mean the characters, structures, etc. of the books). Now I know I can distinguish between these, but what happens in the one always affects the other, in subtle ways. There are resonances. All in my head. (& sometimes in yours, I know.) [Writing] history papers, part of what made me feel perverse & sometimes guilty was that the things I saw & wrote about were things that I felt exposed me—I often imagined people saying what kind of mind does she have that she can see things like that? (Considering how much sexuality was my topic, that made it all the worse.) I remember people thinking my insights remarkable: how did I happen to *see* such a thing, since I'd been looking at the same things no one else had for as long as people had been looking at it. (Interestingly a *lot* of scholars are now seeing those things: feminism & post-structuralism have significantly changed people's angles of vision.)

& so now with this book more than the others, since it gets down into the muck & mire, there's a sense of being polluted with it. That I see & write about those particular things [...] somehow makes me a party to them. Now in my shifted state five days later I can say but we are all a part of that. It's in our world & it's all around us & just because some of us close our eyes to it & pretend not to see it doesn't mean we aren't implicated. Somehow by putting this stuff under the microscope I'm implicating myself. But now when I think about that I realize that I'm only forcing a painful realization upon myself, that I was always implicated (& here I'm not talking about liberal hand-wringing guilt, it's something else, something I don't have words for just yet) whether I looked or not.

Sometime in the last year the conviction has grown upon me that I have to look. That it's essential. As something to do with this process I was trying to name as myself when I started this letter. As something to do with this ontological imperative compelling me to try to understand. Not just torture, but this [relation] that replicates itself in so many different ways, including Alexandra's story, including Kay's story, & so on & so on. [...] calls this repetition, but I don't think that's the word. All their stories aren't the same. They replicate this structure I think I see, but differently. & there are very few people in the world who would compare an Alexandra Sedgewick to a Celia Espin or Kay Zeldin. (& in fact, subtract the incest & what we know about Sedgewick, & some people would see nothing terrible in her story.)

Most of you reading this afterword will have by now finished the entire Marq'ssan Cycle, and some of you will be feeling both exhilarated and bereft at having done so. Exhilarated because you've grasped some intangible sense of a process that will allow you, as my friend Joan Haran said to me when she finished reading *Stretto*, to "write beyond the ending." And bereft, as she also said, with the knowledge that there will be no more text from that world. (Another friend, Ann Hibner Koblitz, persists in trying to tempt me into writing more, all these years later, but I frankly don't see it happening.) A sense of exhilaration and loss were my own reactions on finishing *Stretto*. A letter to Kath dated July 4, 1986, shows how I was feeling after my first exhilaration at finishing had faded:

> & so here I am [...] all hollowed out with the end of the book, end of the series... wish I didn't feel bad about it. Mourning? Or more of the malaise that comes when I'm forced to look at my writing from that certain angle & distance? Probably more of the latter than the former. All this weepiness & mopiness.[...] I'm feeling like this small speck, almost a zero (which would be too glamorous or exalted anyway for this dismal boring gray state of mind, for zeros as extremes bear a certain significance, even if negative) lost in a pile of sludge. Sometimes it's overwhelming being so swallowed up by a reality I try to pretend is only anterior to my own. I don't really have that gift of solipsism, as you call it, & so finishing the series only means losing a world, losing those people who've filled my consciousness for two years. They've impinged on yours, &, you say, won't simply vanish—but that's a different matter from what I'm used to. & that certain sense of power of voice, in one way combating all the crap that I force down my own gullet day after day. (I don't think stopping watching McNeill-Lehrer can be my solution for this. I don't think there's any ignoring it for me, at least not just now.) So here I have this beautiful day & feel as though I'm going to pieces. Absurd.

I felt as though I'd lost a world, a world that would continue to haunt me for months to come. Although I sat down and wrote my first short story ("Welcome, Kid, to the Real World") a couple of weeks after finishing, I only managed to exorcise the ghost of that world through writing a story in which I woke one afternoon from a nap to find Elizabeth Weatherall in my house. In the story, I find her more terrifying than I had ever imagined. She knows all about my reality (including the outcome of the Iran-Contra scandal) because it lies in her past. And then before I know it, the other characters begin to show up, too. They gave me a wild ride in that story (and made me feel like Frankenstein, to boot). It took me about 18,000 words to get rid of them. But then I was free.

A couple of decades later, I find the vision of hope I conjured up for myself in the mid-1980s oddly more credible than it was back then. There are many reasons for this, some of them to do with the changes I've witnessed in many progressives, men and women both, since then, some of them to do with the interesting wave of change sweeping much of Latin America today. I recently had the pleasure of discovering the often painful but also heartening narrative of the activists in Oaxaca, who began powerfully to remake their world when the corrupt regime controlling their state attempted to shut down a teachers' strike. In the 2007 documentary that Jill Freidberg made about them, *Un Poquito de Tanta Verdad,* you can see 1000 people sitting together, making decisions by consensus, visibly demonstrating that a truly democratic polity, like the one I imagine evolving in the Marq'ssan Cycle, is possible. Yes, it's true that the Oaxacan community of activists pose such a threat to the regime that they continually face violent repression from the police and military. But violence is a last resort that will *never* get the final word (unless that violence ends in the total annihilation of our species, of course). The Oaxaca revolution won't be stopped. And in my Marq'ssan Cycle, people *will* learn to embrace complexity and multiple perspectives. And therein, I'm convinced, lies the key to finding our way into a decent future.

Seattle

January 11, 2008

Aqueduct Press Conversation Pieces Volume 10

The Red Rose Rages (Bleeding)

A Short Novel by L. Timmel Duchamp

Sarah Minnivitch, an actor sentenced to prison for acts of civil disobedience, wreaked havoc at the for-profit medium-security facility she was first sent to. When Penco transfers her to a high-security facility, the facility's director assigns Dr. Eve Escher the task of rehabilitating Minnivitch and recovering the corporation's losses. Escher believes she is on the verge of a scientific breakthrough that will not only rehabilitate the prisoner but also win the doctor fame and glory. But the stakes for both Escher and Minnivitch prove to be higher than either of them realize...

"...an intense and gripping read...dense with ideas... Not a comfortable book, but a compelling and thought-provoking one."
—Lesley Hall, *Strange Horizons*, April 24, 2006

"The protagonist's blind faith in the system proves to be a kind of innocence that ultimately can't persist, but her enlightenment won't lead to anything as blatant as protest, martyrdom, or absolution. The irony of this work's ending feels as brutal as its truths."
—Faren Miller, *Locus*, February 2006

"Given the recent revelations of how prisoners of the U.S. government have been treated at Abu Ghraib and Guantanamo, and of the free hand that private corporations like Halliburton have been given by the government to act like independent pocket-states, Duchamp's novel seems as relevant today as any uncensored blog reporting form the Middle East."
—Michael Levy, *New York Review of Science Fiction*, August 2006

Author Biography

L. Timmel Duchamp is the author of *Love's Body, Dancing in Time*, a collection of short fiction, *The Grand Conversation: Essays*, *The Red Rose Rages (Bleeding)*, a short novel, and *Alanya to Alanya*, *Renegade, Tsunami*, and *Blood in the Fruit*, the first four novels of the Marq'ssan Cycle. Her stories have appeared in a variety of venues, including *Asimov's SF* and the *Full Spectrum*, *ParaSpheres*, *Leviathan*, and *Bending the Landscape* anthology series; she has been a finalist for the Nebula and Sturgeon awards and short-listed several times for the Tiptree Award. She has also published numerous critical essays in *The American Book Review*, *The New York Review of Science Fiction*, *Extrapolation*, *Foundation*, *Strange Horizons*, and *Lady Churchill's Rosebud Wristlet*.

She was a Guest of Honor at WisCon 32. A selection of her stories and essays can be found on her website: http://ltimmel.home.mindspring.com.